THE RECKONING

BOOK ONE OF THE INTERTWINED SERIES

KAYLA KNUE

THE RECKONING

BOOK ONE OF THE INTERTWINED SERIES

This book is a work of fiction. Names, characters, places, and incidents are the product of the author's imagination or are used fictitiously. Any resemblance to actual events, locales, or persons, living or dead, is coincidental.

Cover design by: Mandi Lynn- Stone Ridge Books
Illustrations by: Tiffany Davis- CS Designs
Formatting: Enchanted Ink Publishing

ISBN: 978-1-954554-00-9

Printed in the United States of America

TO MY PARTNER, EVAN,

NONE OF THIS WOULD BE POSSIBLE WITHOUT YOUR UNYIELDING LOVE AND SUPPORT.

ALWAYS AND FOREVER.

CHAPTER 1

KI

A woman's scream wrenched my attention from the deer carcass. She stared wide-eyed as I drained the beast of its blood. Its warmth and metallic taste called to my deepest parts, and I couldn't stop. A look of horror was on her face, but my thoughts were only of blood. Hers teased me as it pulsed in her veins.

She ran into tree cover, but branches crunching underfoot made her easy to follow. I stalked her in silence as she flailed through the brush. Eventually she came to a stop and looked back. I was concealed in the trees above, and she let out a sigh of relief.

The creaking branch betrayed me as I dropped to the ground, but by then it was too late. I pinned her under the weight of my body. My hand muffled her scream as my eyes bored into her. The familiar red glow filled my vision. She fell under my spell, and her resistance dissolved. I sank my teeth into her without pause, and a wave of energy ran through me as I tasted her.

I tore my teeth from her flesh when a sound echoed in the distance. Scanning the trees, I saw no movement. Her hot arterial blood sprayed out and covered my face, drawing my attention back to her. The blood was impossible to ignore.

A sound grabbed my attention again, pulling me from the bloodied scene.

"Knock, knock!" Harrison threw open my bedroom doors.

Even in my sleepy daze I recognized his voice. We'd been friends since infancy. I retreated under my black fur covers and pretended he was a dream, more like a nightmare.

"Don't tell me your sorry rump is still in bed!" Harrison teased.

He tugged on my blanket, and I peered over the covers. His mess of brown hair was tucked behind one of his long, pointed ears, and a stupid smile was spread across his face.

I sat up in my bed. "What the bloody hell are you so happy about?" The tightness in my underwear was unexpected, and my blanket did nothing to conceal it.

"Guess I'm not the only one excited this morning." Harrison's green eyes met mine, and heat rose in my cheeks.

I threw my pillow at his face. He took a step back from the force of the impact and laughed.

"Get out!" I stood from my bed with my blanket held up to cover my erection.

"Okay, okay. Just wanted to let you know that breakfast will be ready soon." Harrison's smile never faded as he left.

I slammed the double doors behind him and sighed. My throbbing cock demanded attention. For weeks I'd been plagued by dreams of blood that caused me to wake up at full mast. It had become a problem.

The dreams started right after I manifested a need for blood, a demonic trait that was hard to hide and impossible to ignore. As a dierdre, I expected my body to continue to transform as my dark magic grew, but the bloodlust was a surprise. I couldn't find any books that mentioned it, and no one else in my family exhibited the trait.

I clenched my fists, refusing to yield to my perversion. Blood should not cause arousal, yet I couldn't stop my own thoughts. I recalled the deer I'd killed the night before. Its bright red blood had speckled my gray skin. I remembered the metallic taste of its blood and how it warmed me on the inside, filling me with power.

My cock ached, and my resistance disappeared. It filled me with shame, but I had to relieve myself.

ılı ֍ ʃ ≈

I stood tall as I walked through the palace in my favorite black robe. It was trimmed in silver and had the holy symbol embroidered on the back. Most days I had to wear uncomfortable black suits handpicked by my father, but on the holy day I got a break from my busy schedule. It came but once a week, and I always looked forward to the day of comfort and relaxation.

The dark walls of the palace were lined with portraits, statues, and overly ornate sculptures, all cast with silver detailing to showcase the wealth of the Dark Nation. Servants bowed and greeted me as I passed by on my way to the kitchen. I nodded respectfully but kept my distance from them as much as possible. It was likely they were all spies for my father, or worse.

A young maid greeted me with a bow and a wide smile. "Good morning, Your Royal Highness."

She looked me over with big brown eyes. Her heart rate quickened as her gaze trailed from my feet, all the way up to my horns. Her pale face flushed, making her attraction to me undeniable. It sickened my stomach.

I briskly moved past her without a reply, hoping she wouldn't try to speak to me again. Sexual attraction eluded me. It never made sense, people's sudden sexual desires based entirely off another person's appearance. I wished women wouldn't look at me in such a way. It made me feel unclean, as though they had defiled me with just their eyes.

Harrison's laughter echoed down the hall. He always managed to radiate a positivity that uplifted me, although I would never admit it. I wished I could talk to him about my bloodlust. He'd be able to find a bright side, but I couldn't. My growing powers had to be kept secret from him, from everyone, for fear of my father finding out.

The sweet aroma of syrup greeted me as I entered the kitchen. Pots and pans hung from the dark stone walls with wooden counters beneath them. Usually there'd be a dozen chefs fast at work making food for the entire palace, but it was the holy day, so the kitchen was mostly empty.

Harrison leaned against the only workstation in use while sampling pastries. A bounty of them were laid out upon the counter. His black robe was already dusted in powder from the sugary treats. He was complimenting the head chef in Asudhen when I walked up. Harrison always jumped at the chance to speak his native tongue with fellow asudhs.

Our head chef was a middle-aged asudh. Like most asudhs, he had dark olive skin and pointed ears. His long black hair was pulled back into a tight and perfect bun. No matter what time of day it was, his hair was always slicked back under his hat. Never had a single hair been found in any of the many dishes he prepared for the palace.

"I see His Royal Highness has finally privileged us with his presence," said a familiar voice from the pantry.

"Daniel?" My old friend stepped out of the pantry with a jar of honey in hand. "When the bloody hell did you get back?"

He looked different, bigger. It wasn't unusual for tlalocs to be tall and wide, but Daniel had definitely become more muscular in his time away. Training with the Dark Nation Army had done him well.

"Just this morning!" Harrison said with a mouthful of pastry. I had to step back to avoid the puff of powder that expelled from his lips.

I glared at Harrison. "Is that why you burst into my room unannounced?"

"Oh dear, did my presence cause a disturbance?" Daniel smirked as he placed the honey on the counter.

The head chef placed a platter full of pancakes before us. "Breakfast is served."

Plates and silverware were stacked in a pile next to it so we could serve ourselves buffet style, another benefit of the holy day.

"Chef, you know I don't—"

"And for Your Highness," he said before I could finish my complaint. A plate piled high with eggs, bacon, and sausage was placed before me. "I know you don't like pancakes, but the boys insisted. Nevertheless, I of course saw to your preferred breakfast. Enjoy."

"Thanks," I replied. Chef returned to his morning routine.

Harrison and Daniel insisted that we eat outside. It was late in the fall season, but the morning sun was bright, too bright. I hated how it glared down on me harder in the cold months than it did in the warm ones. Cold and darkness went hand in hand, yet the sun was defiant.

We sat under the dark oak pergola near the poolside. The solid stone table at its center had the most comfortable outdoor chairs around it. They were made of the same hard wood as the pergola, but they were topped with soft black cushions.

I had to squint to bear the morning light and ease the burning in my eyes. Harrison wasted no time, drowning his pancakes in syrup and honey as soon as he was seated. He was a sloppy eater and would be a disgustingly sticky mess in no time.

Daniel had much better table manners, even though tlalocs were usually the messy ones. He was a freak of nature. He was tall, muscular, and green like most tlalocs, yet Daniel had no tusks. He also had slightly pointed ears, whereas all other tlalocs had rounded ones. I thought he looked more like a large green asudh than a tlaloc.

"Are you going to tell us about your summer or what?" Harrison mumbled through a mouthful of pancakes. Syrup oozed from the crack between his lips.

Daniel smirked. "I guess I have a story or two that I could share."

"We do enjoy the free entertainment," I replied.

It may have sounded sarcastic, but I enjoyed Daniel's theatrics. His stories let me experience the world through his eyes, even though I was confined to the palace grounds. They were a welcome escape from my prison.

"Well, it all began many months ago, way back at the break of spring," Daniel said dramatically. "The sun was shining, the flowers were blooming, and the animals were . . . mating. Violently and forcefully mating!" Daniel made inappropriate gestures as he continued, and I couldn't help but smile. Harrison, on the other hand, choked on his pancake.

"As soon as our ships landed on Kilshore Island, I tore into the new recruits without mercy. I made them run the perimeter of the island until bodies started to drop. Of course, like any good leader, I ran with them."

"Is that why you look so good? A summer of running?" Harrison asked. He looked at Daniel with wide eyes.

"You like the way I look?" Daniel said as he smiled at Harrison.

Harrison's gaze quickly turned back to his pancakes, but I could see the flush in his cheeks. Daniel had always had a knack for teasing him. I had to hold back my laugh so that Harrison wouldn't get mad.

"I'm sure he did a lot more than just running to get that kind of muscle definition," I said.

"Indeed." Daniel grinned. "We started and ended our days with a ten-mile run around the island. During the day, I put the recruits through obstacle courses, weight training, hand-to-hand combat training, and magical combat training. Only a handful of the recruits actually made it through the day still standing." He laughed.

"Sounds brutal," Harrison said. He went back to stuffing his face.

"That was merely the beginning. After the first month, the recruits were divided into squads based on performance. The top performing recruits became squad leaders, and surprisingly enough there was a woman among them."

"A tlaloc?" I asked. The tlalocs were a warrior race that prided themselves on strength. Even the women among the tribes were fierce and muscular.

"Naturally. But around midsummer, when the days were the hottest, our female squad leader forgot her place. We were in the midst of a war game between the squads when she questioned my command."

"No!" Harrison said. His mouth dropped open.

I was just as shocked as he was. A soldier questioning a commanding officer was bad news. Add to that the fact that Daniel was a general and the son of the field marshal. The heat must have made her delirious.

"What did you do?" I asked. Breakfast forgotten, I was on the edge of my seat. Daniel had never told a story where someone had questioned him before. My heart raced. I had no idea how he'd react to a slight like that.

"I stared her in the eye and watched the color leave her face. As soon as she finished her words, she realized what she had done. With others around, her insubordination could not go unpunished. I backhanded her helmet off her head and grabbed her by the hair.

"As I dragged her into the middle of the battlefield, she spoke only three words to me. 'Please have mercy.' With her hair in hand, I announced her crime loud enough for everyone to hear and called upon the squad leaders to witness her punishment."

"You didn't kill her, did you?" Harrison asked. He was on the edge of his seat.

The blood in my veins began to tingle as dark magic surged within. I tried to fight it, but my demonic nature had been triggered by the promise of violence.

"Of course not. She was a skilled soldier; killing her would be a waste of talent. Instead, I had to teach her a lesson. She gave no resistance when I stripped her out of her uniform and threw her over a barrier. The squad leaders stood in formation around us as I held her in place.

"She tried to relax, but she felt tight when I forced myself inside her. She must have been a virgin. Tears filled her eyes, but she didn't scream out. I was as rough with her as I could be without causing permanent damage. All her holes were filled with cum by the time—"

"That's *enough*, Daniel!" My chair fell over when I stood. I had to choke back the contents of my stomach. Tlalocs had violent tendencies, but Daniel always took it too far. I swore he made up for his attractive appearance by being unnervingly brutal.

"But we were just getting to the good stuff," Daniel replied. He smiled wickedly.

Harrison's eyes were wide, and his mouth hung open. I swore I could see the wheels turning in his head.

"We don't need all the bloody details. We get it."

"Someone's a bit sensitive today," Daniel mocked. My blood ran cold.

"You did take it a bit far," Harrison replied.

"You two just need to get laid already," Daniel said, leaning back in his chair.

His words cut through me. Dark magic boiled in my blood as I was consumed by rage. My teeth ached, and my vision turned red as the change took over.

Harrison began to look my way, and I turned. I couldn't let them see my face, not like this. "I'm going to the shrine," I said in a cold voice as I walked away from the table.

My dark magic had nearly overwhelmed me. The frenzy of rage was mixed with a burning desire for violence. I needed to keep it under control and stay calm, otherwise my new demonic abilities wouldn't remain a secret for long.

CHAPTER 2

HARRISON

It was a truly beautiful day. Summer had ended, but cool fall weather still lingered. The trees surrounding the palace had changed color, and their leaves scattered the grounds. It was my favorite time of year. I wanted to enjoy every moment of it before the harsh cold of winter came.

Daniel was finally back from his training with the Dark Nation Army. Since his father was the field marshal, the head of the military, he was expected to attend every single boot camp. I had missed his company and was eager to show him how much my magic had grown in his absence.

We stood in the open training field near the palace gardens. Daniel had agreed to my request for a duel after Ki's abrupt departure. Daniel never passed on a chance to fight—it wasn't in his nature. He loved showing off his strength, as most tlalocs did.

"Are you ready?" Daniel asked from across the small field.

A gentle breeze made his long white hair dance about his shoulders. Braids, feathers, and decorative beads were mixed between the coarse rolls of his hair. His light green skin glistened in the sunlight, which only emphasized the thickness of his muscles. Every inch of his bare upper body was defined—his arms, shoulders, chest, and those abs. I'd kill for those abs.

"Yes. Let's do this." I clenched my fists in anticipation. We both bowed to signal the start of our duel. Daniel had the upper hand when it came to physical strength, so I knew to keep my distance from him.

As Daniel moved, I mirrored his steps. Our leather boots matted the grass as we walked circles in the field. We gathered dark energy around us as we moved. My veins tingled with electricity that felt like a million tiny lightning strikes happening simultaneously under my skin. I fought to keep the flow of electricity under control as dark magic radiated from my hands, surrounding me with its dark aura.

"Your aura has grown," Daniel said. "But mine is still stronger."

Energy surged around Daniel as he summoned his dark magic. I watched as the black crackling energy accumulated in his hands and expanded to encompass his entire body. The cloud of dark magic danced around him wildly, ready to strike.

"Are you sure about that?" I replied.

My hands tingled from the dark magic that wanted to rupture them, but I showed no signs of it. I forced my aura to stretch a little farther. It put even more strain on my hands, but I didn't care. I would fight through the pain.

The best strategy for any duel was to let your opponent attack first, and we both knew it. I managed to keep my distance as we circled, but Daniel got impatient and made the first move, a move I'd seen him do a million times before. His hands circled in front of him, forming a solid ball of dark magic. He thrust it straight at me.

It whipped right past my face with a zipping sound as I barely dodged it. The nearness of if shook my concentration, but I still managed to send a bolt of dark magic at Daniel. It ricocheted off his shoulder, and a thin line of red appeared. My bolt had cut through his dark aura. He laughed as he noticed the small drop of blood that trickled down his arm.

"Looks like your power has grown after all. I'll have to stop going easy on you." He smirked, launching a ball of dark energy at me.

"Ha. You never go easy on me," I replied and quickly circled my hands to make a solid shield of dark magic to block it.

The ball of energy broke as it hit my shield, and I prepared to return fire, but another ball was already coming at me. Hit after hit, my shield blocked the attacks, but I could feel the dark magic weakening. My hands ached from the dark energy that flowed through them to keep the shield up. It would break soon.

I released the shield from my hands and thrust it forward. It knocked balls of energy away from me and provided cover for my attack. I shot another bolt of dark magic at Daniel, but my stamina was depleted. The electricity ripped through me as it left my hand. My palm split open, and blood flowed down my fingers.

Daniel dodged the attack and ran straight at me. I continued fire as I moved backward, ignoring the burning in my hands. If he got within melee range, I would be done for. He dashed side to side as he cleared the distance across the field. My attacks missed. I was unprepared for his speed; he had never been so agile in the past. My hands were bloodied, and I needed to reposition.

I turned to run after I sent a final bolt barreling toward him. It missed, but it served as a distraction for me to get away from him. He was fewer than twenty yards away from me when the ground rippled beneath my feet. As hard as I tried to keep my footing, I was lost in the wave of dirt that pulled out from under me.

"Got ya!" Daniel shouted as he threw himself on top of me. I was pinned facedown to the ground beneath the weight of his body. It was over. There was no way I'd be able to escape his grasp. He had won.

"You cheated," I mumbled through the dirt. My face was nearly smothered in it. Daniel lifted slightly and rolled me onto my back. His hair danced in the air around my head as he hovered over me. The beads shimmered in the sun.

"I always do, according to you." Daniel grinned. His hazel eyes stared down at me, and the flecks of pink within them began to glow. "But I don't think using my birth-given earth magic is cheating. It might be an unfair advantage, but you know fights are never fair."

Daniel's smile was softer than I had remembered. As his eyes stared into mine, a warmth washed over me. I was filled with a familiar sense of safety that only he could inspire.

"Don't I know it," I replied. "No matter how hard I try, our fights always end with you on top of me." The words escaped my lips before I could consider how they sounded. Heat burned in my cheeks as Daniel snickered, and I had no way to hide the redness of my face.

"I did have to try harder for it this time, so you have improved," Daniel said. I thought he'd use his words to punish me for my slip of the tongue, but he didn't. He gave me an out, and I readily took it.

"So have you," I replied. "I didn't know you could move that fast. It appears training with your father's army did you well."

It was meant as a compliment, but the pink glow in his eyes faded. He abruptly pulled back, taking the warmth with him, and got to his feet.

"I guess being the field marshal's son has its benefits." Daniel extended his hand to pull me to my feet. He didn't talk about his father much. I wanted to ask why, but I didn't want to push the subject.

"I bet it doesn't have nearly as many benefits as being the grand duke's son," I said sarcastically as he pulled me up. He chuckled, and his shoulders relaxed. My blood streaked his hands, but he just wiped it off on his pants.

"Yeah, I don't envy you one bit. Being forced to marry the princess is a hell I wouldn't wish on my greatest enemy," Daniel said as we began to walk back toward the palace. His usual demeanor returned.

"She's not that bad," I replied. Jess was complicated and confusing, but she definitely wasn't comparable to hell.

"Not that bad? She's been tormenting you for years!" Daniel said.

"I mean, she's been a little harsh, but I think she just doesn't want people to know that she has a good heart deep down."

"A little harsh? I recall you crying for a solid week after she burned your favorite shirt out of spite. If she has a heart, it's at the end of a bottomless pit."

"Let's not talk about Jess. I don't want to fight."

Daniel had never liked Jess and always had bad things to say about her. He said he wanted to protect me, but I was tired of it all. Jess was the princess and my fiancée, and no one could change that.

"Fine. We should head to the temple to pay our respects to the shamans anyway," Daniel said. I nodded in reply. It was always good to thank the gods and shamans after using large amounts of magical energy. We walked in silence as we crossed the palace grounds.

The large black doors of the temple were wide open when we approached. Ancient runes inscribed in gold and silver lined the perimeter of the doors. The whole structure was fashioned from granite and was surrounded by large pillars that held up the roof. I'd always admired the intricate carvings and paintings that filled the holy spaces. The time and care required to create them could only be imagined.

Pausing at the bottom of the granite stairs, we bowed before we entered the temple. Daniel had always insisted that we show respect before we step foot on holy grounds. He was devout in his beliefs, and I admired him for it.

The pink glow returned to Daniel's eyes when we entered. A powerful presence could be felt in the air around us; it tugged at the dormant energy within my veins. We stepped into the washroom just inside the main doors and began to strip. Shelves lined one of the walls for clothes to be placed on. Even though there was ample room, Daniel always chose to use the shelf right next to mine.

We stored our clothes away and stepped into the large bath in the middle of the room. It was customary to cleanse oneself before entering the sanctuary. The water was warm and soothed the ache in my hand, washing the blood away. Daniel was quiet. He never spoke inside the temple, at least not to me.

Holy robes hung on hooks near the sanctuary entrance. Daniel and I put them on after we dried off. The washroom led directly into the sanctuary. I stayed back and let Daniel enter first. He preferred to pray without someone right next to him, so I waited a few minutes before I followed.

Entering the sanctuary, my skin tingled from the energy that filled the circular room. Four altars were placed in the middle—one for each shaman—and the three shrines for the gods were located along the wall with equal distances between them. Daniel was in the center shrine communing with Sibyl, the goddess of spirit.

My worship started in the center of the room with the four shamans. To the north was the altar for Gaia. She was the first to be blessed with the gift of earth magic. I knelt before her idol and thanked her for her sacrifice, then I prayed that she would continue to bless Daniel with the strength and protection of earth magic.

I moved clockwise around the altars, thanking each shaman for their sacrifice. To the east was Ilmatar, the first to be blessed with the gift of air magic. At the south was Vulcan, the first to be blessed with the gift of fire magic. Then lastly, at the west was Nerine, the first to be blessed with the gift of water magic.

The magic of my era was a blessing, but from what I'd read in the history books, it started out as a curse, which was why I always thanked the shamans. They'd been horribly disfigured by the gifts of magic that they received. But the horrid forms of those with magic changed over the decades as our species evolved. Most beings now looked humanoid in origin, so we were blessed with the gift of magic without having a disfigured appearance.

After thanking the shamans, I visited the shrines of the gods. I respectfully thanked Sibyl and Apollo, the sun god, before I entered the shrine for Hecate, the moon goddess. As a dark magic user, I communed with Hecate the most. Her gift of the moonstone was what allowed me to use dark magic.

I thanked the goddess and cut my palm with the athame that sat on her altar. My blood dripped into the bowl before me as an offering to my goddess. I used one of the silver strips of cloth in the basket on the floor to wrap my hand. It was an honor to bleed for the goddess, and I prayed she would continue to bless me with the gift of dark magic. I bowed before I left her shrine.

Daniel had already left the sanctuary by the time I finished my prayers, so I went back to the washroom to change into my regular clothes. I headed outside and found Daniel sitting at the bottom of the steps. The muscles in his back were tensed up. It was strange to see because he was usually so relaxed after communing with the gods.

"Hey, is everything all right?" I asked as I stepped off the last step. Daniel jumped up and turned to look at me. His eyes glowed pink.

"There's something I have to tell you," he said. His face was flushed. If I hadn't known better, I would've thought Daniel was blushing, but that was impossible. He never blushed and was almost never serious, so I knew he was about to mess with me.

"All right, so tell me then," I said with a smile in preparation for the joke I was about to hear. Daniel placed his hands on my shoulders and stared into my eyes before he spoke.

"I love you," Daniel said. His grip on my shoulders was firm.

I sighed, but before I could respond to what was clearly a poor joke, we were interrupted.

"Harrison! There you are. I've been looking everywhere for you." Jess's voice echoed across the grounds. She stood at the rear entrance to the palace and wore one of her casual black dresses.

"Jess, this isn't a good time," Daniel replied. I could hear his teeth grind as he spoke.

"Nonsense. Harrison always has time for me." She smirked. Daniel released me and clenched his fists as his arms fell to his sides. I had never seen him get so upset about her presence before.

"We're in the middle of an important discussion. Why don't you come back later?" Daniel replied.

"Oh please, you boys can talk later. Harrison and I need to go over wedding plans," she said.

"Yeah, all right. I'm coming," I said.

As I left, Daniel sighed. He must have been disappointed that I obeyed Jess, or maybe he really did have something important to discuss. Either way, he'd have to wait. I was obligated to put the princess first, even if I preferred Daniel's company.

CHAPTER 3

TYLER

My eyes stung fiercely as the dust cloud settled around me. The ache in my head was a reminder of what had happened. I'd let my guard down, and my father had landed a hit across my temple. We'd worked on my self-defense skills all summer, but I still had a ways to go.

"Get up," my father shouted at me on a repetitive loop until I staggered to my feet. I raised my sword and tried to regain my focus. His hit came hard as his blade crashed into mine. The power behind it made me stumble back. I landed in the dry dirt again, and another cloud of dust puffed up from the ground. This time I used it as cover to launch a counterattack. It barely fazed him. I swung my sword with all my strength, but he was fast enough to block it. Our swords crashed together again.

"Tyler"—the disappointment in his voice was clear—"you must use your opponent's strength and size against them. You'll never beat out an attacker with a frontal assault." He was right. Even though I trained with him every morning, my strength would never be greater than that of a man.

I hoped I would never have to fight. I had faith that love and kindness could turn around even the most dire situation.

The late fall sunrise washed the land with light. It glinted off our swords as we continued to duel. I was determined to be as great a warrior as my father, but his magical abilities always put me at a disadvantage. He had a connection to the earth. The lands of Alterra were both his ally and his weapon.

Dust lifted from the ground, clouding the air. It swirled around me like a storm. I couldn't see more than a foot in front of me, but I knew my father was coming. The dust storm was merely a distraction. If only I had magic of my own to make the fight more fair. Then I could be as strong as he was.

I ducked when the glint of a sword hilt cut through the dust. It just barely missed my temple. My foot caught on a dip in the ground, or rather the ground dipped out from under me. I fell to the earth, rolling over to meet my father's sword with my own.

"Good," my father said. As the dust fell from the air, I saw the smile on his face. The lines on his forehead almost completely disappeared when he smiled. I wished I had a smile like his, that I had any resemblance to him, but I didn't. He was an asudh, and I was human.

A figure in the distance brought our duel to a halt. My mother walked toward us with a somber expression on her face. Her dark brown hair was tied on top of her head in a frazzled mess, and her olive skin was still darkened from the summer sun. I didn't look anything like her either.

It was obvious that I'd been adopted by them as a baby, though they'd never told me so themselves. I had bright blue eyes and long blond hair that nearly blended in with my pale skin. Even when I'd spend time in the sun during the summer to look more like my parents, I'd only end up burnt and red.

"Honey, come quick," my mother sobbed as she reached us. She tucked a wild strand of hair behind her pointed ears. "It's the cows."

My father's brown eyes widened. The cows were sick or

worse. Every year we lost more and more animals to illness or starvation. We headed toward the barn where we kept what was left of our small herd.

The icy chill of the morning air beat across my face. Winter would come soon, and if the cows didn't survive, neither would we. As it was, we barely got enough milk from the cows to meet the needs of our village. If we lost any more of them, there wouldn't be enough for everyone.

Over the past couple years, a handful of people from our village died from starvation. Most of the families in Addersfield were farmers, and because of that we were all expected to feed ourselves. Unfortunately, every new harvest season was worse than the last. People had to ration their food, but even that wasn't always enough. The lands of Alterra were dying, and without aid from the Dark Nation, everyone in Addersfield would eventually starve to death.

When we reached the barn, I had to stifle back tears. Two of our older cows were dead, their blood staining the floor of the barn. The rest of the herd had lain down. They were all too thin. The grain we harvested was hardly enough to keep them alive.

"How long have they been dead?" my father asked.

"They were warm when I found them, so sometime this morning. I cut them open to start the bleeding but knew I'd need more hands to get this done," my mother replied. She pushed on the rear legs of one of the dead cows, and more blood oozed out of it. My father did the same to the other dead cow. I fought back the urge to vomit. There was too much blood.

"We're running low on salvia. Why don't you see if you can't get more from town?" my mother said. She knew I couldn't bear the butchering process.

"But there's too much work to be done here," I replied. My stomach churned at the thought of helping them cut up the cows, but I knew I needed to help.

"Nonsense," my father replied. "Your mother and I can

take care of things here, but we're going to need more salvia if we hope to keep the rest of the herd alive."

I looked to the cows that were lying in the barn. Foot rot had spread to all of them over the past week. Salvia was the only herb we had access to that could fight the infection. If we ran out of it, they would surely die.

"All right, I'll go to town to get more."

"Be careful out there," Dad said as he waved me off.

I went to the house to grab my pack. We lived in a small wooden cabin that only had two rooms. We had a main room and a bedroom with three cots in it. My pack sat beside my cot. I grabbed it and headed toward town. With any luck, the alchemist would have salvia and I'd be home with it before sunset.

The town was a few miles north of our farm, and it usually took me about two hours to get there if I walked. Even though I moved with urgency, the time passed slowly. When the town was finally in sight, I took a moment to catch my breath and looked back at the lands behind me.

Our town was located at the top of a hill, so it had a beautiful view of the farmlands below. It pained me to see that a large portion of the land was barren. Fields of black nothingness covered more of the land than the fields of green. My heart ached to see how the earth suffered. I prayed the gods may give us a way to save our land.

People filled the town square. There was a live broadcast at the viewing station, which would make it impossible for me to wade through the crowd. I decided it would be easier to cut through the alleys to get to the alchemist's shop. There were only a couple shops between me and my destination when I was stopped.

"Now where's a fine lass like you goin' in such a hurry?" The man slurred his words as he stepped out in front of me.

"I have urgent business with the alchemist, so if you'll excuse me." My attempt to slip past the man failed. He caught my wrist and pinned me to the alley wall. I could taste the liquor on his breath as the smell suffocated me.

"Surely he'll understand if you're a wee bit late." He ran his fingers through my hair as he spoke. His dark brown eyes stared down at me. I could see pain reflected in them as he looked through me. He did not see me as a person, but as a mere outlet for his unfortunate circumstances. I felt bad for him briefly until the gravity of the situation hit me. This man was lost, and I doubted there was anything I could say to stop him from what he was about to do.

He leaned in to kiss me, but I turned away. I rammed my knee into his groin, and he took a step back. It was my chance to run, so I took it. Unfortunately, he was only surprised for a second before he grabbed a fistful of my hair and threw me to the ground.

My body still ached from the duel with my father, and the man was three times my size. I knew I wouldn't be able to fight him off. My heart raced in my chest as I prayed for an escape.

"Ahem." A man's voice echoed down the alley. My attacker turned to look up at him, but his head blocked my view. "Excuse me, sir, but that's my woman you have there, so unless you want me to retaliate, I suggest you leave."

"Aye, I see. I'll be leavin' then." The man's weight quickly lifted from me, and he ran off down the alley. My head throbbed as I looked up at the man who'd saved me.

"Nydden?" I gasped as I recognized him. His skin was tanned from the summer sun, and his black hair had been cut short, revealing his perfectly pointed ears. He extended his hand toward me, and I graciously took it.

"Are you hurt?" he asked as he looked me over for injuries with his dark teal eyes. I'd known Nydden for years. We'd met at the alchemist's shop; he was apprenticing there the first time I walked in. He had been protective back then too, warning me about the more dangerous herbs.

I threw my arms around him, squeezing tightly. "I'm fine, thanks to you. But it was risky for you to challenge that man like that. You could have been hurt."

"He was clearly drunk and no threat to me." Nydden held me at arm's length. "You should be more careful."

"And you shouldn't put yourself in danger for me," I replied, moving out of his grip.

He smiled and shook his head. His gold earring glimmered in the sunlight as it hung from his ear. It drew my attention, and I couldn't help but admire how Nydden's long pointed ears complemented his sharp jawline. He was lucky to be an asudh.

"Why were you in an alley anyway? You know it's best for women to stick to the main streets."

"There was a broadcast on the viewing station, and I was in a hurry," I replied.

"A lot of good that did you. Were you headed to see the alchemist?"

"Yes. I need to get salvia for the cows."

"All right, I'll accompany you the rest of the way," he said as he motioned for me to lead.

I didn't want to be a burden, but I let him escort me anyway. My hands still trembled from the attack, and it was easier to go along with him than it was to fight. Once Nydden made his mind up about something, it was impossible to change it.

When we got to the alchemist's shop, it was mostly empty. The walls were lined with shelves that held glass jars full of different herbs and potions. I checked the shelves for salvia while Nydden went to the back to look for the alchemist.

As I scanned the shelves, the bell to the shop door rang behind me. I turned and glanced at the man who walked in. His pointed ears pegged him as an asudh, and he was dressed in an all-black military uniform. Based on the decorations around his collar, I guessed he was a sergeant in the Dark Nation Army. His beady eyes locked on mine as I stared. Soldiers rarely visited Addersfield.

"You there, where's the owner of this establishment?" He spoke to me in Asudhen even though I was clearly human. Before I was able to reply, the alchemist stepped out of the back room.

"Hello, sir, how may I help you today?" The alchemist smiled as he greeted the soldier. He was completely unfazed by the military presence. His long black hair was braided to one side and had specks of gray throughout it. He was by far the wisest asudh in town.

"Let's get out of here," Nydden whispered as he nudged me toward the door. The soldier spoke to the alchemist, but I could not hear what was said. I was hurried out of the shop before I could protest.

"What was that for?" I asked as the door closed behind us. "I still need to get salvia for my family."

"He doesn't have any," Nydden replied. He led me around the corner of the building so others wouldn't overhear us. His eyes scanned the town the whole way.

"Then I'll have to search the woods," I said. My family needed the salvia, and time was of the essence. I knew of a grove in the forest not too far from town where salvia liked to grow.

"It can wait until the morning," Nydden said. "You shouldn't wander the woods at night."

I looked to the sky. The sun was still high. "It's hardly midday. I'm sure I could make it home by nightfall if I leave now."

Nydden's dark teal eyes stared into mine. "It's not safe. Not with these soldiers around."

"Why are they here?" I asked, looking around the corner of the building.

"I'm not sure, but it can't be good."

A crowd was gathered around the viewing station with a handful of soldiers lined up outside the town hall. If the Dark Nation sent soldiers, then something big was about to happen. But was their presence a threat? I wasn't sure. All I knew was that our cows were sick and that salvia could help them.

"I need to get going." I headed around the back side of the shop, and Nydden followed.

"I'll walk you home," he replied. His words were full of confidence, as if saying them made them true.

"I'm not going home, not until I get salvia for the cows."

Nydden sighed and stopped in his tracks. I continued to walk on past him.

"Tyler," Nydden said sternly, and I turned to face him. His lips formed a thin line, and his eyes stared into mine. A chill ran down my spine.

"The cows need the salvia," I said through quivering lips.

My heart raced. I had only ever seen that look on Nydden's face once before. If I didn't comply with what he wanted, he would use his magic to make me. I could already feel the cold prickle of ice on my skin.

"Your safety is more important," he replied. His dark teal eyes didn't back down.

"All right, fine," I said as the chill overwhelmed me. "I'll go home."

"Good."

The cold prickle of ice vanished. I was powerless against magic and hated that there was nothing I could do about it. Nydden was usually so kind to me, but when it came to my safety, he went too far. I knew he was just trying to look out for me, but I wasn't always in need of protection.

Our journey began with silence. We walked slowly back toward my family's farm, and even though Nydden wouldn't let me get the salvia our cows needed, I refused to let it get me down.

I reveled in the cool breezes that tossed my hair about, taking in deep breaths of the fresh air. It reminded me that the earth was still alive, which meant it could still be saved. I only hoped we would be able to find a way to save it before it was too late.

"How has the harvest been this year?" Nydden asked, breaking the long silence that hung between us. He stared out at the fields of nothingness.

"Worse than last year, I'm afraid." My sigh was audible.

"That doesn't bode well for Addersfield. Your farm has

been the main source of food these past couple years. The other farms hardly produce at all anymore."

"I know. We're doing the best we can. Father has been rationing the family supply in order to give more to the town. He feels responsible for the families that died last winter."

"What?" Nydden stopped and turned toward me. "Is he really that foolish? If he cuts into your family's supply, he puts you at risk for starvation." There was tension in his voice. He sounded much wiser than his years when he spoke out of concern for me. It made me think he was older than he appeared. Asudhs could be tricky that way.

"You know how my father is. He wants to save as many people as possible, and I fully support him. I'd rather be a little hungry than watch another person die."

"Don't be a martyr. Your life is too important." He sighed and began to walk again.

"Being kind to our neighbors does not make us martyrs. It's simply the right thing to do," I said. Nydden had no family, so he only ever had to worry about himself. He didn't understand what it was like to feel responsible for others.

"Kindness isn't right if it gets you killed," he replied. We continued the rest of our walk in silence. Nydden hated it when things didn't go his way.

The sun bathed the land in an orange glow as it began its descent. We reached the farm before dark. Smoke rose from our cabin's chimney, carrying the mouthwatering smell of beef stew with it. Dinner was almost ready.

Nydden stopped a few meters away from the cabin's door. "I'll meet you here tomorrow morning. We'll get the salvia then."

"You should join us for dinner," I replied.

"No. Good night. I'll be back tomorrow." His words were short.

Before I could think of a reply, Nydden turned and walked

away. He traveled back toward town. It would be dark before he made it home. I prayed for his safe return as he disappeared in the distance. Even though he was out of sight, I continued to stare in his direction. He had put himself in danger for me . . . again.

CHAPTER 4

KI

Pressed for time, I walked briskly through the palace halls. My father had summoned the council, and I was expected to be there. It had taken longer than expected to cram myself into the bloody suit he requested, so I had to hurry. Tardiness was unacceptable, especially for a prince.

I sighed in relief when I reached the council room; my father had yet to arrive. The other council members were already there. They stood behind their seats, which were arranged around the long wooden table that sat in the middle of the room. My parents' seats were at the head of the table, while mine was on the opposite end.

Just barely reaching my seat in time, the doors to the council room were thrust open and my father made his grand entrance. He wore a black silk tunic embellished with silver thread and a surcoat that had the Darkblood family crest embroidered on the left chest panel. His silver mantle floated across the floor as he took his place at the head of the table. The silver crown atop his head fit perfectly between his large ram-like horns and was balanced by the many rings he wore on his gray-skinned fingers.

Of all the rings he wore, the family ring was the largest. It was made of silver with our family crest etched into each side, topped with a black diamond at the center. I wore the exact same ring and had always admired our family crest. It was an outline of a dark creature with large feathered wings that held on to a shield. The shield was divided into four sections, a small shield with the letter *D* at its center. Each section had its own representation of the family: a crown to show our royal bloodline, the moonstone to show our power and connection to the goddess Hecate, an inverted pentagram to show our demonic origins, and a ring to symbolize our strength.

My mother trailed behind my father, following him to the head of the table. Made to match my father, she wore a black dress that blended in with her charcoal-colored skin and a small silver crown that stood out against her jet-black hair. Her jewelry was not as decadent as my father's, but she did have an embellished black fur over her shoulders. She looked at me with her fire-colored eyes as she passed by.

"Be seated. We have much to discuss," my father said as he took his seat. The rustle of chairs echoed around the room as we all bowed and took our seats. Once the noise settled, my father began. "Evan, what is the status of Tor Terran?"

"Conditions continue to worsen, Your Majesty. Riots are happening every few weeks. The people are not happy about the food shortages," Evan replied.

Evan was the Tor Terran ambassador, though I never understood how he got elected for it. He was a rather plain light-skinned human who dressed casually compared to the rest of the council. His hair and eyes were the same ordinary shade of brown. The Tor Terran emblem embroidered on his chest was the most interesting thing about him. It was a tree encompassed by a circle that looked like waves on the sea.

"Field Marshal, have your troops been dispatched as requested?" my father asked, looking at Vladimir.

Even though the field marshal was Daniel's father, they looked quite different. Vladimir had the common tlaloc traits that Daniel lacked: large tusks that extended out from his lower jaw and rounded ears. However, they did share the same white hair and hazel eyes.

"Yes, sir. Troops have reached even the smallest towns. They've managed to keep civil order thus far, but the rioters continue to be persistent," he replied. The dress uniform he wore was heavily decorated with colorful bars and ribbons representing his many military achievements. As long as I could remember, he had always been in control of my father's armies.

"You have my permission to use any force necessary. Make an example out of those rioters. I will not have unrest in my streets," my father replied. He was always quick to send soldiers to keep the people in line, but a military presence wasn't going to fix the real problem.

"Pardon me, Your Majesty, but shouldn't we consider rationing the Dark Nation's food supply to give aid to the outer cities and towns?" I said. All the eyes in the room turned to look at me.

"Absolutely not! We cannot raise awareness of the issue. If the farmers can't feed themselves, then they can starve!" my father snapped. I understood that he didn't want the Dark Nation's people to find out about the dying lands, as it would cause panic in our city, but our outer regions needed help.

"Might I offer a suggestion?" Pope Klyn asked. He was a rather thin light-skinned human with dark red hair that was braided back into a bun.

As a holy man, Klyn wore a clergy robe that held representation for all three of our gods. It had a mix of black, white, and purple colors that were trimmed with decorations of silver and gold. I envied him. My attire wasn't allowed to be so colorful.

"Of course, Your Holiness," my father replied.

"The church could sponsor a food drive. We would advertise that donations would go to those in need without bringing attention to the current blight. I'm sure people would be happy to please the gods by helping others," Pope Klyn said. The smile on his face irked me.

"That's a great idea," my father replied, smiling in the pope's direction.

"It won't solve the problem long-term, but it might afford us a little time," Pope Klyn said.

"We should consider asking the other nations for aid as well. If the land continues to die at its current rate, many people won't survive the winter," I added.

"Have you lost your damn mind? Asking the neighboring kingdoms for aid would cause just as much panic as broadcasting the barren farmlands. We'd have a fucking uprising on our hands. Is that what you want?" my father shouted. All the men in the room sat up straighter, shoulders pulled back.

Heat rose within me as I clenched my fists under the table. The familiar electric tingle of dark magic swirled inside my veins, but I forced it down. I couldn't lose my temper, not in front of my father.

"Pardon me, Your Majesty, but I also have a suggestion." Daniel's words broke the tension in the room and drew my father's focus away from me.

My father never listened to any of my suggestions, even though I'd been on the council for over five years. The day I turned fifteen, he insisted I attend the meetings, but I had zero sway. Thankfully, Daniel was part of the council. He often served as a buffer between me and my father.

"Continue," my father replied. His eyes focused on Daniel.

"We should have the Reckoning. It would give the people something to be excited about while they struggle through the winter months. Their misery wouldn't seem so bad in comparison to the people suffering to survive the Reckoning," Daniel said with a grin.

"Field Marshal Darkson, you should be proud of this genius son of yours," my father said.

"Thank you, Your Majesty." Vladimir grinned. He looked at

his son in a way I wished my father would look at me—full of pride. My father only ever looked at me with disappointment.

"Your Majesty, before you make a decision on this, I would like to point out that having the Reckoning now would break hundreds of years of tradition," said Grand Duke Dmitry Darkborne, the voice of reason and my father's right-hand man.

He was Harrison's father, and their likeness was uncanny. They had the same olive-colored skin, long pointed ears, and piercing green eyes. I could only tell them apart because Dmitry had long brown hair that trailed most of the way down his back. He sat beside my father with his hair down with only a few strands pulled back to keep it out of his face. It draped over the front of his black jacket, which was trimmed in elaborate silver designs. He dressed nearly as ostentatiously as my father, with his hands covered in silver jewelry.

"The Reckoning was created so that the original Darkblood and Lightblood families could find warriors worthy of sharing their magical connections with. They designed it to test the loyalty and strength of those who would become the families' protectors. With all the riots in the outer areas, I think the people would understand the king's choice to break with tradition. They'd understand his need for loyal and worthy warriors," Harrison said.

My lips parted, but I said nothing. Harrison dressed like his father and shared the same love of history and tradition, yet he publicly spoke out in opposition.

I looked to Dmitry, but there were no signs of anger about him. No clenched fists, no grinding teeth, not even a raised brow. Harrison's opposition didn't faze him at all. How the bloody hell was he not bothered? If I opposed my father, he'd beat me half to death and throw me in the dungeon for a night.

"Well, there you have it, gentlemen. Spoken from the mouths of babes," my father said as he gestured toward Harrison, a wide grin on his face. "You never cease to amaze me. I'll be proud the day I can call you son."

My eye twitched as I took in his words. Harrison had always

been his favorite. It didn't matter what he did, my father always praised him. I felt the prickle of magic in my veins again, but this time it wasn't caused by anger.

"Guards!" my father shouted, and the doors flew open. A large tlaloc stood in his silver plate mail and looked to my father for his orders. "Send for the seers. Tell them the king requests their audience at once."

"Yes, Your Majesty." The guard bowed and left the room.

My father stood from his chair, and everyone else followed suit. "This meeting is adjourned. I must prepare for my audience with the seers." The council members bowed as my father walked out of the room. My mother followed closely behind him. I wondered what my father had done to break her. She lacked the spirit she had when I was a child.

Senseless chatter filled the room once my father was gone, the Reckoning being the main subject. I didn't care for pointless conversations, so I left. Unfortunately, Harrison caught up to me before I even made it halfway down the corridor.

"Do you think we'll be Called?" Harrison asked as he walked beside me. I had to take a deep breath before I could respond. The electric tingle of dark magic still plagued me.

"Of course we will," I replied. "Even if the seers don't pick us, my father will make sure we're added to the list." My father would use the Reckoning as an excuse to make my life even more miserable.

"You really think so? It's such an honor to be Called."

"He'll use it as a test to make sure we're worthy of our bloody titles." The swirling dark magic within me began to seep out. It created a dark aura around me, but Harrison paid it no mind.

"Well, I'm up for the challenge." Harrison smiled. He was always quick to jump at the opportunity to please my father. His loyalty knew no bounds. A bloody perfect son he was.

"I'll catch up with you later," I said as I turned down the hall that led to my room.

Harrison waved me off without another word. He could

tell when I didn't want to talk, and he respected that. I managed to get back to my room without being stopped.

Locking the doors behind me, I went to my bed. I opened the secret panel in the wall behind it to reveal a journal and several other notebooks. Writing was nearly as useless as feelings were, according to my father, so I had to keep my hobby a secret.

For a moment I thought to grab my journal, to write about how my father had treated me during the meeting. Instead I grabbed one of my notebooks. I'd escape my harsh reality by exploring the lives of the characters in my story. They could go anywhere and do anything.

CHAPTER 5

TYLER

I woke before the sun. My parents were sound asleep in their cots next to me. They had stayed up most of the night butchering the cows in an attempt to save as much meat as possible. I was of no help to them because of the blood, so the least I could do was not interrupt their sleep.

Sliding slowly out of my cot, I was careful not to make a sound. My clothes and pack lay by the front door where I had placed them the night before. I made my way toward them, but at every creak of the wooden floors I froze. Continuing on when I was sure my parents hadn't been disturbed, I slipped into my clothes and out the door.

The cold bite of morning air nipped at me through my tunic, even though I was wearing a thicker one. I hoped the warmth of the sun's rays would be upon me soon. If only the summer days could've stuck around longer.

A crunch in the grass caught my attention as I walked toward the road. Nydden's dark teal eyes reflected the dim light of morning. The sun had begun to rise, but it hadn't yet made it over the horizon.

"You're here," I said as Nydden came up to me. He wore his caramel-brown tunic. It was my favorite one because it made his eyes pop.

"I said I would be," Nydden replied. "It's not safe to wander the forest alone." I noticed the long wooden spear strapped to his back. It had sharp steel blades on both ends.

"It's a good thing we won't be wandering," I said with a smile. "I know a grove were salvia grows, so I doubt you'll be needing to use that." I motioned toward his spear. Weapons only ever made bad situations worse.

It was a long hike through the woods, up and down the hills. Nydden was quiet as we trudged through damp underbrush. I took a deep breath and enjoyed the simple beauty of it. Being in the woods, surrounded by trees, I felt connected to the land. We were one, and I was at peace. The presence of Apollo, our sun god, could be felt in the warmth of the sun's rays trickling through the tree cover. He still blessed the land.

By the time we reached the small clearing, the sun had risen high in the sky. I knew exactly where to find it because I had stumbled upon the dry patch of land earlier in the year. It was closer to town than our farm, but it was an undisturbed area.

Dust lifted from the ground as we walked. Nydden stuck close to my side, his eyes scanning the forest. I searched the area for a few minutes, and then I saw it. Salvia. I gathered as many leaves from the plants as I could and stuffed them into my bag. It was a delicate plant, so I was careful not to disturb its roots. Hopefully the salvia would continue to grow, and I'd be able to collect from it again.

The wind picked up, and the sky darkened. Nydden drew the spear from his back and took a defensive stance. A loud siren blared out across the land, scaring birds out of the nearby trees. The Calling? It was definitely the sound of the Calling, but it was too soon.

I looked to Nydden. His wide eyes and raised brow told me

he was just as confused as I was. The Calling only happened once every five years. It was a ritual spell the king's seers used to select competitors to take part in the Reckoning. But it had only been four years since the last one.

"We should hurry back," Nydden said.

I nodded in agreement and headed in the direction of town. There would be a broadcast on the viewing station about what was happening. Only beings with great magical potential were Called to take part in the Reckoning, so I didn't have to worry. But Nydden was an asudh. He had magic, and I was sure he was within the fifteen-to-twenty-two age range that the competitors were selected from.

An unusual sound came from behind us, and my walk quickly turned into a run. Nydden kept up with my pace as something ripped through the trees. It was getting closer to us. I didn't know what it was, but it couldn't be good.

It hit me hard, and I crashed to the ground. My wrist burned with pain from the impact. Was it broken? No. When I looked down, I found that a solid metal band had fused around my right wrist. It dangled, but the hole wasn't big enough for my hand to fit through. There was no way to get it off. I attempted to slide the band over my hand, and a shock zapped me.

"You have thirty minutes to report to the nearest viewing station," the bracelet said. A thirty-minute counter popped up and began to count down by the second.

Nydden helped me to my feet. His mouth hung open as he stared at the timer ticking away. When his dark teal eyes locked with mine, I saw a desperation in them.

"Run," he said, but I didn't move. I was frozen in fear. "Tyler, you have to run!" Nydden shook me, pulling me back to myself.

Realizing how far I was from town, I ran. My boots were heavy, and the terrain was hilly, but I ran as fast as I could. I wasn't sure if I'd be able to make it to the station in time, but if that shock the bracelet gave me was any indication, I didn't have a choice.

The brush of the forest floor tore at my exposed skin as I forced my way through it. I used my hands to protect my face, and scratches covered them. A thorn caught on my sleeve and tore it open, but I continued to fight through the harsh forest terrain. I had to keep my legs in motion; there was no time to rest.

I could hear Nydden running through the forest behind me. He couldn't keep up with my pace, but he didn't need to. Suddenly, I was grateful for all the long-distance training my father had me do over the past few years. I could outrun anyone in Addersfield.

By the time the town square came into view, I only had five minutes left. I ran faster as my feet found the cobblestone that stretched through the town. People crowded the streets, presumably confused by the Calling.

I crashed into passersby as I shoved between bodies. The viewing station was at the center of the town square. I could see the six large stone pillars that surrounded it. They represented the different types of magic.

Five seconds were left as I made it through the crowd. The clock struck zero right as I passed between two of the pillars. A burning pain shot through my hand, and I collapsed onto the crest carved in the center of the station. I gasped, trying to catch my breath. The searing pain in my hand subsided as the station came to life.

"Congratulations." The Darkblood King's voice filled the square. It quieted the crowd. His image appeared on the flat surface of the government building in front of me. "You've survived the Calling and are one step closer to participating in the Reckoning. It's an honor to be selected for this challenge." The crowd clapped with excitement. It had been many years since someone from our town had been Called.

"From the moment that bracelet found your wrist until the moment it's removed, you are the property of the Dark Nation. A transport will take you to the processing center before nightfall. Be sure to say your goodbyes. I look forward to seeing how well you perform in the Reckoning." The Darkblood King's face disappeared as he finished his announcement. People began to cheer my name. They thanked me for the honor I brought to them. My participation in the Reckoning could help save the town.

I climbed to my feet as two soldiers dressed in Dark Nation uniforms stepped out of the government building. One of the soldiers was a tlaloc. He had one large horn that protruded from the space between his eyes and nasty scars that stretched across his face. It looked as though someone or something had tried to claw his face off. My stomach churned from his grotesque appearance.

The second soldier I recognized from the alchemist's shop. His short black hair and olive skin complemented his uniform. However, he had unnervingly beady brown eyes that seemed to look through me as the two of them approached. Had they known about the Calling before it happened? Was that why they were in town to begin with?

"We're here to escort you to the center," the asudh said. He used the common language this time. It was clear he thought I was uneducated. Eager to deliver me to the king, he grabbed my arm. "Let's go." He growled as he pulled me out of the circle.

"Let her go. This is some kind of mistake." Nydden's voice broke through the crowd as he emerged from the mass. He caught the asudh's attention, and I used the distraction to pull my arm from his grip.

"The king does not make mistakes," the asudh replied.

"Then it was the seer. This girl has no magic," Nydden said as he drew near. He stood between me and the soldiers.

"You can make a formal complaint with your government official," the asudh said. "Now if you'll step aside, I have orders to deliver this girl to the processing center."

"I thought I had time to say my goodbyes? My parents will need to know where I've disappeared to, and I have to get these herbs back to them," I said, loud enough for the nearby townspeople to hear. If the soldiers refused my request, the whole town would surely riot. They'd riot over anything at this point, given the king's refusal to help with the shortage of food.

"Fine," the asudh said. "But don't dally." He shoved me forward. I walked quickly down the street with Nydden at my side. He positioned himself between me and the soldiers, a small comfort.

The soldiers followed us. They kept a close watch on me for the entire journey. I suspected they thought I might run, but that would be pointless. The bracelet that dangled from my wrist would make it impossible for me to hide, and I knew it. A pit formed in my stomach.

When we made it back to the farm, I found my parents in the barn with the cows. They had washed away all signs of the butchering that had happened just the day before and were busy trying to get the herd to stand. I walked toward them with Nydden beside me, and they finally glanced our way.

"Thank goodness." My mom gasped as she took notice of the salvia that stuck out of my pack. "We just used up the last of it." She took the bag from me and immediately began to feed the leaves to the cows. The Calling hadn't fazed her at all. She had no reason to believe her magicless daughter would be Called.

"I was starting to worr—" my father began, but stopped short when the soldiers stepped up behind us. The look of dread on his face was almost too painful to see. They must have heard the alarm after all. "I guess this is goodbye," he said as he pulled me in for a hug.

My mother turned at my father's words and dropped my pack on the floor. She finally noticed the soldiers and the metal bracelet on my wrist.

"No. It can't be." Her eyes filled with tears as the realization hit her. She threw her arms around me, joining in on my father's embrace. "Please come back to us. You have to come back to us."

"I'll do my best," I replied.

I felt the wet warmth of my tears as they slid down my face. It was impossible to fight them back. My reality was fractured, and I prayed it was all a bad dream. I clung to my parents with an ache in my chest—an ache that only got worse as Nydden joined in on the group hug.

"All right, let's go," the asudh said as he pulled me from my family's embrace. I wanted to fight, to have a few more minutes with my parents, but there was no use. The soldiers were ready to go, and even if I would never see my parents again, I had to go with them.

"Goodbye," I cried as the soldiers dragged me from the barn.

My parents and Nydden stood in the doorway. They waved me off with tears in their eyes. Except for Nydden. He stood there with an angered expression. His fists were clenched, and his muscles were tight. I wondered what he was about to do with the resolve I saw on his face.

Once we were out of the view of my parents, the tlaloc threw me over his shoulder. "Put me down!" I cried, flailing my limbs in an attempt to free myself from his enormous hands.

"Shut up, or I'll drag you by your hair," he snarled.

I froze, suddenly aware of the direness of my situation. If I struggled or resisted in any way, they would have grounds to assault me, and tlalocs were known for their ruthlessness. I relaxed and let my arms dangle lifelessly as he carried me back toward the town.

The transport ship was docked at the edge of town. As we got close enough to be seen by townspeople, the tlaloc put me down and let me walk on my own. I was grateful for that small amount of dignity, although I was sure he only did it so he wouldn't look bad.

As we walked closer to the ship, I could see the Dark Nation's crest painted on the side of it. The emblem was painted in silver and stood out against the black color of the ship. It gave off an aura of intimidation.

Inside the ship, an asudh waited for us. I was shocked when

I caught a glimpse of her face. She had a soft smile and rosy cheeks, not what I expected from a Dark Nation soldier. The words she spoke were foreign to me, but the soldiers acted in response. They strapped me into a seat along the back wall of the ship and then did the same for themselves. Once everyone was ready, the door closed and the ship took us into the sky.

My stomach dropped as we shot up into the air. I had never been on a transport ship before, or in the air for that matter. The shakiness of the ride made me nauseous. I was barely able to see out the large window at the front of the ship because the asudh's head blocked most of my view.

Trees covered the hills in the distance, with leaves that had turned colors. The reds, yellows, and oranges blurred together and made the world look like it was on fire. It brought me back to the burning feeling that shot through my hand, to the dire situation I had found myself in. There was no way I would survive the Reckoning. I didn't have any magic.

The pit in my stomach grew. I had to have been Called by mistake, but the soldiers refused to listen. They didn't care that a magicless human girl had been sentenced to death. My heart raced, and dizziness overcame me.

Mountains stretched high into the sky in the far distance. They were the last thing I saw before the world spun out from under me. My vision blurred to black.

CHAPTER 6

KI

I woke in a sea of black feathers. The familiar ache in my back haunted me as I realized my wings had unfurled in my sleep. I barely noticed the dull throbbing of my wrist in comparison. A solid metal band dangled from my arm like a shackle on a prisoner. It was the Calling.

Even though I'd been prepared for the Calling, it came at a less than ideal time. I had only a few minutes to report to the throne room, and I needed to conceal my wings before I left my room. A dread filled me as I reached back to touch the skin on my back where my wings jetted out. I winced from the tenderness of the area, but I had no time to wait.

The pain was unavoidable. I took a deep breath and drew on the dark magic within me. I forced my freed wings to retract into my back in one swift motion. My stomach flipped from the searing pain, and I nearly vomited.

As I staggered to my feet, a trickle of blood ran down my back. In my mirror I could see the two long slits that remained as a bloody reminder. It was unnatural for me to fight against my body's development, and the pain was my consequence.

My back ached as I headed toward the throne room. I tried to keep up my usual appearance as I walked the halls, but my body had other plans. A fit of dizziness consumed me, and I nearly crushed a handmaiden as I stumbled.

"Your Highness," she squeaked as I fell into her. Her arms pushed against me as she tried to hold me up, but her attempt was futile. She collapsed under my weight, and we both fell to the floor.

Dazed, I tried to focus, but the maiden's words were lost in the spinning of the world. She pushed against me, panicked. My senses came into focus as I noticed her rapid heartbeat. I was drawn to it, just as a spider is drawn to a fly caught in its web. The blood in her veins called to me, but I resisted.

"Tell no one of this," I said sternly as I found my way to my feet. Her watery eyes locked with mine for a brief moment before turning to the floor.

"Of course, Your Royal Highness," she replied with a bow. Her unnatural movement caught my attention. She was injured, but to what extent I did not know.

"Take the rest of the day off. If anyone asks, tell them the prince told you to stay out of his sight. Expect to find extra compensation at the end of the week." I turned away from the girl before she could look up at me.

"Thank you, Your Royal Highness," she said.

I continued my journey to the throne room without further incident. Hunger became pain's companion as I walked. My mood was deteriorating, and my patience was thin. I needed to hunt sooner rather than later.

As I approached the throne room, I was greeted by two guardsmen standing at the entrance. They nodded respectfully as they opened the large black doors. I walked in, glad to find the curtains drawn and the candelabrums lit. The dim lighting was easy on my eyes.

A long silver carpet stretched across the room, from the

door's entrance to the raised platform where my parents sat atop their thrones. The king's throne was taller than the queen's, with a spiked back that stretched toward the ceiling. They were made of silver with jewels embedded in the trim and soft black cushions lining the seats.

I made my way down the long aisle lined with empty pews and noticed Harrison and Daniel standing at the foot of the thrones with metal bands on their wrists. No one bothered to look at me. Their attention was focused on a swarm of viewing orbs that hovered before them.

Curious as to what they were watching, I nearly missed the guards and warlocks that lined the perimeter of the room. They wore their black-and-silver uniforms and stood stiffly in place. I wondered if a single one of them could best me in a fight.

"Malaki, you're just in time for the show," my father said with a laugh. He leaned back in his throne, but his eyes remained on the orbs. They streamed live footage of competitors being Called.

My heart raced. Had an orb been there watching me when I was Called? Had my father seen my wings? The thought plagued me as I scanned the footage on the orbs. I saw competitors from all over Alterra being Called. Some were in their homes, others were out in the streets. Ones that resisted cried out in pain from the shock of the bracelet; it would kill them if they didn't comply.

There was a girl deep in the woods. She was so far away from a viewing station that she was sprinting to get to one. The forest's branches scratched at her, but she pushed through with determination. Her fight for survival had already begun.

I looked over every orb, but not one of them showed the throne room. There were no orbs following me, Harrison, or Daniel. I took a deep breath, relieved. No one had seen my bloody wings after all.

"Father, what is the meaning of this?" Jess shouted as she stormed into the room.

Everyone turned to look at her as she approached. Her flat

black hair hung limp around her small face, which only accented the horns that corkscrewed straight out of the top of her head. It annoyed me that her horns looked like an exact replica of mine. Hers were shorter and thinner, but it made us look too similar.

"It's the Calling, child. You know what that means," my father replied. "Or have you grown ignorant with age?" His smirk was cruel, and out of the corner of my eye I could see Jess cringe. She was bratty and mean, but our father was always too harsh with his words.

"But the Reckoning wasn't supposed to happen until next year," she said. "What about the wedding? We've been planning it all summer."

It was hard to believe the words that came out of her mouth. She couldn't really be upset about her arranged marriage being postponed. Since the day our father promised her hand to Harrison, for his father's success on the battlefields, she had done nothing but complain. To top it all off, she treated Harrison like he was her lapdog. He deserved way better than her, but my father wanted him to be his second son.

"The wedding will have to wait. Nothing is more important than the Reckoning," my father said, glaring at Jess from his throne. Jess's eyes began to water, but I had no pity for her. She always cried over the smallest things.

"Dear," my mother said, "couldn't you marry them before the departure? Jess has been waiting all these years, and Harrison just turned eighteen last week." She smiled at Father, and his anger melted away. I wondered if my mother was secretly an empath, given the way she could alter my father's foul mood so easily. It had to be magic.

"Yes, but they've waited this long. I'm sure a few more months isn't too long to wait. Is it, Harrison?" my father asked as he looked toward Harrison.

"No, Your Majesty," Harrison replied with a bow of his head. "I'm honored to have been Called and eager to prove myself worthy of your daughter's hand." Harrison was always so compliant to my father's wishes that he made me look bad. It frustrated me that he never stood up for himself, even when he was made to do things he hated.

"Wonderful." My father laughed. "Let's move on to more pressing matters. Competitors are being rounded up as we speak. You boys can take the night to prepare yourselves, but you must be at the processing center before midday tomorrow. I expect high performance from each of you. Show the people just how strong the Dark Nation is and make me proud."

"Yes, Father," I replied at the same time Harrison and Daniel said, "Yes, Your Majesty."

With that we were dismissed. Daniel stayed behind to have a private talk with my father, but Harrison and I exited through the main doors. Jess followed us closely, unusually quiet. Maybe she really was upset about the wedding being postponed.

Harrison took Jess's hand and gave her a smile. I was sure he only did it to brighten her somber mood; he was too nice to her. She smiled in return, perking up from that small gesture. It made my stomach churn.

"Can I speak with you in private?" Jess said. Her request was for Harrison, but he looked in my direction as if he needed permission.

"We can meet up later," I said as I walked away. No part of me had any desire to hear their conversation. The thought of Harrison with my sister was revolting, and my patience was at its limit. I needed to feed.

Returning from my hunt, I had no worries about the Reckoning. As the prince, I had unlimited access to the recordings of past Reckonings and had studied them closely over the past few years. They all had the same three-phase structure. Each phase had individual challenges that tested competitors' strength and skill, but the real test was staying alive.

The Reckoning took place in the Inbetween, an isolated patch of forest nestled within a perfect ring of mountains. Transport ships were the only way to get in or out, so wilderness survival skills were key, though combat skills were equally important.

There were no rules in regard to interactions between competitors, which meant they could work together or in opposition. However, I'd only ever witnessed competitors sabotaging one another. Unnecessary bloodshed happened quite often. A part of me was excited by the idea of the unknown, of the potential bloodshed, but I kept those desires to myself.

The full moon was rising in the sky as I made my way across the palace grounds. My hunt had restored my energy levels and quelled the hunger that plagued me. It was amazing, the strength I felt after feeding, but it would fade and turn back into crippling hunger soon enough.

With no time to waste, I hurried into the palace. Moving swiftly down the dark halls, I snuck into the secret passage that would take me into the caverns below. The moonstone was kept hidden within the maze of tunnels and would be at its strongest once the moon reached its apex.

It was pitch-black in the passage, but I could see in the dark—one of the more convenient attributes of being a dierdre. Rounding the final turn in the passage, I was greeted by the silver glow of the moonstone. It floated in the middle of the cavern with magic symbols drawn on the floor in a circle below it. The crescent moon shape that symbolized dark magic was the most prominent. Energy swirled within the stone and cast iridescent colors around the room. I was captivated by its beauty, its power.

There was a gravitational pull that drew me to the stone whenever I was near it. The dark magic within me was naturally drawn to its source. In a way, the stone was a part of me and I was a part of the stone. It was the only thing that could bind my power, and if I wanted to keep my abilities a secret throughout the Reckoning, that was exactly what I had to do.

The materials I needed for the ritual were already in the room. I pulled the spell book containing the binding ritual from the shelf along the wall, the page needed marked by a folded corner. I knew this day would come and had gone over the ritual a hundred times. There would be no mistakes.

Grabbing candles and a silver athame from the cabinet, I made my way over to the moonstone. I placed the candles over the symbols on the floor and sat outside the circle with the book open in front of me. A twinge beneath my skin told me the stone knew what I was about to do and did not approve.

I pushed the thought from my mind as I finished my preparations. The last piece of the ritual was my family ring. I placed it directly under the moonstone. It would act as my totem. Instead of casting the binding spell on myself, I would enchant the ring with it. That way if things got too risky, I could take the ring off and access my full power.

Sitting cross-legged, I slit the palms of my hands with the silver athame. My hands rested on my knees, palms to the ceiling as I began to chant in Tenebrisal, the ancient dierdre language. The moonstone responded immediately. Its energy swirled faster, and its power brightened the room.

Dark magic electrified my blood as it radiated from my body. My chant continued unfazed as the power gripped at me. It wanted to pull me apart, but I was in control. I forced the energy to listen to my words, and the silver glow of the moonstone's energy swirled around the dark tendrils that escaped me. The magics intertwined and surrounded the ring.

Sweat dripped from my face as I maintained my chant through to the end. The ritual was almost over. Curling my hand into a fist, I dripped blood across my ring. It absorbed into the ring, along with the black and silver magical energies. The ritual was complete. I relaxed, hunching over as the energy in the room dissipated.

The binding ritual took more out of me than expected. I hesitated briefly before grabbing the ring. In my exhausted state, I wasn't sure how the binding magic would affect me. It didn't matter, though; I knew the risk before I began the spell, and I'd decided a long time ago to take it.

When I returned the ring to its proper place on my hand, relief washed over me. There was no pain. In fact, the constant pull of magic that came from keeping my wings hidden was gone. I still had the discomfort from my wings being trapped within my body, but I no longer needed to actively use magic to keep them in.

I returned the book and candles to their proper places on the shelves before I left the cavern. Even though the ring only gave me a small amount of relief, it felt like a miracle. In that moment, I hoped the ring would prevent my body from transitioning before my ascension. It was a stupid hope, but I carried the thought with me as I made my way to my room, blissfully unaware of the challenges I was about to face.

CHAPTER 7

HARRISON

Jess held my hand firmly as she led me down the dimly lit corridor. Her puffy princess gown brushed against me as we walked. Made of satin and tulle, it perfectly matched the lavender color of her eyes. Black stone walls surrounded us, as if we were headed blindly through the abyss, yet even in the dim light I could see the smoothness of her pale gray skin. It was a beacon in the darkness that drew my eyes to her exposed upper chest.

Making our way to the east side of the palace, Jess was quiet. We stopped in front of the large purple door to her room, and she turned to face me. Her long black hair fell behind her shoulder, revealing the small crescent-moon-shaped birthmark on her neck. It was just below her left ear.

I was greeted with the familiar scent of lavender as Jess stood unusually close to me. It reminded me of a time when we were younger, before we were forced into an engagement. Jess had been a sweet young girl who loved flowers, especially lavender and white lilies. In the summers, I'd made a point of delivering bundles of them to her on my way back from my hunting lessons. I'd handpicked each one.

Jess had given me delicate kisses on my cheeks as reward for being her loyal servant—her words—but my real reward was her smile. Jess was always kept under lock and key in the castle, and it was rare to see her smile. Once I'd realized how happy a few flowers could make her, I made it a habit.

I looked into Jess's shimmering eyes and wondered if she had the same fond memories. Did she know why I brought her flowers all those years ago? I considered telling her. Part of me felt guilty that I hadn't brought her flowers in a long time.

"I have something for you," she whispered as she opened the door behind her. I almost didn't hear her words. Jess squeezed my hand a little tighter as she pulled me into her room.

Everything was purple: the covers on her bed, the rug beneath it, the drapes that hung over the balcony windows, and even the couches that sat in front of her wall of books. Her decor was beautiful, but my attention focused on the stone wall by her balcony. It had an intricate mural of flowers painted on it, mostly white lilies and lavender. She must have painted it herself. Maybe she remembered after all.

While I stared at the beauty of her painting, Jess fished around in one of her drawers. Out of the corner of my eye, I noticed the trembling of her hands. Was she nervous about something? She'd never had me in her room before, so I figured she was just embarrassed. I would have been uncomfortable being there myself if she'd ever shown romantic interest in me. However, in the past she was always uninterested, so I didn't see the harm in indulging her this one time.

"I wanted to give you this for your birthday, but there were too many people at your party," Jess said as she pulled the item from her drawer. In her hands was a thin black-chained necklace with a small crescent moon dangling at its center. I was surprised to see how personal the gift was, since she'd never given me anything before. The charm on the necklace looked exactly like her birthmark, and I couldn't find any words to say.

"May I?" she asked, opening the clasp on the necklace. Her arms were open, and I only hesitated for a moment before dipping my head down so she could reach my neck. The necklace was cold on my skin, but the warmth of Jess's hands lingered at the base of my neck. Her hands had never touched me in such a way before.

Tilting my head up, our eyes locked. The lavender sparkled in her eyes as one of her hands moved to caress the side of my face. My body shivered from her touch, and heat rose to my cheeks. Her hands were soft and warm as she touched me gently.

Without hesitation, Jess pulled my face into hers. I staggered as her lips found mine. A warmth surged throughout my body as her tongue slipped into my mouth. She was deliciously sweet, and her lips were soft. I lost myself in the moment as my mind was unable to comprehend my body's reaction. Her kiss was intoxicating.

When she pulled away, I fell to my knees, crippled by the dark desires that filled me. Dark magic electrified my veins, screaming for the pleasures of lust, but I refused to give in to it. I forced the magic down, regaining control.

My control was tested when Jess's body pressed into mine, joining me on the ground. She placed herself between my knees, and her arms wrapped around my neck. Her breath danced across my skin as she looked up at me with a desire I'd never seen before. I knew I needed to leave.

I forced myself to stand, pulling Jess up with me. Her arms slid from my neck and trailed down my sides. Unable to hide my body's reaction, I trembled. Jess gave me a smile that was so innocent she completely caught me off guard when her hand found its way to my pants. She gripped the bulge I couldn't hide, and a surge of heat hit me again.

"Stop," I said as I pushed her hands away. My heart pounded in my chest. "I need to go; the transport will be waiting." It was then that I realized how heavy my breathing had become.

Taking a deep breath, I pushed past her, eager to leave. Her sudden interest in me made my head spin. Why the heck was she trying to touch me like that? We weren't even married yet. I figured we'd wait until then to do stuff—in fact, I wanted to wait. The thought of doing things with her both overwhelmed and confused me. She was my best friend's sister and four years older than me. I was sure she knew things that I didn't, and the unknown territory of exploring her body terrified me.

"Harrison, wait," she said, closing the distance between us. I stiffened as Jess's hand slid into my mess of hair. She gripped tightly, using her hold to pull my head down.

A small gasp escaped me before her lips reached mine. I felt the surge of warmth fill me again as her body pressed against mine. She tasted like the first meal after a seven-day fast, and her body felt like the sun warming my face on a winter day. Her kisses were relentless. She barely gave me enough time to breathe between them, and I let myself enjoy it a little too much. Before I could wrap my head around the situation, Jess's hands found their way to my pants again.

I took a step back with my sense returned to me. "Goodbye, Jess." Even though my voice was stern, she didn't want to let me go. Her hands held on to mine, and tears filled her eyes. My heart clenched at the sight of them. I'd never seen Jess look so sad.

"But I have one more thing I want to give you," she whispered. Her hands pulled the sleeves of her dress off her shoulders, and the whole dress fell to the floor. Jess had bared herself to me. My mouth dropped open, and I couldn't tear my eyes away. The curves of her body stole my breath as I stepped backward in disbelief.

I stared at her, unable to form words. Was she trying to give me her body? Her virtue? No, there was no way she would want to disgrace herself by having sex before the wedding. Would she? As I stepped back, her bedroom door brushed against me. My hand reached to find its handle. Running was my only option, but when I tried to pull the door open, it didn't budge.

"It's sealed with magic," Jess said with a laugh that was all too familiar to me. I focused my dark magic on the seal, but it was no use. As a Darkblood, Jess's magic was stronger than mine. I would never be able to break the seal or leave the room unless she wanted me to. A sickness churned in my stomach as I realized she had me trapped.

"I really need to go. Please take the seal down," I pleaded. Her laughter filled the room, mocking me.

"Don't be silly, Harrison. You've seen me, and now it's my turn to see you." She grinned. My eyes widened, realizing what she meant. She wanted me to get naked. My heart raced, and I shivered from the horrifying thought. I hadn't asked her to expose herself to me; she'd done that by choice, and my choice was to stay clothed. At least, that was what I wanted.

Jess didn't give me time to respond or comprehend. She rushed me. My back slammed into the bedroom door as she kissed me. Her tongue slid into my mouth while she wrapped me in her bare embrace. I melted into her arms. The feel of her tongue massaging mine broke through my restraint.

There was an ache in my chest when I sank against the door behind us and slid to the floor. My heart pounded, and I gasped for breath, but Jess never let up. I wanted to fight her, but my body was frozen. A mix of fear and desire consumed me. My body flooded with new sensations as Jess slowly unbuttoned my shirt. Every tiny touch she placed on my skin set my body on fire. Dark magic rose within me, drawn to my fear and lust.

When Jess finally released me from her kiss, her mouth found its way to my ear. My long pointed ears extended past my skull and were extremely sensitive. It was common for asudhs to have long ears, but mine embarrassed me. As soon as her tongue touched my ear, a shiver rippled down my spine and a moan escaped my lips. It wasn't right, but the pleasure overwhelmed me.

Her kisses turned into little nibbles, and I thought I would explode from the pleasure. It was unbearable. Magic surged uncontrollably throughout my body. Jess must have felt it because she stopped tormenting me and went to her dresser. Her absence gave me a reprieve.

I fought to control the chaotic bursts of energy that escaped through my skin. The electric tingle of dark magic was hard to force down, but I had to quell the storm before it ripped me apart. Once I got it under control, my chest tightened. I mentally scolded myself for my behavior and regained my strength.

By the time Jess found what she was looking for, I'd staggered to my feet. My breathing was under control, and I was ready to leave, even if I had to jump from her balcony. I refused to stay in this uncomfortable situation, but it was as if Jess could read my mind.

As soon as I took a step toward the balcony door, she threw something at me. A magical bracelet she'd pulled from her dresser attached to my right wrist, just below the one from the Calling. It didn't hurt, but I instantly felt strange.

"Feel better?" she asked. Her voice was like a siren's song. "That bracelet will keep your magic suppressed so it doesn't get out of control again. It should also make you more compliant." The smile on her face was radiant.

My body was heavy as Jess guided me to her bed. I remembered that I wanted to leave, but I no longer had the energy to resist. It was as if her words controlled me. She laid me down and pulled off my boots. I couldn't suppress the moan that escaped my lips when she removed my pants, freeing my member. She had me naked in her bed. It was wrong and made my stomach tighten, but for some reason my body was relaxed. It had to be the bracelet.

I had fantasized about our wedding night many times over the years, but I never once imagined we would have sex before then. So when Jess climbed on top of me and her lavender-scented hair fell around my face, it felt like I was suffocating. My hands caressed her body, even though I didn't want them to, and she returned to kissing my ears. I'd allowed her to find my weakness, and she took full advantage of it.

Overwhelmed by the sickening pleasure tingling throughout

my body, I cried out. Jess clearly enjoyed the sound and continued to make me moan. She even bit down hard on my lip while she kissed me, causing it to bleed. It hurt, but I liked the pain. I deserved the pain.

When I could no longer bear her touch, Jess slid onto me. I gasped as I felt myself slip inside her. Dread washed over me. It wasn't right. I shouldn't have let her do that. Why had I let her do that? I wanted to fight, to make her stop, but I couldn't. That damn bracelet had me weak. She was in control.

Jess was merciless. Even though tears filled my eyes, she continued to ride me. She pulled my head to her and took my ear into her mouth. I couldn't handle it. The pleasure was cruel and so intense I thought I would explode. And then I did. Unable to stop myself, I released all of my tension and misery into her. She moaned, no doubt excited by her victory over me. I felt the tears roll down the sides of my face as I went limp on the bed.

I turned my head to the side in an attempt to hide my shame, but I knew she could see it. Jess remained on top of me for a while. She admired my body with her hands, but I couldn't look at her. I was too ashamed. Tears were pouring down my face when she finally rolled off of me.

Jess removed the bracelet, and my will returned. I was surprised that she released me, but I quickly found my clothes and dressed. Even with my skin covered, I was exposed. My stomach tightened.

Guilt consumed me as I rubbed my wrist where the bracelet had been. It ached, and when I looked down, I was horrified to see an exact replica of Jess's crescent moon birthmark on the underside of my wrist. It was solid black; there was no way Ki wouldn't see it. My breath escaped me as I froze. People would know what we did. I choked as the tears came faster.

"Well, that's unexpected," Jess said as she noticed the mark. She didn't seem at all bothered by the fact that people would know our shame. She just dressed and released the seal on the door. I kept my head down, avoiding eye contact with her as I headed out of the room.

"Be safe," she said as I walked out into the hall. Her words cut through me like a knife. After what had just happened, she dared to pretend to care about my well-being. My heart ached, and I regretted ever entering her room.

I took off in a run down the hallway. My heart raced as thoughts plagued me. With no regard for the presence of others, I ran until I made it out of the palace. I never stopped to see if anyone was around; I just ran.

When I reached the woods at the end of the palace gardens, I hunched over and gasped for breath. I retched into the brush, and wooziness filled me. As I stumbled to the ground, I found myself seated at the base of a large oak tree. Without any restraint, I cried. It felt as though my heart would burst from my chest. I was sure I would die from the force of it. My heart hurt more than I thought was ever possible as I sat there with my face buried between my knees. Rocking back and forth, I hit my head on the tree repeatedly.

What had I done?

CHAPTER 8

TYLER

A fierce stinging in my face was followed by foreign words as I regained consciousness. The female asudh had hit harder than necessary to wake me. Her soft features furrowed as she unbuckled me from my seat. Even though I couldn't understand her language, she was clearly annoyed.

My stomach clenched as she pulled me upright. A fit of dizziness overwhelming me, I struggled to stand on my own. She cursed in Asudhen as she pushed me out the door of the transport ship, into the blinding light of the morning. I stumbled to the ground and would have landed on my face if not for the other asudh. He caught me by the arm mid-fall and pulled me to my feet.

"Thanks," I mumbled as I finally caught my bearings. The asudh sighed and led me away from the ship. We were only a few feet from the transport when it took off into the air. The force of the wind blown by its departure nearly knocked me over, but once again the asudh's strong grip saved me from meeting the ground.

"If you can't walk on your own, I'll be forced to carry you," the asudh grumbled. I was close enough to feel his breath on my face as he stared down at me with his beady eyes. The afternoon sunlight glimmered off something on his chest. It was a name tag that I hadn't noticed before.

"Thank you, Sergeant Seskel, but I think I can manage on my own now," I replied as I read his name tag.

"Just get moving," he said as he released my arm and nodded toward the direction ahead. I started to walk and finally got a chance to look around.

Before me stood a rectangular and vastly ornate building that was larger than my entire town. I gasped at its beauty. Huge marble columns lined the perimeter of the structure and held up the solid roof, which was lined with intricate carvings. Never had I imagined I would see a building with such a massive infrastructure up close.

History books had depicted structures like the one in front of me. It was definitely the processing center, built by the original families, though it was hard to believe there had ever been a time when the Darkblood and Lightblood families worked together to create something beautiful. Part of me wished I'd lived during that era of peace and prosperity.

"Move it along." Sergeant Seskel shoved me in the direction of the entrance.

Competitors were arriving from all directions. They were ushered toward the stairs that led up to the building's platform, forced to fall into lines as they approached the doors. Soldiers were scattered about the grounds, keeping the competitors in motion. If anyone stopped to look around, a soldier was there to nudge them forward.

My heart raced, but I quickly fell in step, eager to be free of Sergeant Seskel's rude temperament. Climbing the shallow steps, I thought a command had been shouted, but between the hustling footsteps of competitors and their confused conversations cut short by forceful soldiers, I couldn't be sure. It wasn't until I stepped through the overly tall double doors and into the center that I finally understood what was said.

"Ladies to the right!" a soldier yelled, shooting daggers at me.

I had accidentally stepped toward the left hallway, distracted by the intricately painted ceiling. It was impossible not to admire the beauty of the artwork before me. The high dome of the main lobby had the story of the four shamans and the creation of magic depicted at its center. Positioned around it were depictions of both dierdres and liusaidhs. It was mesmerizing, the way the demonic creatures were intertwined with the angelic ones, creating balance.

Correcting my course, I headed down the large hallway to my right. Ornate paintings and statues were placed evenly along the hall. They alternated between being lined with gold and lined with silver, a perfect blend of light and dark. The sun and moon gods were praised well within the center. I would have spent hours in admiration of each piece of art if not for the soldiers who patrolled the hall.

With the soldier's not-so-polite directions, I made my way through the maze of hallways and doors. When I turned to enter the waiting room, shouts down the hallway drew my attention. Distracted, I bumped into the girl in front of me.

"Watch your step," the pale-skinned asudh said as she turned to face me. She had a small pointed nose and intimidating dark gray eyes. Her black hair was buzzed on the sides but long enough on the top to fold back on itself. I had never seen a girl with hair that short before.

"I'm sorry," I replied. Her eyes looked me over head to toe before she smiled.

"I'm not. Name's Keerla."

"Tyler. It's nice to meet you," I said.

Keerla's attention was drawn away by the older lady sitting at the desk in front of us. It was her turn to check in. The lady held what appeared to be a piece of glass with names on it. When she touched Keerla's name, it disappeared from the list. Magic. The piece of glass must have been enchanted. I wondered where the names were going as I stepped up to be checked in.

"Name," the lady said, not bothering to look up at me.

"Tyler Skyy, but I think I've been Called by mistake. I don't have magic," I said, hoping she'd be more helpful than the soldiers who removed me from my home.

"The Calling makes no mistakes," she replied as she found my name on her list. My chest sank as I watched it disappear. Would no one listen to reason? The Reckoning was supposed to be for magic users, and I wasn't one of them.

I was instructed to take a seat; the lady would hear no more of my complaint. Looking around the room, I found myself surrounded by books. The walls were lined with shelves full of them, most of which I hadn't heard of. Addersfield could never afford such a vast collection. If I hadn't found myself in such a dire position, I would have been eager to read them all.

"Come sit with us." An asudh with a nasally voice waved me over. There was a seating area in the middle of the room made up of plush chairs and couches arranged in a circle. Competitors filled most of the seats, but there was a spot open next to her.

"Thanks," I said as I sat on the couch.

The friendly asudh introduced herself as Ilythyrra. She had bronze sun-kissed skin and long blond hair. Her soft rounded face was complemented by the large hoop earrings that dangled from her pointed ears.

Each of the girls briefly introduced themselves. As I listened to their names, I noticed that I was the only human in the room. All the other girls were either asudhs or tlalocs. It made me wonder if I was the only human Called.

"Did you see him?" asked Kih. She was a tlaloc and had two small tusks that curved downward on either side of her nose.

"Did I see who?" I replied.

"The prince," she replied with an eye roll.

"No. Was I supposed to see him before I came here?" I asked. No one had mentioned anything to me about the prince when I arrived. My breath caught in my throat. Had I offended His Royal Highness? I hoped not, as dierdres were quick to violence.

"Don't worry the poor girl, Kih. No one has seen the prince, so stop asking everyone who comes through the door," Lexa said, relieving my worry. Her blue eyes and blond hair were similar to mine, but her tan skin and pointed ears marked her as an asudh.

"Kih," said a female voice from the door. The tlaloc standing in the doorway wore a traditional maiden's outfit. Holding a sheet of glass identical to the one the lady at the desk had, she stared at the group of us.

"Guess I'm up," Kih said as she stood from her chair. She followed the tlaloc into the hallway with her head held high. I stared in confusion.

"What was that about?" I asked, looking to Ilythyrra.

"They've been calling us back one at a time, but no one ever returns," she said.

"I wonder where they're taking them," I said.

"I've been secretly hoping they're giving us tests," she said. "That way I can just fail mine and return home." She sighed heavily.

"Are things not good at home?" I asked.

"I have six brothers and nine sisters waiting at home for me. I'm the eldest, so it's been my job to educate them, and if I'm gone too long, I know they'll start to skimp on their studies," she explained. Her duty to her family made a day on the farm seem like a breeze. I had no idea what it must have felt like to have so many siblings to take care of.

"I'll pray for your swift return home," I said with a smile.

"Thanks," she replied. "That's a nice thing for you to say, but I know how this usually ends for females. It's likely that most of us will never make it home."

I wanted to reply but couldn't find the words to say. It didn't matter that I hoped for the best outcome for everyone; the truth was that most of us would likely die. Even women gifted with magic had a slim chance of surviving the Reckoning, which meant my being Called was practically a death sentence. The metal bracelet on my wrist felt tighter. I was trapped.

"Speak for yourself," Lexa said. "I plan on living in the palace when this is all over." Keerla laughed, and Lexa glared her way. "Did I say something funny?"

"I'm just curious as to why you think you'll be living in the palace. Plan on seducing the prince or something?" Keerla said.

"I plan on winning. And once I've proven my warrior skills, I'll be welcomed into the Royal Guard, securing my place within the palace. Though for you ladies with lesser magical abilities, you may want to consider seducing the men for protection. It's been known to work," Lexa said.

"You can't be serious," I replied. The footage of the past Reckonings never showed competitors having sex.

"Oh, believe me, it's true. The few women to survive past Reckonings either slept with men for protection or were well-trained tlalocs. I did my research," Lexa said.

It was hard to believe. Was that really how those women survived the Reckoning? Could Lexa be right? Did they really use sex to survive? I had so many questions that I wanted to ask, but I didn't get a chance to.

"Tyler." A voice came from the door again. This time it was an asudh. She wore a maiden's outfit identical to the tlaloc's. I rose from my seat and walked over to her slowly, my stomach twisting into a knot.

"Follow me," she said and headed down the hallway. I trailed behind her, my heart racing as we passed many doors, each marked with a unique number. She stopped in front of a white door with the number fourteen engraved into it.

"You're number fourteen," she said as she nodded toward the door.

I hesitated, but a beep came from my bracelet and the door opened on its own. The room was dark, so I couldn't see what was inside. Standing at the doorway, a fear crept over me. There was no way to know what waited within.

The asudh must have been in a hurry because she shoved me into the room. It caught me off guard, so I tripped, falling onto the cold hard floor. I regained my composure, and the room responded to my presence. A dim white light radiated from the translucent floor, and a voice came from the walls.

"Welcome, number fourteen," the voice said. "Remove all personal items and place them in the bin." A drawer opened out of what appeared to be a seamless wall. Magic. It had to be some kind of enchanted room, and the enchanter who created it must have been very gifted.

"I've brought nothing with me," I replied. An orb of light emerged from the wall, and its beams scanned my body.

"Incorrect," the voice replied. "Remove all articles of clothing, including shoes, and place them in the bin provided." I froze. Had the wall just asked me to get naked? A few minutes must have passed, because the floor glowed red and the voice came back. It was angry. "Number fourteen, noncompliance will have repercussions!"

The bracelet shocked me, and my entire body convulsed. When it finally stopped, I immediately began to disrobe. I placed my clothing in the drawer, and it retracted back into the wall, leaving no trace that it had ever existed. I stood there, naked in a glass room, thankful that my hair was long enough to cover my chest. My heart raced as I waited for instructions. A few painfully long minutes went by before the orb of light came back to scan my body.

I must have passed its inspection because a counter slid out from the wall with a folded robe on it. Eager to be covered, I grabbed the robe. It was thin and made of paper, but anything was better than being naked.

As I tied the robe, an exam table emerged from the floor. Without needing to be instructed, I took a seat on the table. It was strangely comfortable. I was able to remain mostly upright, even in the reclined position.

My concerns about my nudity dissipated, as it became clear that I was about to have a medical exam. Every few years my father's seer friend would come by the village and perform exams on the kids, so I was used to them, although the seer's equipment wasn't as comfortable or magical.

During my wait, I became hopeful. A medical exam would prove that I had no magic, that I shouldn't have been Called. The doctor would see that they had made a mistake. I could get back home to my family.

The door to my room opened, and a doctor walked in with a sheet of glass in hand. She was a slender asudh with slightly pointed ears and an overly pointed nose. The white jacket she wore had her name embroidered on it, Dr. Rella.

"Good afternoon, I'll be taking care of you today," she said with a smile. A stool rose out of the floor beside the exam table, and she took a seat on it.

"I'm glad you're here," I replied. "I tried talking to the soldiers and the lady who checked me in, but no one would listen. I've been Called by mistake. I have no magical abilities."

Dr. Rella looked at the glass sheet. Swiping her finger up it, she scrolled through a series of pages containing information about me. My words had no effect on her. After a moment of reading, she looked at me pointedly.

"You are Tyler Skyy of Addersfield?" she asked.

"Yes, but I shouldn't be here. I'm magicless," I replied, hoping she'd see reason.

"Magic or no, you have been Called. There is no way around it, so I suggest you focus on the challenge ahead of you rather than wasting energy trying to plead your way out of it." Dr. Rella's words held a seriousness within them. She was telling me the facts, pure and simple.

"But it's a death sentence for magicless beings." Tears filled my eyes as my reality overwhelmed me. There was no way out.

"I suggest you make friends then," she replied, beginning her exam.

My chest sank as thoughts plagued me. How could I

possibly survive? I would be helpless against competitors' magic, but would they hurt me if I was kind to them? Maybe us girls could team up and fight the odds. But would that even work? Past competitors rarely worked together, but considering I had no magic, what options did I have?

I was confident that I could survive in the wilderness on my own, but surviving other competitors was a different issue. Maybe Lexa was right. Seducing one of the men might be my best option. The idea wasn't appealing, but for the sake of survival, it would be worth it. I'd do anything to get back to my family.

Dr. Rella finished her exam. She was putting her equipment away when someone knocked on the door. "The ladies will clean you up," she said as the door opened and three ladies walked in.

"What are we having done today?" asked the largest of the three ladies.

She was a human with round ears and wide hips, clearly not from a starving village. The other two ladies were asudhs. In fact, they looked as though they could be twins. Their olive skin and wide eyes matched perfectly.

"Give her the full treatment," Dr. Rella said. She walked past the group of ladies and out the door.

"We'd better get started," one of the twins said. The other remained quiet.

"Wash station, please." The larger lady projected her voice, and suddenly the room began to change. A wall opened, revealing a tub, while the medical table vanished into the floor. I barely got to my feet before it disappeared. The magical room confounded me. It had completely changed into a washroom.

I was ushered into the tub without a moment to think, and the ladies began their work. Every inch of my skin was scrubbed clean with a bristle brush. The water they dumped over my head was just as warm as the water in the tub. It soothed the tension that had built in my body.

My scalp was massaged as one of the twins rubbed soap

into my hair. It felt great to have someone wash my hair for me, and I wondered if this was a normalcy for nobles. By the time the ladies finished, I smelled of strawberries.

I was towel dried quickly and asked to lie down on a massage table. The quiet twin fought to untangle my mess of hair. She brushed hard trying to get out a knot and her comb broke. I thought that would give her a reason to let my hair be, but she had a slew of combs with her.

The other twin focused on my hands. She had a stockpile of metal utensils that she used to cut and file my nails. Layers of dead skin were removed from my hands. My well-earned calluses were nearly gone by the time she finished. She left me with perfectly rounded nails and soft hands. The cream she rubbed into them also smelled of strawberries.

Worst of all was what the large lady did to me. She lathered wax all over my legs and covered it with thin strips of cloth. The warmth of the wax wasn't too bad, but then she began to rip the strips off. I shrieked from the shock of pain, but it didn't faze her. She continued to remove all of my body hair, including the hair that covered my private areas.

The burning irritation left from the waxing was quelled by the cool cream the ladies covered me in. My skin was smooth, smoother than it had ever been, and it shimmered in the light. It was a magical sensation. I wondered if Dark Nation ladies felt this way all the time.

My nails were painted black, and my hair was twisted up into a bun of curls. The black flowered hairpin they used was gorgeous. It sparkled in the light, and I wondered what the gems were made of and if they were expensive. I was nervous I might lose it.

When the larger lady presented me with a black formal ball gown, my breath escaped me. It fit snug around my torso and puffed out at the waist, flowing elegantly to the floor. It was a gown for a princess. There were no sleeves, so my chest was more exposed than I would've liked it to be, but when they showed me my reflection, I was taken aback. I looked like a completely different person.

Makeup was put on my face to emphasize my eyes, and a solid black choker made of lace was fastened around my neck. When the ladies slipped my feet into black high-heeled shoes, I could hardly walk. I was ready to go when the door to my room opened and an asudh walked in.

"A flower for the lady." He smiled and extended a white rose corsage to me. It was wrapped beautifully with a silver ribbon. I presented my left wrist for him to place it on, so that it wouldn't get caught on the metal band that dangled from my other one.

The man towered over me, even in heels, and wore a well-kept black suit. His white undershirt had ruffles that flowed down from his neck, and his shoes shined in the light. He stood tall with his shoulders back as he motioned toward the door.

"Right this way, miss," he said with a smile.

I followed him out into the hall, and as soon as the ladies in the room were out of earshot, his smiled faded. His eyes glaring down at me, the asudh walked at a pace that I struggled to keep up with in heels.

"Not that you deserve the honor, but the Darkblood Prince will also be participating in the Reckoning. Do not speak to him unless spoken to. He should be addressed as Your Highness or Your Royal Highness. Don't look him directly in the eye, don't stare at him, and for the love of all things holy, do not touch him. Is that clear?" the asudh said as we weaved through a maze of doors and hallways.

"Yes, sir," I replied through gritted teeth, struggling to maintain a smile.

"Good. If I were you, I would stay clear of him entirely. Your presence alone is a disgrace. His Royal Highness shouldn't have to lower himself by conversing with commoners." The asudh's words made my jaw clench.

I tried to distract myself from his insulting words by focusing on the path we took, but it was hopeless. There was no way I'd be able to find my way back to the room we came from. Looking ahead, I was thankful to see a line of girls wearing dresses identical to mine. I recognized most of them from the waiting room.

Lexa stood at the front of the line, next to a large set of double doors. There was an elegance in the way she held herself. She was no stranger to formal attire and was likely highborn.

Keerla stood with less confidence a few girls behind Lexa. Her fists were clenched, and she mumbled curses under her breath.

The asudh instructed me to take my place at the back of the line before disappearing down the hall. Thirteen girls were in front of me, making me number fourteen.

In front of me was a small aeni girl who had light pink skin and periwinkle hair. Her hair was tied into two long braids that draped over her shoulders. There was a childlike presence about her, and I wondered how old she was. People as young as fifteen had been Called to the Reckoning.

All of the girls were quiet. Had they been told to be quiet, or were they just nervous? I decided to risk it and spoke to the aeni girl in front of me.

"Do you know what's going on?" I asked.

"I don't think anyone does," she replied. Her voice was high-pitched and quiet.

"Did they talk to you about the prince?" I wondered if I was the only one talked down to by the asudh.

"Yes. I assumed it was protocol," she replied and snuck a peek at me over her shoulder. I caught a glimpse of her cloudy blue eyes. It was nice to know that I wasn't the only one being treated like an ignorant commoner.

Footsteps came from behind me. I turned to see the asudh heading toward us with Ilythyrra walking beside him. He shot daggers at me as he instructed her to take her place behind me. I smiled at Ilythyrra, glad to see a friendly face, before facing forward.

"Listen up, ladies!" A raspy female voice came from our

bracelets. I nearly toppled over. "The prince will be walking by shortly. You are not to speak to him or move from your place in line. He's passing by as a mere courtesy to those who have never been in the presence of a dierdre before."

Her voice cut out, and whispers rose from the girls. One of them jumped excitedly, as if seeing the prince would be the highlight of her existence. I lacked her enthusiasm. The prince had never done anything to help my starving town, and though I had never seen a dierdre in person before, it didn't seem like a preview was necessary. I was wrong.

When the prince came into view, I didn't know if I should run or faint. My jaw dropped, and a gasp escaped my lips as I tried to reconcile his appearance. His skin was gray like the ashes of a fire, and he had solid black eyes that matched his hair. Most unsettling of all were the large corkscrewing horns that jutted out of his skull. This was a dierdre? I knew they had blood ties with demons, but I'd never thought they'd look so menacing.

He hardly glanced at the women as he passed them, but when he got to me he stopped. His dark eyes bored into me and changed from black to red. Were his eyes actually glowing red, or was I hallucinating? A shiver ran down my spine, giving me gooseflesh.

"Please try to keep your mouth closed when you're inside. A gaping trap is undignified, and I doubt you want that to be recorded for all to see." His words made my face burn. I wanted to disappear from existence as I realized I'd been staring at him with my mouth open the entire time.

Even though he was right, his words didn't have to be so cruel. I wanted to both apologize and reprimand him, but the bracelet's words played back in my head. If I spoke to him, there'd be repercussions. I remained silent and closed my mouth.

His eyes lingered in my direction for a moment before he continued down the line. Why had he gazed at me for so long? I hoped I hadn't offended him. Even if he was cruel, I had to be respectful. He would be king one day, and no one wants to be the enemy of the king.

Part of me hoped I wasn't the only one to make a fool of myself. If the other girls were as surprised by his appearance as I was, then I wouldn't stand out. He would have no reason to remember me. My actions would fade from his mind. With any luck, I wouldn't have to be around him much.

CHAPTER 9

KI

My fists were clenched so tightly that my nails dug into my palms. I'd been made to perform many bothersome acts as prince, but parading myself in front of the female competitors was pure degradation. The way they all stared at me, as if I was a bloody prize they could win. Their all-too-desperate smiles for my attention. I could hardly stand to look at them.

But even worse than the fake smiles was the look of pure terror on that human girl's face. Her widened eyes and open mouth gave me chills. The way her body trembled when I spoke to her revealed her horror. She stared at me with her bright blue eyes as if I were a bloody monster. Maybe I was.

My blood tingled with dark magic. The unwanted attention from the girls made my rage that much harder to control. I breathed deeply and exhaled slowly. It eased the tension in my muscles, and by the time the line of male competitors came into view, I was almost completely relaxed. My day had been terrible, but I had to push it from my mind.

Ignoring the stares of my competition, I made my way to the front of the line where Daniel stood. He wore a black suit with a white rose pinned to the lapel. All of the competitors were dressed exactly the same, the only difference being the silver crown that sat on top of my head.

"Have you seen Harrison?" I asked Daniel as I took my place in front of him. It was concerning that I hadn't seen Harrison since leaving the palace.

"No. I heard he had a fight with the medical staff," he replied.

"Really? He's usually so obedient." I wondered what the medical staff could have done to make Harrison angry enough to fight them.

"It sounded like they had to sedate him, so I don't think he'll be here for the opening announcements," Daniel said. He was lacking his usual enthusiasm.

"We should go check on him," I said, worried about what the doctors had done to him.

"No. You're the prince, so all eyes will be on you tonight. I'll check on him after introductions and make sure he joins us later."

His confidence gave me peace of mind. The evening would be stressful enough without worrying about Harrison. My father was unpredictable. I could only imagine the gruesome tasks he would have us all perform.

"Gentlemen, it's time," said the asudh by the door as he opened the large doors before me. Bright lights from the room flooded the hallway, burning my bloody eyes. Momentarily blinded, I stood tall, not knowing how many people looked my way.

"Follow me, Your Highness."

I walked a few paces behind the asudh, using the sound of his footsteps as my guide. My eyes adjusted to the lights as he led our line into the enormous ballroom.

The female competitors filed into the room from a door directly across from ours. There were two large staircases between the sets of doors that led down to the black marbled ballroom floor below. The curve of the stairs created a half circle with a stage in the middle on the lower level.

Walking down the stairs, I watched the women. The asudh at the front of the line matched my pace perfectly, staying even with me as our lines descended. When one of the females stumbled on the steps, I nearly laughed. It was the human who'd stared at me in the hall. Served her right.

On the stage between the circling stairs were my father and his entourage. They'd already taken their places. My father sat on his throne with my mother beside him. Seated to the sides of the stage were Jess and the rest of the king's council. Jess's eyes were fixated on the steps. Was she looking for Harrison?

At the bottom of the steps, our line crossed behind the women's, and we ended in two rows curved around the front of the stage. We all turned to face the stage while recording orbs floated about the room. They would capture the whole ceremony and broadcast it to the masses. My father rose from his throne.

"Everyone, please join me in welcoming the Called," my father said. He spoke loudly so that his voice would be heard by the recording orbs. I was surprised that the room lacked a crowd. In the past there were crowds of people at the opening ceremony for the Reckoning, but it appeared that, for the most part, the only people in the room were workers, competitors, and a handful of nobles.

"We break from tradition this year as a need for warriors has come. And with this opportunity for change, I've decided to mix things up a little." I flexed my jaw in frustration as my father grinned. He was great at manipulating the people, but his genuineness was completely fake. "In the past, female competitors were targeted and as a whole rarely survived the Reckoning. In order to prevent that from happening again this year, we will have teams of two. Each male competitor will be paired up with a female competitor. Neither will be able to complete the first phase of the Reckoning without the other. This should help even the odds for our female warriors."

"Bloody hell," I grumbled softly. A female partner would only slow me down. My father pretended he made the new rule to help save female lives, but it was most likely done to penalize me, though the crowds probably loved it.

"Gentlemen, you will receive a paper with your partner's name on it shortly. The teams were arranged based on magical ability so they'd be as evenly matched as possible. Tonight you have the chance to mingle and feast. Tomorrow the Reckoning will begin. Enjoy the evening." My father closed out his speech with a smile and returned to his throne. He was a master showman.

"For you, Your Highness," an asudh said from behind me. I turned, and he handed me a slip of paper.

"Tyler Skyy," I read out loud. "Are you sure this is a female competitor?"

"Yes, Your Highness." The asudh bowed as he walked away.

The two perfect rows quickly dissolved into a swarm. Competitors began to socialize as they searched for their partners. I sighed heavily as I worked up the nerve to do the same, but before I could even take a step to begin my bloody search, I was approached.

"Hey there, handsome. Is that my name in your hands?" The woman before me had ebony skin and piercing green eyes. Her wicked smile made my spine tingle. I could feel the pull of her magic and realized she was a succubus. My dark magic was strong enough to overcome her powers of persuasion, but that didn't stop her from tracing a finger down my chest.

"What's your name?" I asked as I pushed her hand away from me, sickened by her touch. Her smile was unfazed.

"Jadette. But you can call me Jade," she replied. Relief washed over me. A succubus could be a powerful ally, but since my ring limited my magical abilities, I would have a hard time fighting her aura. Her constant presence would be a drain on me.

"Sorry, I'm not your partner," I replied.

"Pity," she said.

Before she could continue to speak, I turned away from her. I held my breath as I walked away and hoped she wouldn't follow. She didn't, but there were plenty of other competitors who were eager to talk to me. Their introductions swirled together in a blur. I caught a few names, but most I forgot nearly as soon as they were spoken.

Every interaction was more exhausting than the last. I kept my paper concealed out of fear that the women would pretend to be the person I was looking for. They all wanted my attention, and I hated it. It made my stomach churn, causing my dark magic to stir within me.

Hands slammed into my back, knocking me forward. I sucked in a breath as the small hands gripped the back of my jacket. Rage warmed my entire body, and my dark energy threatened to erupt. Who would dare place a hand on me?

"Oh gosh. I'm so, so sorry." The woman's soft voice distracted me from my rage. "I've never worn heels before." I turned to see her bright blue eyes looking up at me. It was the bloody human again. "These things are so hard to walk in. Surely you can understand. Not that I think you've worn heels before or anything."

"It's fine," I interrupted, afraid she would talk all night if I didn't say something. Light radiated off of her pale skin as if she were a porcelain doll. Its brightness was hard to look at and contrasted greatly with the black gown she wore.

"Please let me make it up to you. I could get you a drink from the table over there," she said, pointing to the buffet. My chest tightened as I realized she was the only woman I hadn't spoken to yet.

"You're Tyler?" I asked, already knowing her answer.

"Y-yes," she stuttered. Her eyes looked away from me, but I could still see the redness in her cheeks. The paleness of her skin made it impossible to hide. "How did you know?"

"It's right here on my paper," I replied, holding the slip out for her to see. Taking it from me, she stared in stunned silence. "Guess I'm not the partner you were hoping for." Her eyes darted up to look into mine.

"It's not that, it's just—"

"*Hey* there!" said a pair of asudhs in unison, interrupting us. They had the same blond hair, blue eyes, and tan skin. Siblings, no doubt.

"I'm Lux," the male asudh said, extending his hand to me. I ignored it.

"And I'm Lexa," the female asudh said with a big smile. Her hair was pulled back into one long braid that draped over her shoulder.

"We just wanted to come over and introduce ourselves. I'm sure we'll be seeing each other a lot when the Reckoning is over," Lux said as he ran his hand through his short spiky hair.

"How presumptuous of you," I replied.

"Based on the competitors I see here, I'm quite confident my sister and I will make it to the end," Lux replied with a grin.

"We've been training together since we were five," Lexa added. "Now that this is a partnered competition, we're bound to dominate."

I sighed. "Well, good luck to you both, but if you don't mind, I'd like time alone with my partner." They both looked at Tyler and smiled at each other. I could tell they were communicating without words.

"Of course, Your Highness," they replied in unison, bowing before they departed. I took a deep breath and tried to calm myself. Tension built up inside my head. Between the lights and the constant interactions, I couldn't catch a break. I rubbed my temples to try to soothe myself.

"Why don't we grab drinks and sit down? I could use a break from these shoes," Tyler said. Even though her words made it sound like she needed a break, the warmth in her smile told me otherwise. My mood had been too transparent. A bloody human was able to notice it.

"Right. We should grab some food before it's all gone," I

replied. Her eyes widened at the mention of food. She walked briskly toward the buffet, stumbling all over herself in her eagerness. I followed behind and struggled to not smile when she tripped approaching the table.

Collecting herself, Tyler's eyes widened when she got a look at the buffet's spread. As she piled her plate high with food, my humor quickly faded. Finally noticing the thinness of her frame, I realized she must have been half-starved. A pit grew in my stomach. There would be many others just like her in the outer villages and smaller towns. I knew how dire the food situation was in the kingdom, but I'd never witnessed it firsthand before.

"Are you going to eat anything?" she asked after she made it all the way around the buffet.

"No. I ate earlier," I lied. "But I'll sit with you while you eat." She smiled, and I led her to one of the tables that lined the room. I tried not to stare, but I couldn't help watching as she stuffed her face. Her hunger clearly outweighed her concern for proper etiquette. Such a thing would usually bother me, but instead I just felt bad for her.

"May we join you, Your Highness?" Daniel mocked as he sat down next to me. He had a plate piled high with meat in his hand.

"Of course. How could I possibly refuse your company?" I joked. My friendly smile quickly faded when I caught a glimpse of his partner. She sat down in the chair across from me, and I instantly recognized her. The succubus.

"We meet again." She grinned. I turned my head to hide the sigh I couldn't hold back. Tyler must have heard it because she finally looked up from her plate, sneaking a peek in my direction.

"Do you guys know each other?" Tyler asked as she looked at the succubus. Tyler's eyes widened, and an excited smile spread across her face.

"We briefly connected earlier," Jade replied, winking at me. "You can call me Jade."

"That's such a beautiful name," Tyler said as she moved her chair closer to Jade. The succubus's thrall had her.

"Ki, it looks like your girlfriend is interested in my partner." Daniel laughed as he elbowed me in the side, clearly amused by my less than ideal partner. My eyes filled with a red glow as I shot daggers at him. Tyler was not my girlfriend.

"Your hands are so soft," Tyler said as she massaged Jade's hand with hers.

"What a beautiful white rose you have there," Jade replied. Her eyes bored into me as she rubbed on Tyler's arm.

"All right, that's enough," I said as I stood. "Come on, Tyler. We're leaving." I grabbed hold of Tyler's arms and gently pulled her to her feet.

"But—" she gasped as she tried to pull out of my grip.

"Aw, come on, man. Don't interrupt the show. Girl on girl is so hot," Daniel teased. Dark magic surged within my veins.

"Shouldn't you be checking on Harrison?" I snapped, my patience thinned.

"Don't worry, I'm on it," Daniel replied.

"It was nice meeting you," Jade said as I walked away from the table, dragging Tyler along.

Tyler hardly resisted as I led her across the room. The succubus's thrall was strong, but it didn't cloud people's survival instincts. I was sure Tyler knew better than to fight against me. The biggest challenge was keeping her upright; she really couldn't walk in those bloody shoes.

Once we were far enough away from the succubus, I took Tyler behind a large pillar. The massive marble structure hid us from the view of others. I was tired of socializing, and by the way Tyler favored one leg, I could tell her feet hurt. High heels were such pointless footwear.

"Let me help you with your shoes," I said as I knelt down. Tyler's eyes widened, and her face turned bright red as I lifted the bottom of her dress. The black heels she wore left her toes completely exposed. Her nails were painted black, and the polish glimmered in the light.

My hand grazed her skin as I unbuckled the shoe's strap. Her skin was soft and completely smooth. Tyler trembled from my touch, and I realized my hands had lingered on her ankle. A warmth spread throughout my body.

Gripping her ankle, I lifted her foot out of her shoe. She grabbed my shoulders for balance. When her foot was free of the shoe, my body stiffened. The sweet scent of blood drew my attention. Her heel had been cut by the back strap of her shoe, and the wound taunted me. My skin crawled as I was compelled to taste her.

Tyler's foot pulled from my grip as she stepped down onto the floor. If she hadn't moved, I was sure I would've tasted her. I quickly removed her other shoe and made my way back to my feet. The temptation would have been too strong if I hadn't.

"Better?" I asked as I held her shoes in my hand. Her cheeks were still bright red.

"Yes, but I'm sure the ladies will be displeased," she replied.

"Don't worry about it," I said as I tried to calm my thirst. It hadn't been that long since my last hunt, but the scent of her blood awoke my hunger. She looked up at me, and her lips parted slightly. Her body trembled, and her eyes widened.

"What is it?" I asked.

"Your . . . your eyes," she stuttered. I turned away from her once I understood what she said. My bloodlust made my eyes turn red. The glow hypnotized my prey, making them calm. I hadn't even noticed the change.

Tyler's heart raced, and her breath quickened. I could practically taste her fear in the air, and it consumed me. My movements were instinctual. In one swift motion, I turned and pinned her against the large marble column. Her body was still, frozen in fear. My senses were heightened by the dark magic within me that fed on her fear, fueling my hunger. When the discomfort of my teeth growing into sharp points hit me, I knew I couldn't stop. My body was ready to feed.

"Everyone, please report to the dance floor!" My father's voice echoed throughout the room. His sudden announcement broke through the frenzy of hunger that had overwhelmed me. I stepped away from Tyler, hiding my face.

"Are you all right?" Tyler stuttered. I forced the change to revert before I looked back at her. Questions lingered in her eyes, but the other competitors had already gathered on the dance floor.

"Let us close out tonight's festivities with a dance. I'm sure the people would love to see the partners dancing together," my father said as he glanced in my direction.

A pit grew in my stomach. How was I supposed to dance with Tyler after nearly feeding on her? I was surprised she hadn't run off the second I'd turned away. I wouldn't blame her if she had.

"We should join the others," Tyler said as she folded her arm into mine. Her calm composure was unexpected, considering her heart was still racing.

I stood tall as I led Tyler onto the floor. Her hand trembled, but a smile was on her face; she was good at faking it. Between the competitors' stares and the recording orbs, it felt like the whole room was watching us. I bloody hated being watched.

When the music began to play, Tyler's eyes widened, her entire body trembling. "I don't know how to dance."

"Just follow my lead," I said as I took her hand into mine. My other hand wrapped around her waist, and I began to lead her around the dance floor. She was quite short without her shoes on, so if I looked down I'd be able to see what was hidden beneath her dress, though I had no desire to do so.

All of the other partners danced beautifully, but not us. Tyler couldn't dance to save her life, and after she nearly tripped me, I had no choice. I picked her up and placed her bare feet on the top of my shoes. It required her to be pressed up against me, which was a discomfort, but at least we were able to look competent in our dance.

"Smile," I whispered in Tyler's ear as a recording orb approached. Her smile looked remarkably genuine and took me by surprise. There was a warmth about her, and I wasn't the only one to notice it. One of the tlaloc competitors had his eyes on Tyler throughout the entire dance. He watched her way too closely. I could see the obsession in his eyes. He practically drooled all over himself.

When the orbs had their fill of dancing couples, they departed. As soon as they were out of sight, I put Tyler down; she had trembled in my arms for far too long. I was disgusted by the way the tlaloc had stared at her, but I was no better. My hands had touched her body way too many times in the short period I'd known her.

My father announced that we were allowed to return to our rooms at our leisure, and then he departed. He disappeared up the stairs, my mother and sister following behind him. Most of the competitors were happy in their celebrations, but I knew better. It would be an early morning for us all, and I wanted to be well rested. The Reckoning would commence tomorrow, and I had no idea how difficult the next several weeks would be.

"Let's turn in for the night," I suggested. Tyler's eyes twitched, and her face reddened. I extended my arm, and she reluctantly took it. We headed toward the exit. Tyler struggled to hold her dress up as we climbed the stairs; I had to lend her a hand every few steps. If she could be bested by stairs, then the rest of the Reckoning would be a real challenge.

Once we got out of the ballroom and headed down the winding halls of the center, I noticed Tyler had a limp. I instantly wondered if it was because of the cut on her foot. Had it gotten infected? Had she injured her ankle dancing? She wasn't exactly graceful.

"Are you all right?" I asked. Her limp had caused her to lag behind me.

"Could we maybe rest for a bit? I think those heels did quite a number on my feet," she replied. I swooped my arm down the back side of her dress and under her knees. She fell into my arms as I lifted her up.

"You don't have to do this," she said as I cradled her in my arms and carried her down the hall.

"I'd like to get back to my room as quickly as possible." To win the Reckoning, I had to keep Tyler alive, which meant not letting her out of my sight

Tyler's eyes locked onto mine, and her cheeks turned red. She was quiet as I carried her. When we neared the door to my room, I noticed she was fiddling with her hands. Was she nervous?

Her eyes stared up at me. "Do you have a girlfriend?" Her question caught me off guard.

"No," I replied swiftly as we approached my door. "I don't have time for women."

"So you've never been with a woman before?" she asked as I set her down. My heart stopped as I took in her words.

"Excuse me?" I said in disbelief.

"I just figured with you being the prince that you would've had lots of women. But based off what you just said, it sounds like we're both virgins." Tyler's face had been red before, but when she spoke her whole body blushed.

I stared at her in stunned silence, unable to deny the accusation. What the bloody hell? Why would she say something like that? My blood ran cold as she stood there silently.

Taking a deep breath, I pushed her words from my mind and stepped in front of the door. My bracelet pulsed, and the door opened, a dim glow from the floor illuminating the room. Tyler walked in without hesitation, but her heart was racing.

The door automatically closed behind me, and Tyler sucked in a breath. Her eyes darted around the room, and her body trembled. I kept my distance so that I wouldn't add to her uneasiness. She was far from home and probably not used to enchanted rooms.

"Bedroom, please," I said, and the white glow of the room turned red.

"Of course, Your Highness," the room responded. As the walls and floor moved, Tyler stepped closer to me. Her heart still pounded in her chest, and she breathed heavily. Was she panicking?

An overly large bed rose up in the middle of the room. It looked similar to the bed I had back home. Covered in black silk sheets with two large feather pillows, it had everything I liked. There was even a black fur blanket folded up at the end of the bed.

Tyler gasped as she stared at it. I assumed it was a lot more extravagant than anything she'd ever slept on before. Then it finally came to my mind. There was one bed and two of us. Could I really share a bed with a bloody woman? What if I accidentally fed on her in my sleep?

"Um, you'll have to help me with my dress." Tyler's voice was quiet. Her eyes appeared watery as she stepped near me. I froze, not sure what to do. She turned her back to me. "I can't untie it by myself. I'm not even sure how the ladies got it on me." A lump caught in my throat. I was a bloody prince, and she wanted me to undress her.

"I'm not exactly familiar with women's clothes, but I'll give it a try," I conceded.

My hands shook as I reached for the ends of the ribbon that laced her dress, and my heart beat nearly as fast as hers. Humans were quite frail, so I worried I'd accidentally hurt her trying to get the dress off.

Tyler held the front of her dress in place as I slowly unlaced the back. As the ribbon pulled out, her dress loosened and more of her skin was exposed. I tried to avoid it, but my hands grazed her bare back, and heat rose to my face. My hands had never touched a woman in such a way before; it was humiliating.

I wasn't sure if Tyler had anything on under the dress, but then I caught a glimpse of the black panties she wore. The sight surprised me as I pulled the ribbon through the last loop of her dress. Holding the ribbon in my hand, I admired the curve of Tyler's back as she stood motionless. She continued to hold the front of the dress against her. It covered her chest, but the back had fallen open. I could see her entire naked back.

Tyler took a deep breath, and even though her hands trembled, she let go of her dress. It fell to the floor in a pile at her feet and left her completely exposed. I quickly turned away from her. My face burned, and my heart raced. I knew I shouldn't look at her, but her footsteps approached. What the bloody hell was happening? She gently touched my shoulders, and I jolted.

"Do you also need help with your clothes?" she asked as she pulled the jacket from my shoulders. It slipped down my arms with ease, and she tossed it to the side.

"I can manage on my own," I replied and began to unbutton my shirt. My hands shook, which made it hard to do, but I managed to get it off. I held it out to the side. "Here, take this. You can wear it to sleep in."

Tyler hesitated, but she took the shirt from my hand. Her fingers lingered on mine, and heat flooded my body. Had she done that intentionally? No, that couldn't be possible. Why would she want to touch me?

After a few moments of silence, I turned to look at her. She was in my shirt, and it was big on her. The top few buttons were fastened, but the bottom hung open. It left her panties exposed in the front but covered them in the back. I couldn't stop my eyes as they wandered over her body. Her pale skin looked smooth, and I remembered how soft her ankle had felt in my hand.

She stood there shaking while I took off my shoes. I didn't understand why she hadn't just gotten into the bed to warm up. In fact, she could wrap herself in the shirt to cover more of her body if she wanted. Maybe she didn't want to be covered.

"Are you cold?" I asked as I peeled my socks off.

"A l-little, but I-I figured y-you'd . . ." she stuttered. Her face was red, and her eyes stared at the ground. She couldn't say the words.

"Don't worry about me. Just get in the bed and warm up. You're shaking," I replied. She nodded and climbed into the bed. I didn't want to take my pants off, but I knew I wouldn't sleep well with them on, so I stripped down to my underwear and quickly climbed into the other side of the bed.

It was a large bed. There was a good chance if we slept on

opposite sides we would never come into contact with each other. I thought it best to lie on my side so that I faced away from her. She still trembled, and the sight of my face would only make it worse. At least that was what I thought.

Tyler moved around, causing the bed to shake. I was curious as to what she was up to but was afraid to look. My hunger had finally dissipated, and I didn't want to do anything to change that. The hairs at the base of my neck stood on end when her cold hand slid around my chest.

My heart skipped a beat when her hand slid lower. I jumped out of the bed and looked back at her. She'd taken off the shirt I'd given her and sat up in the bed with the sheets held against her chest. Her eyes were wide as she stared at me.

"What's going on here?" I asked.

Her face reddened. "I'm giving myself to you."

I nearly choked on my own saliva. "Excuse me?" The bloody girl couldn't be serious. Could she really believe I'd bed someone I'd just met?

"I'm sorry. I thought that—"

"You thought *what*?" I cut in. "That the Darkblood Prince would bed some commoner girl he just met? As if I'm desperate enough to lower myself to that. Did it ever occur to you that I'm a virgin by choice? There are thousands of girls who would jump at the opportunity to sleep with me, so why the bloody hell would I do it now?" Dark magic boiled in my veins, and the glow in my eyes was so intense that all I could see was red.

"I didn't mean to offend you," she said with tears in her eyes.

"Keep your bloody hands to yourself, and don't you dare speak another word about this. Not to anyone. Do you understand me?" There was venom in my words, and it only enticed the dark magic more. I needed to leave that room.

"Yes," she squeaked.

I slipped into my pants and went to the door. It opened without hesitation. I needed fresh air to calm the wrath raging within me. The ignorance of that bloody girl was confounding.

There was no way I would go back into that room with her. I'd much rather sleep on the bloody floor.

CHAPTER 10

HARRISON

Medical instruments crashed to the floor and scattered across the room as my dark magic unleashed. Rage had consumed me. The doctor's invasive questioning was bad enough, but when he placed his hands on my body, I couldn't take it anymore. I refused to be fondled.

"Take it easy," the doctor said as he inched away from me. He acted reassuringly, but I could see the fear in his eyes. My dark aura continued to expand, electrifying every fiber of my being.

"Don't touch me," I spat as medical assistants rushed into the room. They were all burly tlalocs, sent to subdue me.

"Just relax, Harrison. We aren't going to hurt you," the doctor said, moving farther away from me to grab a syringe. His words were lies.

Dark magic shot out from my hands as the tlalocs drew near, causing them to hesitate, though it was merely a brief pause before they continued to close in. Hands grabbed me, but not before I took out a handful of the tlalocs. My magic blasted them across the room as it erupted from my body.

"Hold him steady," the doctor instructed as I wrestled with the tlalocs. More streamed into the room. For every one I blasted away, there were two more to take their place.

"Get off of me!" I screamed. There were too many of them, but I wouldn't give in. I writhed against their hold as they pinned me to the cold translucent wall.

"Just breathe," the doctor said. A pinch in the side of my neck told me it was over. He'd stabbed me with the syringe. I pulled my arm free and backhanded the doctor. His bloodied face was the last thing I saw before the darkness took me.

Footsteps echoed down the hall and drew near. I fought to open my eyes as they entered my room, but my eyelids were too heavy to lift. My mind was foggy from the drugs, and I was cold, so very cold.

The cold reminded me of the woods, of my encounter with Jess. It haunted me and made my chest ache. Even with the doctor's drugs, I hadn't managed to rest. Not that I deserved to after ruining everything.

"How are you feeling?" I recognized Daniel's voice as soon as he spoke, and my eyes finally managed to open.

He wore a black formal suit that made him look regal as he stood by my side. His long braids of white hair had been pulled back out of his face, which only brought more attention to his eyes. They glowed pink as he smiled.

"Woozy," I mumbled as I tried to sit up. The doctor had left me half-covered on an exam table. Its surface was firm and cold against my bare skin. With nothing but a thin paper sheet over my private areas, most of my body was exposed to the cool air. My body trembled uncontrollably. "What are you doing here?"

"I came to check on you and help you get dressed. You've

already missed the opening announcements," Daniel replied. A black suit identical to his hung on a rack behind him.

I hopped down from the table, but my depth perception was off. My feet slid out from under me, and I fell toward the ground. Daniel caught me in his arms, pulling me close. I braced myself against his warm chest. His muscles bulged through his suit, threatening to rip his jacket.

"Your skin feels like ice." Daniel's smile was gone. "Blanket!" he shouted, and the room complied. A drawer slid out of the wall, and Daniel pulled a blanket from it. He wrapped it tightly around me, continuing to hold me close.

It took a long time for me to stand steadily on my own feet and even longer for my shivering to stop. Daniel didn't complain, though. He just rubbed my back as the warmth slowly returned to my body. I wanted to continue to steal his body heat, but he was quick to help me dress.

Struggling into my clothes, I realized the crescent moon mark on my wrist was completely visible. There was no way Daniel hadn't seen it. He had a keen eye and noticed everything. A pit grew in my stomach as I waited for him to ask the question I didn't want to answer. When he didn't, I was truly grateful.

Daniel caught me up on the king's announcements while I finished dressing. I was surprised to hear we would have to compete with partners and could only imagine how pissed Ki was about it. My stomach twisted as I thought about Ki. How could I face him after what I'd done with his sister? He'd figure out what had happened with Jess and would never forgive me. I could never look him in the eyes again.

I thought we were ready to head out when Daniel presented me with a small box. Within it was a white flower identical to the one he wore on his lapel. It was tradition for the Called to wear them during the opening ceremony. I took it from the box as Daniel's eyes studied me.

"What happened to you?" he asked, staring me in the eye.

"What do you mean?" I replied, turning my gaze from him.

I tried to pin the flower to my lapel but only managed to poke myself with the needle.

"I was told you fought with the medical staff. That's not like you," he replied, helping me secure the flower in place. There was no accusation in his voice, but I got defensive anyway.

"Is it a crime to not want a physical exam?" I yelled. "I'm clearly healthy, so there was no need for one." My heart raced, and dark magic stirred within me.

"Hey now, there's no need to yell. I'm just worried. Did someone hurt you?" Daniel spoke in a soft tone as he placed a hand on my shoulder.

"No!" I snapped, pushing his hand away. *Why the hell would he think that? Am I really that transparent?* My heart skipped a beat. People were bound to figure out what had happened. The room grew darker as my chest tightened. I struggled to take a breath.

"It's okay, Harrison. Just take a deep breath," Daniel said as he pulled me into him. "I'm here for you, no matter what."

Daniel held me in a tight embrace. A pink glow filled the space around us, and the tightness in my chest lessened. I could breathe again. Taking a deep breath, I exhaled slowly, allowing myself to take comfort in his words. Maybe people wouldn't find out after all. I could pretend nothing had happened. It wasn't like Jess would say otherwise. Or would she? I wasn't sure I knew her very well at all anymore.

My chest sank. The panic was gone, but a weight pressed down on me. I caught a glimpse of Daniel's glowing pink eyes, and my spirit lifted. Daniel was an empath; he could sense and manipulate others' emotions. Mine must have caused him concern, otherwise he wouldn't have used his gifts on me.

"I'm fine now. You don't have to use your gifts on me. We should get going," I said, releasing myself from our embrace.

I was completely vulnerable when Daniel was in tune with my emotions. He could feel what I felt and either make me feel better or worse. Even though he always chose to make me feel better, I didn't want to return to our previous conversation. I headed toward the door.

We walked in silence down the halls that eventually led to a large ballroom. As we opened the doors, we were greeted with the sounds of music and laughter. It appeared the competitors were enjoying their last night of freedom. With the amount of wine provided, I was sure at least a few competitors would be drunk by the end of the night.

Daniel led me down a large set of stairs, and I held on to his arm for support. There appeared to be two of everything. I didn't know what those damn doctors had given me, but the world spun.

I caught a glimpse of Jess. She wore a lavender ball gown that made her look radiant. Yet when I looked at her, it sickened my stomach. I feared I might retch if I looked at her for too long. Luckily, Daniel refocused my attention when he pointed at the dancing competitors.

Ki was easy to spot in the crowd since he was taller than most of the people in the room. My mouth dropped open as I took in the spectacle. The tiny human girl he was dancing with was so pale that she looked like a beacon of light against Ki's dark appearance. I nearly laughed. Her look of innocence was refreshing in comparison to the competitors who looked menacing. It was ironic that Ki, the Darkblood Prince, was partnered with her.

"It's shocking, isn't it?" Daniel said. He must have seen me staring at Ki. "I figured Ki would've been eager to have his way with his partner, but he clearly hates how close she is to him."

"Maybe he's saving himself for marriage," I replied with a heavy heart. My guilt cut through me. I'd wanted to wait until marriage, but that was no longer an option for me.

"Or he just thinks he's above it all." Daniel laughed. "His Highness wouldn't dare tarnish his reputation with impotent girls." He nearly crumpled over with laughter, and for a moment I smiled.

His perfect smile and the tears in his eyes made everything seem less important, as if my broken moral code wasn't that big a deal. He laughed, and I saw a glimpse of beauty in my life. When he recovered from his self-induced hysteria, Daniel grabbed me by the shoulder and pulled me close.

"Let's get some food." He smiled as he led me toward the large buffet.

We ate straight from the buffet, wasting no time with plates. Food helped to fill the void within me. I hadn't realized how hungry I was until I bit into one of the sandwiches. Thoughts of my encounter with Jess had plagued me so much that I hadn't eaten anything since. The pit that grew in my stomach every time I thought of her squashed my hunger, but now that I had food in my mouth, my body was grateful.

The dizziness from the drugs had just started to subside when I noticed the king leaving the room. The queen and Jess followed closely behind him, and my hunger disappeared as I watched Jess climb the stairs. The sickness returned. I couldn't eat anymore, not after the things I'd done to her. My body didn't deserve food.

Ki and his partner left shortly after the king, and I was glad. I wasn't ready to face him yet. There was no way I could lie to him, so instead I would avoid him, at least until I figured out what I would say. Or maybe I would just hide forever.

No longer able to eat, I turned to walk away from the buffet and fell into an aeni competitor. All I saw was the blue tint of his skin as we tumbled to the floor. He grunted when we hit the hard stone surface. I landed on top of him.

"What the—" he started, but his words slowed as his eyes locked onto mine. "Oh. Hey there, cutie. I don't recall seeing you earlier." His gray eyes lit up as he smiled at me.

"I'm sorry," I said as I climbed to my feet. Daniel was already at my side and had a hand extended to help me. "I'm a bit woozy from some meds the crazy doctor injected me with."

"That's quite all right," the aeni replied as he stood. "I'm Wynter, and you are?"

"Leaving," Daniel cut in. "Let's go find our partners. Talking to him is a waste of time."

"Don't be rude, Daniel," I said as I turned to reply to

Wynter. "I'm Harrison. It's nice to meet you, but he's right. I really should go find my partner."

"Oh, I see. I didn't realize you were already spoken for. My bad." Wynter winked at me, then turned and trotted off. What had he meant by spoken for? I stood confused for a moment, but then Daniel nudged me.

"The girls are over there," Daniel said. A small aeni girl sat next to an ebony goddess at a table not far from us. The ebony goddess waved us over, and I walked toward her.

I'd never seen such an enchanting creature before. Her dark skin was topped with a head full of orange hair. She was beautiful, like a sunset. It was impossible to look away from her piercing green eyes. In fact, I was so mesmerized by her that I couldn't hear the words Daniel said. His presence completely faded away.

Pain exploded in my jaw, and I stumbled. My eyes fell onto Daniel's, and his furrowed brows relaxed.

"I told you not to look her in the eyes. She's a succubus, you idiot." Daniel shook his head at me. A succubus. No wonder I was so captivated by her. I'd have to be more careful in the future.

"You didn't have to hit me so hard," I complained as I rubbed my aching jaw.

"Is everything all right over there?" the aeni girl said, rising from her seat. She had light pink skin and long periwinkle hair tied into two large braids. Her eyes shot daggers at Daniel.

"Yeah, I'm fine," I replied. With her small round face and cloudy blue eyes, she looked like a child—a glaring child.

"I was just teaching your partner here a lesson on how to avoid a succubus's thrall," Daniel said. The girl completely ignored him.

There was bad blood between aeni and tlalocs. Since the creation of magic, tlalocs had persecuted the aeni and raided their land. The tlalocs hated the aeni for their beauty. Aeni were small, delicate, brightly colored people, whereas tlalocs all had the same green skin color and tusks that protruded from their faces. Most would consider tlalocs ugly in comparison to the aeni, though Daniel was an exception. His lack of tusks made him quite appealing to most.

"I'm Emm," the young aeni said, extending her hand to me. I shook it.

"I'm Harrison. I hear we're partners for the Reckoning." I took a seat at the table next to her.

"I guess we are," she said, relaxing back into her chair.

"I don't want to start off on the wrong foot, but you don't seem like you're old enough to be called," I said. Her lips formed a thin line.

"I'm fifteen," she replied. As I'd suspected, she was at the bottom of the age range. "And I can hold my own. It's not like I asked to have a partner."

"Right, 'cause you'd do so well on your own," Daniel mocked. Emm's eyes narrowed as she glared at him with clenched fists. She began to rise from her seat, but the succubus's words distracted her.

"Um, hello? What does a girl have to do to get some attention around here?" the succubus said. I almost turned to look at her but caught myself at the last second.

"Don't pout, Jade. It's not a good look on you," Daniel said sarcastically.

"How rude," she replied, playing along. I got the sense that Daniel and Jade would get along quite well.

The four of us spent most of the night at the table. Daniel and Jade swapped stories of their conquests, and I wasn't sure which of them was more twisted. Their tales of sex and violence made me squirm in my seat. It brought my thoughts back to Jess and the things that had happened in her room. I tried to force it from my mind.

Luckily, Emm kept me distracted for most of the night. She asked dozens of questions about my magical abilities: what my affinities were, how long I could channel for, how long I'd been practicing. It was like she was giving me a practitioner's exam at the table. She was all about strategy, and I couldn't blame her.

We both had tiny frames, especially in comparison to the other competitors, so it would be best for us to utilize our intelligence rather than our physical strength.

After Emm's interrogation ended, she decided to go back to her room. Jade was tired and left with her, but I was dazed. I'd had a long conversation with Emm, yet I hadn't learned anything about her. All of her questions had been focused on me. Thankfully, Daniel stayed behind. I was sure he only stayed because he thought I couldn't get back to my room on my own, but I was glad to have the company.

We sat in peaceful silence while watching the other competitors. They all appeared to be in high spirits. Some danced while others drank wine and ate the food. It was smart to enjoy the food while we could. After tonight, we wouldn't have a good meal for a long time.

Even though I wasn't hungry, I knew I needed to eat as much as I could, so I headed back to the buffet to get more food. A strange sound came from a nearby pillar, and I walked over to check it out.

My eyes could hardly register what I saw. Wynter, the aeni I'd knocked over, was tongue-deep in another competitor's mouth, and the other competitor was a *guy*. The asudh had his fingers wrapped in Wynter's short black hair, and their bodies were pressed together against the pillar. I sucked in a breath, and my heart skipped a beat when Wynter's hand pressed against the asudh's crotch.

It was wrong of me to watch, yet I couldn't tear my eyes away. A nobleman had once bragged to me about his male conquests, so it wasn't uncommon, but I'd never witnessed two guys together before. It was captivating how they just openly made out in a place where anyone could stumble upon them. Their quiet moans and rough movements made my face burn.

"See something you like?" Daniel whispered, and I nearly jumped out of my skin. He stood right behind me. My heart raced.

"Fuck, don't sneak up on me like that," I said quietly.

Turning my gaze away from the men, I prayed my arousal wasn't obvious.

"I'm sure they wouldn't mind the extra company if you wanted to join in," he teased.

"Excuse me?" I replied defensively.

"Hey, don't get mad at me. You're the one who was staring." He laughed.

"Shut up. I have a fiancée. I wouldn't do that," I snapped.

"If you say so." Daniel's smile made me clench my fists.

"Whatever. I'm heading back to my room," I said, walking away.

What the hell was wrong with me? Why was I excited by two men being together? I was engaged to the princess. How could Daniel possibly think I would do that sort of thing? Of all the stories he'd told, he'd never once mentioned guys. It must have been a joke. He'd teased me because I'd gotten excited. I'd never even considered the possibility of being with a man before, but those guys had been enjoying themselves.

Fuck, what was I thinking?

CHAPTER 11

TYLER

I ran as fast as possible. It was dark, and I had no idea where I was, but I sensed that I was being followed. If I could just get far enough away, I would be safe. There was no time to stop. I had to run.

A dark force surrounded me. It wanted to consume me entirely. The thick fog caught in my throat. That was it. I would choke to death on the darkness. At least that was what I thought until I saw the fiery eyes that burned through the fog.

The darkness slithered away. All that was left were the brightly burning eyes. They drew closer to me, and I began to see the shadow of the beast. Large horns protruded from its skull, adding to its already intimidating height. It easily towered over me.

I tried to scream, but there was no sound. My voice was gone completely. Then I realized that I couldn't even move. The monster surrounded me. Baring its sharp teeth, it bit into my shoulder. Its teeth cut through my skin with ease . . .

A loud bang stirred me from my nightmare. I jolted upright in bed. Was I alone? My heart raced as I looked around. Ki was nowhere in sight.

I slipped out of bed and headed to the door to investigate. When I tried to push it open, it didn't budge. The door refused to open for me, and I knew any further attempt was pointless. I'd tried to command the room earlier after Ki stormed off, but it hadn't even lit up. The room completely ignored me whenever I spoke.

I pressed my ear to the door. It was quiet in the hall. Maybe a competitor couldn't find their own room and had tried all the doors. Regardless, there was nothing I could do, so I went back to bed.

As I lay down, I worried about Ki. I was surprised he hadn't returned. My failed attempt to seduce him had caused him to leave in a fit of fury, but surely he needed to rest. Had he found another room to sleep in, or was he forgoing sleep because of me? It had been stupid to try to bed the prince; of course he wouldn't want to sleep with me. Why had I listened to Lexa's suggestion? I didn't have the skill to seduce a man into protecting me.

My actions had been thoughtless, careless even. Ki had been so offended by it that he couldn't bear my presence. How was I going to make it up to him? I needed to make things right, but my eyelids were heavy. Giving in, I closed my eyes and drifted back to sleep.

I'd never been so relaxed upon waking before. The softness of the bed and the smoothness of the silk sheets were godsent, especially in comparison to the rickety, scratchy cot I had back home. Even though strange dreams and loud noises had disturbed my sleep, I was still well rested, rejuvenated.

The three ladies from the day before came into the room to wake me, but my body refused to get out of bed. I was so comfortable that I ignored the larger lady when she threatened to throw water on me. Surely she wouldn't want to ruin such a nice bed. I was wrong.

Cold water had me jumping out of the bed in a flash. My body shivered as I joined the ladies by the tub. They didn't even try to hide their smiles. Grateful that the water was warm, I climbed in without complaint. As soon as I was seated in the tub, the twins questioned me.

"How did you get so lucky to be paired with the prince?"

"Was he nice to you? Did you guys talk?"

"Why were you sleeping in his bed?"

"Did you two have sex?"

The questions came so quickly I couldn't make out who was asking what. My mind raced as I tried to come up with a response. I definitely couldn't tell them the truth—that I'd offended the prince.

"Let's not overwhelm the poor girl. This is a big day for her," the larger woman said, rescuing me.

"Yes, miss." The girls sighed in unison.

They continued their work quietly, which gave me time to think. I still had no idea what I would say when I saw Ki. It was just a momentary lapse of judgment? There must have been drugs in the food? *Maybe I should just apologize for my own stupidity.*

The ladies scrubbed me clean, leaving no trace of the makeup from the night before. I looked like myself again when they helped me into a fitted white spandex suit. There was a single zipper on the front that extended from the neck to just above the crotch. It was long-sleeved and lightweight, which made it oddly comfortable to wear.

I was given a pair of knee-high leather boots that matched the color of the suit perfectly. With my skin being so pale, I was concerned I'd look naked from a distance. My concerns deepened when the larger lady stared at me. Maybe I'd put the suit on backward.

"Something's missing," she said, thinking out loud. Her eyes lit up, and she went to the drawers in the wall. She pulled out a long white ribbon and walked over to me. "Here, for your hair," she said, handing me the ribbon.

Taking the ribbon, I used the reflective wall to tie my hair up. There was even enough length left to make a cute bow with the tails of the ribbon. I loved it, and the smiles on the ladies' faces told me they agreed.

As I stared at my reflection in the wall, I thought I looked like a child. The color of the suit and the girlie bow made me look innocent, as if that would somehow save me from my fate. There was a high probability I would die, even with a partner, although being paired with the prince definitely increased my odds of survival.

I was lucky to have been paired with such a strong partner, yet the thought of being alone in the woods with Ki made my stomach twist into knots. Not only had I made a fool of myself in front of him, but my knowledge of dierdres was limited. On top of that, Ki had a dark aura. In the ballroom, he'd looked at me with those red eyes like he wanted to devour me. I'd obviously been mistaken, thinking sex was what he desired. But what else could he have wanted?

"Number fourteen." A soldier appeared at the door of the room.

"I have a name," I replied.

"Number fourteen, it's time to go."

I sighed heavily, realizing I was nothing but property of the state to these people. It made me miss my family that much more.

Following him into the hall, I gasped. Bloodstains were everywhere. The walls, floor, and ceiling had all been bathed in blood. I recalled the loud noise from the night before. Had there been a fight outside the room? What the hell had happened? I started to ask the soldier, but he silenced me with a motion of his hand. Apparently, I wasn't to speak.

We passed through the halls and strolled out the front entrance. Stepping outside, I could see the other competitors being gathered. They were lined up with their partners wearing suits identical to mine, though half of the teams' suits were black. I broke away from the soldier and joined the group.

As I scanned the crowd, I spotted Ki. He walked toward me with his fists clenched and the veins in his arms bulging. A crackling aura of dark energy radiated from him, causing competitors to step out of his way. The scowl on his face was almost comical against the white of his suit, and his gray skin looked even darker in contrast.

Stopping beside me, he didn't say a word. My skin tingled from the magic in the air. Ki breathed deeply, but his tightly clenched fists were ready to fight. I figured it was a bad time to try and apologize, so I stood quietly by his side, praying I wouldn't add to his aggravation.

"Ki, buddy, you should wear white more often. It suits you," Daniel said from behind me. I was surprised that his green skin looked pale in the daylight. He was nearly as tall as Ki, but his appearance was nowhere near as intimidating.

I thought it odd that Daniel had pointed ears and no tusks. He looked quite different from the tlalocs I'd seen, yet he still had huge muscles that were plainly visible, especially in the tight black suit he wore. He'd definitely be able to shatter my bones with one blow.

"Keep your bloody mouth shut, Daniel," Ki snapped. A vein near his eye enlarged, and his aura thickened. It touched me, forcing me to step back to rid myself of the sickness it caused. My stomach twisted into knots.

"At least it shows off your figure." Daniel laughed.

"I'll have your tongue," Ki said as he stepped close to Daniel.

"You'll have to catch it first," Daniel teased. He stuck out his tongue. Just as a fight was about to break out, they were interrupted.

"Now, now, boys, there's no need to fight over me. There's enough to go around," Jade said. I avoided eye contact but got a glimpse of the wicked smile on her face.

"Don't flatter yourself," Ki said as he backed away from

Daniel. His hostility had changed targets. "Men don't fight over whores."

"Oh, so you're fighting over Tyler then?" Jade accused. My chest tightened as they all looked at me. I suddenly wished I hadn't tied the cute white bow into my hair.

"Oh, please. As if either of us would be interested in a frail little human." Daniel laughed as he slapped Ki on the back.

His words pierced through me like a sword. Ki had already rejected me, and now a tlaloc I'd hardly met mocked me. My eyes stung as I fought back tears. They all thought I was useless, and they didn't even know I had no magic.

"Leave her out of this," Ki said. His eyes avoided mine when I looked toward him. The tension in his body eased as he relaxed his hands. His dark aura calmed, the crackling energy around him dissipating.

"Hey, Harrison, over here," Daniel called across the crowd.

A thin olive-skinned asudh waved and headed toward our group. He had an aeni girl with him, and I recognized her cloudy blue eyes and light pink skin from the hallway line. Both of them wore black suits. Ki's gaze fixated on Harrison as he joined our group.

"Did you hear about the girl who got sent home this morning?" Daniel asked in a sarcastic tone. "She was disqualified because her partner died."

"What?" I gasped, surprised at how casually he spoke of a death. Then I remembered the bloodied hallway outside of Ki's room.

"Apparently, the idiot thought he could have his way with one of the ladies, but her partner got to him first." He laughed, as if the whole situation was child's play and not murder.

"Shut your bloody mouth," Ki snapped. His eyes glowed red as he glared at his friend.

"I saw blood outside your room," I said, glancing up at Ki. He turned his fiery gaze toward me as I pieced together what Daniel had said. Had a competitor been trying to get to me last night? And had Ki killed him for it? Daniel laughed about the whole thing, but the expression on Ki's face looked serious. His eyes bored into me, and I couldn't look away.

"I will not lose," he said as his eyes faded to their normal shade of black. His words chilled me.

"The Reckoning hasn't even started yet," I said, thinking out loud. My stomach twisted as I thought about what could have happened if that man had gotten to me. Was I a target? Would others come for me? If I died, what would become of my family? We could hardly keep the farm running with the three of us. I hoped they'd get along all right without me.

"The Reckoning began as soon as that bracelet found you." Ki's words haunted me. I rubbed my wrist as I recalled the pain the bracelet had inflicted on me. We were all prisoners.

I searched the faces of the remaining teams. All of the girls who'd been in front of me when we'd been lined up in the hallway were present. That meant Ilythyrra was the one who got sent home. She would be returning to her family unharmed. I wished I could be returning home to my family, but I was still happy for her. At least the man's death wasn't completely in vain.

"Listen up!" The king's voice blared across the grounds. He stood atop a wooden platform at the front of the group, dressed in all black. Recording orbs circled around him like a swarm of bugs. The morning sunlight reflected off his silver crown as he continued to speak.

"Unfortunately, one of the teams has already been disqualified. It's a tragedy when a life is lost, but it shall not delay things. Today you will all be transported to the Inbetween. If you can survive the harsh wilderness, it will be a testament to your fortitude, which as you all know is the foundation of any good warrior. The suits you're wearing are of the latest magical enchantments. They work like light armor but have self-mending and self-cleaning properties. These properties mean the suits are also waterproof. Challenges will appear to you at random and are to be completed in teams of two. Successful completion will earn you supplies vital to your survival. Failure to complete a challenge could prove fatal." He paused for dramatic effect, and his eyes scanned the crowd of competitors.

"To begin your journey, you will select one of the five items set out on the tables by the transports. Take time in deciding what you choose; it could make a huge difference in your ability to survive out there. Once in the Inbetween, you'll be on your own. Good luck, and may the strongest survive!" Cheers rose from the crowd of competitors. They were all eager to win and gain favor from the king, except for Ki. He stood with a silent stillness.

"Let's take a look at the items," Ki said as he nudged me toward the transport ships. They were lined up in a long row behind the king's platform.

I led the way with Ki walking closely behind me. He towered over my shoulders when I stopped at one of the equipment tables. Before us was a stockpile of canteens, twine, hunting knives, flint and steel, and hatchets. Any of the items would be helpful in the wilderness.

Knives and twine would be vital if we wanted to catch and kill animals for food, but the hatchets and flint and steel would make it easy to start fires. Our suits weren't very thick, so we would likely need the warmth of a fire. However, the canteens were the best choice. Water would likely be hard to find and nearly impossible to store without a canteen. There was no way to know how far we might need to travel, so we would definitely need the means to take water with us. Without water we would die quickly.

Ki must have shared my logic because we both reached for the same canteen, accidentally touching hands. He pulled away quickly. I grabbed the canteen and strapped it to one of several gear loops on the side of my suit. Ki did the same, which meant we were ready to go. My heart raced as I thought of the unknown. What were we walking into?

Soldiers herded us onto a transport ship. There were three teams on each ship, and we ended up on the same one as Ki's friends. At least, I thought the guys were his friends. I didn't think Ki would let just anyone talk to him the way Daniel did. They constantly taunted each other.

Daniel made crude jokes as the crew instructed us to take our seats. I finally caught the young aeni girl's name in passing when Harrison helped her strap in next to me. Ki eyed Emm as he checked to make sure my straps were secured. Did he think she might hurt me?

"How are you holding up?" I asked Emm. She was the only competitor who was smaller than me, so I thought she would understand the intimidation, especially with the large men who surrounded us.

"I may not look it, but I can hold my own," she replied with a smile. "What about you?"

"This bright white suit may be an issue when it comes to hiding, but I'm sure we'll figure something out," I replied, hoping my smile held the optimism I lacked.

"Maybe it'll snow," she said. Her innocent smile lifted my spirits. My odds of survival were low, but I wasn't going to just lie down and accept it. I had faith. Love and kindness would give me the strength to survive; they had to.

With everyone strapped in, the transport ship was ready to go. We launched into the sky, and my stomach dropped. I fought the urge to vomit as the ship leveled out. The large window at its front was a welcome distraction from my sickness. We were headed toward a range of mountains. White clouds surrounded the ship, blocking our view, but the pilot kept going forward. When the sky cleared up, there was a perfect circle of mountains surrounding a patch of forest below us.

"The Inbetween," Ki said as he gazed out the window.

With mountains surrounding us on all sides, there would be no way to escape. The slopes were too steep to climb over. My wrist ached from the weight of the bracelet. If I wanted to make it home in one piece, I would have to survive until the Reckoning was won.

"All right, teams. You may exit at any time," the pilot called out. I froze in my seat. Exit at any time? But we were still in the air. Did he want us to jump? I tightened my grip on the harness that kept me strapped to my seat.

"What are you doing? It's time to go," Ki said. I swatted his hands away as he reached for my harness. The other competitors had already started to put on parachutes. *Crap.*

I was still in my seat when the first team jumped. Daniel and Jade both smiled fearlessly as they leapt out the side door. As I watched them fall, my heart skipped a beat and my breath caught in my lungs. They were there, and then they were gone.

Harrison and Emm weren't wearing enthusiastic smiles like the other two, but they approached the open side door. My heart raced as I watched, secretly hoping they wouldn't jump. If they didn't jump, then it would be reasonable for me to refuse the jump as well.

I had no such luck. They stepped out of the ship and vanished into the clouds. The loud sounds of wind had me paralyzed in my seat.

Distracted by the jumpers, I lost the fight against Ki. He released the straps holding me in place and pulled me from the safety of my seat. My entire body shivered with fear as my eyes darted to the two parachutes that remained on the ship's wall. Both had been cut through cleanly with a knife. But how? Had one of Ki's friends done it? Or maybe the girls? It didn't make any sense.

"Hold on to this," Ki said as he slipped a ring into my hand. It was silver with a large black diamond embedded into it. There was a crest engraved into each side—the Darkblood family crest.

"What?" I shouted, confused as to why he thought it was a good idea to hand me something so valuable at a time like this.

"Whatever you do, don't let go of that ring!" he shouted, unfazed by the damaged parachutes.

I'd barely gotten the ring onto my finger when his arms slid under me. He lifted me up, cradling me close to him, and my arms wrapped around his neck instinctually. My fist was clenched tight so that his ring wouldn't fall off. When his eyes locked on mine, heat rose to my face. He held me so close that I could feel his breath on my skin. I didn't know what he was thinking.

Ki ran toward the ship's open door, and suddenly I didn't care about the closeness anymore. I clung to him as he dove into the sky. My stomach fell out from under me, but I clenched my fist hard. If it was my time to die, I'd die with the ring still in my hand.

I struggled to take in a breath as we fell from the sky. The horrid sound of Ki's flesh tearing filled my ears as a scream that sounded more like a growl escaped his lips. After a few of the longest seconds of my life, our descent stopped abruptly.

We jerked upward, and I squeezed tighter for fear that I might slip out of his arms. My eyes were closed tightly the whole time; I didn't dare to open them. Flight did not agree with me, and I was sure I would've been sick if I'd looked down.

Our motion stopped, but my body trembled uncontrollably. I was frozen in fear, unable to think or move properly. Was it truly over, or had my mind tricked me? The ring was my only savior. It distracted my mind from reality.

"You can let go now." Ki sighed. His arms had released me. When I finally opened my eyes, I discovered that we'd made it to the ground in one piece. Removing my arms from his neck, I stepped down and crumpled into a pile in the dirt as a spell of dizziness hit me. The world spun.

"Let's never do that again," I said as I dragged my hands along the surface of the earth. Ki's ring shined in the light. It was an extraordinary piece of jewelry.

Ki was quiet. When I looked up at him, he had a pained expression on his face. Two large black feathered wings protruded from his back that hadn't been there before. Then I remembered the horrid sound his flesh had made. The sound would haunt me for the rest of my life. Blood trickled onto the ground, and I gasped.

"Are you all right?" I got up to check his injuries, but he turned them away from me.

"Just give me my ring," he said. I did as he asked. He held the ring in his hand but didn't put it on. "Turn around. I don't need an audience."

Even though I didn't understand what his concern was, I turned around. If he wanted a moment of privacy, I wouldn't deny him. His groans made me curious, but I didn't turn around until he gave me the okay.

When I finally looked back at him, his massive wings were gone and his ring was back on his finger. He looked as though nothing had happened. There wasn't even a spot of blood left on his suit. Magic. I was sure the ring was enchanted, but I had no idea as to what it did. When I'd worn it I'd felt nothing, not even the slightest tingle, but it brought about a change in Ki—one I might never understand.

"I saw water north of here. We should head that way first," he said as his eyes scanned the area. Competitors could have landed anywhere, and the woods were dangerous on their own.

We found moss on a nearby tree and agreed on which direction was north. I half expected Ki to disagree, but he didn't. Maybe our partnership could be mutually beneficial. I vowed to find a way to be of help to him and earn his forgiveness.

CHAPTER 12

HARRISON

After jumping from the transport ship, I'd assumed the hard part was over, but I was wrong. The parachute was nearly impossible to control. I spiraled in circles as strong winds ripped me away from Emm. We'd jumped at the same time so we could stick together, but I quickly lost sight of her.

I was tossed side to side as I rapidly descended toward the ground. A dense forest spread far below me, but I noticed a small clearing. Gliding toward the clearing, I thought I would land smoothly, but unfortunately the winds had other plans for me.

As I dropped below the treetops, the wind pulled me hard to one side. My parachute caught in the branches of a tree, and I dangled helplessly. I was only a few feet from the ground, but I couldn't get my harness unbuckled; the damn thing had jammed. It was pointless to try to use my magic on the harness, as the parachute was made of a fire-resistant material, making it immune to dark magic. Struggling to wiggle free, I realized my efforts were futile. I was stuck. As I hung helplessly, the wind rocked me back and forth, taunting me.

My legs became numb from the harness cutting off circulation. I must have been hanging in that tree for at least an hour before snapping branches gave indication of someone's approach. The footsteps stopped behind me, but I couldn't turn far enough to see who it was. I prayed it was Emm.

"Isn't this a pretty picture?" Daniel said with a laugh as he appeared in front of me. I knew he would never let me live this moment down, and I almost wished I'd never been discovered.

"Would you just cut me down?" I pleaded, but his laughter continued.

"But it would be so much better if I waited till the girls found you," he said between chuckles. He was so amused I could see tears in his eyes.

"Just get me down. I can't feel my legs," I said. The harness had dug deep into my groin, and I worried my circulation had been cut off for too long.

"All right, don't pout," he replied, still grinning. "I'll come to your rescue, fair maiden." His laughter ate at me. A fire burned under my skin, and I had to stop myself before I gave a spiteful response.

Daniel cut the parachute cord with a knife, and I fell to the ground, landing on my ass. When I looked up, his hand was waiting to help me. I welcomed the aid, as I could barely feel my legs. His grip was firm and warm as he pulled me to my feet.

I stood shakily as the intense tingling sensation of circulation returned to my legs. The harness still clung tightly to me and squeezed my tender bits in the worst way. Daniel grabbed the strap of the harness near my crotch without hesitation. My face burned as he cut through it, freeing me from my discomfort.

"As my reward, I ask ye fair maiden for but one kiss." Daniel smiled as he spoke. He stood close, looking down at me with his hazel-pink eyes. I didn't find him to be the least bit funny. He had already joked about being in love with me, and now he was asking me for a kiss. I was sure he was just trying to get a rise out of me, but I wasn't going to fall for his tricks.

"Seriously, though, we should probably find the girls," I replied as I looked away from his eyes. It was hard to keep eye contact when he said such embarrassing things.

"I don't really care if we find them. Ki will win, after all, so let's just have some fun." Surprised by his words, I looked back at him. His grin was even bigger, and I couldn't help but admire his perfect teeth. They were the perfect shape and size to complement his supple lips. Why was I thinking about his lips? I hoped he hadn't noticed my stare and tried to cover it up.

"By fun do you mean raping innocent girls?" I said, my tone full of judgment.

"I don't do that for fun," he replied. His smile faded.

"Well, you sure as hell talk about it like it's a game," I said angrily. Thoughts of Jess plagued me. It had all been a game to her, just like it was to Daniel. My chest tightened.

"You know I just tell those stories like that to tease Ki." Daniel tried to place his hand on my shoulder, but I pushed it away.

"If it's not a game, then why do you do it?" Tears filled my eyes. How could Daniel hurt people like that? I never understood how much damage it did until Jess. A knot formed in my stomach.

"Because I have to. Do you think a tlaloc with a face like mine could ever be respected without being merciless? Think of what the soldiers would do if they caught even a whiff of weakness." Daniel stared me in the eye as he spoke. He didn't show any emotion on his face.

As I thought about it, I knew there was a truth in his words. Tlalocs gained the respect of their people by proving their strength. Large tusks were always a sign of strength, but Daniel had none. It made sense that he would need to be merciless and brutal in battle. But was he really okay with raping people? He couldn't be. My chest ached just thinking it.

"You could at least show a little remorse," I replied, wiping the tears from my eyes. Daniel had always been kind to me, so it was hard to imagine him being like Jess.

"I can't," he replied. His eyes began to glow pink.

"What?" I took a step back, but my eyes couldn't leave his gaze. My heart raced as tears fell from my eyes. Could Daniel not feel remorse? But he was an empath. I recalled all the years we'd been friends and realized I'd never once seen him cry, not even when his mother had died.

"I think you're just a little sensitive to the topic right now," Daniel said. He closed the distance between us, and the tightness in my chest lessened.

Sensitive? Why would he say that? Did he know about Jess? Maybe he could sense it with his empath abilities and was looking for a confession. I couldn't give him one, even if I wanted to unburden myself. If I told him about what had happened, it would tarnish Jess's name. It would ruin her, and I couldn't do that to the princess. I couldn't stain the Darkblood family's reputation.

"I don't know what you're talking about," I lied, trying to walk away from him. He caught my arm in his hand and turned me to face him. The look in his eyes made my heart hurt. He'd never looked so concerned for me before, had he?

"You can trust me, Harrison," he said as he stared into my eyes. I swore he looked straight into my soul. I wanted to melt into his arms and tell him all my secrets. He always knew the right words to say to me.

"I can't," I replied. Tears flowed freely down my cheeks, but I wiped them away.

"I always keep your secrets, don't I?" he said. Daniel always had my back, even when we were kids. There were many times that he'd taken the blame for something I'd done, rather than ratting me out. He'd suffered harsh punishments on my behalf without any complaint.

I fell apart.

"It's all my fault," I cried, unable to hold it in any longer. Daniel pulled me to him, wrapping me in a hug.

"No, it's not," he replied. His embrace was strong and comforting. It eased the pain that weighed heavily on my chest. I struggled to take in air as I cried uncontrollably. As I thought about the night with Jess, my stomach twisted. Everything about it was wrong. I was wrong. It never should have happened.

"I should have prevented it. Why wasn't I strong enough?" I wept into his shoulder. My words were muffled, but he understood them anyway. He had always understood my feelings, sometimes better than I did.

"Just let it all out," Daniel whispered into my ear as he held me tightly in his warm embrace. I couldn't hold it back anymore. Through my tears, I told him everything, every single horrid detail. As I revealed my shame to him, my legs felt weak and I crumbled to the ground. He came with me, holding my head to his chest the whole time. His soft whispers kept me grounded.

"It's going to be okay. You'll get through this," he said repeatedly in a loop until I had no more tears left to cry. One of his hands caressed my hair, while the other one gently rubbed my back in circles. Had he always been so caring? I didn't deserve his kindness.

Looking up at him with tears in my eyes, I discovered a softness that hadn't been there before. His eyes glowed pink as he stared back at me. He had the most beautiful eyes I'd ever seen. How could a tlaloc be so beautiful? My arms were wrapped around him, so I pulled him closer. A sudden desire came over me. I wanted to kiss him. It seemed like he felt the same way as he leaned in closer to me, but when his lips were nearly touching mine, noise in the woods spooked us.

We both jumped to our feet. Daniel pulled his knife out, and I wiped the tears from my eyes. I scanned the trees as the noises came from multiple directions. It could have been anything: a bear, a trap, other competitors, or perhaps even a challenge.

Emm appeared out of the bushes to our right, while Jade came stomping through the trees to our left. I sighed in relief and waved Emm over. She hesitated, but once Daniel tucked his knife back into his boot, she approached us. He was completely calm.

"How nice of you ladies to join the party." Daniel grinned. I couldn't believe he was being so casual. Was he unfazed by what had just happened? Heat still burned in my cheeks. We almost kissed! What if the girls saw?

"It wasn't a party until I got here." Jade winked. She had a sharp tongue, but Daniel just laughed in response. Neither one of them were serious; they just fed into each other's nonsense.

"We should get out of here," Emm said, speaking directly to me. She was dwarfed as she stood near Daniel, her head barely coming up to his mid-chest. Of course, at six and a half feet tall, Daniel towered over most. My head barely reached his shoulder, and Ki was the only person I knew who was taller than him.

"The transport was headed north when we jumped, so if we head that way we're bound to find Ki," Daniel replied.

Emm pulled me to the side. "We should go south and put as much distance between us and them as possible." She whispered so the others wouldn't hear.

"It's better if we stay together," I replied, not wanting to leave Daniel's side.

"Tlalocs can't be trusted," she said, glaring at Daniel.

"He's my best friend, and our odds of survival are greater if we work together."

Emm sighed. She knew I was right. We moved back to where Jade and Daniel were waiting. Daniel flashed me a knowing smile.

"All right. Let's go," Jade said. I fought the urge to look at her, but Daniel didn't. He stared in her direction, unaffected. I wondered if his empath abilities made him immune to her succubus charm.

Jade led us north with Emm by her side. Daniel and I trailed a few paces behind them, as I was in no hurry to meet up with Ki. We didn't need his help in order to survive, and I still didn't know how to act around him. He would be able to tell something was wrong, just like Daniel had, and I'd die if he found out about Jess.

Our group was quiet as we made our way through the forest. Wind tossed the trees around and got worse by the minute. As its strength increased, the girls struggled to walk. I was worrying Emm might get swept away into the storm when suddenly they screamed. Daniel rushed forward and pulled the girls back. Their hands were bloodied from cuts.

"What happened?" I asked.

"There was glass in the wind," Jade replied. "Luckily, we had our hands up protecting our faces from the gust when it happened." The wind picked up again.

"Run!" Daniel shouted as a funnel of wind came at us. It had to have thousands of shards of glass within it because it glimmered in the light. I might have thought it to be a beauty of nature if it hadn't been headed straight for us.

We ran south. Struggling to run through the underbrush, I slowed to jump over several fallen trees. At the rate our group was moving, the wind would catch up to us soon. To make matters worse, I discovered that we weren't alone.

Lux and Lexa, the asudh sibling duo, crossed our paths. They were highborn, and I'd met them during the king's gala last year, but they didn't hesitate to make matters worse for us. Trees fell down around me, and I was nearly crushed. It was magic. Lux and Lexa worked together to throw obstacles into our path. I avoided as much as I could, but I inevitably stumbled to the ground when a root caught my foot.

It was worse than just being tripped. The root had grabbed ahold of my ankle and pulled me down. I called upon my dark magic, forcing the electric energy into the root, but the spell was strong. One of them must have had an affinity for earth magic.

A stray shard of glass sliced my arm as I fought with the root. I screamed out in pain, and Daniel was at my side in an instant. His earth magic ripped the root in half, freeing me. He grunted as glass cut into him. The wind had caught up to us.

It made my stomach clench to hear Daniel's grunts of pain. He pulled me from the ground, and we ran. Glass shards shot out at us at random as we continued. They cut into our skin, but we kept ahead of the worst of it.

By the time the storm cleared, my leg muscles were ready to give out. I breathed heavily as I collapsed at the base of a tree. My lungs burned, and my chest ached. Lux and Lexa were nowhere to be found now that the storm was gone. I wondered if they'd been the cause of it to begin with.

"What the hell was that?" Jade asked as she gasped for air. None of us had an answer for her. It definitely hadn't been a natural storm. Maybe it'd been a trap, or part of the Reckoning.

"Whatever it was, it didn't want us going north," Daniel said, and I understood what he meant. The king must have made sure Ki would be isolated from his friends, to make it as hard on him as possible. He made every part of Ki's life a challenge. I'd bet his partnership with a human wasn't by chance either. The king had likely handpicked the most vulnerable girl on purpose.

"We should find a place to rest," Emm said as she approached me. "How bad are your injuries?" I had several cuts along my back, but the gash on my forearm was the worst of it. Blood trickled from it, pooling on the ground at my feet.

"He'll be fine," Daniel replied as he stepped between me and Emm. He knelt next to me, examining my arm.

"What are you doing?" Emm raised a brow. She stared at Daniel with fire in her eyes, and I could see the tension in her shoulder blades.

Without a word, Daniel scooped dirt from the ground and channeled his magic through it. A green glow radiated from the dirt as it turned to paste in his hand. He spread the compound over my wounds. The bleeding stopped completely, and the pain vanished. It astonished me.

Daniel's affinity for earth magic was unparalleled. Even some of the Dark Nation's highest-ranking warlocks couldn't match his gifts. It was as if he were one with the earth, and

I envied how effortless it was for him. But he rarely used his earth magic. I wondered why that was.

"Thanks," I said as I looked into his hazel-pink eyes. A sly smile spread across his face.

"Of course, my damsel," he whispered into my ear. A shiver ran through my body. His closeness made me think of our almost kiss.

"We should keep moving. Who knows if that storm will come back," Jade said, scanning the area.

Daniel struggled to his feet and then helped me up. Maybe the magic had taken more out of him than I thought. The earth shook around us.

"What the hell?" Jade gasped. The girls moved closer to us.

Dust clouded our view as we stood back-to-back in a tight circle. Daniel's muscles were clenched as he moved to stand directly in front of me. He was ready for a fight.

When the dust settled, I was shocked by the obstacle before us. Two wooden platforms towered overhead, and two glass mazes stretched across the land. It was a challenge.

"Welcome to your first challenge." A dark priestess appeared. Her face was hidden by the hood of her cloak, but the silver amulet that hung from her neck was unmistakable. She was a member of the holy order, a true priestess.

"Your task today is simple. One person from each team will be the eyes that guide the other member through the maze. You may use any commands you like, but just know that one wrong turn could be fatal for your partner. You'll be linked so that you can communicate telepathically. I'll give you a moment to decide who will be in the maze and who will be atop the tower."

A lump caught in my throat as I took in her words. The challenge was deadly. If one of us died while our minds were linked, we'd both die. My heart raced as I looked to Emm. Her eyes were wide as she stared at the maze. I tried to see what had caught her attention, but it was too far away for me to make out. My visual perception was only good for about ten meters. Anything past that was a blur to me. I knew what I had to do.

"I'll be the one in the maze," I said. Emm looked at me and nodded.

Daniel and Jade discussed between themselves, but when I spoke, Daniel's attention turned to me. Was he unhappy with my decision? It didn't matter. There was no turning back.

"I'll also be in the maze," Jade said. I was surprised Daniel hadn't volunteered to go into the maze, but his movements were a little sluggish.

"All right, you've made your decisions, so it's time to begin. Maze runners, take your positions at your entrances. You will be blinded for the duration of the challenge, but don't worry, your sight will return once it's over." My heart stopped as the dark priestess's words sank in. Not only were we headed into a deadly maze, but we'd also be blind. *Fuck.*

"The mazes are set up on a timer, so the longer you take to get through them, the deadlier they become. You'll want to move as quickly as possible. As a bonus, the team that gets through their maze first will get an extra reward. Good luck, and may the strongest survive." The dark priestess spoke with no emotion in her voice.

A cold sweat shivered through me as I took my place at the entrance to one of the mazes. Jade stood at the other. Without thinking, I looked into her eyes and saw the fear that was hidden there. Her piercing green eyes were the last thing I saw before the world went dark. I sucked in a deep breath and clenched my fists to try to calm myself. My heart beat wildly as I waited for the horn to sound. I silently prayed to the gods for strength, hoping they'd guide me safely to the other side.

The deafening sound of the horn echoed in my ears, and I darted straight forward. Emm warned me of the step up, but I still gashed my shin on it. *Fuck.* Darkness surrounded me as I climbed into the maze. The air was warm inside, and it was hauntingly quiet. My footsteps and Emm's voice in my head were the only sounds that filled the void.

Emm screamed directions at me with her mind as I ran through the darkness. "Left, right, straight, left, your other left."

Her commands were getting scrambled in my mind. I wanted to reach out and touch the walls for guidance, but I kept my arms at my sides, afraid of what might happen if I touched them. Deadly traps could be anywhere. I could lose a limb, or my life even. My stomach churned at the thought.

"Duck!" Emm shouted.

Not expecting that sort of command, my response was slow. A heavy object hit the side of my head as it swung past me, knocking me to the ground. The wetness of blood trickled down the side of my face, over my eye, and into my mouth. My body trembled from the impact, but the metallic taste of my own blood brought me back to reality.

"Get up! Run!" Emm shouted. This time I was fast enough. The ground trembled as something crashed behind me. *Fuck, that was close.* "Sharp left!" Her commands were perfectly timed as I continued to weave through the maze with objects crashing behind me.

When the crashing stopped, I prayed I was near the end, but my prayer went unanswered. The sound of machines whirring made my heart skip a beat. Vibrations reverberated around me, as if the entire maze was in motion.

"Move faster. The walls are closing in," Emm said. *Fuck.* I hated small spaces.

The ceiling grazed the top of my head, forcing me to duck down as I ran. Even in the pitch-black darkness, I knew the path was narrowing. My hand accidentally brushed across the wall, and my chest tightened. Emm's constant commands kept me from giving in to my paralyzing fear. I had to focus on moving. If I thought too hard about the shrinking space, I'd be done for.

My heart raced, my lungs burned, and my head throbbed. I was forced to crawl through the maze on my hands and knees as the ceiling continued to push me down. The hard surface of the glass bruised my knees, but I pushed through the pain. I knew I'd be crushed to death if I didn't.

Emm's commands pushed me forward. "You're almost there. It's a straight shot to the exit. Keep moving!"

I crawled as fast as I could, but the ceiling pressed into me. My elbows met the glass floor as I pulled myself through the last stretch of the maze. Crawling on my stomach, my hand found the exit. I didn't know how far the drop was to the ground, but I pushed off the wall with my hands anyway.

The cool breeze hit me as I launched myself out of the maze. I tucked into a ball and rolled out onto the grass. My sight was still consumed by darkness, but I didn't care. I breathed heavily as I lay on my back. Every inch of my body hurt, but the damp grass soothed me.

Footsteps drew near as I sat up. The darkness over my eyes slowly lifted, and Emm's voice dissipated. Jade lay in the grass not far from me, looking just as relieved as I was. It was over, and we'd both made it out in one piece. My head throbbed, and I instinctually touched it. The side of my face was bloodied, and a lump had already started to form near my temple. I tried to wipe the blood from my face as Daniel and Emm approached with the dark priestess.

"Congratulations. You've both made it to the end." The priestess's voice lacked sincerity, but Daniel's smile did not. His hazel-pink eyes stared into mine.

"As your reward, you will all get small first aid kits and your choice of one item from the table." A table appeared before us. The items on it were the same as the items we'd chosen from before. "And for the winning team, a map of the Inbetween." She handed the map to Daniel.

I staggered to my feet. My head injury had me a bit off-balance, but I managed to walk to the reward table with the others. Since I already had twine, I grabbed a canteen along with my first aid kit. It was in a little backpack, which made it easy to carry. The others all grabbed the same thing; apparently none of us had grabbed a canteen to start with.

Once we'd made our choices, the table vanished, along with the entire challenge. We were left in the middle of the woods, and it was as if the challenge had never existed. My head throbbed, and a sickness rose in my stomach, causing me to hunch over.

"Are you all right?" Daniel asked. He drew near and examined my head.

"I feel sick," I replied. The world spun, but Daniel's warm hand on my back kept me grounded.

"Let's camp for the night," he said.

"Sounds good to me," Jade replied. She had to be just as tired as I was. I wondered if she'd been injured in the maze too, though there wasn't any blood on her.

"There's better coverage over there." Emm pointed to a dense patch of trees. It wasn't a bad idea to stay as hidden as possible. We still had no idea what could be waiting in the woods, especially at night.

Daniel helped me over to the covered area while the girls gathered wood for a fire. I sat at the base of a wide oak tree, and Daniel immediately went to work. Opening his first aid kit, he pulled out a jar of antiseptic cream. It burned when he smeared it into my head wound.

"Ouch, that hurts," I complained with tears filling my eyes. My body had reached its threshold for pain.

"Don't be such a baby," he teased, giving me a warm smile. I tried to fight it, but I couldn't stop the smile that crept across my face. Daniel's presence was always comforting.

"Just be gentle," I replied. He stared into my eyes and caressed the side of my face. The warmth of his touch made my skin tingle with gooseflesh.

"I'm always gentle with you," Daniel said, whispering in my ear as he placed a bandage over my wound. His breath tickled my neck and made my body tremble. Heat rose to my cheeks. His face was so close to mine; he was too close. I thought of how I'd nearly kissed him. What was wrong with me?

"Are you almost done?" I asked as I looked away from him. Securing the bandage with a wrap around my head, he released me.

"All done," he said. I knew his eyes were on me, but I didn't dare look at him. He would tease me for the redness of my face.

"Thanks," I replied. The throbbing in my head was calmed by the cream he'd applied.

"Of course. I'd do anything for my fair maiden." He laughed. His humor was lost on me. I couldn't tell if he was joking or being serious. The whole "damsel in distress" joke had gone on too long. I wasn't some girl who needed a hero to save her.

"I'm not a damned maiden!" I snapped as I looked into Daniel's eyes. "I'm a man, and I don't need to be saved." His smile wavered for a moment but quickly returned.

"I'll save you whether you need it or not because you're my maiden," he replied as his hand touched my face. A fire rose within me as his thumb traced along my bottom lip. He pulled me toward him. Was he going to kiss me? Did I want him to kiss me? He had to be messing with me.

Swatting his hand away, I climbed to my feet. Daniel looked up at me from where he sat on the ground, his eyes glowing pink. He was never serious about anything, and I wouldn't get caught in his trap. I walked away from him, needing to clear my thoughts. A walk in the woods would do the trick.

CHAPTER 13

KI

I glanced at the map one last time before turning our path to the east. Tyler followed closely behind me without complaint. I still couldn't believe how helpful she'd been during our first challenge. She'd given clear, concise, and perfectly timed commands that had made navigating the glass maze a breeze. My inhuman speed hadn't thrown her off at all. Her sharp performance had allowed us to beat the other team and win the map of the Inbetween.

Having a map of the area should've been helpful, but I'd spotted the waterfall when we'd jumped from the ship. It was likely that other competitors had won the same map and would be headed toward the waterfall. I just hoped we had enough of a head start to get in and out without any conflict.

We'd been walking for two hours without rest when running water sounded in the distance. As we drew closer to the source of the sound, a small lake came into view. A large waterfall poured into the lake before us. It originated from the mountainside and ended in what appeared to be a bottomless lake—a marvel of nature.

Tyler eagerly ran to the water's edge to fill her canteen. I had more restraint. Something in the air didn't seem right; it was too quiet. I walked the lake's edge and came upon two freshly dead bodies. The tlaloc and his asudh partner lay belly-up with pale faces covered in black veins. Their bodies were soaking wet. Poison?

"Don't drink the water!" I yelled. The water source must have been poisoned. I ran back to Tyler. She was clearly deaf and about to take a drink from her canteen. Electricity ripped through my hand as crackling black tendrils extended from it, snatching the canteen out of Tyler's hands just before it touched her lips.

"What was that for?" she asked as I emptied the water from her canteen. Her bright blue eyes stared at me.

"It's poisoned," I replied, directing her attention to the bodies down the bend.

"Oh my god," she gasped, spotting the corpses. I handed her back her empty canteen, and she looked up at me. "You saved me. Thank you." The look in her eyes was unsettling, so I ignored her.

"You should clean that out before reusing it," I said, moving away from the lake. She nodded in agreement and returned the canteen to its holster on her hip.

"Are there other water sources on the map?" she asked, hopeful.

"No. But we should get out of here. This place has a bad energy about it," I replied, heading back in the direction we'd come from.

"Leaving so soon?" an eerie voice called from the water. A hurricane lifted from the middle of the lake, spiraling upward. The water settled, and an ugly devil of the sea appeared. She floated on top of the water with three layers of tentacles where her legs should have been, each tier larger than the last. It looked like a horrid ball gown made of tentacles.

"What is that?" Tyler shrieked as she took in the sight of the sea witch.

The witch's chest sagged and was strapped to her by a web of seaweed. She wore a pet octopus on her head like a hat, and the poor thing was tangled in her stringy black hair. What disturbed me the most were her solid black eyes, which looked more like sunken holes in a skull than eyes. Did people see my eyes that way?

"Run!" I said as I grabbed Tyler's hand and pulled her toward the woods.

She tried to keep up with my pace but couldn't move fast enough. One of the sea witch's tentacles caught her foot, pulling her to the ground. Her hand slipped from my grasp, and she was dragged swiftly toward the water. I jumped back and caught her hand in mine just before she fell over the lake's edge. The sea witch cackled as I tried to pull Tyler free.

Realizing the tentacle's grip was too strong, I launched a ball of dark magic at it. The tentacle broke in half, and the witch screamed in agony. Pulling Tyler away from the water, I practically carried her as I ran for the woods with inhuman speed. She struggled to stay upright, but I didn't stop until I knew we were out of the bloody sea witch's reach.

We crashed to the ground when we finally stopped, breathing heavily. As I caught my breath, I noticed that part of the tentacle remained attached to Tyler's leg. I grabbed it in an attempt to rip it off, but she screamed in agony. The tentacle tightened around her ankle, and she flailed her leg in a feeble attempt to shake it off.

"Hold still," I said as dark magic crackled in my hand. It was harder to control with my ring on, and I didn't want to hurt her.

Tears rolled down Tyler's face, but she held still. I placed my hands over the tentacle and commanded my dark magic to burn it from the inside out, incinerating it. The smell of its burning flesh nauseated me, but it released Tyler's leg and withered on the ground.

"Thanks," Tyler said, wiping the tears from her eyes. She rubbed her freed ankle and winced.

"Did the tentacle break through your boot?" I asked. The tentacles of a sea witch contained a deadly poison.

"I don't think so," she said. I was skeptical, but if the poison had been introduced into her system, she would've already been writhing in pain.

"Is your ankle broken?" I asked.

"I'm not sure," she replied. Her eyes were fixated on her ankle, as if she could will it to heal. I noticed that she hadn't moved her foot at all. She must've been scared to do so.

"Remove your boot; we need to assess the damage," I said, and her face paled. It must've hurt more than she was letting on.

"Are you sure that's a good idea?" she asked. Even at a distance, I could hear how her heart raced in her chest.

"Just do it," I said. She stared up at me with tears in her bright blue eyes. I sighed in resignation, realizing I would have to do it for her. Moving closer, I reached for her foot, and she instinctually pulled it away.

"Trust me," I said as I held my hands open to receive her foot.

Tyler hesitated before extending her foot toward me. Carefully loosening the strings first, I slid her boot off. She bit her lip to muffle her cry of pain, but the sound still shook me. My stomach twisted from having caused her pain, even though I knew it was the only way to help her.

I slid her suit leg up, and she turned her head away. She didn't want to see her injury, and I couldn't blame her. A dark black bruise surrounded her ankle, looking grotesque in comparison to her pale white skin. Most people would've been sickened by the sight of it. Her foot dangled loosely in my hands; it was definitely broken.

Tyler shrieked when I twisted her foot back into its rightful place. Her scream was so loud that it echoed through the trees. I cringed from the sound but continued on. Dark magic flowed through my hands and surrounded her ankle. It solidified and held her foot in place while I riffled through my first aid kit. Splinting her ankle, I wrapped it tightly with cloth from the kit. It wasn't perfect, but it would have to do.

"How did you know how to do that?" Tyler asked as I tucked the kit back into my bag.

"Broke a lot of bones as a kid," I replied, scanning the trees for movement. There was a good chance that one of our competitors had heard Tyler's scream.

"But the palace has doctors," she said, confused.

"We need to relocate," I said. "Danger could be headed our way." Tyler nodded and went to stand up but immediately fell to the ground with a screech. "You're in no condition to walk, so I'll carry you."

Tyler's face reddened as I handed her the boot. I slid one arm around her back and the other under her knees. She trembled from my touch, but I lifted her up anyway. Without any resistance, I carried her through the woods. She weighed very little, reminding me how malnourished she was.

I headed west, following the line of the mountains, hoping we'd come across a cave to take shelter in for the night. If the cool evening winds were any indication, the temperature would drop with the sun. My skin was thick and could withstand freezing weather, but the same wouldn't be true for the human. Her body shivered from the wind alone.

Unfortunately, I hadn't found so much as a bloody alcove to hide in before the sun began to set. My arms had tired from carrying Tyler all day when the trickling of a stream caught my attention. I shouldered my way through a thicket of bushes and came upon the small stream. It ran along the mountain's edge. Setting Tyler down, I checked the water for poison, not wanting to make the same mistake twice. I drew on the magic within me to create fire. When the water didn't burn, I knew it was clean.

Tyler's eyes lit up when I drank straight from the stream. She joined me, and we drank our fill of water before filling our canteens. We moved on quickly, as there wasn't much daylight left. I needed to find a place for us to sleep that wouldn't leave us completely exposed.

Carrying Tyler, I spotted a ledge along the mountain's cliff. It was twenty meters up and the best resting place I'd seen all day. With the cover of darkness, it would be hard for competitors to see us from the ground, and it would give us the upper hand should there be an attack. There was no way to know what would come out of the woods at night, be it animals or other competitors, so we needed to be prepared.

I scaled the cliff with ease and placed Tyler on the ground. She smiled as she thanked me, but I ignored her. I'd only done what I had to. If I wanted to win the Reckoning, I would have to keep her alive, so there was no need for her to thank me. My actions were for my own benefit.

A tall tree stood nearby, providing us shade and protection from the wind as the sun fell from the sky. We sat in silence with our backs against the mountain's smooth stone wall. I appreciated the quiet and closed my eyes to relax, my body sore from carrying Tyler. My moment of peace was short-lived. A cool breeze brushed through my hair and made Tyler shiver.

"We should make a fire," she said. I looked at her in disbelief. Was she really that ignorant? A fire would give away our position, especially at night.

"Don't be a bloody idiot," I replied. She complained as she shivered, but I still refused.

A few hours later, a fire appeared in the distance. Its smoke rose high in the sky, and its light was a beacon in the dark. Tyler's eyes widened when she spotted it. Her eyes pleaded with me, but I shook my head. I knew she was cold, but her constant complaints were annoying. A piercing scream came from the direction of the fire. The screaming carried on for some time before it finally stopped. Tyler never asked for a fire again.

Unable to bear the sound of Tyler's bloody teeth chattering, I positioned myself closer to her. I loathed physical contact, but I placed my arm around her and pulled her into me. She huddled against me, clinging to my body, and her teeth quieted. My stomach knotted, and my heart raced. The suits we wore were so thin that it was as if she were touching my skin.

"I'm sorry for being such a burden," Tyler said as she nuzzled her head into my chest. I didn't reply. My energy was focused on staying calm. I fought the hunger that begged me to taste her. Luckily, the heat that radiated from my body comforted Tyler enough for her to fall asleep.

Once I was sure she wouldn't wake up, I placed my family ring on her finger for safekeeping and then leapt into the night sky. My wings released from my back; I was whole again. The night breeze soothed the ache in my back as I glided in circles. I didn't want to venture too far from Tyler, but I needed to hunt. It had been two days since I'd last fed, and my hunger was becoming a burden.

The forest was oddly quiet. It was late enough in the season for the bugs to be gone, but where were the animals? I hadn't come across one the entire day. If they were out there, they were hiding well. It would be difficult to find one, but I had to try. I couldn't risk losing control and feeding on Tyler. Only the gods knew what would bloody happen if I did.

It took too long, and I traveled too far away from Tyler, but I managed to catch a rabbit. I drained its blood in seconds. My body wanted more, but it was enough to stave off the hunger, and it would make a good meal for Tyler in the morning.

I headed back to the cliff as quickly as possible, but I spotted movement in the trees not far from it. A competitor was headed straight for Tyler. Swooping down low, I approached the competitor from behind. It was a tlaloc. She stomped loudly through the brush.

"Isn't it a bit dark to be wandering through the woods?" I asked, startling the tlaloc. She turned quickly in my direction with a hellish grin across her face.

"Why, if it isn't the Darkblood Prince," she replied. Her eyes lit up in the moonlight.

"Go back to where you came from, or you will die this

night," I said with hope that she wouldn't be stupid enough to challenge me. But the bloody fool chose to charge at me.

I stepped to the side, avoiding her tusks as she passed me. With my leg extended, I tripped her. She crashed to the ground but quickly recovered with a roll to the side. Light reflected off the knife in her hand as she swiped at me. I dodged her attack, kicking the knife from her hand. It flew into the woods and disappeared in the darkness.

"Damn you," she grunted and tackled me. A scream came from above; there was more than one attacker. "She's as good as dead now." The tlaloc smiled.

Realizing her attack was just a distraction, I wrestled my way on top of her. With my hands wrapped around her throat, I squeezed tight. Her limbs flailed in the air as I cut off the blood flow to her head. It only took a few seconds for her to lose consciousness, but I didn't have time to spare. I needed to get to Tyler.

Another one of Tyler's screams pierced the silent night. It was louder than the first, and the sound haunted me, but it meant she was still alive. I scaled the side of the cliff with one jump, landing on the ledge. Tyler writhed under the man on top of her. He had her pinned to the ground and half-undressed. It sickened me as I saw him grab at her private areas. The vile human lowered his pants, and rage consumed me.

My sight turned red as a pulse of dark magic radiated from my body, electrifying my blood. I was upon him in an instant. I stepped onto his back and grabbed a fistful of his hair. Pulling with all my strength, his bones cracked. It was like music to my ears, and I couldn't stop. I ripped his head from his body in triumph. Blood sprayed out like a fountain from his neck. The smell of it was intoxicating.

Tyler's shriek drew my attention. She wiped at her eyes fervently. I'd acted without thought. She was drowning in the man's sweet blood as it poured from his body straight onto her. Realizing I still had his head in my hand, I threw it to the side and pulled his body off of Tyler.

Hovering over Tyler, I stared at her exposed chest. Blood pooled between her breasts and trickled down the curves of her body. It left a tantalizing trail as it dripped to the ground. The brightness of it stood out against her pale skin, making it more vibrant and enticing. My body desperately wanted to taste it.

Heat rushed through me with a swirl of new desires. I wanted to lick the blood off her skin—no, I *needed* to. I touched Tyler with a single finger, tracing a trail of blood from her stomach down to the side of her hip. She whimpered, and her eyes opened.

"Ki?" Her cry brought me back to my senses. What was I doing? My intentions redirected, and I zipped her suit up in one quick motion. The blood was too tempting.

"Let's get you cleaned off," I said as I lifted her from the ground. She was silent and trembled in my arms as I carried her. Was it shock or fear? No one else had witness my changed face before, and with all the blood still on her, I couldn't get my teeth to revert.

Careful not to jostle Tyler, I moved quickly toward the nearby stream. When we got there, the blood had mostly dried, which meant it would be difficult to wash off. I set Tyler on the bank and removed the one boot she still had on. She didn't say anything, just stared downward. Her blue eyes lacked their usual brightness and were filled with tears.

I stripped down to my underwear and slid into the water. The gentle flow of the stream was cool on my skin. If only it could wash away my shame. I turned to Tyler, and her eyes avoided mine. Why had I touched her like that? The thought plagued me as I pulled her into the stream.

The water came up to Tyler's shoulders, but she remained quiet. I gently dipped her head underwater and was glad she wiped at her face. Chunks of red clouded the water around her as I brushed my fingers through her hair.

When she came up for air, bloodied water dripped from her chin. Her hands immediately covered her face. Did she not want me to look at her? With the thick layer of blood gone, I could see the redness of her cheeks. Was she embarrassed?

I pulled the white ribbon out of Tyler's hair, and a mess of bloodied blond hair fell around her shoulders. Tying the ribbon to Tyler's wrist so that it wouldn't get lost, I leaned her back again to rinse more blood from her hair. It took a while, and Tyler kept her face hidden, but I finally got her head clean.

Clumps of blood still clung to her body. She refused to remove her hands from her face, so I had no choice but to undress her myself. My heart raced as I pulled at the zipper on her suit. It was wrong, but I had to do it. I had to get rid of the blood that tempted me. Just the scent of it made my mouth water, even when it was dried up.

Keeping my hunger at bay, I slowly unzipped Tyler's suit. I waited for her to complain, but she remained silent and gave no resistance. Her hands only moved from her face for the brief moment it took for me to get her arms out of her suit sleeves. Once the suit was off her shoulders, she sobbed quietly.

She refused to look at me, and I hoped that made the situation easier for her. I hated the fact that I had to place my hands on her after such an attack, but she wouldn't do it herself. With caution, I rubbed my hands over her body, washing the blood away. I started at her shoulders and was surprised by how soft her skin was. The blood came off with the gentlest touch, but Tyler still trembled. As I ventured down her body, I had to force myself to think about the severity of the situation. I had to fight the desires that rose within me.

An arousal I hadn't known I was capable of overwhelmed me. Her smooth skin was inviting, and her silent obedience excited me. I had complete control over her, and it made my heart race. This must've been the feeling that made men lose their reason, what made them attack women, but it couldn't be the same. I wasn't like those men, and I wasn't trying to hurt Tyler.

Once the blood was washed away, Tyler's hands finally fell from her face. She covered her chest with her arms, but it made no difference. The image of her blood-covered chest would be imprinted in my mind forever. Her face was red, and her eyes stared downward.

The scent of fresh blood distracted me, my body still ready to feed. There was a small cut on Tyler's shoulder that I hadn't noticed before. In fact, there were several scratches and bruises along her arms and chest. It was clear she'd fought hard against her attacker, which made me feel better. She hadn't fought against me, so my actions couldn't have been bad.

Tyler must've been in shock from the attack. That was why she was silent and compliant. Any other possibility was too hard to think about. I convinced myself that she hadn't minded when my hands lingered on her body. It was harmless. After all, she'd tried to cling to me the night before, hadn't she?

Wrapping my arms around her, I pulled Tyler into my chest. Our bare skin touched, and the water rippled around us. Her eyes finally looked into mine, and her trembling eased. She stared up at me with slightly parted lips. A hunger burned deep within me. I needed to feed.

Tyler's blood smelled even sweeter than the man's. I was completely consumed by the cut on her shoulder. It teased me. Breathing in its deliciousness, I couldn't resist any longer. I was starved. Just one taste, that was all I needed. One drop of blood, and I could drive away my hunger. She would be okay.

Leaning down, I licked the blood from Tyler's cut. She sucked in a breath, and an unexpected wave of ecstasy took over me. My razor-sharp teeth sank into Tyler's skin like a hot knife through butter. I bit hard into her shoulder, losing all control.

The pleasure from drinking her blood intoxicated me. She relaxed into my arms and let out a soft moan. An intense surge of power filled me, engulfing me with dark magic. The energy was too strong to contain. It flowed out of me like a black flame. My head spun.

Tyler's heartbeat began to slow, and I found my will. I withdrew my teeth from her, but my blood still vibrated with energy.

Her hazy eyes looked at me as she smiled. When she went limp in my arms, I realized I'd taken too much blood.

As I held Tyler in my arms, the events of the night finally set in. Over the course of one day, I'd killed two men and drank the blood of a human. How many more would I have to kill to keep Tyler alive?

CHAPTER 14

TYLER

Screams pierced through the silent night, waking me. I jolted upright, afraid there was another attacker. My throat burned as I swallowed. Ki stared at me, eyes searching for an explanation. The screams must have been my own. His gaze traveled down my body as if he expected to find an injury, but my pain wasn't physical.

Sure, my ankle throbbed and my shoulder ached, but my real pain was internal. I would never forget the horrors I'd witnessed. There'd been so much blood. It had blurred my vision and seeped into my mouth. The metallic taste still lingered. My stomach twisted as I thought of the man's face, how his eyes had practically popped out of their sockets when Ki had ripped his head from his body. It haunted me.

Tears built in my eyes as I remembered that night. I'd fought as hard as I could, but I still hadn't been able to get myself free. Ki had saved me just in time, though I hadn't been able to thank him. The sight of blood had paralyzed me. I'd tried not to look at it, but it'd been everywhere.

"Are you all right?" Ki asked, sitting up next to me. We'd been huddled together for warmth before my nightmare had woken me. My heart was still racing, and my breath came heavy. I couldn't remember my dream, but the fear was real.

"No, I'm not," I replied. Ki's eyes widened. Several days had passed since that night, but it still plagued my thoughts and dreams. It was impossible to process what had happened with Ki. He'd saved me from the man, from the blood, but then he'd bitten me. To top it all off, he hadn't said a word about any of it.

Ki stared at me silently. It had become a habit of his, but at least his eyes weren't red. I could never tell what was on his mind when he stared at me with glowing red eyes and a blank expression on his face. He was a mystery to me, much like Nydden was. I wondered if he would give honest answers to questions like Nydden.

I took a deep breath to steady myself. Thoughts of my nightmare had passed, yet my heart still raced. Ki was unpredictable, but I needed answers.

"Why did you bite me?" I asked, meeting his gaze.

Ki's lips parted as he continued to stare. "I hadn't intended to, but there was a cut on your shoulder," he said. His eyes fell to the ground. "My energy was low, and I couldn't control it."

The look of shame on his face was clear, but his answer only left me with more questions. "What couldn't you control?" I asked. His eyes darted up.

"The change. I know you've seen it—in the ballroom, and that night," he replied.

"Is that why you don't eat? Because you survive off blood?" I said, needing to know more. Ki sighed and lay back on the ground with his eyes looking to the sky. "I'm sorry if this seems like common knowledge to you, but I don't know anything about dierdres."

"I don't have the answers," Ki said. "My need for blood didn't present itself until this summer, and there's no mention of a trait like it in my family records. I can eat regular food, but my body only hungers for blood. It gives me strength. Until you, I satiated that hunger with animals. No one knows about this, and no one can find out."

Lying down, I joined Ki on the cool ground. "Will you do it again? Feed on me?"

Ki turned, and his eyes fixated on me. "The sun will be up soon," he replied, avoiding my question. I wanted an answer, but I didn't press the matter. Ki had already been more forthcoming than I'd expected.

"I'll gather wood for a fire," I replied, climbing to my feet. It hurt to walk, but I managed. The tight splint Ki had made kept my foot in place.

Morning was the only time we made fires. It was less noticeable when the sun was up, and there was a chance the other competitors would still be asleep. Of course, we only made the fires as a means to cook the small animals Ki caught at night, and once we were done Ki made sure to cover up any trace of a fire having ever been present.

After I gathered wood, Ki lit the fire. It amazed me every time, how he was able to summon fire from within. He didn't speak any words at all. The fire simply appeared in the palm of his hand, and he threw it onto the wood pile. I was sure he had great magical ability, but he hardly ever showed it. He was secretive.

I'd just finished eating when our bracelets vibrated. The sensation startled me, and I jumped to my feet, worried it would shock me again, but it didn't. Instead, it announced that there were only twelve teams remaining and that we were to follow its directions. It would lead us to our next challenge.

A lump formed in my throat. My body wasn't ready for a challenge. My ankle was weak, and my shoulder soreness made it difficult to raise my arm overhead. I'd examined my shoulder when Ki wasn't looking and had found black marks in the shape of a bite on my skin. Originally, I'd thought they were bruises, but the marks hadn't changed in days. In fact, when Ki lay close to me at night, the area would tingle. It was as if the mark could sense his presence.

My worries multiplied as we trudged through the forest, following the bracelet's directions. A tunnel appeared in the ground before us, and we were to go inside it. I hesitated. There could be any number of deadly traps within the dimly lit tunnel. Thoughts of my family rushed in. I had to survive so I could make it back home to them.

"Don't worry. I'll keep you safe," Ki said. Could he read my mind? His words were of no comfort; in fact, they made my stomach twist. I knew he needed me alive for the first phase, but I lost my certainty after the other night. Ki was dangerous. He had the power to do anything he wanted to me, and I had no way to stop him. What would happen when he no longer felt like protecting me?

Having no choice, I continued to move forward. The darkness of the tunnel consumed us, and I could hardly see a few feet in front of me. Ki's eyes glowed red as he stuck close to my side. He was unaffected by the darkness.

The narrow tunnel opened up into a large underground cavern. Torches lined the walls, lighting up the area. A huge pit as wide as the cavern loomed before us. Three other teams filed in, each coming from a different tunnel at the back of the cavern.

A large muscular tlaloc named Adakk had a nasty underbite and two large tusks that jutted out of his lower jaw. He was accompanied by a rather large female asudh named Ghilanna. They both wore black suits and matching grins as they looked around at their competition. Adakk chuckled when he looked my way, and my shoulder tingled. Ki's dark aura filled the space around us. I was caught inside his dark tendrils of crackling magic, but they didn't hurt me.

One of the teams was a pair of twins. They were aeni with dark purple skin and long silver hair. The only notable difference between them was the color of their eyes. Moonshine had blue eyes while Midnight had orange. I almost envied how their white suits complemented their skin tone.

The last team to arrive consisted of a rather flamboyant

aeni named Wynter and his tlaloc partner, Kih. They wore black suits, and the scowl on Kih's face was hard to miss. I'd heard that tlalocs and aeni didn't get along, but I didn't see much of either race in my village.

Recording orbs flooded the area as the dark priestess appeared. I recognized her from the first challenge. She wore the same hooded cloak and silver amulet. Ki's dark aura dispersed as the priestess began to speak.

"Congratulations on making it this far. Today's challenge will require teamwork, and I don't just mean with your own partners. You will be paired with another team and will work together as a group for the duration of this challenge." Adakk groaned loudly. I guessed he wasn't a big fan of teamwork.

"This will be a timed challenge. You will have five minutes to get all of the members of your group to the other side of the pit. Take a moment to get to know your teammates. Midnight and Moonshine, you're with Ki and Tyler. Adakk and Ghilanna, you're with Wynter and Kih."

I was relieved that we weren't paired with either of the tlalocs, but we didn't get much time to confer with the other team. Midnight and Moonshine, the aeni twins, were quiet. Ki took the lead, and none of us were about to oppose him.

We approached the pit to examine the challenge before us. I looked down into the endless abyss, and my heart skipped a beat. High places were no friend of mine. My hands trembled as I thought of how easy it would be to fall. Would I fall forever, or was there a bottom to the pit of darkness?

Floating square platforms made of stone moved about the pit in various directions: up and down, side to side, and diagonally. There were several different levels of platforms, and only a handful of them hovered statically in place. Ki studied the movement of the platforms and mapped out a strategy for us to get across. It would require moving downward into the pit before coming back up to get to the other side.

"Time starts now," the priestess said, and a five-minute timer popped up on all of our bracelets.

Ki led the way into the pit by jumping to a platform that was moving up and down. At the bottom of the platform's movement, he jumped to another one, which moved side to side. His eyes looked to me. It was my turn to come down. My heart raced as the platform came my way. I leapt onto it, and it carried me downward.

Taking a deep breath, I prepared for my next jump. All I had to do was follow Ki; his instructions were specific and calculated. I could make it across, as long as I didn't look down. It was just like jumping stones in the creek back home, and I always made it to the other side without getting wet. I just had to stay focused on the platforms.

After a few jumps, my ankle was throbbing. Moonshine was close behind me, and Midnight brought up the rear. I had to keep moving; they were all counting on me. Jumping onto a static platform, I wobbled from the pain in my ankle. I managed to stay upright, but I looked straight down into the abyss. My heart stopped as I sucked in a breath. Frozen in place, my body trembled.

"Tyler, you have to keep moving," Ki said, but his words were lost on me. My attention was focused on the dark depths below me. I couldn't breathe.

Moonshine landed on the platform behind me. They grabbed me by the shoulders and turned me to face them. "Look at me," they said. My eyes locked on theirs. I was lost in the sea of blue. "You can do this. Don't look down."

I nodded in reply. Moonshine had pulled me from the paralyzing fear. We only had two minutes left to get to the other side of the pit. I didn't even want to think of what might happen if we were still in the pit when the timer ran out.

Taking a deep breath, I jumped to the next platform, and again to the next, and so on. Ki was at the other side of the pit helping me off the final platform before I knew it. I could hardly stand when I took my place beside him. My head was foggy from the pain in my ankle.

All I could do was watch as Moonshine and Midnight made

their way across the platforms. The other group was already across, and Adakk looked our way. Ki was helping Moonshine off the last platform when Adakk focused on Midnight. I saw the ball of dirt in his hand just before he launched it straight at the back of Midnight's head. Midnight was in the middle of a jump when I screamed.

"Look out!" I waved my hand in Midnight's direction, and a fierce pain of tingling electricity shot through it. Dark magic expelled from my hand, colliding with the ball of dirt that was headed for Midnight. The ball was knocked away just in time. Midnight continued their jumps with only seconds left. They made it over the side of the pit just as the timer struck zero.

"Thank you," Moonshine said as they went to check on Midnight.

My hand and shoulder both tingled as blood dripped from my palm. It had split open from the magic. Pulling my hand to my chest, I looked to Ki. He stared at me with wide eyes and a slightly open mouth. We needed to talk about whatever had just happened, but the pain in my ankle overwhelmed me. A sickness rose in the pit of my stomach. My leg gave out, but Ki scooped me into his arms before I hit the ground.

"Congratulations on your victory here today. Be sure to grab your rewards on your way out," the dark priestess said, pointing to the table behind us. There were backpacks stuffed with tents, bedrolls, and blankets along the table.

Ki set me gently on the ground as he grabbed our rewards and consolidated our equipment into two packs. He threw one over each shoulder before picking me back up and carrying me out of the cavern.

We exited the cavern just as we had arrived, through separate tunnels. As Ki carried me back to the surface, the afternoon sunlight burned my eyes. It was hard to see anything, but at least we were above ground. The tunnel closed up as soon as we were out of it, and Ki set me down under a tree to examine my ankle.

"It hasn't healed yet?" he asked, confused.

"Of course not. It could take months for it to heal fully," I replied.

"Seriously? Humans are so frail." He sighed. "Can't you just use your dark magic to heal it?"

"I don't have magic," I replied. Ki stared at me with a raised brow.

"I witnessed you using dark magic."

"I have no idea how that happened. I've never been able to use magic before. I swear I was born magicless. My being Called was a mistake."

"The Calling makes no mistakes. It's more likely that you didn't know how to access your own magic."

My jaw clenched. Did he really think I was that stupid? That I wouldn't have noticed an affinity for dark magic until I was eighteen? Everyone knew magic began to display during infancy.

"No, it's more likely that you infected me with your magic when you fed on me!" I pulled open my suit to reveal the black bite mark that remained on my shoulder.

Ki stared at me in stunned silence. After a few minutes passed, he sat back on his heels and scratched his head. "I could try to fuse your bones together with my magic. Since my magic is already inside you, a little more shouldn't hurt. It won't actually heal you, but it should hold your bones together while they heal themselves."

"What? I just said you infected me with magic, and that's your response?"

"You're no good to me in your current condition. Your ankle needs healed."

I sighed. He wasn't going to acknowledge what he'd done to me, so I conceded. Placing my foot in his hand, I figured anything was worth a try if it meant saving me from the constant pain. Ki removed my boot carefully and rolled up my pant leg. What remained of the splint unraveled without my boot keeping it in place.

"Have you done this before?" I asked as dark tendrils

crackled around his hands. He placed his hands around my ankle before he replied.

"Not exactly." My breath caught in my throat, and my heart raced. I braced myself for the worst. A tingling charge of electricity surged through my ankle. I tensed my muscles, but when my pain vanished, I relaxed. The tingling subsided as Ki released my ankle. His handprints lingered on my skin. They were a faded shade of black, a shadow of the hands that had touched me.

"Will it fade away?" I asked. My thoughts turned to the black bite mark that still lingered on my shoulder.

"Time will tell," he replied. His eyes avoided mine as he sat beside me.

"How do you not know? Have you not left a mark before? Will there be lasting effects?" I had so many questions. Dark magic wasn't something I was familiar with, and I had no idea what it would do to me. After all, I'd just used dark magic and had never possessed any magic abilities before. It had to be from the mark.

"I don't know!" he snapped. "It's not like I've ever used my magic on a human before." His head was turned away from me as he spoke, and his muscles were tense.

"Hey, it's okay. We can figure this out together." I smiled, hoping to cheer him up. It would've been nice to get answers, but I didn't want to upset him more. I remembered the look of shame on his face when I'd asked about the bite.

Thoughts of that night filled my mind. I didn't want to think about it—how his hands were warm on my skin, how my body tingled from every touch, the intense pleasure that came when his teeth sank into me. It made no sense; it had to be magic.

"I'm sorry," he whispered. "This whole mess is my fault." His somber tone pulled at my heart.

"If you want to make it up to me, you can teach me how to control the magic," I replied. There was no guarantee I'd actually be able to use magic. What happened during the challenge could've been a onetime thing. Either way, it was worth a try. If I could use magic, it would definitely be useful in the days to come.

"Deal, but we must relocate first," he replied after a long pause.

Ki helped me to my feet, and I was thrilled to have no pain in my ankle. It appeared that his magic had worked. My ankle wouldn't be a hindrance anymore. I only hoped it would last. Magic could be unpredictable.

The sun was setting by the time we found a decent place to rest. Ki made fast work of setting up the small tent we'd won in the challenge. It was just big enough for the two of us to sleep in. I was thrilled to get a night's sleep without the constant chill of a breeze cutting into me; however, as I lay there next to Ki, my mind raced.

Ki slept soundly, but I couldn't lie still. I was restless. As quietly as I could, I snuck out of the tent, hoping a short walk would clear my head. I was surprised to find snow softly falling to the ground. A thin layer had already formed, but I continued anyway. There was so much that I didn't know about Ki, about the magic that I suddenly had access to. Was it permanent? Was Ki really that unaware of what he'd done to me, or was it a lie? Could I die from it?

A soft melody pulled me from my spiral. It was a song I didn't recognize. I followed the sound, curious as to who was singing. The voices led me to a small clearing where I found Midnight and Moonshine. Snow had been pushed to the side so that they could draw a circle in the dirt. They sat inside the circle holding hands. I crouched behind a tree as I watched them.

A ball of magical energy floated in the space between them.

It's glow dimly lit the clearing. I could vaguely recognize the words they spoke; it was the ancient language. They were praying to the four shamans.

"Gaia, mother of the earth, please continue to shelter us with your body," Midnight said aloud in common.

"Ilmatar, father of the air, please continue to fuel us with your breath," Moonshine said.

"Vulcan, father of fire, please continue to warm us with your fury."

"Nerine, mother of water, please continue to refresh us with your touch."

"May the power of the original shamans continue to flow," they said in unison.

"Fire, I thank you for your strength," Midnight said.

"Water, I thank you for your resilience," Moonshine said.

Their arms rose toward the sky, and the ball of energy between them separated. A ball of blue light hovered over Moonshine while a ball of orange light hovered over Midnight, matching their eye colors. My breath caught in my lungs as I took in the beauty of it all.

"Won't you join us?" Moonshine asked as the balls dissipated. My heart skipped a beat as their glowing eyes turned to me.

"We don't bite," Midnight added.

"I'm sorry," I said as I stood up. "I didn't mean to interrupt."

"Would you like to pray with us?" Moonshine asked.

"Oh, no. I'm not very religious. I wasn't blessed by the gods," I replied.

"Are you sure about that?" Midnight asked. I wondered why they would ask such a thing. Did they know something that I didn't?

"There you are!" Ki said from behind me. He grabbed my arm before I had the chance to turn. "It's not safe to run out in the middle of the night like that." Ki's head turned as he finally noticed the others.

"Sorry, I couldn't sleep. I thought a walk would help," I replied.

"Let's go," he said as he pulled me away from the aeni. They both waved as we departed, and I hoped I would see them again.

CHAPTER 15

HARRISON

"Watch out, long ears," Urmicca said as she cut me off on my way to the reward table.

She had small perfectly pointed ears and had made fun of me throughout the entire challenge. Her harsh, unprovoked insults had nearly made me lose my footing when jumping between platforms. I tried to appear unaffected by her words as I fought back the tears that built in my eyes. As a fellow asudh, she knew how cruel it was to insult one's ears.

Filing in behind her, I grabbed my rewards from the table—a tent, a bedroll, and a blanket, all things that would make it easier to sleep at night, especially since the temperature was steadily dropping.

I'd just finished packing my backpack when Urmicca shouldered me, leaving the table. Losing my balance, I bumped into Quaeth. He was also an asudh and about my height, though he had a thicker build. His short pointed ears were perfectly shaped, unlike mine, which were abnormally long. I wished I had ears like his.

"Hmm, it's a shame you don't look my way more often," he said as he smiled at me. Heat rose to my face.

"Excuse me?" I replied. His brown eyes looked me up and down, and I recognized him from the welcoming night. He was the asudh who'd openly made out with Wynter.

"You're cute, but I doubt that tlaloc of yours would ever let me get near you," he said while he stuffed his reward bag.

"Daniel? He's just an old friend," I replied, confused. Was he flirting with me? And what did he mean by that tlaloc of mine? I didn't own Daniel.

"Hey, no judgment here," he said as he zipped up his bag and walked away.

I struggled to understand his words. What was there to judge about me and Daniel being friends? Or had he sensed something else? Could Quaeth tell that I'd had thoughts about kissing Daniel? My thoughts plagued me as I walked over to my group.

"Was that guy bothering you?" Daniel asked. He stared daggers at Quaeth.

"No. He was just misunderstanding something," I replied.

"Right, and that Urmicca bitch was just playfully teasing you?" he said. Daniel's eye bored into Urmicca's back as she headed down one of the exit tunnels with her partner, Zugak. He was an average-size tlaloc, a little smaller than Daniel, with tusks that curved upward from his cheeks.

"We should get going. We'll want to find a good place to camp before the sun sets," Emm said, looking only at me. She avoided speaking to Daniel whenever possible, even though she had agreed that teaming up with him and Jade would be advantageous for us.

"We'll want to walk a good distance from these tunnels too, make sure we have some distance between us and the other competitors," Jade added.

"Follow me," Daniel said with clenched fists. He led our group down the narrow tunnel that eventually brought us back to the surface.

The sun was high in the sky, just past midday. Daniel kept his fists clenched as he weaved through the underbrush. I wondered how long it would take for his anger to dissipate. It was all my fault. He always got angry and defensive when people made fun of me. I'd never forget the time he challenged a schoolmate to a duel. He'd said it was to restore my honor, but he used it as an excuse to beat the poor boy half to death. I prayed we wouldn't run into Urmicca again.

Daniel's muscles still held tension as the sun fell from the sky. He selected a small grove of pine trees to be our campsite for the night and immediately began setting up. With only two tents between the four of us, we all decided that Emm and Jade would share one, while Daniel and I shared the other. The way Emm's shoulders relaxed when we made the agreement told me she was relieved to be sleeping with another female.

Emm and Jade went to collect wood while Daniel and I assembled the tents. He was oddly quiet as we made fast work of it. I couldn't stop myself from admiring his body as he worked. His muscles flexed as he hammered the stakes into the ground with the hilt of his hunting knife.

Sweat glistened on his forehead as he looked up at me from where he knelt. His hazel-pink eyes caught me mid-stare. "Are you going to help, or do you plan to just stand there staring?" Daniel nodded toward the last rope that needed tied down.

"Sorry," I said as I quickly grabbed the rope. Pulling it over to him, we secured the tent in place.

"We should pray to the gods. Their blessings helped us survive yet another challenge today," Daniel said as he wiped his forehead with his sleeve.

My heart raced. "It would be my honor to pray with you," I said. Daniel always worshipped alone in the temple, but we were in the wilderness, and forming a holy circle on your own wasn't as respectful to the gods.

"At midnight," he replied. I nodded with a smile, shocked that he'd actually agreed.

The evening passed quickly. When the girls came back, they

carried more than just wood with them. Jade and Emm had stumbled upon a fox and had managed to kill it. We made a fire to warm ourselves and cook the meat. It had been two days since our last real meal, so I savored every bite.

With midnight being several hours away, Daniel suggested we get some sleep. The girls agreed to take the first watch and would wake us when the moon was high in the sky. I'd slept in the same room as Daniel many times when we were young, but things were different.

The tent was barely big enough for us to squeeze into. My back was pressed into his side as we lay on our bedrolls, and my heart raced. His every movement made me tremble. I thought about how we'd almost kissed. Would he try again now that we were alone? It was odd that I couldn't get it off my mind. Did I really want him to kiss me?

Daniel rolled over in his sleep, and his arm wrapped around me. He pulled me into his chest, and I sucked in a breath. His skin was warm as it pressed into my back. His strong arms held me tightly to him. My heart raced, refusing to calm down and making it hard to sleep. I quietly enjoyed the comfort his touch brought me.

After a long while, I drifted off to sleep.

"Harrison, wake up." Daniel's breath was warm on my neck as he whispered into my ear. He knew how to wake me gently, but his nearness made my heart leap. His chest was pressed into my back, and his lips nearly touched my ear.

"I'm up," I replied.

We crawled out of the tent to find a thin layer of snow had dusted the ground and continued to fall from the sky. Daniel stared up at the full moon, waiting for the girls to quiet down as they settled into their tent. Without a word, he motioned for me to follow him.

Walking a short distance through the trees, we came upon a clearing illuminated by the full moon's light. My body trembled—partly from the cold breeze, and partly from the spiritual energy that filled the air. It was the perfect place to create a holy circle. The gods would be pleased, which meant Daniel would be pleased.

"Wait here," Daniel said and then disappeared into the trees.

I stood alone in the clearing with snow falling down around me. There was something almost magical about the peaceful silence of it all. My problems with Jess seemed so far away.

Daniel returned with two large sticks in hand. I took one from him, then we moved to the middle of the clearing and stood back-to-back. We walked in opposite directions, creating a small circle just big enough for the two of us to sit within. After three full rotations, one for each god, we stepped inside the circle.

With the holy circle created, our ritual had begun. Daniel sat at the north end of the circle, as he was more in tune with Gaia, and I sat to the south, closer to Vulcan. We sat cross-legged with our hands on our knees and palms toward the sky. Daniel began the prayer. His eyes glowed pink as he spoke.

"Blessed are we by the gods that give us day and night. May the everlasting powers of the sun and moon continue to shine down upon us. To our god Apollo, we thank you for the earth that gives us shelter and the fire that keeps us warm. To our goddess Hecate, we thank you for the air we breathe and the water that cleanses us." Daniel's voice was commanding.

"For without light there can be no darkness, and without darkness there is no light," we chanted in unison. Daniel took my hands into his, and our fingers intertwined. My heart skipped a beat, his touch unexpected.

"Blessed are we by our mother, the goddess that gives us life. May the spiritual power continue to be eternal, and may the rebirth of reincarnation continue to cleanse our souls. To our goddess Sibyl, thank you for the spirit that makes life worth living," Daniel said.

"For without life there can be no death, and without death there is no life," we said in unison as Daniel squeezed my hands. He never looked more beautiful than when he was speaking to the gods.

Keeping a firm grip on my hands, Daniel pulled me into him as he leaned forward. My eyes stared into his. His lips parted. He was going to kiss me; I was sure of it. My body trembled, and I became completely aware of my own desire. I wanted to kiss him.

Daniel's lips found mine, and a fire burned throughout my body. His lips were warm, his kiss rough. With the power of the gods and the falling snow around us, it was perfect. Our kiss was perfect. It should have been my first kiss. I wished it had been, but it wasn't. Thoughts of Jess crept in, and I pulled back.

"Do you believe me now?" Daniel asked with a smile.

"What?" I replied, confused. Thoughts of Jess continued to plague me, and my stomach twisted. I couldn't get that night out of my head.

Daniel's smile faltered. "I love you, Harrison."

Looking into his pink eyes, I was overcome by déjà vu. He'd said it before, outside the temple, but I'd thought it a joke. When? When had Daniel started to feel this way? Had he always felt this way, and I was too oblivious to notice? My head spun as thoughts of Daniel and Jess overwhelmed me.

"I don't deserve love," I said as I scrambled backward out of the circle. Daniel's eyes widened as I climbed to my feet. My chest tightened, and my stomach threatened to spill its contents. I'd done bad things: sex before marriage, stealing a princess's virtue, kissing someone other than my betrothed.

"That couldn't be further from the truth," Daniel said. He rose to his feet, and I took a step back. "What happened with Jess isn't your fault. You shouldn't punish yourself for it."

Tears flooded my eyes. "Yes, I should. I'm the man, so it's my fault." My chest continued to tighten, making it hard to breathe.

"She used magic against you. There's nothing you could

have done to stop her," Daniel said. His words made sense. I'd told him the whole story, and he didn't think it was my fault, but it had to be my fault. If it wasn't, then I was the victim. Men weren't supposed to be the victims.

I hunched over, gagging as reality set in. Jess was the predator, and I was the victim. I hadn't wanted to do it, but I'd been too weak to defend myself. How could I honor my family name or the king if I couldn't even stop Jess? My mind struggled to reconcile the fact that Jess had raped me.

"It's going to be all right," Daniel said. His arms wrapped around me from behind, but I couldn't breathe. My heart raced, wanting to burst out of my chest, and tears streamed down my face. It hurt. It hurt so bad that I wanted to die. I begged the gods to spare me of the pain.

A pink glow radiated from Daniel's hand, covering the clearing with pink light. My chest warmed, and the weight lifted. I sucked in a deep breath as the pain lessened. Exhaling slowly, my heart rate returned to normal and my tears stopped flowing. I wiped the water from my eyes as my body relaxed completely. My mind remembered why I was upset, but the overwhelming emotions were gone.

Daniel sank to his knees in the snow behind me. The pink glow dissipated. He breathed as though he'd just sprinted a mile.

"You idiot. How much energy did you just use?" I said as I turned to check on him.

"It's fine, I'm fine. I just need to rest. Help me back to the tent," he replied.

I took Daniel's arm over my shoulder and helped him to his feet. It was reckless for him to use so much of his magical strength on me. He'd be vulnerable should a competitor try to attack. If he got hurt, it would be my fault.

We struggled to stay upright as we walked through the snow. It was falling harder by the minute. Soon we'd be in the middle of a blizzard. Luckily, we got back to the tents before the worst of the storm.

Daniel lay on his side facing away from me, and for a

moment I thought I saw tears in his eyes. We lay back-to-back, and even though his skin barely touched mine, his warmth filled the tent. I was safe and comfortable wrapped up next to him. That had to mean something. I trusted Daniel with my life. Maybe it would be all right to trust him with my body too. After all, it wasn't like I was saving myself for marriage anymore. That hope was long gone. I couldn't possibly have a happy marriage. Thinking of Jess only brought me pain, but Daniel took that pain away and he didn't shame me for what had happened.

The next day Daniel was completely normal. It was hard not to overthink every interaction we had. One minute I would think he was about to kiss me, and the next I would think he was making fun of me. I couldn't remember if he'd always teased me in such a way, or if he'd been different since returning home from his military training. Was it because he didn't feel remorse for anything?

"Did you dream of me last night?" Daniel whispered in my ear while we worked together to take down our tent. His warm breath on my neck made heat rise to my cheeks. I tried to ignore him, but he continued. "You woke up with a stiff boner this morning, so you had to have dreamt of me." He chuckled as my body tensed up.

"Shut up," I said a little too loudly. Jade looked over at us from where she and Emm were busy with their tent. Avoiding her eyes, I tried to look casual. After a moment, she turned away.

"We should head south and try to stay ahead of the storm," Jade said as they finished stuffing their tent into a bag. Snow had covered the land overnight and just kept coming. The cold breeze was hard to endure in our thin suits.

"Sounds like a plan," Daniel said as I helped him stuff our

tent into his bag. I watched him closely, wondering if he'd fully recovered from using his empath abilities on me.

After we packed up our supplies, we headed south. I trailed behind Daniel as he led the group through the trees. The sun was high in the sky by the time we stopped to rest. I sat against a tree and ate a handful of snow. We'd just prepared to venture on when a shout echoed through the mountains. I couldn't tell what the voice had said, but it had definitely been female.

"Oh, shit," Daniel gasped as snow near the top of the mountain closest to us cracked. I watched in shocked horror as it broke free and slid down the slope. My body froze in fear, but Daniel grabbed my hand and pulled me with him as he ran.

The snow rumbled down the slope behind us as we ran. I wanted to turn back to see how close it was, but I knew that would only slow us down. I struggled to run, barely able to keep up with Daniel's stride. When the snow swept under our feet, I clung to his hand. He pulled me close as we were engulfed. I was sure we would die from the weight of the snow, but we were pushed to the side.

When the snow settled, Daniel punched through it, pulling me up with him. I gasped for air as we rolled down the hill of snow. We slid to the bottom and were able to catch our bearings. The snow came up to my knees. It was hard to wade through, but we made our way to a large boulder that stuck out of the sea of white.

Daniel climbed the boulder with ease, and for a moment I envied his strength. How had he built so much muscle over the course of a single summer? I'd have to ask him after the Reckoning was over. He extended an arm to me, and I accepted it. I was so tired from the walk through the snow that I had no strength to climb the boulder. Daniel pulled me up with one arm, and I collapsed on the stone's surface. The cold feel of its smooth surface soothed my exhausted body.

"That wasn't a natural avalanche," Daniel said. He stood at the highest point of the boulder, scanning the area. "I don't see the girls anywhere."

"We should look for them," I said, sitting up. Daniel stared at me for a moment, and his furrowed expression gave way to a smile.

"We can rest here for a while. If we aren't disqualified in a few hours, we can search for the girls. No point in wasting energy if they're dead," he replied, taking a seat next to me. My exhaustion must have been transparent because Daniel pulled me close. With his arm around me, I rested my head on his shoulder. We didn't speak, but the silence was peaceful. I fell asleep.

When I woke up, the sun was high in the sky. I had a clear view of it from Daniel's lap. He was awake, staring down at me with a smile. I sat up quickly, checking my face for drool; luckily, there was none. What the heck had he been staring at?

"How long was I out?" I asked as I tried to ignore the questions that plagued my mind.

"I'd say a couple hours. We can look for the girls now, if you're up for it," he said with a glimmer in his eyes.

"All right, let's go," I replied, sliding down the side of the boulder into the pile of snow that covered the area. He followed closely behind me, and we headed south. With any luck, the girls would still be heading that way as well.

I was glad when we finally got through the knee-deep snow and onto ground that only had a few inches of coverage. My boots were heavy, and the sun's rays tired me. It wasn't until the sun began to set that Daniel finally broke the silence.

"Let's camp for the night," he said as he pointed toward what appeared to be an opening in the mountainside.

We'd found a small cave. The cave's opening curved around stone before opening up into a cavern. It was more than big enough for the two of us and a fire, but more importantly, it blocked the harsh winds of the blizzard. I unpacked the bedrolls and blankets while Daniel went to get wood.

With a fire lit, the cave was quite warm. Daniel and I stripped out of our suits before lying down on the bedrolls. We decided to share our blankets so that we could keep each other warm. Lying on his back, Daniel pulled me over to him. My head found his chest, and my leg draped over top of him. His warm skin pressed against mine, making my whole body tremble. I relaxed into him.

My hand rested on his chest, and he placed his hand over mine. Our fingers interlaced. We didn't speak, but my spirits rose. I hadn't realized how desperately I needed to be held. It quieted the dark magic inside of me that wanted to lash out. I snuggled peacefully against Daniel's bare skin, and it confounded me. Even though I didn't understand it, I let myself drift into the comfort of sleep.

CHAPTER 16

KI

It had been five days since the last challenge, ten since the night I'd fed on Tyler, and every day got more painful. My hunger ate away at me even though I fed on a small animal every night. I had foolishly agreed to teach Tyler how to use magic, and no matter what tactic I tried, she failed miserably. The worst part of it all was how bloody cheerful she was about the whole thing. My patience was at its limit, and I couldn't take the frustration any longer.

"Are you even trying?" I shouted as Tyler fell to the snow-covered ground. She'd nearly knocked herself out with a ball of dark magic. It had exploded in her hands due to a lack of concentration.

"I'm sorry. I'll try it again," she replied, staggering to her feet.

"Don't be a bloody idiot. Take a rest before you seriously injure yourself," I replied. She stared at me without a response. Pacing back and forth, I made tracks in the snow as I tried to calm the surge of electricity that flooded my veins. Hunger made it hard to control.

"You do realize that you'll likely die before the Reckoning is over, right?" I said, my frustration taking over.

"Yes, I know," she replied. "That's why it's so important for me to learn how to control this magic, so I have a better chance of surviving." She examined her hands for cuts.

"How the bloody hell are you so positive all the time?" I shouted as my magic crackled around me, escaping my body. My heart raced.

"I have hope," she replied with a smile. Her positivity was unfazed by my shouts. The crackling tendrils of darkness expanded around me. They flowed from my body uncontrollably, and a sharp pain erupted from my horns, causing me to wince.

"Are you all right?" Tyler asked. Her smile faded.

"Do I look all right?" I shouted, then walked away as Tyler tried to come toward me. My frustration had turned into pure wrath, and it fueled my dark energy.

It was all because of her. If she hadn't been my partner then I wouldn't have had to kill those men. I never would've been tempted by the scent of their blood, and I wouldn't have fed on her. She was the reason I couldn't control my magic. Something inside me had changed when I'd drank her blood. My magical abilities had magnified, and it took all of my focus to contain them.

"Just breathe," Tyler said, approaching me. Between the pain in my horns and my current frustration, I hadn't noticed my heavy breathing. I took a deep breath, exhaling slowly. The wrath within me calmed as I continued to take deep breaths.

Tyler's hand touched the middle of my back. She likely thought it would help to calm me down, but it had the opposite effect. My heart skipped a beat from the warmth of her touch. I couldn't understand why she was so kind, especially when I'd just shouted at her.

"Let's continue the training," I said, stepping out of her reach. It was hard to be near her. The blood pulsing through her veins taunted me. Every inch of my body ached, begging me to feed on her. All I wanted was her blood. It was hard to think of anything else when she was around.

Tyler concentrated and had just created a tiny ball of dark energy when our bracelets vibrated. The energy shot out of her hand, nearly grazing me. Her body tensed as we listened to the bracelet's instructions. It was time for another challenge.

We walked through the snowy forest. It was quiet aside from the crunching sounds made by our footsteps. I thought it odd that there were no signs of life: no animals, nor birds, nor even any bugs. It was strange for a forest to be so silent.

I was worrying we were headed into a trap when the challenge course appeared in front of us. Six rows of four large glass tanks covered the area. Each tank was roughly ten meters tall and fifty meters long. The dark tint of the glass made it impossible to see through, so there was no way to know what was inside them. I noticed the increase in Tyler's heartbeat. She was anxious.

Five teams of competitors were gathered at one end of the tanks. Keerla, a female asudh with short black hair, stood next to her partner, Haleth. He was a muscular human. Beside them stood Zugak and his asudh partner, Urmicca.

Daniel, Harrison, and their partners were among the group. I was glad to see them well, though Daniel's glare and clenched fists concerned me. He was staring at Urmicca from across the group. The obnoxious asudh sibling duo from the opening ceremony stood between them. Immediately spotting me, they waved me over.

"Hello, Your Highness. It's nice to see you again," Lexa said as I approached the group. Tyler stood beside me with a friendly smile; the concept of competition was lost on her.

"If you say so," I replied, my tone intentionally cold. The glass tanks lit up, and a dark priestess appeared before she could respond.

"Welcome to your third challenge. Today's test is primarily for the women. The four tanks before you represent the four elemental magics and have been enchanted accordingly. Your goal is simple: get to the other side of the tanks. Be warned that if you fall into a tank, you will be killed by that element, either buried by the earth, crushed by the air, burned by the fire, or drowned by the water. There is no time limit for this challenge, but the first to make it across earns a hot meal for her team." The dark priestess spoke casually about the deadly challenge.

"And what will we be doing?" Daniel asked.

"You may support your partners from the ground. If you're fast enough, you may even be able to save your partner should they fall into a tank. Everyone who survives the day will receive winter suits. Ladies, please take your starting positions," she said, motioning toward the ladders at the front end of the tanks.

I caught Tyler's arm as she walked by me. "Don't worry about trying to be the fastest. Just take your time and stay safe. The extra reward isn't worth your life," I whispered, hating that all of the risk fell on Tyler.

"Don't worry. I'll do my best," she said with a smile, pulling out of my grasp. All I could do was watch as she climbed the ladder.

My heart raced as I stood beside Daniel between the rows of tanks. Tyler was in the middle of the cluster with Jade to one side and Lexa to the other. Beside Jade was Urmicca, and on the other side of Lexa were Keerla and Emm. A pit grew in my stomach as I waited for the challenge to start.

The dark priestess sounded the horn, and I watched in silent horror. Tyler took off full speed across the course. She leapt from platform to platform with no regard for what I'd told her.

"Bloody hell," I grumbled. She was going to get herself killed.

"I didn't think your girl could move so fast," Daniel said as we jogged along the base of the tanks, following our partners.

"I told her not to go too fast," I replied. Daniel's eyes lit up as he smiled.

"You told her to throw the challenge." He laughed. I glared at him for a brief moment before my focus returned to the tanks.

"If she dies, I'll lose more than just a hot meal," I said. My eyes were fixed on Tyler. The platforms shook like earthquakes, but she managed to clear the first tank without so much as a stumble. Her ankle was unaffected by her jumping. I prayed my magic would hold. If it didn't, she would be done for.

"It looks like you telling her to lose had the opposite effect. She appears to be quite determined," Daniel said. I could hear the humor in his voice. Tyler was ahead of the others as she jumped to the second tank.

"She's a bloody fool," I snapped. How could Tyler risk her life for food? I knew she was from a poor village and half-starved, but it was reckless. Maybe it was my fault. I'd hardly been able to hunt enough animals to provide her with one small meal a day. If I'd found more food, she wouldn't risk her life so carelessly.

My chest tightened as the winds from the second tank blasted Tyler. She teetered on the beam that ran the length of it. If I didn't do something, she was going to fall. Tapping into the dark magic within, I shot dark tendrils at Tyler. The electric tingle ripped through my hands and increased my hunger, but the tendrils made a sphere of dark energy around her. My magic protected Tyler from the winds as she crossed the tank.

Shouts from the other competitors indicated sabotage, but I kept my focus on Tyler. As long as my dark energy surrounded her, she would be protected from magical attacks. My hands trembled as I continued to jog to keep up with Tyler's pace. Hunger ate away at me, but Tyler moved on to the third tank without hesitation.

The heat of the raging fire within the third tank hit me. Sweat dripped down Tyler's face as she jumped platforms between the bursts of flame. My veins burned with electricity, and my body begged for blood. The sphere of dark energy wouldn't last much longer.

Screams came from behind me as Urmicca fell into one of the tanks. Daniel chuckled, but I had to stay focused. My energy levels were exhausted by the time Tyler reached the fourth and final tank. The sphere around her dissipated as I took a knee in the snow, breathing heavily.

Tyler was still in the lead, but Lexa was right behind her. They leapt with speed across the stones floating atop the water. When Lexa tapped into her dark magic, I sensed it. My energy was drawn to it, much like I was drawn to the moonstone. My heart stopped as Lexa created a ball of dark magic and threw it straight at Tyler.

The ball hit Tyler as she was just about to clear the final stone. It knocked her into the tank. I was already on my feet, sprinting, when her body hit the water. The sounds of splashing filled my ears as Tyler flailed about. I didn't even know if she could swim. Not that it mattered. The water swirled, forcing Tyler underwater. She sank to the bottom in defeat.

I made it to where she was in the tank by the time her feet touched the bottom. With all of my strength, I beat against the glass with my fists. Punch after punch, I laid into it. I couldn't let Tyler die, not when I was supposed to protect her. Lexa never should've been able to hit her. It was my fault for not having enough energy.

Tyler's bright blue eyes looked into mine as I tapped into my dark magic. It was a risk to do with my energy depleted, but I didn't care. I had to save her. My hands split open as the crackling energy ripped through me. Blood dripped from my hands as I punched the glass with the strength of my magic. The thick glass cracked, and I continued to beat into it, not caring that my knuckles were busting.

I prayed for Hecate to lend me her strength as Tyler's eyes closed. Using every bit of energy I had left, I threw the weight of my body into the glass, and it gave way. The glass exploded as water poured out of the tank. It knocked me back, but I managed to grab ahold of Tyler as the water raged by. She wasn't breathing.

Laying her on her back, I pushed on Tyler's chest with my bloodied hands. She couldn't die; I wouldn't allow it. I tilted her head back, opening her mouth, and forced air into her lungs. My heart raced as I went to press on her chest again. She coughed.

Water rushed out of her mouth as I turned her onto her side. She was breathing. Relief washed over me. I held her in my arms, kneeling on the ground. Her body shivered as she continued to cough. When her blue eyes looked up at me, I couldn't help but smile. She was alive, and that was all that mattered.

"Ki, are you all right?" Harrison asked as he ran up to me with Daniel right behind him. They both stared at me with wide eyes. I realized I was covered in blood.

Recording orbs swarmed around us as I assessed the damage. Glass had sliced up my body when the tank exploded, but I'd been too focused on Tyler to notice. My blood stained her white suit as I held her in my arms. The suit had already self-repaired, keeping the severity of my wounds hidden from the others.

"Congratulations!" The dark priestess's voice drew everyone's attention. She walked toward me, and the rest of the competitors gathered around. "The challenge is complete. Lux and Lexa have earned the extra reward, but those of you left should consider yourselves victorious for being alive." I glared at Lexa. The smug expression on her face made my jaw clench. I wanted to annihilate her and her brother, but I was in no shape to do so.

"You're bleeding," Tyler said quietly. The dark priestess took Lux, Lexa, and Zugak to the side to talk to them, while Keerla and Haleth headed for the reward table.

"I'll be fine. Let's get out of here," I replied. Helping Tyler to her feet, I stood. My head spun, but I kept myself upright.

"You guys should stick with us," Daniel said as he came to my side. "The others are grabbing suits for us, so let's find a place to camp and get you guys dried off."

"Sounds good," I replied. A pit grew in my stomach as my vision blurred. I needed to lie down.

Our group walked for what could only have been a few minutes before Daniel picked a spot to camp. Struggling to stay upright, I leaned against a tree while Tyler set up our tent. She watched me the entire time, never letting me out of her sight.

"Let me tend to your wounds. It's the least I can do," Tyler said after she finished. She shivered in the cold air, her hair wet from the tank. The others had already finished setting up their tents. I was useless to them.

"In the tent," I replied, eager to lie down. Tyler nodded and followed closely behind me. I stumbled as I crawled into the tent. My body was heavy, but I managed to lie down on one of the bedrolls.

"It's bad, isn't it?" Tyler asked as her hands grabbed the zipper of my suit. I didn't have the energy or will to stop her. She unzipped my suit and helped me out of it. Her eyes widened as she stared down at me.

Dried blood coated the majority of my body. Shallow cuts covered my arms and upper chest, and a large piece of glass was stuck in the side of my abdomen. Tyler's eyes were focused on it. If I'd been human, it probably would've killed me.

"Just take it out and stitch me up. There are sutures in the first aid kits," I said. Exhaustion and hunger pulled at me. Tyler unfroze. She went to our packs to get the kits.

I lay on my side, giving Tyler better access, and she placed a blanket under my head. She took care to make me comfortable. My chest tightened as her hands touched my body. She pulled the glass out of my side, but it didn't hurt. Warm blood flowed out of me.

My consciousness faded in and out as she stitched me up. Tyler spoke to me, but I couldn't understand her. She pressed up against me, and I caught the scent. It was blood, but not just any blood; it was her blood.

With a heavy body, I could hardly move. Tyler grabbed my head, pulling my face into her shoulder. Her warm blood touched my lips, causing the change to happen. My teeth turned into sharp razors, and I couldn't stop myself from biting into her. A frenzy of hunger took over. As her blood flowed through me, my magical energies restored. My body healed as my strength returned. All of my senses heightened. Pleasure consumed me as my power magnified, spilling out into the air, surrounding us.

Wrapping my arms around Tyler, I held her against me. The warmth of her body pressing against my bare skin intoxicated me. My primal desires begged for more than just her blood as my dark energy crackled around us. I wanted to touch every inch of her, to feel every part of her body. The need to be inside her shook me as soon as I had the thought. With all the willpower I had left, I released her, holding her at arm's length.

Blood dripped down her chest as she stared at me. My heart raced, and I breathed heavily. I fought against my hunger and desire with the familiar red glow filling my vision. Forcing my dark energy to dispel, I struggled to revert the change.

Tyler's eyes were filled with desire, and her smile invited me to proceed. She was in a trancelike state, rubbing her hand along my arm. Her gentle touch enticed me as she pushed against my hands, trying to get closer to me. I couldn't let that happen.

Taking several deep breaths, I let the bloodlust and desire pass. My mind cleared. I was back to normal, and Tyler was too. Her face turned bright red as she pulled away from me. Wiping the blood from her shoulder, she quickly covered up.

My eyes lingered on the black bite mark on her shoulder. It had grown. Black tendrils were extending from the small black lines created by my teeth. It was as if dark magic was taking root, trying to weave its way into her.

Tyler caught me staring. Her eyes widened when she glanced at her shoulder, but there was a smile on her face when she turned back to me. "Don't worry. I feel fine."

"Are you sure?" I asked, skeptical. She had lost a lot of blood from me feeding on her, and I had no idea if there would be other side effects. My stomach twisted as I worried what my magic could be doing to her.

"We should join the others if you're feeling better," Tyler said as she straightened herself.

"How are you smiling right now? I could have killed you, and only the gods know what that bloody mark is doing to you."

Tyler took my hand in hers, and her bright blue eyes stared into mine. "I promise I'm fine, and you could have died if you hadn't fed on me. We're a team, so if this is how I can be helpful, then this is how I'll help."

Heat rose to my face, and I pulled my hand away. "This isn't happening again."

I got dressed and exited the tent before Tyler had the chance to respond. She didn't understand how hard it was to control the change, how easy it would be for me to give in to it. My demonic nature wasn't satisfied with just tasting her; it wanted to drain every last drop of blood from her body. But I didn't want her to die.

Tyler followed me out of the tent. The sun was nearly gone from the sky, and snow had started to fall again. It just kept getting colder. Thankfully, the winter suits we'd received had hoods and were lined with fur. Everyone was seated around a fire, lost in conversation. Daniel motioned for me to join him. I sat between him and Jade, while Tyler took a seat opposite of me next to Emm.

"Looking good, man," Daniel said as he slapped me on the back. "You had me worried for a minute there." His eyes looked from me to Tyler. Did he know what had happened? Had he seen us?

"It'll take a lot more than a few cuts to bring me down," I joked, hiding the severity of my injuries.

"We're glad you're okay," Harrison said, but his eyes avoided me. I wondered why.

"If there's *anything* I can do to make you feel better, just let me know." Jade winked at me. Her flirtations lacked subtlety; it was disgraceful. She knew nothing about me beyond the fact that I was the prince.

"Is it okay to have the fire burning this late? Others might see it," Tyler said. Her eyes scanned the area.

"Don't worry. With all of us together, no one will bother us," Daniel replied.

I stared into the flames, admiring the fire's intensity. The swirls of orange and red distracted me from my thoughts. It was hard to keep my eyes off of Tyler. She'd seen my wings and the change. I'd even fed on her, yet she was always kind and positive toward me. My thoughts drifted to the desire that had overcome me when I'd fed on her. Why had that happened? It had to be the blood. Desperate to focus on anything else, I focused on the fire.

Jade continued trying to talk to me, but I mostly ignored her. Small talk was unnecessary, and I didn't want to tell her any details about my life. I was afraid that if I mentioned even one interest she would latch on to it and become even more bothersome than she already was. Luckily, Emm and Tyler were content. They sat quietly by the fire while Jade practically talked to herself.

Daniel and Harrison mostly talked to each other. I'd occasionally laugh at one of Daniel's jokes, but half the time he whispered to Harrison. I'd know what he said if I really focused my senses, but I had no interest. Every inch of my body tingled from the strength of the magic within me. It had magnified from feeding on Tyler, and I had to focus to keep it controlled.

Snow continued to fall as the night dragged on, and the others eventually went to sleep. I stayed up with Daniel even after Harrison left. We sat by the coals. The fire had died down and barely glowed. The night sky was lit by the moon, and it didn't take long for Daniel to start prodding.

"I can tell something is on your mind," Daniel said as he stared at the embers. He spoke quietly so that he wouldn't disturb the others.

"Is that so?" I sighed.

"We've been friends a long time, so why don't you just tell me what's burdening you? Is it the human?" Daniel asked. I tried not to react when he mentioned Tyler, but he could read me so well. Damn bloody empath.

"So it is the girl. You'll feel better if you talk about it."

"I seriously doubt that," I said.

"Your energies are in turmoil. Did something happen between you and the human?"

"No!" I said defensively, and Daniel smiled.

"Oh, something definitely happened," Daniel said. "It would be more unusual if something didn't happen, considering the amount of time you've spent together."

"Shut your bloody mouth. Not everyone is a pervert," I snapped. His questions ate away at my composure. I didn't want to tell him what had happened, but I also didn't want his sick mind twisting the events into something perverted.

"Prove me wrong then," he replied. He knew exactly how to manipulate me. There was no way I couldn't bloody tell him, not after he made it sound worse than it was. Then I remembered how I'd touched Tyler; maybe it was perverse.

"I have nothing to prove," I replied as I stood to leave.

"There's no shame in liking the human. I mean, it's only natural to have certain desires, especially when we're out here with nothing better to do." His smile cut through me.

"Good night, Daniel," I said as I walked away.

The conversation wouldn't continue after that. Daniel knew better than to push me too far. My dark magic swirled within me as my anger built. I wasn't just mad at Daniel—I was mad at myself. How could I have let myself lose control over a human girl? Why did her blood have such a strong effect on me? I refused to let anyone or anything have control over me and forced myself to think straight. Once the Reckoning was over, I wouldn't see Tyler again, and that was the way things were meant to be.

CHAPTER 17

TYLER

I woke up to the sound of Ki's heartbeat, my head moving with every breath he took. We were sharing the blankets when we'd lain down, but I'd rolled onto him in my sleep. My head rested on his chest, and my leg was wrapped over his. I sucked in a breath, realizing my thigh was resting over his crotch. Had he noticed that I was on him?

Ki's bare skin was warm against mine. He always radiated heat, and it made me want to stay. I wanted to steal his warmth and go back to sleep, but I was afraid of how he'd react if he woke up. He'd gotten upset every time I'd touched him. It was best to sneak out while I had the chance.

Moving slowly, I rolled off of Ki and slipped out from under the blankets. I slid into my regular suit before pulling my white winter suit on over it. I stared at Ki while I laced up my boots. He looked so peaceful as he lay there. It was strange to see a demonic being looking so content. A few weeks ago I wouldn't have thought it possible for him to look peaceful. I wondered when I'd stopped being intimidated by his appearance.

Leaving the tent, I headed toward the fire that the others had already built. Jade stood near it, poking at the coals with a large stick. The cold snowy breeze made me eager for the fire's warmth. Winter was upon us, and I doubted it would let up anytime soon. I knew Jade's eyes were on me as I took a seat near the coals.

"Sleep well?" she asked sarcastically. I fought the urge to look at her and answered anyway.

"It wasn't my worst night of sleep. Luckily, Ki radiates heat," I said.

"Don't get too comfortable," Jade snapped.

"I'm not sure I understand what you mean," I said.

"You're just a tiny human girl. You aren't worthy of the Darkblood Prince."

I had no argument against her.

"I know. I was just lucky to be paired with him," I replied.

"Lucky? They obviously paired you with him because you're the weakest competitor. You're only his partner so that he'll be challenged," Jade said.

The truth of her words cut through me. Could the seers have Called me for that reason—to challenge the Darkblood Prince? That couldn't be true, and even if it was, I wouldn't let it get to me. I wouldn't let Jade's hurtful words bring me down. My mother had taught me to always respond with kindness.

"It's true that Ki has saved my life, but I haven't been useless in our partnership. I'm doing my best to keep him safe," I said.

Jade burst into laughter. "You keep him safe? That's a good one. If anything, you put him at risk. He was injured during the last challenge because of you." Her words stabbed at me.

"I know. I feel terrible about it, but I think I made it up to him," I said without thinking.

"Excuse me?" Jade stepped in front of me, and I couldn't avoid her eyes. "How exactly did you make it up to him?"

"I . . . uh . . . I . . ." I stuttered as her eyes enchanted me. Their piercing green glow pulled me in. My thoughts of Ki dissipated, replaced by thoughts of Jade. She was an ebony goddess with hair the perfect shade of orange. I reached out to touch it.

"All right, break it up, ladies." Daniel's hand broke my line of sight. The fog in my mind lifted. I needed to be more careful around Jade, having no defenses to fight off her thrall.

"Did you hear what she just said?" Jade complained, but Daniel just laughed.

"Maybe you should go look for wood and cool off a bit. It won't do you any good to fight with Ki's partner," Daniel said. The grin on his face complemented his sharp jawline. He was quite attractive, especially for a tlaloc.

Jade grumbled under her breath before she stormed off. I didn't understand why she hated me. Was it because I was a human, or because she didn't think I deserved to be part of the Reckoning? I couldn't blame her. After all, I didn't understand it myself.

"I think Jade is warming up to you," Daniel said as he plopped down in the snow by what was left of the fire. White ash had covered the embers, but when he blew on them they turned orange. Fires were so magical.

"You think that's warm?" I asked. Daniel braided the ends of his long white hair.

"She's just jealous. Pay her no mind."

"Jealous? Of what? I'm just a magicless farmer. There's nothing to be jealous about," I said. Jade was a succubus; she could have any man she wanted with that thrall of hers, so there was no reason for her to be jealous of me.

"You've gotten to spend quite a bit of time alone with Ki, and he's the Darkblood Prince," Daniel said.

"So? We were forced to be partners. It's not like he wants to spend his time with me."

"If you say so," Daniel replied. His words left me questioning myself. Was he implying that Ki would actually want to spend time with me? I was sure I was just a burden to him.

"Good morning!" Harrison greeted us cheerfully, but his smile was directed at Daniel.

"You're finally up. Did you get the beauty sleep you needed?" Daniel said playfully.

"I would've slept longer, but it got cold in the tent after you left," Harrison replied.

"I'll warm you up with my body anytime. All you have to do is ask," Daniel said with a teasing smile. Harrison's entire face turned red. They must've been really close.

As the guys continued to tease each other, I got lost in thought. Daniel was one of Ki's close friends; if he thought Ki would want to spend time with me, then there was a chance it could be true. I was sure Ki had only saved me from drowning because of the Reckoning, but then again, he'd let me see the injuries he'd hidden from everyone else, including his friends. He'd even trusted me to tend to his wounds when he was in a weakened state. If I hadn't made him drink my blood, he might have died.

Heat rose to my face as I thought about the way he'd looked at me with fire in his eyes, enchanting me. I remembered how his hands had trailed along my body when he'd bitten into my shoulder and the white-hot pleasure that'd followed. I wondered if it had felt the same for him. His crackling dark energy had filled the space around us, so at the very least he'd felt a surge in power. Maybe he did desire me. I could've sworn he'd looked at me with desire after feeding on me, but I'd mistaken his hunger for desire once before. It couldn't be true. Why would he want me? He was a prince.

The others gathered around the fire, and the morning escaped me. It was nearly midday, and Ki still hadn't left the tent. He'd never slept in this late before. I was concerned about his injuries and wanted to check on him, but I also didn't want to bother him if he was just asleep. I eventually couldn't stand it any longer and headed toward the tent.

"Hey, where are you going?" Jade asked. Ever since coming back with firewood, her eyes had been glued to me.

"I'm going to check on Ki," I replied, continuing to walk.

"You shouldn't bother the prince," Jade said. Her words chilled me.

"Give it up, Jade. Tyler is Ki's partner; she can check on him if she wants to," Daniel said. I was relieved he was on my side. Crude jokes aside, he seemed to truly care about his friends.

"Be careful waking him—he lashes out if you startle him awake," Harrison added.

I smiled at them and continued on my way. No sound came from the tent, and I wondered if Jade was right. If he was sleeping and I woke him up, he would probably get mad, or worse. Harrison's warning echoed in my head. I needed to be careful to not startle him.

I crawled into the tent as quietly as I could. Ki was curled into a ball on his side with his hands wrapped around his head. His eyes were closed, but he wasn't asleep. The sounds of his muffled groans became clear as I crawled closer to him.

"Are you all right?" I asked, kneeling next to him.

"It'll pass," he grunted. His face was scrunched in pain.

"Is it your injuries? Are they infected?" I asked as I tried to examine his abdomen. Even though I pulled at his side, he refused to roll onto his back.

"No. It's my head. It'll pass. Just leave me alone," he replied. There was an unbearable pain in his voice.

"Would my blood help?" I asked, hoping I could ease his suffering.

"No!" he snapped. "Just go. My friends will keep you safe."

Ki curled into a tighter ball, and my chest squeezed. He was suffering, but there was nothing I could do to help him. I didn't want to go, but I decided it was best to respect his wishes. It was the least I could do. I just hoped his agony would end soon.

As I left the tent, I heard Ki's groans. I had no idea what had happened to him, but he definitely didn't deserve it. When I finally pulled myself together, I walked back to the fire. I was surprised to find Harrison by himself, fiddling with his wrist. Had he gotten burned by an ember?

"Where are the others?" I asked as I approached. Harrison jumped.

"They're out hunting," he replied.

"And you stayed behind?"

"I just stayed here to keep watch for you and Ki, in case you were tending to his wounds for a while."

"That's very kind of you. Ki must be glad to have such good friends," I replied. Harrison's eyes fell to the fire, but he didn't reply. He wore a somber expression. "Have you been friends for a long time?" I asked, taking a seat in the snow next to him.

"For as long as I can remember. We grew up together in the palace since our fathers are close," he said.

"Really? I'm curious, has Ki always been so cold toward others? He's very careful with his words, and it always seems like he's holding back."

Harrison turned to stare at me with his green eyes. "He's not cold, he just doesn't trust people. But who can blame him? He's the prince, so people always want something from him."

"That makes sense. I could never begin to imagine the pressures he faces. At least he has you and Daniel. I'm sure your friendship means a lot to him."

"I don't really know anymore. Ki has always been secretive, but he used to share those secrets with me. I think my engagement to his sister hurt our friendship."

"You're engaged to his sister?" I asked, surprised.

"The king made the arrangement when we were young. He's bestowed a great honor on my family."

"But aren't you and Daniel together?" The way they carried on, I was sure they were more than just friends.

"What makes you say that?" Harrison said defensively.

"I'm sorry, it's not an insult. You guys just look so happy and carefree together."

"We're just friends," Harrison insisted.

"Does he know that?" I asked. Harrison looked at me with

one eyebrow lifted. "I see the way he looks at you, like you're the only thing in the world that matters."

"Even if that's true, we could never be together. People would talk."

"So what? If you two love each other and make each other happy, then why does it matter what others think? Isn't your happiness more important than the opinions of a stranger?"

Harrison's face turned bright red. "It doesn't matter. Daniel isn't actually interested in me. He just likes to mess with people for his own amusement."

"Or maybe he's just waiting for you to make a move," I replied.

Harrison was quiet after that. He stared into the fire, and I assumed he had a lot on his mind. I hoped he'd find his happiness. Everyone deserved to be happy. My thoughts drifted back to Ki. He was still in the tent and likely still in pain. I hoped he'd feel better soon, but he remained in the tent for most of the day. If he truly was injured, I wondered if he'd recover before the next challenge. If he didn't, we would be in big trouble.

CHAPTER 18

HARRISON

Thoughts of Daniel plagued me as the days blurred together. He'd kissed me and said he loved me, but he hadn't made any mention of either of those things since, not even when we snuggled together in the tent at night. How could he just return to his usual jokes? Had he not been serious about any of it? He'd sounded serious when he said it. Tyler even mistakenly thought we were together. Could he really just be waiting for me to make a move?

The land was bathed in an orange glow as the sun made its descent. I would've enjoyed the view had the snowy breeze not been so frigid. Daniel and I trudged through the thick snow together in search of food. We'd been walking around for hours with no signs of life to be found.

"This is pointless," I snapped as the bitter wind cut through me. Even in the fur-lined winter suit, my body shivered.

"We need food," Daniel replied. He was right. Everyone in our group had hardly eaten in days, and there would be another challenge soon. There had been five days between the past ones, and I was sure it was a pattern. If we didn't find something to eat, we would all be at a disadvantage.

"I know, but there're no tracks. Where are all the animals?"

"I don't know," Daniel replied, glancing back at me. He was a few paces ahead, but his worried expression was clear. It brought all of my lingering questions to the surface, and I couldn't hold them back anymore.

"How can you love me if you don't feel remorse?" I asked. Daniel stopped in his tracks, but he didn't turn to look at me.

"They're two separate emotions," he replied. As his words sank in, I realized I'd asked the wrong question. Daniel may have been able to love me, but how could I truly love him if he couldn't feel remorse, if he wasn't whole?

"Why can't you feel remorse?" I asked as tears filled my eyes. Daniel meant more to me than I'd realized. It broke my heart to know that he wasn't entirely himself.

Daniel turned to face me. His eyes met mine, and tears trickled down my face. "Why do you think? I'm an empath, Harrison. The guilt from the things I've done would kill me."

"Then why do you do them?" I asked.

He sighed. "We've been over this before. Tlalocs must be merciless."

"But you don't have to rape people," I replied. It sickened me to know that Daniel had done to others what Jess had done to me. I'd never fully understood how terrible it was.

Daniel closed the distance between us and took ahold of my hand. "Is that what you need to accept my feelings for you? I swear I'll never do it again."

My heart raced. Daniel never broke his promises. I couldn't believe he would change his ways without a second thought. He must've really loved me.

A twig snapped nearby, drawing our attention. Before us stood a large grizzly bear with dark brown fur that perfectly matched the trunks of the trees behind him. Standing on his hind legs, he revealed his teeth and growled fiercely. We had no time to respond as he charged us.

Daniel shoved me to the side as the bear attacked. It swiped at him with its large paws, and Daniel grunted in pain. Blood trickled from his arm, staining the snow at his feet. My heart clenched as I watched in horror.

The bear lunged again, but this time we were prepared. Daniel created a shield with his dark magic, and the bear bounced off of it. Landing in the snow, the bear shook its head in confusion. It clearly had never seen magic before.

"Aim for the heart," Daniel said as he widened his shield to protect both of us.

Summoning the dark magic within me, I created a small ball in my hand. My energy levels were low from the lack of food, but I managed. It would be a challenge to create more, so I needed to make my first one count. I waited patiently for the bear to attack.

When the bear came at us again, it barreled straight through Daniel's shield. A sharp pain pierced my lip as the shield shattered, but I stayed focused. As the bear nearly clawed me, I shot my ball of dark magic into it. The bear roared and stumbled, falling to the ground. As its blood poured out, the snow around it melted. I'd hit the heart.

"Nice shot," Daniel said through heavy breaths.

"Thanks," I replied, trying to catch my breath. My heart raced as I tasted the blood on my lips.

"Are you all right?" Daniel asked as he drew close. He tilted my chin up to get a look at my lip, and my heart fluttered.

"I'll survive," I replied. Heat rose to my cheeks. His face was so close to mine. "You're the one who took a hit." Examining Daniel's arm, I could tell the scratches weren't deep, but they still bled.

"Aw, are you worried about me, Harrison?" Daniel smiled. His hands were warm as they touched my face.

He wiped the blood from my lips with his thumb. The gentleness in his touch and the concern in his eyes overwhelmed me. I no longer doubted his love; his affections had always been there. Through the years I'd relied on his unyielding support, telling myself he was just a friend, that I was engaged, but it was more than that. I loved him. Every moment I spent with him brightened my day. He had a good heart, and I believed in him. How had I not realized my feelings sooner?

My restraint disappeared. Daniel's hand brushed the base of my ear as I leaned into him. My lips found his, and a rush of emotions flooded my system. The cut on my lip stung from the force of the kiss, but I liked it. Daniel's arms wrapped around me as my hand slid up his neck, firmly gripping the base of his braided hair. The world fell away as we kissed.

I was consumed by the sound of Daniel's quickened breaths, by the warmth of his touch. My body begged for more, but he pulled away. The absence of his lips left me dazed.

"We should get the bear back to camp," Daniel said. His eyes glowed pink as he looked at me.

"Of course," I stuttered. It made sense to get back to camp as quickly as possible. Everyone was hungry, and it was getting dark.

Daniel was quiet as we carried the carcass back to camp, but he smiled the whole way. I wondered what he was thinking. Had he enjoyed our kiss? The more he smiled at me, the more I wanted to kiss him again.

As we approached camp, the others came over to assist us. I was exhausted. Between the fight and carrying the bear back, I could hardly stand. Daniel, however, looked fine. His eyes still glowed pink, and the blood on his arm had dried up. Was he even out of breath? I couldn't believe how easy he made it all look.

"I trust you guys can take care of this while Harrison and I rest," Daniel said.

"Of course," Ki replied. As soon as we laid the carcass down near the fire, Ki immediately began the skinning process. He was good with a knife.

Daniel put his arm around my back and led me to our tent. Was he in a hurry? He definitely moved faster than someone in need of rest. It didn't make sense to me; he couldn't possibly be eager to sleep. The sun had just set.

We crawled inside the tent, and Daniel sealed the flap tightly behind us. I'd just gotten my boots off when his glowing pink eyes focused on me. There was a hunger within them, a desire he'd never shown me before.

My heart skipped a beat when he grabbed the collar of my suit and pulled me to him. His lips pressed hard into mine. The roughness excited me, but not as much as his tongue slipping into my mouth. He tasted like maple syrup. A quiet moan escaped me.

I was out of breath when Daniel finally pulled back. He quickly pulled off his boots and stripped down to his underwear. My heart raced as I stared at his bare skin. I could hardly see its pale green tint in the dimly lit tent. The fire outside provided only a little bit of light.

Daniel moved back to me. He unzipped my winter suit and had it pulled off my shoulders before I could even think.

"What are you doing?" I asked. He removed my winter suit without pause.

"I'm making love to you," he said, unzipping the regular suit that was still on me. "Unless you don't want me to?"

My arms were already free from my suit, so I pulled him in for a kiss. His hands trailed across my skin, making my heart race, and I leaned back on the bedroll. Daniel came with me. His erection pressed into mine, and I trembled. He pulled back from our kiss with a smile. My heart melted as I admired his beauty.

"Are you sure you want this?" Daniel asked in a soft voice as he kissed me right below my ear. My skin tingled with desire. I couldn't have wanted anyone more.

"Yes, I want you. All of you," I replied, breathing heavily.

My heart raced as I anticipated his touch. He pulled my suit and underwear off in one fluid motion. Slipping out of his underwear, his eyes lingered on my body, but I wasn't ashamed.

I trusted him completely, and I wanted to be the cause of his pleasure.

He was a gentle and passionate lover. After trailing kisses along my neck, across my chest, and down my abdomen, Daniel's mouth stopped at my erection. His eyes looked up at me, questioning if it was all right to proceed. My nod and smile were all the confirmation he needed before taking me into his mouth. Pleasure tingled through my body as his warm tongue massaged me.

I was on the verge of release when Daniel came up for air, a huge smile on his face. His saliva dripped between my legs as he wetted his finger. Placing his finger at my entrance, he paused.

"If it hurts, let me know. We'll stop if it's too uncomfortable for you," Daniel said as he massaged the area.

"I don't want to stop," I gasped between heavy breaths.

Daniel kissed me as he slid his finger in. It was a new sensation that took me a few minutes to get used to, but Daniel made me comfortable the whole time. He kept asking if it felt all right, and it did.

My body relaxed, loosening as Daniel continued to slide fingers into me. He had the area dripping wet with his saliva when the tip of his cock pressed against my entrance. My whole body trembled.

"Keep going," I moaned when Daniel hesitated.

His caution only made me want him more. I hadn't realized how much I needed permission to be confirmed, to have a choice over what was done to my body, to have the opportunity to say no and be listened to. It made saying yes that much more satisfying.

Daniel pushed himself inside me slowly, filling me with his warmth. I moaned from the mix of both pleasure and pain. He was large. I was made to stretch around him, and I loved every minute of it. There was nothing between us. His skin was against my skin, his lips pressed against mine, and his hand stroked me as he moved back and forth.

Pleasure consumed me, and I fought the urge to moan

loudly. I gripped his thick back muscles, knowing I wouldn't last long. His every movement made me desperate for release, so when he asked if he could cum inside me, I begged for it. We found release together. I'd never experienced such intense pleasure before.

I chuckled, bubbling with happiness. Daniel smiled as he moved to lie next to me. I snuggled into the safety of his chest, and we lay naked beneath the blankets. As the comfort of sleep took hold of me, I hoped I could spend every night this way, in the strong arms of the man I loved.

Waking first, I found myself still wrapped in Daniel's arms. I admired his peaceful beauty for a moment before he woke. I wasn't ashamed when he caught me staring. He greeted me with a kiss before moving to get dressed. My smile was uncontrollable as we made our way out of the tent.

Bear meat was skewered on sticks next to what remained of the night's fire. The embers were still warm. Grabbing meat, I took a seat by the coals. Daniel joined me, and we ate together in peaceful silence. The others were all still asleep in their tents.

I stared at Daniel as we ate and noticed that his eyes had changed. They weren't glowing, but they were a solid shade of pink. The hazel color that was once there was completely gone. His eyes had never looked that way before.

"Your eyes," I said, breaking the silence. Daniel smiled as though he knew exactly what I was talking about.

"I'm an empath. Your love has changed me," he replied. I wanted to confirm that his statement was true—that I loved him—but just as I was about to say the words, Jade popped out of her tent.

"You guys are up early, but you did sleep through the whole night. Ki couldn't even wake you when the bear was served," Jade said as she plopped down by the fire between me and

Daniel. I sighed. Why did she have to walk up at this moment? It wasn't like I could tell Daniel how I felt in front of her. I'd tell him later when we were alone.

Soon after we finished eating, our bracelets vibrated. There were only ten teams left, and it was time for another challenge. It'd been five days since our last one, so it was definitely a pattern. Thankfully, we were all rested and well-fed.

We quickly packed up camp before following the bracelets directions through the woods. We trudged through the thick snow for over an hour before coming across the clearing. Ten circles had been drawn in the snow, a dark priestess standing by each. They all wore the same black hooded robes and silver amulets. The only distinction was that of the head priestess. Her black robe was trimmed in silver, with the holy symbol embroidered in the middle of its back.

"Gather round," she said as teams arrived from all directions. Once all ten teams were gathered in a circle around her, she continued. "Welcome to your fourth challenge. Today we will put your combat skills to the test. No doubt you're all tired, but a true warrior must be able to fight at any time.

"You'll be competing in a two-and-out tournament with females and males having separate brackets. Two losses puts you out of the running, but one loss puts you into the losers' bracket. The winners of the losers' bracket will fight the winners of the main bracket in a final showdown. Two of you will prove to be the top warriors, and as a reward you and your partner will get to enjoy the comforts of a warm bed as well as a feast." The competitors got hyped from the mention of food.

"But just as there will be two winning teams, there will also be two losing teams. The two teams with the worst performance will be eliminated from the Reckoning. Our merciful king has decided to have the weakest sent home rather than leaving them out here to die." Murmurs rose from the crowd. There had never been an elimination challenge before. I wondered if the rioting had gotten worse.

"The rules are simple: be the last one standing in the circle."

The head priestess's voice commanded the crowd of competitors. She listed off the pairings for round one, and we took our places in the rings.

Taking a deep breath, I prepared myself for the first round. I was up against Quaeth. He smiled from across the circle, but I didn't let it distract me. Though we were both asudhs, Quaeth was larger than me. Not by much, but it would still make a physical fight challenging. I was just grateful I hadn't been paired with Daniel. There was no way I could fight him after the night we'd shared together. The dull ache in my low back was a constant reminder of it.

"Is everyone ready?" the head priestess asked, looking around at the rings. Each of the dark priestesses gave her confirmation when she looked their way.

A dark priestess stood halfway between me and Quaeth just outside our ring. I couldn't see her face, but I knew she was watching us closely. My heart raced in anticipation. What type of magic did Quaeth have an affinity for? His brown eyes gave no indication.

"Begin!" the head priestess shouted.

Snow crunched as Quaeth charged me. Waiting until the last second, I jumped. The power of my dark energy aided me in my flip. When my boots hit the snow, he'd already turned. His fist hit me square in the chest, knocking the wind out of me. I stumbled back, gasping for air.

He swung at me again, but I twisted away, kicking him in the face as I moved. Cursing, Quaeth wiped away the blood that trickled from his nose. The ground rumbled beneath him as it broke apart. Dirt rained down upon me, but the dark energy that flowed through my hands shielded me from the worst of it. My hands tingled with electricity as I reinforced the shield with more magic.

Summoning a ball of dark energy in my hand, I waited for the rain to stop. The burning tingle in my hand intensified as the dirt settled. I threw the ball straight at Quaeth's chest, and he didn't move. He was either caught off guard or too weak from using his magic. It hit him hard in the chest, throwing him backward.

"Winner!" the dark priestess called out. My blast had knocked Quaeth completely out of the ring. He sat up in the snow with his hands on his knees.

The head priestess gave us all a few minutes to recover while she determined the pairings for the second round. The dark priestesses distributed clean water for us to drink. Unsurprisingly, Daniel and Ki had both won their fights. Neither of them looked the least bit tired. Their first fights must have been easy for them.

I hadn't had any expectations for the girls, but Jade, Emm, and Tyler all managed to win their first rounds as well. In fact, I overheard Keerla cursing about her loss to Tyler. She hadn't expected a human to be so quick on their feet.

With the uneven number of competitors moving forward to the second round, Emm and I both got randomly chosen to move forward to the third round. Since we had to wait until the second round was over in order to have an opponent, we got to watch the fights. Emm watched one of the female fights to check out her competition, but I decided to watch Daniel's fight.

Daniel was up against Adakk, the only other male tlaloc that remained in the competition. Their strength was comparable, and even though Daniel was a bit taller, I wasn't so sure he'd win the fight. Fights among tlalocs were usually long-winded and aggressively bloody. As a proud warrior race, neither opponent was ever willing to concede.

Adakk looked like a typical tlaloc. He had dark green skin and mellow brown eyes that almost looked golden. His two sets of tusks protruded out of his mouth, curving toward the sky. He had one set on his lower jaw near his canine teeth and one set on his upper jaw near his back teeth, giving him a nasty underbite.

Daniel and Adakk took their places in the ring. Adakk had a hunger in his eyes that unsettled me, and he stared at Daniel as if he was his next meal. I quickly looked to Daniel; he was staring at me with a big smile on his face. Heat rose to my cheeks, but luckily no one paid any attention to me as the round began.

The fight was hard to watch. Daniel and Adakk matched each other blow for blow. My heart leapt every time Daniel took a hit. His grunts of pain made my stomach clench. They were both bloodied and bruised after only a few minutes in the ring together, but neither showed any sign of backing down.

Watching Daniel closely, I realized he was letting Adakk hit him on purpose. He was slowly wearing him down. Adakk tapped into his magic and launched boulders at Daniel, while Daniel used minimal amounts of energy to dodge. The constant attacks eventually drained Adakk to the point of exhaustion.

Daniel smiled through the blood trickling down his face when he saw his opening. He blasted Adakk out of the circle with a ball of dark magic. Adakk grunted, landing on his back in the snow. The dark priestess announced Daniel as the winner, and I was glad the bloodshed was over. Daniel's victorious smile was contagious.

After another short break, the head priestess announced the pairings for the third round. I was up against Ki. We'd sparred with each other many times in the past, but I wasn't ready to face him. What if he noticed the mark on my wrist while we fought? I couldn't let that happen. He'd ask questions that I wasn't ready to answer.

Taking my place in the ring across from him, I took a deep breath. Ki greeted me with a friendly smile. I returned the smile even though I knew I was about to make him angry. The round began, and Ki moved slowly around the circle. I matched his pace, keeping as much distance between us as possible. When Ki finally lunged toward me, I backed out of the circle.

"Winner," the dark priestess said. She didn't say anything about me throwing the match, probably because she figured Ki would have won anyway. Ki, on the other hand, wouldn't let it go that easily.

"Bloody hell, Harrison! What was that?" he asked as he

marched over to me. I tucked my arms behind my back, keeping my composure.

"It would have been useless for us to waste energy fighting each other. This way we can both reserve our strength for our next fights," I replied. Did it sound strategic enough? Would he buy it?

"We could've at least given the dark priestess a bit of a show. I don't think she was happy about how quickly it ended," he replied. I was relieved he believed my story.

"Don't worry about it," Daniel cut in as he joined us. "I'm up next, and I won't let you win so easily," he said with a smile.

"Try not to kill each other," I said. They both laughed, mocking my words.

I didn't get to watch their fight, but I already knew what the outcome of the match would be. Ki would win. Daniel would surely make him work hard for it, but in the end Ki would be the victor. I wondered if Daniel was strong enough to actually beat Ki. Did he let Ki win, or was Ki actually the stronger of the two of them? I'd never know for sure.

My round in the losers' bracket didn't go well. I was put against Lux, a particularly egotistical asudh. He acted like I was worthless, like he would hardly have to try to win. I proved him wrong, of course. If he wanted to beat me, he would have to use all of his magical energy. I wasn't about to let a punk show me up.

Lux went straight for a magic attack when our match started. A small boulder barreled at me, but I dodged it. Knowing I had an affinity for dark magic, Lux only used earth magic during our fight. It was a smart move on his end, as I could've deflected dark magic attacks back onto him.

The earth beneath me lurched up. I rolled to the side as Lux tried to capture my limbs in the earth. Moving too quick for his magic to catch me, I shot a ball of fire at him. The earth at his feet extinguished the flames before they reached him. His concentration was better than I'd anticipated.

Focusing on countermoves, I lost the fight. Lux moved the

circle out from underneath me without me noticing. It was a brilliant move. I clenched my fists when the dark priestess announced him as the winner. To think I'd let a jerk like him best me. It was humiliating.

My day only got worse after that. Daniel lost to Ki, as predicted, but that meant he had to fight Adakk again. He'd used a great deal of his energy during his first few fights and ended up losing. It was hard to watch. Adakk thrashed Daniel brutally, and I wished he'd just stepped out of the ring. His damn pride got him beaten half to death. My heart couldn't handle it. I couldn't stomach Daniel's pain.

Luckily, Adakk had to fight Ki in the last round. Ki was ruthless. He took no pity on Adakk, not after what he'd done to Daniel. Adakk lasted longer than I'd expected, but in the end Ki forced him out of the ring. Ki was the male victor. As for the females, I really thought Jade would win it all since she'd won all of her fights in the main bracket. However, she had to go up against Lexa for the final round. As the winner of the losers' bracket, Lexa would have to beat Jade twice to become the female victor, and to my dismay, that was exactly what happened.

Lexa was the female victor, which meant she and her self-absorbed brother, Lux, would get to enjoy the spoils of victory along with Ki and Tyler. Quaeth, his tlaloc partner Kih, and a pair of asudhs were eliminated from the competition for their poor performances. I almost envied them. It would've been nice to go back home, to enjoy the comforts of the palace, but I was glad to move forward.

Things with Daniel had just started, and I didn't want to face Jess. I feared what might happen if she found out about the night I'd spent with Daniel. Would she tell the king? Would we be punished? I couldn't even begin to think about that. The present was my only concern. And presently, Daniel was greatly injured. It was my turn to take care of him for once.

CHAPTER 19

KI

The falling snow and frigid air helped to calm the throbbing in my head. I'd won the fourth challenge, but headaches had been plaguing me for days. The pain made it hard to enjoy my victory. In fact, Tyler's wide smile told me she was more excited about our reward than I was. As soon as the head priestess had mentioned food, Tyler's eyes lit up. Everyone was hungry from the lack of wild animals to hunt, but Tyler had been starved before the Reckoning started. She'd probably do anything for a good meal.

Tyler walked cheerfully beside me as we followed the dark priestess through the woods. Lux and Lexa trailed behind us, whispering between themselves. It bloody sucked that we had to share our reward with those two. I was sure they would try to talk my ear off all night, as if my head didn't hurt enough already.

As the sun began to set, we approached a large cabin. Smoke lifted from its chimney, filling the air with the smell of roasted chicken. Tyler's stomach growled, and I shared in her hunger. I hoped eating my fill of meat would help to curb my appetite for blood, though I doubted it.

Excited gasps came from the others as the dark priestess led us inside. Warmth consumed me as we entered the large main room. It had high ceilings and a table filled with food stretched the length of it. Plush chairs and couches were positioned around the fireplace, and several doors branched off the main room: four bedrooms and two washrooms in total.

"Enjoy the night. You've earned it," the dark priestess said as she disappeared out the door, leaving us alone with our competition.

"I say we dig in," Lux said. Tyler and Lexa were already at the table. Their eyes were wide as they filled their plates with food. I sighed, joining them. It was a reward, so I supposed we should all enjoy it. I could handle socializing for one night.

To my surprise, there were several bottles of wine on the table—more than we could all drink collectively. Grabbing a bottle and a pair of glasses, I joined Tyler by the fireplace. She sat on the couch closest to the fire, her mouth already full of food.

"Join me for a drink?" I asked as I set the glasses on the table in front of her. She nodded in agreement. Setting my plate down, I opened the bottle. Lux followed my lead, popping the top off the wine bottle in his hand. We poured glasses for ourselves and our partners before setting the bottles to the side.

"To the Reckoning," Lux said, lifting his glass to us.

"To the Reckoning," we all replied, raising our glasses in unison before drinking. It was odd to celebrate with the competition, but I figured I should get used to being around them. If their performance had been any indication, they would likely be top competitors and receive offers from my father.

The night continued on peacefully. Everyone made several trips to the buffet table, eating as much food as possible, and empty wine bottles started to stack up. After the first bottle, Tyler refused to drink any more wine, but I kept drinking with the others. In fact, I drank more than I ate. The alcohol liberated me from my headache and dulled my thirst for blood, though that deep-rooted hunger never truly went away.

A warm, tingling sensation filled me, the alcohol in full effect. Lexa walked over to join us on the couch. I slid closer to Tyler, giving Lexa room to sit. My shoulders and legs brushed against theirs. Lifting my arms up, I laid them along the back of the couch. Lexa looked at me with a smile, while Tyler looked at me with a raised brow.

"Is Your Royal Highness enjoying himself?" Lexa asked, scooting closer to me. The warmth of her nearness made my skin tingle.

"As a matter of fact, I am. And please, call me Ki," I replied. The room vibrated around me, and I was overcome with a floating sensation. It was a welcome relief.

"All right, Ki. Was everything to your liking? Is there anything I can get for you?" she asked, placing her hand on my thigh. A shiver ran up my spine. I was pressed between the two women, and every part of my body that they touched hummed in pleasure. Why had I always kept a distance from others?

"I'm quite content," I said as I slipped my arms around them. Tyler tensed, but Lexa relaxed into me.

"Oh, but content isn't good enough. Someone of your stature should be happy, or very pleased, if you will," she replied. Her fingers walked up my chest and touched the side of my face. Every touch set fire to my skin, and I could hardly stand it. The room spun around me.

Lexa turned my head toward her. She was so close. The rhythm of her heartbeat and the pulsing of her blood overwhelmed me. Her exposed neck teased me, begging to be torn into. I was sure she was offering herself to me.

"All right, Lexa, that's enough," Lux said. "Don't bother the prince while he's trying to relax." Lexa turned to look at her brother.

His words barely registered as I stared at Lexa's neck. If she wanted me to have her, then a quick taste wouldn't hurt. The change took hold of me, my vision turning red.

"I'm not bothering him, Lux," Lexa said.

When she turned back to me, she flinched. I didn't care the slightest bit that my appearance had bothered her. The fogginess in my mind freed me from my usual worries. There was an intoxicating pleasure that came with not caring.

"Are you all right?" Lexa asked, leaning away from me.

"You'd do anything to make me happy, right?" I asked with a smile. Tyler pulled at the collar of my suit, but I ignored her.

"Of course, Your Highness," Lexa replied, staring into the red glow of my eyes.

"Then you'll let me feed on you?" I asked. My heart raced, anticipating her reply. Tyler pulled harder on my collar.

"Of course, Your Highness. Anything for you," Lexa stuttered as she replied.

"Excuse me!" Lux yelled as he came toward us. He grabbed Lexa by the arm, pulling her from the couch. "How drunk are you, sis? Have you lost your damn mind?"

"I can make my own decisions, Lux," she replied.

"Yeah, Lux. She can make her own decisions," I mocked as I rose from the couch. The room spun around me, and I swayed. Tyler's grip on my arm steadied me.

"Prince or not, I won't let anyone lay a hand on my sister," Lux said.

"Why would I lay a hand on her when I could just sink my teeth into her flesh?" I replied.

My laughter took me over. That silly little asudh thought he could take me. He clenched his fist as if he would swing at me, but Tyler slid herself between us. Her body brushed up against me, and my skin tingled.

"Everyone, just calm down. We've all had a bit to drink, some of us more than others. Let's just call it a night and get some rest." Her commanding words thrilled me. She'd never taken charge like that before. A warm sensation spread throughout my body, arousing me.

"Let's go, Lexa," Lux said as he walked away. He pulled

Lexa by the arm, dragging her with him. She didn't resist at all. Maybe she didn't want me to bite her after all.

A deep sadness came over me. Was I not good enough? Was I a monster, like my father? Nobody would ever want to kiss a mouth full of razor-sharp teeth. My true form was hideous. People only pretended to like me because I was the prince, but in reality I terrified them.

"Let's get you to bed," Tyler said. Her bright blue eyes stared up at me, and even though my eyes were red, she wasn't afraid. She'd seen the change multiple times but was still kind to me, even after I'd fed on her. Tyler was a true goddess.

"You're so kind to me. I don't deserve it," I said as I pulled her into a hug. She didn't try to pull away. She wrapped her arms around me and rubbed circles into my back. My body tingled from her touch.

"Everyone deserves kindness," she replied. My heart fluttered from her words, and I was overwhelmed with emotion.

"You're too good, and it's selfish of me to ask, but please stay with me. I can't stand the loneliness any longer," I said as the change reverted. Tears fell from my eyes. An overwhelming emptiness ate away at me.

"Come on, let's get to bed," Tyler replied. She led me to one of the bedrooms and helped me undress. It was hard to balance with the room spinning, but I managed to get into the bed with her assistance.

I'd grown accustomed to sleeping with Tyler by my side, so I asked her to share my bed. She crawled in behind me, pressing her bare chest into my back. Her arm wrapped around me, and her leg rested over mine. I trembled from the warmth of her skin touching mine. Relaxing into her tight embrace, I found comfort and welcomed the pull of sleep. She was too kind to me.

I remembered everything the next morning, much to my dismay. I couldn't believe I'd tried to feed on Lexa. Thankfully, Tyler had stopped me before I'd done something I surely would've regretted. Her kindness was more than I deserved. She smiled warmly at me when I woke up next to her.

"You have five minutes to vacate the premises." The voice came from our bracelets as soon as we stirred.

I caught myself admiring Tyler's form as she dressed. She didn't look any different than the day I'd met her, but I was drawn to her. I wanted to touch her and take comfort in her touch. The desire was foreign to me, so I pushed it from my mind.

The cabin had been cleared out by the time we got up. Lux and Lexa were nowhere in sight, and the cabin vanished as soon as we stepped outside. It was as if it had never been there. Snow-covered trees surrounded us, and the bite of the winter breeze cut through me. I squinted from the bright morning light.

As Tyler and I trudged through the snow, my headache returned. It was a dull but constant pain. We had only walked a short distance through the trees before our bracelets vibrated. Was there another challenge already? Several days had passed between the previous challenges. The bracelet didn't give us any information aside from a direction to travel. Maybe the Reckoning was nearing the end? We'd been out here for several weeks already.

The bracelets led us to a large clearing. A few competitors were already there, while others continued to arrive. At the center of the clearing was a viewing station. We all gathered around it. People whispered questions and wondered what was happening. No one had any answers, of course. My father was surely up to something. I kept Tyler close as we waited for instructions.

Once all the teams were near the viewing station, it came to life. It lit up, giving us a view of my father, who immediately began another one of his speeches.

"Congratulations! You should all be very proud of yourselves for making it this far. It's an honor to be Called, but a greater honor still to make it to the second phase of the Reckoning. There are only sixteen competitors remaining, and only ten of you will continue on to the third and final phase. Your fate is no longer tied to your partner's as we move forward. Ten familiars have been set free in the Inbetween. To move on to the third phase, you must find and capture one of them. Take caution when approaching a familiar; they all have their own test you will have to pass in order to capture them. Good luck to you all, and may the strongest survive!"

My father's image disappeared. Everyone was quiet for a few moments as they processed his words. We were no longer required to stay in teams. In fact, with only ten familiars and sixteen competitors, the competition was heating up. Teammates would now be competition. My thoughts were only of Tyler. I'd spent time each day teaching her how to control her dark magic, but she'd made little progress. She would be vulnerable on her own, and I didn't want to leave her.

"Listen up!" The dark priestess's voice echoed through the trees. She appeared from behind the viewing station. "As the king just informed you, it is every man for himself. In order to help you all survive on your own, and as a reward for making it this far, there are a variety of weapons scattered among the trees. At the sound of the bell, you will have five minutes to find and grab what you can. Prepare yourselves; things will only get harder from here."

I pressed my hand into the small of Tyler's back and led her to the side of the group. Once that bell rang, chaos would ensue. Unaware of how much time we had, I quickly whispered in her ear.

"Stick close to me. I don't care what my father says, I will not abandon you," I said. Tyler's bright eyes lit up, but she didn't get a chance to speak. The bell rang loud across the clearing, echoing in my ears.

Competitors took off in all directions. Grabbing Tyler's

hand, I ran toward the trees. Out of the corner of my eye, I could see Lux and Lexa. They rooted others in place with their earth magic, which only caused fights to break out.

Tyler and I reached the tree line before the worst of it. Magical energy was thrown about the clearing in all directions. Competitors were foolishly focused on sabotage rather than the real task. I wouldn't make the same mistake.

"If you see a weapon you know how to use, pick it up. If you can't use it, don't waste your time," I said to Tyler as I released her hand. She kept close to me as we jogged through the woods, scanning the area. The weapons would likely be concealed in some way, so we needed to stay vigilant to spot them.

"Ki, up there," Tyler said as she pointed into the trees. I spotted it before she'd even completed her statement: a long sword sheathed in a leather back strap tied to a high limb. Without a second thought, I leapt into the tree, jumping from branch to branch until I got to the sword. It was easy to untie.

With the long sword in hand, I dropped to the ground. Tyler was wide-eyed when I handed it to her. She took it and strapped it to her back with ease. It was a surprise to me, but it appeared she knew how to use it.

We continued through the woods, and a timer popped up on our bracelets. Only two minutes remained. I quickened my pace as we jogged through the trees. I almost missed it in my haste, but out of the corner of my eye there was a reflection of light.

The handle of a great sword stuck out of a large boulder. I grabbed it with both hands and pulled. It was stuck in place. With all my strength, I couldn't get it to budge, which only irritated me. There wasn't enough time left to find another weapon, so I had to get this one. I would not be defeated by a rock.

My dark magic flowed through me, and I forced it into the sword. Cracks emerged from the boulder. They stretched out from where the sword was stuck. I pulled hard once again, and this time the sword slid free.

The timer on the bracelets hit zero, and another loud bell

rang through the trees. I had the sword in hand, barely clearing the stone in time. Tyler stood nearby and smiled at my victory. A sheath for the sword magically appeared, and I strapped it to my back.

I wondered if my friends had been as successful in their search. They were both strong, so I knew they would be fine on their own. In fact, Daniel would probably watch over Harrison as he always did. The two of them always had each other's backs. It gave me comfort to know that I didn't need to worry about them.

Tyler was a different story, though. Her light could easily be snuffed out by any one of the competitors, and the thought of that bothered me. I'd gotten used to her light. Her kindness and hope for the world soothed me. If someone as fragile as she was could survive the Reckoning, then maybe there was a way to restore the land and save the kingdom from starvation.

CHAPTER 20

TYLER

His skin was hot like fire as his hands wandered across my body. I yearned for his touch, wanting to be consumed by it. My entire body trembled when he pressed into me with his naked flesh. Desire burned deep within me, begging for him to be closer, for there to be no space between us.

I ran my fingers through his hair, grabbing hold of his horns as he kissed my neck. His gentle kisses trailed down to my chest. When he took my nipple into his mouth, it was unbearable. I moaned loudly as he teased me with his tongue. My body ached for him to be inside me.

"Please, Ki," I begged as I wrapped my legs around his. He looked up at me with a smile. His eyes glowed red, and his teeth turned sharp.

My breath caught in my throat as he bit into my shoulder. Every inch of my skin tingled. I wanted him even more. Blood trickled down my back, but I didn't care. He held me tightly to him. The bulge in his pants pressed against me, and I reached for it.

"Tyler, come eat!" Ki's shout woke me. I jolted upright, breathing heavily, my thoughts cloudy. It was just a dream. Taking a deep breath, I tried to calm myself.

"Are you up?" Ki asked as he popped his head into the tent. Warmth rose to my cheeks, and I sucked in a breath. His black eyes stared into mine as I gripped my blanket tightly to me. "Is everything all right?" he asked, looking me over.

I nodded, unable to form words. Could he tell what I'd just been dreaming? My warm face was completely obvious. *Crap.* Why was I so awkward? Thankfully, he left me alone in the tent to dress after looking me over once more.

Ki's thoughts were a mystery to me. He'd been drunk when he revealed his loneliness, but it had still come as a shock. I never would've guessed a prince to ever be lonely. Didn't he have a bunch of friends? And didn't he prefer to keep his distance from people? He was always cold and distrusting in his interactions with the other competitors. Maybe it was because of his secrets. He'd made it clear that I wasn't to tell anyone about his wings or his need for blood—not even his friends. I guessed I'd be lonely too if I couldn't confide in anyone.

Exiting the tent, I went to join Ki by the fire. He sat cross-legged on the snowy ground, staring at the flames. I wondered what was on his mind. His attention turned to me as I took a seat next to him.

"Eat up. We have a lot of ground to cover," he said, motioning to the cooked rabbit that hung from a stick near the fire. Once again he'd gone out during the night to catch a meal for me. I understood his reasoning for the extra effort when we were partners, but the Reckoning no longer required him to keep me alive. So why had he refused to abandon me? Could Daniel have been right about Ki wanting to spend time with me?

"Thanks," I replied. Grabbing the stick, I peeled off strips of meat and stuffed them into my mouth. It warmed my stomach as I ate it. Ki stared at me intently.

"Were you having a bad dream earlier? You made strange sounds," Ki said. His eyes pierced through me, and a lump caught in my throat. What noises had I made? My face burned as I laughed nervously.

"I don't remember," I lied, my heart racing. Could he tell I wasn't honest? I had to change the subject quickly. "So what was it like growing up in the palace?" Ki's gaze turned to the fire.

"Why do you want to know?" he asked. His voice was filled with suspicion.

"I just realized that I hardly know anything about you," I replied. His dark eyes looked to me in disbelief. I smiled at him, and his shoulders relaxed.

"Let's get moving first. We should cover as much ground as possible," he replied. I quickly finished off what was left of the rabbit, and we packed up camp.

As we started our trek through the snow, Ki finally told me stories about his past. He told me he'd been taught to control his magic since as early as he could remember, and that he'd studied hard for most of his life to not only learn the typical educational standards but to also learn as much about his kingdom as he could. He took a particular interest in current events, wanting to be prepared to rule.

I shared my own stories with him as well—not that my life in a small village could come close to the life he had in the palace, but we had similar interests. He spent a lot of time in libraries, and I absolutely loved books. We talked for a long time about the few books we'd both read.

The day passed by quickly. As we walked through the snow-covered forest, we didn't spot any signs of familiars. I'd just finished telling Ki about my favorite romance story plot when his reply made me stop in my tracks.

"I wrote something similar to that once," he said.

"You write stories?" I asked. Most of the people I knew didn't have the luxury of being able to write. In fact, the majority of the people in my town couldn't even read.

Ki froze in place. When he turned to look back at me, his face was red. "Promise you won't tell anyone I said that. No one can ever know."

"I won't say anything," I replied with a smile. "But why

would you want to keep something like that a secret? It's a privilege to be able to write."

"My father wouldn't see it that way," Ki replied, resuming his walk. During all of the stories he'd told me, Ki had never mentioned his father. The thought ate at me as I followed behind him.

"Do you ever get to spend time with your father?" I asked. The muscles in Ki's back tensed. "I've always loved spending time training with my father, and with your father being the king, I didn't know if you got to do the same kind of thing."

Ki clenched his fists. "My duties as prince force me to spend time with my father, but outside of that I avoid him."

"Is it okay for me to ask why?" I replied as snow began to fall from the sky.

"I know you have a good relationship with your father, but my family matters are complicated."

"If you want to talk about it, I'll listen," I replied. Ki looked around at the setting sun and falling snow. His fists relaxed.

"Let's make camp for the night," he said.

We struggled to push through knee-deep snow as we approached a cluster of trees. Digging out the snow around them, we made a barricade and set up our tent inside it. My legs were exhausted by the time we finished.

Crawling into the tent, I collapsed onto our bedrolls. They were placed together with the blankets since we'd been huddling together for warmth at night. My legs throbbed as I lay on my back, but at least I was out of the snowstorm. Ki joined me in the tent and immediately began to undress, placing his clothes to one side of the tent with the rest of our gear.

"Are you going to sleep like that?" he asked, staring at the clothes I still wore. We usually slept in our underwear so that his body heat could warm me under the blankets, and I got the impression that he didn't want that to change.

"Of course not," I replied and began to undress.

Ki made himself comfortable under the blankets. Placing my clothes beside his, I joined him under the covers. His body radiated a warmth that soothed my aching muscles. When he rolled onto his side, facing away from me, I knew what he wanted. The past two nights he'd asked me to hold him. I pressed my chest into his back and slid my arm around his waist.

My thoughts returned to last night's dream, the warmth of Ki's skin impossible to ignore. I knew he had no interest in sex, but I couldn't stop myself from imagining it. His lips had made my skin tingle when he fed on me, so I wondered what it would be like if he kissed me. My cheeks warmed, and my heart raced. I needed a distraction. If Ki knew my thoughts, he would be offended.

"Do you think anyone has found a familiar yet?" I asked.

"Maybe, but I doubt it," he replied. "Familiars are good at hiding when they don't want to be found, and this snowstorm only makes it easier for them."

"Even if I found a familiar, I wouldn't know what to do," I said. Familiars could only bond to people with magic abilities, so I'd never bothered to learn much about them.

"I'll teach you the binding spell tomorrow. It's simple and doesn't require much energy, so you should be able to manage it." Ki spoke as if it was nothing, but it wasn't. He was going out of his way to help me. Maybe he felt obligated to teach me how to control the dark magic he'd infected me with, but teaching me how to catch a familiar was too much. Wasn't I his competition?

"Why would you do that for me?" I asked as I sat up to look at him. His dark eyes glanced at me, annoyed that I'd moved.

"I promised to protect you."

"But that was when we were partners. You'd cover a lot more ground without me. With your wings you could probably canvas the whole Inbetween in one day," I replied, needing a real answer. There had to be a reason he was letting me stay with him.

Ki rolled onto his back. There was a fire in his eyes that turned dark. "You're the only person who has seen my wings and still lives. Remember that." His words were cold, but he grabbed my arm and pulled me into him.

My head rested on his shoulder as I snuggled into the curve of his body. I was surprised that he held me close to him. Wasn't he mad about my question? Why couldn't he just admit that he liked having me around? That had to be the reason he was helping me.

Thoughts of Ki continued to plague me, but I had to push them from my mind. I needed to sleep. We would be up early in the morning to continue our search. I hoped the familiars would be found quickly. The Reckoning had already gone on for several weeks, and I missed my home. I wondered what my parents would think of Ki as I drifted off to sleep.

Ki's warm hand was pressed firmly over my mouth when I awoke. It was still dark outside, and I was exhausted. His eyes glowed red as he held a finger to his lips. He was fully dressed.

"Competitors are headed this way. Pack up the gear quickly; we need to move now," he whispered as he released me. No sounds came from outside the tent, but I trusted his instincts.

As quickly as I could, I dressed and packed up my gear. Ki grabbed his gear, slipping out of the tent before me. He said he would distract the competitors while I took down the tent. When I stepped outside, frigid wind and snow greeted me. The storm made it hard to take down the tent alone, but I managed to get it rolled up and strapped to my back with the rest of my gear.

When footsteps drew near, I pulled the long sword from my back. Ki stepped into view, breathing heavily. He paused for a moment when he saw the sword but continued to approach me. Sweat trickled down the side of his face as he caught his breath.

"Put that away. We need to run. Lux and Lexa are out for blood," he said.

"What? Why?" I asked.

"It doesn't matter. We need to move now," he said as he took the tent from me.

"Well now, look what we have here." Lux's voice broke through the silent night's air. He jumped down from a tree and was only a few meters away from us. The smile on his face was wicked as he stared at me with a sword in hand.

"You'll leave now if you know what's good for you," Ki said, stepping in front of me.

"But what fun would that be?" Lux replied as he walked toward us. Ki drew the great sword from his back.

"Just as I thought, he's obsessed with that small human girl," Lexa said. She stepped out of the shadows to join her brother. The howling wind blew her hair about wildly.

"How pitiful. The Darkblood Prince has fallen under the spell of a commoner," Lux added. Their words made no sense. Ki wasn't obsessed with me, and I hadn't used magic on him.

"Don't bring her into this. Your sister is the one who begged for my attention. It's not my fault she couldn't handle it," Ki replied.

"You sick bastard! How dare you talk about my sister that way," Lux said as he charged straight for Ki.

"Run," Ki said as his sword crashed into Lux's.

There was fury in Lux's eyes as he continued to lunge at Ki. With no good options, I took off into the woods. The snow was thick, but I waded through it as fast as I could.

"Not so fast!" Lexa shouted. I turned to see that she had a short bow in hand. An arrow came straight at me, but Ki's ball of dark magic knocked it off course. Lexa cursed as the arrow flew into the snow.

I ran for cover between trees while Ki fought them both off. The sounds of clashing metal echoed in the wind. A blast of magical energy was followed by curses from Lux and Lexa.

My attention stayed focused on moving forward, but then Ki was at my side. What had happened?

"Keep moving. That won't hold them back for long," Ki said, running beside me.

My legs burned from pushing through the knee-high snow, and my mind wandered. What had he done to the asudhen duo? Why were they even after us in the first place? They should've been focusing their energy on finding familiars, not attacking competitors.

Ki grunted as an arrow pierced his back. Lexa was close. We stumbled into a small clearing as the pair caught up to us. Ki tried to keep me behind him, but it was no use. There was no way to escape them, not with the snow slowing us down. Our only option was to fight. I drew my sword.

"So the little mouse wants to play." Lexa laughed. "Have you ever even used one of those before?" She mocked me, but I didn't care. I didn't want to hurt anyone, but I wasn't going to die without a fight.

A series of growls cut through the howling winds as over a dozen wolves emerged from the shadows. They had bright yellow eyes and sharp teeth. Lux and Lexa were just as surprised as we were when the wolves began circling us. They were so thin that they must have been starved.

"On my signal, take out the one on the left and run," Ki whispered to me as we faced the wolves. I nodded in reply, lifting my sword.

"Go," Ki said as one of the wolves lunged at Lux. I cut down the wolf nearest to me and ran. Ki swung his sword full circle as I passed him. Several wolves whimpered, but I didn't look. Ki's footsteps closed in behind me. We'd made it past the circle, but we weren't in the clear yet.

"Oh no you don't," Lexa shouted as she loosed an arrow. Ki stepped into its path to block me, and it pierced his shoulder. He grunted in pain but pushed me forward. A couple wolves followed us, but the rest were focused on Lux and Lexa. The ground shook as the duo used their earth magic in unison.

We ran through the trees with the wolves hot on our trail. Ki fought them off to the best of his ability, but he was clearly hurt. I had to do something. There was no way he could handle any more wounds. I gripped my sword in both hands and waited for the perfect moment. A wolf lunged at Ki, and I stabbed it through the chest. It fell to the ground, a bloodied corpse. The wolves behind it tripped over its body.

"Nice hit," Ki said. He breathed heavily as we continued through the thick snow. My legs burned from the effort, but I willed myself to continue on.

I killed three wolves before they stopped their pursuit. It was a shame we weren't able to collect any of the bodies. Such a waste of life and resources. I would pray to the gods later for the wolves' sacrifice.

We only slowed our pace once we were sure the wolves were gone. My heart pounded in my chest as I breathed heavily. Ki came to a stop next to me, his blood trickling into the snow. He had two arrows sticking out of him and struggled to catch his breath.

"We have to keep moving," he said through gasps.

"First we need to get those arrows out," I said, pointing to his wounds.

"Fine, but do it quickly. Lux and Lexa could be on our trail," he said as he knelt in the snow, giving me access to the arrows.

The arrows were embedded deep in his skin, but they hadn't gone all the way through. I had to be careful. If the tips broke off inside him, I'd never be able to get them out. Grabbing as close to the skin as possible, I pulled on the first arrow. My arms weren't strong enough to pull it out, so I placed my foot on Ki's back for leverage. Using my weight, I pulled on the arrow again. It slid free from his flesh as I fell back into the snow.

Ki let out a groan of pain. After pulling the second arrow out, I unzipped Ki's suits, placing gauze pads over his wounds. They wouldn't last for long, but I hoped they'd slow the bleeding until we got to a safer location. He definitely needed stitches. We were back on the move in no time at all.

Time moved slowly as we trudged through the storm. The temperature dropped steadily, and I struggled to breathe in the frozen air, but at least the heavy snowfall covered our tracks. We walked for hours in the frigid weather before the sun began to rise. The sun had never looked so beautiful before. It warmed my frozen skin as the storm calmed.

Ki collapsed in the snow. His suits hid the severity of his wounds, but his forehead was on fire. His wounds must've gotten infected. We should've stopped sooner to tend to them. It was foolish to have walked so far; he could die. I couldn't let that happen.

The frozen air made me shiver as I unzipped my suits to expose my shoulder. Ki stared at me with wide eyes as I knelt before him. "Let me help you." Ki was speechless, but he shook his head in disagreement. "You can't protect me if you're dead."

Ki's eyes fell to my shoulder, and a familiar red glow burned within them. His teeth turned sharp as he pulled me against him. He held me close, brushing my hair to the side gently, and my body trembled. I wasn't sure if it was because of his touch or the cold air.

"I'm sorry," he whispered before he bit into me. Fire burned in my veins as his hold on me tightened. My body tingled with pleasure, and I wrapped my arms around him. Relief washed over me as I relaxed into him. My lips fell to his neck, and I kissed his light gray skin.

Ki bit harder, and the world around me spun. My breath matched his, but then my vision began to blur. Darkness took over, and I gave in to it completely. I welcomed the peacefulness of it.

CHAPTER 21

HARRISON

Being the first to wake, I admired Daniel's body while he slept. Several days had passed since the second phase of the Reckoning had begun, and Daniel had made a full recovery. His injuries from his fights with Adakk were gone completely. Thankfully, tlalocs healed faster than asudhs and humans.

It had been a challenge to get past competitors to find weapons at the start of the second phase, but Daniel and I worked well together. Our injuries had hardly slowed us down. Working as a team, we'd been able to find a sword for me and a great axe for Daniel. I would never understand it, but Daniel loved to use axes for battle. It was a testament to his tlaloc heritage.

Even though I was snuggled against Daniel, it still didn't seem real to me. We'd made love every night since the first time, and he'd confessed his love for me over and over again. I wanted to tell him what he meant to me, but I could never make the words come out.

With the endless blizzard that blew across the land, we'd

taken shelter in a cave. We would venture out and search for familiars when the sun was up and would return once the sun set. Our nightly fires would stave off the frigid air. Embers from the night's fire still warmed the air around me.

"Good morning." Daniel smiled as he pulled me in for a kiss. My body trembled from his gentle touch.

"Good morning," I replied. Daniel stared into my eyes as he rolled on top of me. The bulge in his underwear pressed firmly against my leg. He'd just woken up but was already eager to take me. Morning light had not yet reached the cave, so I gave in to him.

I loved every second I spent with Daniel. His touch drove me mad, and I could never get enough of it. We got lost in waves of passion until light crept into the cave. It was nearly impossible to keep our hands to ourselves, but we dressed and journeyed from the cave.

We trudged through the snow, but there were no signs of familiars or other competitors. The snow fall made finding tracks difficult, but I didn't mind it at all. Being alone with Daniel was pure bliss. In fact, I wished we could've stayed in that little cave together forever. We wouldn't have to worry about the world or my pending marriage to Jess; we could just live a peaceful life together. If only that had been our destiny.

"Harrison, over here," Daniel said. He pointed out a set of rabbit tracks in the snow.

"A familiar?" I asked.

"If not, it'll make a nice meal." He smiled as he followed the tracks through the trees.

We moved quietly through the snow for at least an hour before we spotted the rabbit. It definitely wasn't a familiar. There was nothing magical about it; it was just a plain brown rabbit. Unfortunately, it spotted us and took off. We chased after it.

"You remember that game we played when we were kids?" Daniel shouted as we chased after the rabbit.

"Of course," I replied. We would make bets on who would catch an animal in the woods first. Back then they were silly bets, like the loser had to do the winner's chores or the loser had to wear a dress for the day, but we were older now.

"Winner gets to be on top tonight!" Daniel shouted. He broke away from me as he pursued the rabbit. His bet caught me off guard. Daniel was always on top anyway. He didn't think I could win.

"Deal!" I shouted. That rabbit would be mine. I'd prove to him that I was just as powerful as he was.

We ran through the woods, and the rabbit dipped back and forth. Daniel tried to encase it in the earth, but the rabbit jumped out of the way. It managed to avoid my blasts of dark magic as well. That little sucker was crafty.

After we'd both made several attempts to catch the rabbit and had failed, I finally figured out a plan. I'd wait for Daniel to attack and then attack simultaneously while the rabbit was distracted. Teamwork was the only way to trap the rabbit, even if Daniel didn't know he was aiding me.

I watched as Daniel forced the earth to move. As expected, the rabbit jumped to the side to avoid it and was hit by my ball of dark magic. I'd timed it perfectly. The rabbit fell to the ground and lay motionless in the snow. Victory was mine.

"I won." I smiled as I picked up the dead rabbit. Daniel laughed at me as I danced around in excitement. It was rare that I ever beat him in a challenge. He closed the space between us.

"Fair is fair." Daniel smiled as he pulled me toward him. His lips pressed into mine, and I melted. I'd nearly forgotten about the rabbit when he finally pulled away. If only I'd been lost in Daniel's kiss forever.

We didn't spot any other tracks the rest of the day. The sun was setting when we decided to head back toward the cave, and the winds changed. A strike of lightning in the distance caught our attention. It wasn't the right time of year for thunderstorms, so there shouldn't have been any lightning, yet it managed to get closer with every minute that passed.

The winds raged around us, making it difficult to walk. Daniel grabbed ahold of my hand and practically dragged me through the snow with him. The lightning was headed straight for us.

When it was fewer than a hundred meters out, I could tell it wasn't normal lightning. Shocks of electricity filled the air as the lightning struck a tree. Its trunk caught fire, and smoke obscured our vision. The storm was upon us.

Daniel ran toward the cave, pulling me with him. It wasn't far away, but the storm moved quickly. The static in the air made my hair stand on end. I could feel the energy all around us. There was no way the storm hadn't been created by magic.

We leapt to the side when lightning touched down nearly on top of us. My heart raced, and breath caught in my lungs. That was too close for comfort. We dashed for the cave as it came into view.

The storm covered the area as we dove into the safety of the cave. Energy showered down upon the land. Its electricity crackled. The sound echoed in my ears along with my rapid heartbeat. We were safe.

Breathing heavily, I struggled to catch my breath. Daniel lay on the cave floor beside me, breathing just as hard. He smiled in relief. Footsteps came from behind us, and we both jumped to our feet.

"I guess great minds think alike," Wynter said as he came into view. He had gear strapped to his back and an iguana draped across his shoulders. Its body blended in perfectly with his black suit. *A familiar!*

"What are you doing here?" I said. The cave had been a home away from home for Daniel and me for days, and I wasn't ready to give it up.

"The same as you, it would appear. I'm hiding from the storm," Wynter replied as he nodded toward the entrance. Icy rain had begun to pour from the sky. It was ugly out there.

"Shit," I mumbled under my breath, but I was pretty sure Daniel heard me.

"There's nothing to be done about it now. We'll have to share the cave for the night," Daniel said. His gentle smile didn't make the situation any better. I wanted my reward for capturing the rabbit, and that couldn't happen with Wynter around.

Daniel was quick to get a fire going. We'd stocked the cave with plenty of wood earlier in the day, so we'd be able to keep the fire going all night. Wynter and I unpacked our gear. We stripped out of our heavy winter suits and placed our bedrolls near the fire.

Wynter sat on his bedroll next to me, and I was surprised to see how muscular he was without his suit on. He was slender but fit. In fact, his muscle definition was almost as chiseled as Daniel's. I tried not to stare, but his blue skin twinkled in the firelight.

"I guess now is as good a time as any to bust this bad boy out," Wynter said as he riffled through his pack. He pulled out a bottle of wine. The smile on Daniel's face was impossible to miss. He loved to drink. It was probably his favorite thing to do, aside from teasing me.

"Where did you get that?" Daniel asked with wide eyes. Wynter popped the cork out with a knife. He made it look easy, but I knew better. I could never get away with taking wine from the palace cellar because I could never manage to get the damn bottles open. In the end I'd have to ask a servant for help, and more often than not they'd just rat me out.

"I stole it from the victors' buffet when they were all asleep in their cozy beds. It pays to be unnoticeable," Wynter said. He smiled warmly at me before taking a drink. With a wink, he passed the bottle to me.

When I hesitated to take a drink, Daniel pulled the bottle from my hand. He took a drink and handed it back to me. I took a sip and gave it back to Wynter. We continued to pass the bottle around as we made conversation.

"When did you find the iguana?" I asked. Wynter's fingers touched mine as we passed the bottle. I thought of how he'd made out with Quaeth at the opening ceremony, and heat rose to my cheeks. Wynter's soft moans had captivated me.

"This little guy? It actually felt more like he found me." It was as if the iguana knew we'd mentioned it. The color of its skin changed to match Wynter's as it crawled onto his lap. I swore it stared at me with its giant eyes. Why were its eyes so damn big?

"You don't say," Daniel replied with a smile. Wynter's cheeks grew flush. Why was Daniel being so friendly? He usually ignored most people. I didn't like that his attention was focused on Wynter, and the alcohol had my head spinning.

"Don't you have a boyfriend?" I said. Wynter's focus turned to me. "I saw you making out with Quaeth."

Wynter laughed. "That doesn't make him my boyfriend. We were just having fun."

"I told you they wouldn't mind if you joined," Daniel added. My thoughts spiraled. Had Daniel wanted me to join them? But he was in love with me. Didn't he want me for himself?

"I can't speak for Quaeth, but the way I see it, the more the merrier." Wynter's words sank in slowly. I snatched the bottle from his hand and took a long drink before handing it to Daniel. His pink eyes were as enchanting as his smile.

"I don't mind sharing," Daniel said as he looked from me to Wynter.

Wynter moved closer to me. His hand rubbed across my thigh, and my body trembled. The alcohol made his every touch burn like fire on my skin. Daniel watched with eyes full of desire. He wanted to share me with Wynter.

When Wynter tried to climb on top of me, I fought back. We wrestled near the fire, and Daniel didn't bother to stop us. I managed to pin Wynter down, and he lay helplessly beneath me. His small whimper of defeat pushed me over the edge. I kissed him hard.

It was strange to kiss Wynter. I didn't love him, but it made my body tingle. Holding him down while kissing him gave me control. I liked the control; it aroused me. Wynter moaned in response to my kiss, and Daniel stared with a smile on his face.

"I'm not usually a bottom," Wynter said as I released him from our kiss.

"Neither am I," Daniel added, "but Harrison did win our bet today, so fair is fair." He moved closer to us.

They both wanted me to be on top. They wanted to give me all the control, and I welcomed it. I never wanted to be powerless again, not like I'd been with Jess. Wynter told me he liked it rough, that I needed to make him suffer if I wanted to top him. It was the only way he could enjoy bottoming. He wanted me to use and abuse him.

"You'll do what I tell you to do, yes?" I asked Wynter.

"Of course." He smiled.

"You can start by sucking my cock," I said as I stood up. Daniel stood behind me, caressing me with his hands. The bulge rising in his pants pressed into my back.

Wynter got to his knees. He pulled my underwear down and went straight for my cock. There was no hesitation. He took me into his mouth while massaging my balls with his hand. I could tell he'd done it many times before. How else would he have been able to take the entire length of my cock into his mouth?

Grabbing a fistful of his short black hair, I pulled him into me. He choked as my cock hit the back of his throat. The sound of his gargled moans delighted me. As I continued to fuck Wynter's mouth, Daniel trailed kisses along my neck. They were both focused on me, and the thought of them being at my disposal filled me with an overwhelming pleasure.

Wynter was eager to please me, but I had to try something different. His gray eyes stared up at me pleadingly. He wanted it to be rougher. I needed to make him suffer more. His power was mine for the taking, and it intoxicated me.

Forcing Wynter back, I pulled out of his mouth and gave commands. Daniel smiled as he went along with my commands. He lay naked on his back, giving Wynter access to his cock. Wynter kneeled between Daniel's legs and took him into his mouth. I smiled as he struggled to take Daniel's size.

Without warning, I knelt behind Wynter and slid myself inside him. He grunted as his body tensed up, but his mouth was too full with Daniel's cock for his complaints to be heard. I enjoyed his grunts of pain more than I should have.

Daniel forced Wynter's head up and down while I thrust myself deep inside him. We used him as if he only existed to give us pleasure. He enjoyed it, though. His loud moans and erect cock told me just how much he liked being penetrated.

Fluids leaked from all of Wynter's orifices, so I decided to take pity on him. Grabbing his cock, I stroked him while continuing to pound him from behind. He gasped at my touch.

"If you cum before Daniel does, I'll make you take my cock until the sun rises," I whispered into Wynter's ear. He moaned as I tightened my grip on his cock. It twitched in my hand, and I knew my words had aroused him even more.

Wynter sucked Daniel's cock with vigor. To my surprise, Daniel released inside him, and Wynter didn't spill a single drop. He swallowed all of it. It amazed and excited me. How many cocks had Wynter taken in the past? The thought only made me want to hurt him more. How much could he really take?

I flipped Wynter onto his back, making him lie on top of Daniel. Daniel rubbed Wynter's chest and twisted his nipples. With his mouth finally free, Wynter moaned loudly. I covered his mouth with my hand, letting Daniel take over the cock stroking.

Wynter grunted as I forced myself deep inside him. His body clenched tightly around me, and I neared release. I fucked him even harder. The more he tried to cry out through my hand, the harder I fucked him. His moans brought me to the edge, and I finally found release.

When I filled Wynter with my cum, it was too much for him. He released into the air as his body convulsed with pleasure. I couldn't help but grin.

I wanted to do it again.

CHAPTER 22

KI

The dull ache of pain woke me from my sleep. Tyler had been lying peacefully next to me until my groans woke her. My head throbbed, and I couldn't think about anything else. It was my horns; they were growing. But why now? It was the worst time for my body to be transitioning.

"Are you all right?" Tyler asked, sitting up. Her eyes widened as she took in the sight of my horns. I guessed they looked as bad as they felt.

"The wounds from the arrows have healed completely," I replied as I began to dress.

"But your horns. They're cracked," Tyler said as she reached up to touch them. I leaned back, pushing her hands away.

"Don't touch me," I snapped.

Backing away, she looked up at me in confusion. Instead of trying to explain anything to her, I just made my way out of the tent. My mood was foul, and I couldn't bear a bunch of questions—especially questions I didn't have answers to.

In the past my horns had grown quickly, never causing me

great pain. Most of the time I didn't even know it was going to happen. I'd just fall asleep at night and wake up with pieces of my old horns scattered about my bed, my new horns having grown in larger and darker, protruding from my skull exactly how my old horns had. So why was this time different?

"Did Lux and Lexa do this to you?" Tyler asked as she stepped out of the tent and walked toward me. "It's my fault for not being more helpful in the fight against them."

"Everything isn't about you," I snapped, unable to control my anger. "I'm going to hunt. Wait here." I stormed off into the woods, hoping a hunt would calm me. My dark magic fed off my anger and tingled throughout my body. It made the throbbing in my head worse.

My senses were dulled. Half of my focus was spent coping with the pain in my head. The rest of my focus tried to spot signs of life in the trees. After a few hours, I caught sight of a small fox emerging from a hole in the ground. I stalked it through the trees.

I tried to throw a ball of dark energy at the fox, but it missed completely. My magic split apart midair as my concentration was interrupted. The pain in my head doubled. I could hardly keep myself upright. There was no way I would catch anything in this bloody condition.

Defeated by the small fox, I headed back to camp, hating that I had to return empty-handed. Tyler would be disappointed—as if my guilt for being cold to her that morning wasn't enough. She'd risked her life to heal me from my injuries with her blood, and I couldn't even catch a meal for her. It was because of my horns. The pain had started not long after I'd fed off Tyler. Had her blood caused my body to transition?

When I got back to camp, Tyler was sitting by a small fire. She'd packed up all of our gear while I was gone. I couldn't believe she'd done all of that while I hadn't even been able to catch a small fox. A pit formed in my stomach as I approached her. She looked up from the flames and smiled at me. I didn't deserve her kindness.

"Are you feeling better?" she asked.

"I'm fine," I lied. A throbbing pain radiated from my horns while my guilt ate away at me. Never before had I been so useless.

We both startled when our bracelets vibrated. The sensation reverberated throughout my body, intensifying my pain. We were informed that two familiars had been caught already, which meant there were only eight left. The day had gotten away from us. We needed to continue our search.

"We should move out if we hope to find a familiar," I said. Tyler agreed, and we gathered our equipment.

As we walked through the woods, I had Tyler memorize the familiar binding spell, but the farther we walked, the heavier my gear became. I could hardly walk straight as the weight of the great sword pulled me to one side. Why had I picked such a heavy weapon? Every muscle in my body ached, and my stomach sickened. The pain was too much for me.

"Are you all right?" Tyler gasped as I hunched over to retch. Blood stained the snow at my feet. That wasn't a good sign.

"Don't touch me!" I snapped as Tyler rushed to my side. Even though I knew she was only trying to help, I couldn't stop my words. The pain made it impossible to comprehend anything. My entire body burned from the magic in my blood.

"Something is clearly wrong with you," Tyler said, gesturing to the blood-covered snow.

"Bloody hell. I'm not your boyfriend, so stop making a fuss about it!" I replied. Tyler winced from the harshness in my voice, and I sighed. It was easy to push her away.

I lay in the snow, and its cold touch soothed my horns, if only for a moment. I wished I could stop the pain. Why had my body turned against me? It had terrible timing. I would've cut my own horns off if I'd thought it would end the pain.

"Why don't we make camp for the night?" Tyler suggested. She stared at me intently, as if I would break. I wasn't some fragile human.

"No. We will continue our search. There's lots of daylight left," I said as I rose to my feet.

We continued our trek through the snowy forest. As time passed, my vision became hazy. It phased back and forth between normal and red. I couldn't control it. My senses were completely thrown off by my pain. One moment I swore I couldn't hear, and the next my own footsteps were so loud I wanted to make myself deaf. It was the worst day of my life.

I thought I was hallucinating when a wolf came into view, appearing out of thin air. Tyler's eyes widened, and she stopped in her tracks when she spotted it. That meant it was real. As I stared at the wolf, its eyes glowed yellow. It had to be a familiar. If my senses hadn't been so messed up, I would've noticed its magical energy sooner. It was the only familiar we'd come across, and we needed to be smart to catch it.

"What should we do?" Tyler whispered. I put my finger to my lips to indicate we should be quiet. She understood and followed my lead.

Walking silently through the snow, we snuck up on the wolf. It was only a few yards away when my vision blurred. I tripped over a tree root, alerting the wolf. It glanced back at us before taking off into the woods.

The wolf had a head start, but we chased after it anyway. Its gray-and-white fur blended in with the snowy landscape, making it hard to keep sight of. I could see it clearly when my eyes turned red, but my vision kept phasing back and forth. Our pursuit came to a stop when a loud clink echoed through the trees.

I fell to the ground as a large bear trap captured me. Its teeth had closed around my leg, but I couldn't feel the pain. My body was numb, and my vision turned dark. Tyler cursed. I wasn't sure what she'd said, but I imagined it wasn't very ladylike.

She was suddenly at my side, examining the trap. My blood splattered the snow as it spurted from my leg. It covered Tyler's hands as she tried to free me. She didn't have the strength to pull the trap open—not on her own, anyway.

Tyler helped me to stand on my one good leg, and I pulled my great sword from my back. Sticking it into the teeth of the trap, I used the blade for leverage. As the trap opened, Tyler guided my injured leg out. I was free, but the pain of it washed over me, and I collapsed to the ground. Tears threatened to escape my eyes.

"Is it broken?" Tyler asked. I couldn't bring myself to look. My bones had broken before, but it had never hurt so bad.

"You tell me," I replied.

Tyler poked at my wound. Her every touch was excruciating. "It doesn't look broken, but I can see bone."

Blood oozed out of my leg, and I was overcome with light-headedness. It was good I was already on the ground. "Just stitch me up."

Without hesitation, Tyler pulled the med kit from her pack. She rinsed the wounds with water from her canteen before stitching them up. The stitches hurt like hell, but they made the bleeding stop. I'd already lost too much blood, and my hunger consumed me.

As Tyler wrapped bandages over my stitches, I fought against my hunger. Feeding on Tyler was dangerous. Not only did it put her life at risk, but it also made the pain in my horns worse. I couldn't let myself feed on her again.

We were forced to make camp for the night since I could hardly stand. Tyler didn't complain once. She made fast work of setting up the tent, with hardly any help from me. After dragging our equipment inside, she left me in the tent to rest. I could sense her practicing magic outside while I faded in and out of consciousness. She had the binding spell memorized.

The sun had set by the time Tyler joined me in the tent. "Your wounds aren't healing like they usually do," she said as she changed my bandages.

"What do you mean?" I asked. The constant pain in my horns confused my thoughts.

"You usually heal within an hour or two, but this hasn't healed at all. In fact, it looks worse."

"Fuck," I mumbled as I closed my eyes. It was hard to focus on anything but the pain.

"Do you need blood?" she asked.

"No!" I snapped. My horns cracked, and my entire body was electrified with pain. It was because of her. I never should've fed on her in the first place. Giving in to my desire for blood was my weakness, and I had to be strong. I would suffer through the consequences.

"I'm sorry," she said as she left the tent. It was easier with her gone. I didn't have to hide. My body gave in to the pain as tears fell from my eyes. They were impossible to hold back any longer. I was just glad Tyler wasn't there to witness my weakness.

CHAPTER 23

HARRISON

I woke from the heat. Daniel's arms were wrapped around me, and his chest was pressed against my back. Wynter lay in front of me, my arm resting over him. I was stuck under a blanket and wedged between the two of them, and their body heat was more intense than a fire's flame.

Thoughts of the night played through my mind. I couldn't believe the things I'd said and done. It was the wine. Yeah, I could definitely blame the wine. After all, I did have a slight headache from it, and given the size of my body, a low tolerance level was expected.

Wynter groaned as he squirmed next to me. His hand rubbed on his lower back; he was in pain. I'd been too forceful with him. Why had I let myself get so carried away? He'd asked for it, but I still shouldn't have been so rough with him. Heat burned in my face when Wynter rolled onto his back. His gray eyes stared into mine as he smiled.

"Good morning," he said. I tried to wriggle free, but Daniel's grip was too strong.

"Morning. Are you all right?" I replied. Daniel stirred from his sleep.

"My whole back side hurts, and I'm not sure how well I'll be able to walk today, but I'll be fine," Wynter replied with a playful wink.

"Sorry about that." My heart raced in my chest. I wanted to be free from the situation, from the humiliation. After all the nasty things I'd done to him, how could he just lie there and smile at me?

"You weren't the least bit gentle with me last night," he said with a teasing grin. "And I thought Daniel was the brute." Wynter's laughter struck a nerve, and I froze in place, wanting to disappear entirely.

"You begged for it," Daniel added. I couldn't believe how easily they joked about it. What we'd done was wrong on so many levels. It didn't matter that we'd all enjoyed it. That never should've happened. What had I been thinking?

Squirming free from them, I pulled on my clothes. They both stared at me with a brightness in their eyes, which held no judgment. It was all too much. My thoughts overwhelmed me. I was in love with Daniel, I'd fucked Wynter, and worst of all, I was still engaged to Jess. What the hell was I doing?

My mind struggled to comprehend it all. How had I gone from wanting to wait until marriage to fucking two guys at the same time? Something was wrong with me. Like, seriously wrong with me. It had all started with Jess. If she hadn't stolen my virginity, none of this would have happened. I would've been blissfully committed to our forced engagement.

"Are you all right, Harrison?" Daniel asked.

I'd been unconsciously pacing the distance of the cave, but I couldn't stop myself from doing it as they dressed. Wynter moved slowly. His pain was easy to see. He winced as he bent down to put on his boots. I realized I was admiring his body, and heat rose to my face.

Looking to Daniel, I didn't know what to say. There were so many things on my mind, but I couldn't put any of it into words. I hadn't even told him I loved him before fucking another guy. Daniel walked over to me, pulling me into a hug. His warm embrace was comforting, and it slowed my thoughts. I let myself enjoy it.

"I'm going to head out. It was fun, but it looks like three might be a crowd," Wynter said as he scooped up his iguana. Its big eyes were filled with judgment as it stared at us.

"Good luck out there," Daniel replied. I remained quiet. What was I supposed to say? Thanks for letting me violate your body, hope you don't die? Nothing would sound good. I'd used him, and it was a terrible thing to do.

Wynter smiled and waved as he left the cave. Finally alone with Daniel, I broke down. Tears streamed from my face as I crumbled to the ground. I was a monster just like Jess. Had I not just done the same thing she'd done to me to someone else? My chest heaved.

"It's okay, Harrison. You didn't do anything wrong," Daniel said. I swore he could read my mind. Why was he so good to me? I didn't deserve it.

"What have I done?" I cried. There was no way to go back. The morals once so dear to me were now destroyed. I'd never be able to take back the things I'd done. My chest tightened as if my heart would implode. The plan I had for my life was completely ruined. I would never be the loyal, faithful husband I'd hoped to be. Not anymore.

"Did you want him to stay? I'm sure we could catch up to him," Daniel said. Maybe he couldn't read my mind after all. Did he really think I was upset about Wynter leaving?

"It's got nothing to do with him. He'll be fine on his own," I mumbled through my tears.

"There's no need to beat yourself up about last night," Daniel said. "We all wanted it."

His words pierced through me. We all wanted it? Could that be true? Had I really wanted it? Sure, Wynter was all smiles when he left, but I'd made him suffer so much. There'd been blood and tears. How could he have wanted that?

"But I—"

"Nope, none of that. I won't let you torment yourself," Daniel said. "What happened last night was 100 percent consensual, and that's that." He smiled as he wiped my tears away. The weight in my chest lessened.

"If you say so," I said, catching my breath. Daniel was right—I didn't have time to overthink things. We needed to focus on the Reckoning, on finding familiars.

We packed up our gear and headed out of the cave. There were no signs of the electric storm. In fact, it was snowing once again. We trudged through the knee-deep snow as we searched the woods. Our journey had just begun when our bracelets vibrated. They informed us that four of the ten familiars had been found. There were only six left, and we hadn't caught sight of a single one.

"Do you think we'll be sent home right away if we don't find familiars?" I asked.

"I don't know," Daniel replied.

"I'm not ready to go home just yet."

"Are you worried about Jess?"

"What'll happen when she finds out about us? The king will be pissed," I said.

"Things will sort themselves out eventually," Daniel replied.

"How? I'm so happy being here with you, but I'm supposed to marry Jess. How will that sort out? Someone will get hurt no matter the outcome," I said. Guilt consumed me. Even though Jess had hurt me, I still shouldn't have betrayed her. I was supposed to be the loyal one.

"You know it's okay to love us both," Daniel said. "Having many loves is a blessing."

"What?" He couldn't possibly be telling me it was okay for me to love multiple people. Wouldn't that hurt his feelings? Then again, he'd been more than happy to share me with Wynter.

A sound in the trees interrupted our conversation. We drew our weapons as someone dropped down from a nearby tree.

My heart skipped a beat, anticipating a fight, but it was just Emm. She had a long sword in hand, prepared to strike.

"Hey, Emm. It's just us," I said in a friendly tone. She stared at me with a furrowed brow, but then her face relaxed.

"Hey, I didn't realize it was you. I've had some bad run-ins with other competitors," she replied. Daniel and I sheathed our weapons and walked toward her.

"That's okay. We aren't looking for a fight," I replied.

"You aren't, but I don't trust that tlaloc friend of yours," she said, eyeing Daniel. Her grip on her sword stayed firm.

"Have you seen any familiars out there?" I asked.

"Nope. And if I had, I wouldn't tell you. This is a competition, after all," she replied. There was tension in the air as Emm and Daniel glared at each other.

"We haven't seen any either," I said.

"I better get going. No offense, but I intend to succeed on my own," she said.

"All right. It's nice to see you're doing well," I replied.

Emm ran into the woods, quickly disappearing from sight. I was glad she was still alive. She'd been a good partner for the first phase of the Reckoning. If it weren't for her, I might have already been sent home.

"Pleasant as always," Daniel grumbled. I'd assumed he didn't like any aeni, but I was starting to think it was personal. His motivations were a mystery to me. He never said so, but I knew he had a reason for everything he did. It was as if he knew way more than he let on. Daniel was wise beyond his years.

We walked in silence. I was lost in my own thoughts, but Daniel was focused on the trees. It was impossible to ignore what he'd said to me. To even suggest that I'd love Jess like I loved him was crazy. Sure, I'd known Jess just as long as I'd known him, and I had fond memories of her, but did I actually love her? How could I after what'd happened between us?

If he'd asked me a few months ago, I probably would've said that I loved Jess. I'd practically been obsessed with her from a young age. She'd been the cute older girl who always doted on me, at least until we became engaged. Though she'd been cold toward me, I still cared about her. I'd hoped to prove myself worthy of her. What a silly thought. How had things gotten turned around so quickly?

"It's okay to forgive her," Daniel said, breaking the endless silence.

"Why are you saying this to me?" I replied, stopping in my tracks. "How can you say something so heartless? It's like you want me to go back to her, but I can't. I won't leave you."

"I'm not asking you to, but if you don't move past this, it'll eat at you forever. I watched it destroy my mother, and I won't let the same thing happen to you," he said as he turned to me. I could see the concern on his face.

"I don't understand what this has to do with your mother. Didn't she die from illness?" I said. His face saddened.

"That's just the lie my father tells to save his reputation. My mother killed herself. She suffered abuse similar to yours when my father was fighting in the king's war. It ate at her every day until she couldn't bear it anymore. Her obsession with her pain killed her. She just couldn't let it go. I won't let that happen to you. You have to find a way to make peace with what happened," Daniel said. His eyes filled with tears. I'd never seen such a look on his face before. It confounded me.

"But she hurt me," I said, and the tears began to fall. "She disregarded my feelings and took away my power. I had no control over what happened to my own body, and she humiliated me. How do I make peace with that? I trusted her, and she violated me."

"It won't be easy, but you need to find a way to forgive her," he said as he pulled me into a hug. His large arms held me tight as I cried. As much as I'd tried to convince myself otherwise, the truth was that I'd loved Jess. I just couldn't admit it to myself because she'd broken me. Even if Daniel was right and I could find a way to forgive her, I could never trust her again. How could I love her without trust?

"I'll never love her," I mumbled into Daniel's chest. He

held me tight as I cried my pain into him. I let it all out, and he let me stay in his arms until I was calm again. My mind became clear. Once the Reckoning was over, I would find a way to be with Daniel. I refused to live a loveless life with Jess. No matter the cost, I would find a way out of our engagement.

CHAPTER 24

TYLER

Ki's anguish was insufferable. His groans of agony pierced through me as he tried to find a comfortable position to sleep in. I desperately wanted to end his suffering, but he wouldn't let me help. He refused to feed off of me, even though his condition grew worse with each passing day.

It had been three days since Ki had stepped in that bear trap—three long days of traveling slowly through the snow without food. Ki could hardly walk, let alone find a familiar or hunt, yet he was still insistent on searching every day. I was met with harsh words any time I offered him aid or tried to convince him to rest. I knew he was in a wretched state, so I tried not to take his words to heart, but the more he said them, the more truth they held.

Lying beside Ki in my underwear, I waited for him to fall asleep. I'd already decided that I would help him at any cost—even if it meant he would hate me. We couldn't continue on in the way we were. I couldn't stand any more cruel words from

Ki, and the pit of hunger in my stomach was eating away at me. Something had to be done.

My heart raced when the sound of Ki's shallow breathing reached me. He was finally asleep. Moving slowly so as not to make a sound, I grabbed the hunting knife I'd hidden under my bedroll and sat up. I dug the knife into my shoulder in the exact place where Ki had left a mark. A gasp of pain escaped my lips, and I froze, holding my breath. When Ki didn't stir from his sleep, I let it out. A warm trickle of blood dripped down my chest. I needed to be quick.

Without hesitation, I turned to Ki. He lay on his back with his arms at his sides. I gently put a leg over him, straddling his body with my shoulder just above his lips. Blood dripped from me, and I hoped it would land in his mouth.

"Bloody hell!" Ki said as his dark tendrils filled the tent. He grabbed my arms and pushed me away. My blood had dripped across his eyes. Their red glow drew me into them as he sat up. I watched speechlessly as my blood ran down his face and over his lips.

Ki licked his lips. His eyes fell to my open wound, and his face changed. I was greeted with a mouth full of razor-sharp teeth. My plan had worked. I knew he was about to feed on me as he had before, but a sudden sense of terror came over me. Ki's eyes held a hatred within them that made my body tremble.

Before I could even think to scream, Ki's teeth pierced into me. The intense pain of it lasted but a moment before the pleasure took over. I'd intended to resist it, but there was no use. Ki held me close to him, and I took pleasure in his embrace. My arms wrapped around him as I brushed my face against his.

A crackling sound filled the tent as black flames engulfed Ki's horns. Bits of horn showered down from Ki's head, causing me to close my eyes. When I reopened them, the flames were gone and Ki's horns were whole again. They were darker and larger than they'd been before, but they were whole. The sight of them thrilled me. I somehow knew that Ki would no longer be in pain, and that made me happy.

Ki pulled back, and I stared into his eyes. Blood trickled from his lips, enthralling me. I wanted nothing more than to taste his lips—the lips that had just been on my skin, that had just brought me so much pleasure. I leaned into him.

"Don't," Ki whispered as my lips neared his. He pushed me away and looked down at the ground.

"Are you still not well?" I asked as I sat on his lap, exposed. The presence of his dark magic amplified as the tendrils in the air multiplied.

Ki pushed me from his lap and began to dress. I pulled my suit on but couldn't stop myself from staring at him. He moved with such speed and grace. His injuries no longer affected him. He must have healed completely.

When Ki ducked out of the tent, I followed him. It was instinctual. I wanted to be near him, to make sure he really was all right. After days of worrying about his health, I couldn't help but be concerned.

"Don't follow me," Ki growled, and his wings burst from his back. He didn't even flinch when they fully extended. I gasped as he leapt into the sky, quickly disappearing into the cover of darkness. The only remainder of his presence was a lone black feather that fell from the sky and landed in the snow at my feet.

My fears were confirmed. He was definitely mad at me. Part of me wondered if he would even return, but I quickly pushed the thought from my mind. He'd left all his supplies here, so he had to come back eventually. I'd known that my actions might make him hate me. It was a consequence I'd been ready to accept in order to restore his health. I just couldn't understand why he hadn't let me give him blood in the first place when it clearly healed him.

Plucking the feather from the snow, I returned to the tent. Its dark beauty captivated me, so I tucked it into my boot for safekeeping—a reminder of the glorious wings I rarely got to see. Would Ki be mad if he discovered I'd kept it?

As much as I needed sleep, my mind wouldn't stop racing.

It was impossible to get Ki out of my head. I couldn't believe I'd tried to kiss him and that he'd rejected me. It wasn't the first time I'd made a move on him, but things had been much different that first night. I'd been scared then, but I wasn't anymore. Ki and I had been together for weeks; we'd bonded. Didn't he like me?

A few short days ago I'd been sure that Ki liked me. He'd confided in me and asked me to stay with him, plus he'd told me all those stories about his childhood. I doubted he'd told anyone else about his life at the palace aside from the people who lived there with him. He was always so guarded all the time. Weren't we past that, though? Didn't he trust me?

Tears fell from my eyes as I lay awake with worry. I only wanted to help him, but in doing so I may have driven him further from me. My chest tightened as I thought about it. *What if he never forgives me for my actions? What if he never trusts me again? What if he never comes back at all?* My fears consumed me as I cried, but eventually I drifted off to sleep.

ılı ֍ ≀≀ ≈

"Tyler." My name echoed through the darkness.

"I'm here," I replied as I fumbled around. Ki's voice called to me, but I couldn't see. Reaching out blindly, my hands grazed across his bare chest. He pulled me into him.

"I found you," he whispered in my ear. "I'll always find you, no matter how dark it is." I relaxed into Ki's warm embrace. His strong arms held me tight, and I took pleasure in it. Every touch burned like fire on my skin.

A light appeared in the distance. It called to me, but I didn't want to leave. I wanted to stay in Ki's arms forever. Why would I want to leave? The light called to me again. It beckoned me to walk toward it. I didn't move.

"Will you go?" Ki asked as he looked in the direction of the light.

"No. I won't leave you," I replied.

"You'll stay in the darkness with me?" he asked. I wanted to reply—to say yes, always—but I couldn't speak. My words came out as silence. Smoke filled the distance between us and the light. I choked on it. I couldn't breathe. Was I being punished?

I startled awake. The smell of smoked meat surrounded me. My stomach growled, and I jumped up. Forgetting my dream, I pulled on my clothes and exited the tent.

The cold morning air chilled me, but I could see the fire only a few meters away. Ki sat beside it with his wings still unfurled. He'd hung a small carcass across the flames, and it smelled delicious. As I walked up, Ki remained focused on stoking the flames. He didn't even look at me when I sat down beside him.

"I see you had a successful hunt," I said cheerfully. If I acted normally then maybe we could just move past what had happened in the night.

"It's for you," he said without so much as a glance toward me. "You haven't eaten in days." There was concern in his words, but his tone was cold.

"Thank you," I replied with a smile, but he still didn't look at me. Things definitely weren't normal, and I just wanted him to look at me. "I'm surprised you still have your wings out." Ki's grip tightened on the stick in his hand, and his dark aura roused. His family ring reflected the morning light, and I thought it odd. He'd never had his ring on with his wings out before.

"Eat up quickly; we have a lot of lost time to make up for," Ki replied through gritted teeth. I could tell he wanted to say more, but he held himself back. He was guarded once again, and it was my fault. Guilt consumed me. I knew I'd broken his trust, but it'd been to save him. It was an impossible choice that I'd had to make. When Ki stood to leave, I finally spoke up.

"I'm sorry," I said, and he stopped in his tracks. His back was to me, and he didn't turn around, but I knew he'd heard me. "I'm sorry I went against your wishes. I just couldn't bear to see you in pain any longer."

Ki growled as he finally turned to face me. His eyes glowed

red, and dark flames of magic flowed around him like an inferno. I could even see a sharpness in his teeth. If we'd been strangers his appearance would have horrified me.

"You know nothing of my suffering!" he spat. His words were laced with hate and disgust. "If you try what you did last night ever again, it'll be the last thing you ever do!" Ki's eyes pierced through me as the sting of his words sank in. He hated me.

Tears filled my eyes as I realized my fear had come true, but Ki just turned away. He'd turned his focus to our equipment. I sat back down by the fire, and the tears trickled down my face.

Ki packed up camp while I ate the meat he'd cooked for me. I tried to tell myself that I could fix it, that in time Ki would open back up to me. He wouldn't have gone out of his way to provide me with food if he didn't care. I clung to my hope, as I always did. No matter how bad things appeared, there was always a silver lining, a light in the dark. We were both alive, and I was grateful for that.

CHAPTER 25

KI

Things with Tyler had gotten out of hand. I knew I was slowly losing control. My words pushed Tyler away, but I couldn't let her get close to me. The dark magic within me was rapidly increasing in strength, and I could hardly keep it at bay. My ring was useless. I couldn't hide my wings anymore and could hardly stand to be around Tyler. Her blood called to me. Every fiber of my being wanted to taste her, to drink every last drop of her blood. I had to keep my distance.

We continued our journey through the woods. The wolf familiar we'd spotted was nowhere to be found. It was as if all traces of it had vanished in the night, and we'd yet to spot another one. The odds of us finding familiars grew slimmer with every passing day, but the bracelets reminded us of our mission every morning. We would remain in the cold depths of the wilderness until all ten familiars were found and captured. How many days had it been? The days—or was it weeks?—had jumbled together in my poor health.

"Your ankle has healed, hasn't it?" I asked Tyler without a look in her direction. She trailed behind me by several paces as we trudged through the snow.

"I believe it has, though your magic does still linger there, so I'm not completely sure," she replied. I didn't have to look to know there was a smile upon her face. Her cheerfulness was clear in the tone of her words.

"But it has been long enough for it to heal on its own, yes?" I asked.

"Yes," she replied, picking up her pace to close the distance between us. She walked by my side.

I ignored her nearness to the best of my ability. She'd confirmed that we'd been in the woods for many weeks. Time had gotten away from me. At full strength I should have been able to find a familiar in hours, yet I hadn't. I'd let Tyler distract me from the mission. She only slowed me down, but I couldn't rid myself of her.

"Why did you push me away?" Tyler asked as we walked side by side. Her hand nearly grazed mine.

I said nothing, but I couldn't stop my eyes from glancing in her direction. She looked up at me with her bright blue eyes. They stood out in the sea of white that surrounded us. By the time I realized what I'd done, it was too late. Tyler smiled as she caught me staring at her. I'd tried so hard to ignore her, but her question had caught me off guard.

"You said you were lonely, and you asked me to stay with you even after the teams were dissolved. So why? Why did you push me away last night?" Tyler asked. Her words felt like a knife as she shined a light on my own weakness. I'd shared secrets with her, things I didn't want anyone else to know.

Realization hit me like a slap in the face. I'd let my guard down around her. This girl had gotten way too close to me. In fact, she knew me so well that she knew when I'd be the most vulnerable. She'd even used that knowledge against me to force me to drink her blood. It had been so easy for her to manipulate me. Her words were manipulative even in this moment. She wanted me to explain myself to her, and a sense of obligation plagued me.

"I do not answer to you," I replied through gritted teeth. She would not win. I refused to let her have any control over me. I would not be weak.

"I didn't mean to upset you. I'm just confused," she replied.

Upset? Had she really just laid claim to having control over my emotions? No, that wouldn't do. Emotions were the greatest weakness, and I was not weak. My dark tendrils radiated from me in waves. Tyler stepped back.

A twig snapped underfoot, and Tyler was swallowed by a net before I could react. It lifted her into the trees in one swift motion. Her startled scream pierced through my rage, and I returned to my senses. Laughter filled the air, and I turned toward the sound. Jade stood a few meters away. She leaned against a tree with a dagger in her hand.

"Well, this isn't what I was hoping to catch." She laughed. The sound was grating.

"Jade?" Tyler said as she swung back and forth in the net. "Let me down."

"Now why would I do that?" she said with another laugh. "Surely you can get yourself down, or at the very least I'll get amusement in watching you try."

"Just cut her down," I snapped. Jade's eyes fell on me, and her laughter dissipated.

"You two are still traveling together?" Jade replied.

"That's none of your concern," I said. "Cut her down."

Jade cut the rope, and Tyler fell to the snow. I helped her out of the tangled mess of a net.

"You have wings now?" Jade asked. Her eyes looked at us in judgment. I was sure she'd come to many incorrect conclusions about me and Tyler.

"Is that an accusation?" I asked.

"Of course not, Your Highness. Merely an observation," she replied.

"You can be on your way then," I said. She hesitated in her departure.

"You know you two don't belong together, right? You're the Darkblood Prince, and she's just a weak, useless human," Jade said. I didn't bother to acknowledge her statement as she faded into the trees.

Tyler was quiet after that. I knew that meant she was upset. Whether it was about me or Jade, I wasn't sure. Asking would mean that I cared, and I couldn't do that. A pit grew in my stomach as I held back my own words. I had to be strong.

We trudged through the snow in silence. The sound of snow crunching underfoot was our only company. It was too quiet. There were no sounds of life at all. No birds, no bugs, nothing. I'd hoped it was just a result of the frigid weather, but we weren't that lucky.

The earth trembled and shook around us. Snow fell from the trees and rolled off the land as it shifted. Tyler stumbled backward as the land below our feet began to slope. I grabbed her by the hand, pulling her into me.

"Is this an earthquake?" she asked.

"Stick close to me," I replied as I began to run away from the moving slope. Tyler stuck to my side, but we weren't fast enough.

A shock wave rippled through the ground, toppling us both. The snow made for a soft landing, but Tyler was no longer at my side. She'd been tossed several yards away from me. There was a look of horror on her face as she caught a glimpse of the huge earth golem that stood behind us. My chest tightened.

The golem was nearly five stories high and two stories wide, one of the largest I'd ever come across. Made of solid earth, it was a force to be reckoned with. A normal magic user wouldn't stand a chance against it, but I had a direct link to the moonstone. Dark magic flowed through my blood.

In a flash, the golem's rocklike fist swung down at me. Rolling to my feet, I dodged it just as it smashed into the ground. My dark magic amplified as I allowed my rage to fuel me. All of my frustrations from the past few days surfaced to my mind: How I'd been injured and unable to provide for Tyler during my weakened state. How Tyler had betrayed me by feeding herself to me when I was vulnerable.

The pain of her betrayal was the worst. I focused my anger, making the golem its target.

Forcing my dark energy to flow through the earth, I aimed for the golem. My veins tingled with electricity as my magic came up under the golem's feet, grabbing ahold of them. With its feet fixed in place, the golem let out a roar.

The golem swung at me again, but I was out of its reach. My dark magic climbed up its legs, threatening to consume the golem completely, but Tyler's unmistakable scream made my heart skip a beat. She was tangled in a cluster of vines that extended from the golem's other hand. The vines tightened around her, pulling her toward it. If the golem got ahold of her, she would be crushed in an instant.

My magic stopped its climb as I leapt through the air. Dark magic solidified around my wings, turning them into blades as I came upon the vines. I slashed through them with ease. The golem screeched as the vines fell lifelessly around Tyler's feet. She was freed.

"Ki!" Tyler screamed as the golem's fist crashed into me. I'd barely gotten within its reach.

It happened so fast that the pain didn't register. The sound of bones cracking filled my ears as I was pushed forward. Falling into Tyler, I shoved her away from the golem's reach. When my hands touched down on the ground, the pain consumed me.

"Run!" I yelled at Tyler. She scrambled to her feet and looked back at me in hesitation. "I said move, damn it!" This time she listened.

The golem tried to swing at me again, but I was out of reach. My magic still held it in place, but I knew it wouldn't last much longer. I had to get away from it before it got free. Pain kept me from moving, and if I didn't move it would surely kill me. Out of options, I knew I had to cast a forbidden spell.

"On this day, sun or rain, make this body feel no pain. On this day, sun or rain, make this body feel no pain. On this day, sun or rain, make this body feel no pain!" I chanted the words in the ancient language.

Magic surged within me, and the weight lifted. The pain was gone, but I knew the injuries were still there. I'd studied the forbidden spell book for years after finding it hidden in the moonstone's cavern. It had been used on soldiers in ancient times so they would fight with vigor until they dropped dead. They would die unaware of the spell cast upon them, and the whole time they fought the poor bastards never even knew they'd been injured.

Pain free, I got to my feet and ran after Tyler. I caught up to her easily, and we took refuge in the cover of the forest. The golem wouldn't destroy trees to get to us. It was one with the land and fought to preserve it. In fact, it had probably only attacked us because we'd walked across its back.

Once we were sure the golem would no longer follow us, we found a place to rest. Tyler wasted no time in fussing over me. She dropped her equipment to the ground and was at my side.

"Are you all right?" she asked.

"Do I look like I'm all right?" I said as I let my equipment slide to the ground. The pale look on Tyler's face meant I'd probably made my injuries worse in doing so, but I couldn't feel it. She stared at me speechlessly, which only pissed me off. "Are you going to reset my bones or not?"

My words broke through her trance, and she immediately pulled out the med kit. I knew it was likely that the majority of the bones on the right side of my body were broken. In fact, I'd probably made the injuries to my wing worse when I'd run through the dense forest. It had likely caught on branches without me feeling it.

Realization that I could be at death's door and not even

know it hit me. I stood motionless while Tyler searched the area for sticks to use to splint my bones. Broken bones wouldn't kill me, but if they'd broken through the skin I could bleed out. What if one had penetrated a vital organ? I wouldn't know. The spell would last for twenty-four hours. I'd be long dead by then if I'd sustained a severe internal injury.

"How bad is it?" I asked as Tyler reappeared from the woods. "I need to know the extent of the damage." If I knew what was wrong, I could use my dark magic to slow the progression.

"I think your wing is shattered, and until I get it back into a somewhat normal direction I won't be able to tell how bad the rest is," she replied. The grimness in her voice was hard to miss.

"Just talk me through the extent of the damage as you go," I replied.

"Okay, but it's going to hurt," she said. "I'll try to be quick."

"Don't worry about speed, just do it right," I replied. Since I couldn't feel anything anyway, her speed didn't matter. All I could hope was that she didn't accidentally make things worse. I would much rather she take her time.

Tyler went to work on my wing. I heard the occasional snap and hoped it was the sound of bones moving back into their proper place. Tyler would pause momentarily every time but would quickly move on to the next when I gave her no response indicative of pain. After the fifth loud snap, she stopped.

"I'm so sorry," Tyler sobbed. "This is all my fault. You may never be able to fly again because I couldn't defend myself." I carefully looked over my shoulder toward her. My wing appeared to be in a normal folded position.

"What are you talking about? From here it looks like you got everything back in place," I said.

"I did, but you didn't feel any of it." She continued to cry.

"You forget my magic can regenerate my body," I replied, hoping to stop her tears. The sound of her crying twisted my stomach. "Are there any big gashes back there? Did any of the bones penetrate my torso?"

"If your magic can restore your wings then you must feed

from me at once," she said without answering either of my questions.

"That's not going to happen," I replied sternly as she stepped in front of me. "My magic can fuse my bones in place until they heal, provided they're back in their correct place. I don't need your blood."

"Don't be so stubborn. My blood healed you completely in only a few moments last time. Why would you make yourself suffer when I can help you now?"

"I don't need your help. I can take care of myself." As I spoke, my dark aura radiated from me. Feeding on her again in such a short time could kill her.

"Even if you don't need my help, it's okay to accept it," she replied.

"No!" I spat. "I will not be weak." I had to be cruel, otherwise she would never give up.

"Please just let me help you. It's my fault you got hurt in the first place, so really I'm just paying back the favor," she pleaded.

"You're right, it is your fault!" I yelled. "If I hadn't been partnered with you I never would have gotten hurt. You've been nothing but a liability to me since the Reckoning began. I would have been much better off on my own!" Tyler flinched as I lashed out at her. She stepped away from me, and I could see the tears in her eyes again.

"If I'm such a liability, then why did you ask me to stay with you?"

"Because I felt sorry for you. A weak human like you wouldn't stand a chance out here on your own," I lied.

"You're wrong. I can take care of myself just fine," she said. "In fact, since I'm such a liability to you, then why don't I just leave!"

"Go ahead and leave. That's the best idea you've ever had!"

"Fine then," she replied. The tears had disappeared from her face; only anger remained. Tyler grabbed her gear and headed off into the woods.

I shouldn't have let her go, but I wasn't about to let her risk her life. She would be safer in the woods than with me. If I fed off of her again I might not have been able to stop, and I wouldn't be able to live with myself if I caused her death. I'd be fine on my own. I would make camp until the spell wore off, and then I'd find a familiar. The sooner they were all found, the sooner Tyler would be sent back to the safety of her home.

CHAPTER 26

HARRISON

The days passed in a blissful blur. I was safe with Daniel by my side. Even though the Reckoning loomed over us, I made sure to appreciate the time we had together. There was no guarantee that I'd get to spend my time with him once we returned home. As much as I wanted to be with him, I doubted the king would let me out of my engagement.

Daniel slept soundly beside me. We'd spent the night passionately making love to each other for as long as our bodies would allow. I'd memorized every inch of his body—from the hardened muscles and battle scars to the sparkle in his eyes when he was truly happy. It was a sparkle I'd become accustomed to and would never forget.

I lay awake, taking in the cool morning air. It was as though I'd found my own slice of heaven in this cave. Part of me hoped to never leave it. If I could've spent the rest of my days alone with Daniel in the wild I would have. Unfortunately, fate had other plans.

The vibration of our metal bracelets woke Daniel from

his slumber. His arms left my body as he sat up. The bracelet alerted us that there were only five familiars left, and I couldn't ignore the look of concern on Daniel's face. Neither of us had found a familiar yet, and our chances grew slimmer every day.

"We should head out early today," Daniel said as he stretched.

"It'll be all right if we don't find familiars," I said as I gathered my clothes from the cave floor.

"Speak for yourself. I have a reputation to uphold," Daniel teased as he nudged me. I was in the middle of putting on my boots, and his nudge nearly knocked me over.

"I'm pretty sure my reputation as the son of the grand duke is equally as important as yours."

"Maybe, but your father is much less likely to rip you in two for the dishonor." Daniel laughed.

"Let's just call it a tie." I finished packing my bag and threw it over my back.

"Fine, but you get to lead the way today since my navigation has gotten us nowhere." Daniel motioned toward the cave entrance. His pack was secured firmly to his back. Daniel had always been a better tracker, but I led the way.

We walked quietly through the woods as the sun began to rise in the distance. The forest was silent, as it had been for days. It was like time had stopped. We continued to trudge through the snow, but it was as though life had been frozen in place, as if we'd just repeated the same day over and over again, never moving forward.

A wet ball of snow slammed into the side of my face, pulling me out of my own head. Laughter filled the air around me as I spun, dazed from the impact. Daniel had managed to leave my side unnoticed and was hidden somewhere within the snow-covered trees.

I scanned the area in an attempt to find him. Even though he was large, Daniel was oddly good at hiding. It wasn't until another snowball hit the back of my head that I finally spotted him. He continued to laugh at me, and the sound filled the cool air.

"Daniel!" Another snowball was lobbed at my head, but I ducked out of the way. Scooping up a handful of snow, I returned fire. Things quickly escalated into an all-out war. Snowballs were being thrown about wildly.

Daniel continued his assault, drawing closer with each attack. He never wavered in his forward siege. His pink eyes glimmered in the sunlight, an irresistible distraction. In a flash he leapt onto me. Our bodies collapsed into the snow. I was surrounded by a cold wetness, but I didn't care.

Our bodies were pressed close together as Daniel pinned me down in the snow. I looked up at him with a smile in surrender. His breath was warm against my skin, and the sensation made me quiver. My body was warm from the battle and became increasingly hot from Daniel's touch. His eyes stared into mine as he leaned down for a kiss.

When his lips met mine, a burning desire rushed through me. I wrapped my arms around him, pulling him into me. He moaned into my mouth, and a sense of pride filled me. I was the cause of his pleasure. Rolling over in the snow, Daniel pulled me on top of him. His hard cock pressed against mine through our fitted suits. Straddling him, I got to enjoy the view of his chiseled body. He pulled me close with another kiss, but when his hands grabbed hold of my zipper, I had to stop him.

"We still need to find familiars," I said, reminding him of our mission.

"I'll make it quick," he replied with a teasing smile. It was impossible to say no to him when he looked at me with a glimmer in his eyes.

"Not here," I said. We were completely exposed and would've been easy to spot if anyone happened by.

In one fluid motion, Daniel stood and scooped me up in his arms at the same time. I squeezed my legs tightly around his waist as he walked. My heart raced as he carried me through the snow. With my head resting on his shoulder, I clung tightly to him, relaxing into his strong embrace.

We found cover behind a dense cluster of trees and bushes. Daniel's grip on me was strong yet gentle. He held me against a tree as he kissed me wildly. The desire in his eyes made me putty in his hands. He would've taken me right there if we hadn't been interrupted.

The sounds of a whimpering animal reached me long before I spotted the wolf. It was massive in size, larger than any normal wolf I'd ever seen. There was no doubt in my mind that I'd spotted a familiar, and he was injured.

"Wait, Daniel." I nodded in the direction of the injured wolf. Daniel sighed loudly as he released me from his embrace.

"Go get him," Daniel said in a soft voice, shaking his head. I doubted he'd expected us to find a familiar amidst our moment of passion. He watched me closely as I went after the wolf.

The wolf's whimpers grew louder as I neared the beast. Its eyes bored into mine as I got close, but it didn't run. Blood speckled the snow around the wolf's front paws. He was definitely injured, but I had to get closer to find out how bad it was.

When I got within a few feet of the wolf, he stood. He inched away from me as I closed the distance. His right leg was tucked under, and he favored his left as he crawled backward.

"It's all right now. I won't hurt you." I spoke to the wolf in a soft voice. He stared at me but didn't growl. I had to take a deep breath before I got within biting distance.

The wolf lay back down as I continued to whisper words of encouragement to him. I was finally within touching distance when I spotted the broken piece of arrow sticking out of the wolf's leg. Someone had shot him.

I glanced around quickly, worried the perpetrator might be near. The only other sign of life in the area was Daniel. He kept his distance so as not to frighten the wolf, but his eyes were focused on us. I caught his eyes with mine, and he gave me a reassuring smile.

My focus returned to the wolf, and I slowly extended my hands toward him. He sniffed me for a bit before he relaxed his head onto the ground. I gently shifted the injured leg so that I could get a grip on the arrow. It had broken off inside the wolf's leg, and only a tiny piece stuck out.

"I'm sorry, buddy, but this is going to hurt," I said to the wolf, letting out a sigh. There was a high probability that the wolf would attack me after I took the arrow out. That didn't matter, though. I had to help him; he didn't deserve to suffer.

On the count of three, I pulled the arrow from the wolf's leg. He cried out in pain, but to my surprise he didn't snap at me. His eyes glowed yellow as they stared into mine.

Thank you. The wolf's thoughts invaded my mind. My body was engulfed by the yellow glow that radiated from him. I was completely consumed before I even knew it was happening.

"What's going on?" I spoke mostly to myself in confusion, but the wolf chose to reply.

Your courage and kindness makes you worthy of my company. If you have the strength and will to withstand my power, I will be your companion.

The air in my lungs escaped me as the wolf's magic pressed in on me. If I didn't act, the pressure would crush my organs and break my bones. I pushed back against the wolf's magical aura with my own. Dark magic flowed through me. It strengthened my body and alleviated the pain caused by the wolf's suffocating force.

A tornado of energy rushed around us wildly. The swirl of yellow and black energy was impossible to see through. I stood at the still center of the storm with the wolf and began chanting the binding spell. His eyes softened; he was submitting to my will.

As I placed my hand on the wolf's head to bind us, a loud blast came from behind and footsteps approached. I was unsure of what it was until the binding spell was complete. The wolf turned into pure energy and was absorbed into my hand. It left a yellow paw print in the center of my palm and a swirl that wrapped around my wrist. The wolf's true name revealed itself to me: Razor.

I'd done it; I'd captured a familiar.

My excitement disappeared instantly when warm blood tricked down the side of my face. Reality hit me like a brick wall as I sank to the ground. A heavy weight had fallen into me. It was Daniel. Blood dripped from his chest, pooling on the ground. I pulled him into my arms.

"Look out," Daniel wheezed as a dozen sharp rocks came at us. I deflected them with a wall of dark magic, but the pained look on Daniel's face shook me to my core. My mind couldn't make sense of what my eyes were seeing.

Across the way stood Emm. Her magic swirled around her as she focused her energy. She'd been the one to attack us? How could she have possibly caught Daniel off guard? None of it made sense. She was my friend. Wasn't she? Daniel's eyes fluttered closed.

"No! Stay with me, damn it," I cried out as I pulled him close. He was badly hurt. Blood flowed steadily from his chest. I covered the wound with my hands, applying as much pressure as I could, but blood still managed to seep out. There was so much blood. I radiated dark magic through my hands to try to stop the bleeding. It was a futile attempt that barely slowed the blood flow.

"There's no use, Harrison," Daniel said slowly. His words were strained.

"You can't die," I cried. "I won't let you." Tears streamed down my face, dripping onto my hands.

"Just remember that I love you," he said as he placed his hand on my neck. "I'll always be with you."

"I love you too, but you have to fight," I sobbed. "I can't survive without you." Daniel pulled me in for a kiss, but it wasn't like any of the other kisses we'd shared. It was powerful. Thc world around me disappeared as time stalled. A whirlwind of magic consumed me, pulling my insides in every direction.

The magic swelled as if it would blow my body into a million pieces, but then it settled.

Daniel's lips parted as he slipped back onto the ground, lifeless. I stared in shock at the body of my love. He looked so different without his glowing pink eyes. It was impossible to understand that I would never see their familiar glow again, or feel the warmth of his skin, the gentleness of his touch. Daniel was gone, but it didn't seem real. He couldn't be gone; he'd been there for me my entire life. Our time together had barely just started. It wasn't real.

"Stay down!" Wynter's voice called through the trees. A bolt of earth shattered against a wall of ice right in front of me. Wynter had stopped Emm's attack. Why was he here?

I slumped onto Daniel's body. My head found its way to his shoulder as I lay on the ground beside him. We were surrounded by bloodied snow, and the warmth left his body quickly. A battle raged on around me, but I paid it no mind. Nothing mattered without Daniel, nothing.

Despair and a sudden surge of emotions hit me. My head throbbed as fear, anger, confusion, and love consumed me. There were too many thoughts that weren't my own. I could hardly bear it. Drowning in a sea of emotion, I clung to the strongest one and pushed it to the front of my mind: hopelessness. It took hold of me, and the voices disappeared. There was no hope of happiness, not without Daniel. My chest ached, but my mind was completely numb. I let my eyes close, giving myself to the darkness. The last wish I had was to never wake again.

ılı ֍ ⟆ ≈

It was so warm when I woke that I thought I was in Daniel's arms. A fire burned brightly a few feet from where I lay, and next to it sat Wynter and his iguana. Snow was piled up in a circle, surrounding us. It gave us shelter from the cold winter night's wind. Reality hit me like a brick wall. Daniel was gone.

"Where is he?" I demanded as I spun in a circle. Daniel's body was nowhere to be seen.

"Don't worry. The Royal Guard collected him not too long ago. I was assured they'd return him home. He will have a warrior's funeral once the Reckoning is over," Wynter replied.

"He can't be dead. I'm sure he'll recover. He'll recover," I rambled. Wynter closed the distance between us.

"Just breathe," Wynter said as he rubbed his hand on my back. I hadn't even realized I'd been gasping for air. "Things will get better with time. I promise."

"Don't!" I shoved Wynter away. "We're not friends, and I don't need false promises from you." Anger consumed me. He tried to comfort me like Daniel had many times over, but the weight didn't lift. I wanted to hit him, to make him feel the pain I felt. He knew nothing. Things weren't going to get better—not without Daniel.

"I know you're hurting, and it wouldn't be right to leave you on your own right now, especially not with that aeni girl out there. She seemed quite intent on killing you," Wynter said as he composed himself.

"She killed him," I replied, still unable to believe it. Emm had been so nice when she was my partner. I knew she didn't like tlalocs, but how could she kill Daniel like that? She'd even attacked me. Why would she do that? Did she really only care about winning? How had I not seen it?

"I'm truly sorry for your loss," Wynter said, interrupting my internal spiral.

"It's all my fault."

"Don't say that."

"Daniel would've killed her on the spot if it weren't for me. I was naive to trust her just because we were partners. It's my fault." Tears started to fall from my eyes again. They melted holes in the snow as they fell to the ground, so I covered my face.

"Please don't blame yourself. The aeni girl is the one

responsible," Wynter replied. His arms wrapped around me, and my tears fell away. He was right—Emm was the one I should blame. She'd killed Daniel. Rage filled me as I thought of revenge. Emm deserved to die a miserable death for what she'd done. I would pay her back tenfold for the pain she'd caused me.

"She will pay," I mumbled through Wynter's embrace. He had me wrapped in a tight hug. The strength of his grip surprised me since he was only slightly larger than I was. My thoughts drifted to the night we'd spent together. I couldn't recall him holding me in such a way before.

"Why are you here?" I questioned aggressively. My skin tingled as the dark magic within me swirled. Wynter released me from his embrace and sat back on his heels.

"I didn't think you'd be all right on your own," he replied.

"Why should you care? You hardly know me."

"So what? We both have familiars, and being alone out here sucks."

"I know what you really want," I said, leaning toward him. My dark magic escaped me, and dark tendrils swarmed around us.

Wynter's face grew timid as I stared into his gray eyes. He turned his gaze away, and a rush of anger and lust took hold of me. I pushed him onto his back and crawled on top of him.

"This isn't a good idea. You're not yourself right now," Wynter complained as I unzipped his suit. His hands gripped at mine, but I pushed them away.

"Shut up and get naked," I commanded.

Wynter's resistance fled as he stared at me with his gray eyes. I could see the sadness within them, and it made me angry. My life and emotions were out of control. I didn't want to think about any of it—I couldn't think about any of it—so I focused all of my energy on Wynter. I would find solace in controlling him.

CHAPTER 27

TYLER

My shoulder tingled with electricity as I drew on the dark magic within me. Ki was infuriatingly stubborn and hardheaded. I hated that he refused to let me help him, but my anger made the magic within me stronger. He'd said I was a liability, that he felt sorry for me, but I could take care of myself. I would find a familiar on my own—*without* his help.

Creating a ball of dark energy in my hand, I scanned the area for movement. I'd been hunting a small rabbit for two days straight, and I couldn't miss my chance to kill it. After all, I'd wandered through the woods alone for four days before spotting any signs of life. If I lost the rabbit I would surely starve.

The rabbit hopped out from behind a bush only a few meters away from me. It was within range. I'd practiced my magic every day, even more so since leaving Ki, and I knew exactly how far I could throw it. Launching the ball of dark energy at the rabbit, I sucked in a breath. When the ball hit its target, I exhaled in relief.

My control over the dark magic wasn't perfect. It singed off all the rabbit's fur, and electric fizzles of magic clung to the carcass, but at least it was dead. In my half-delirious state, I almost ate the rabbit raw. The time it took to skin and cook the small carcass was torturous.

I hadn't realized how hard it would be to find food on my own. Ki had made things easy for me. He'd kept me fed, and I should've been more grateful for that. I hoped to see him again, to take comfort in his presence and not let the cold empty forest be my last companion.

As the days passed, I found myself wondering how Ki was doing. Had his wounds recovered? Had he already found a familiar? Could he have possibly died from his injuries? Was it possible that the Reckoning was already over and that I was lost in the woods forever? My mind imagined the worst possible scenarios, but I held on to hope—the hope that I'd make it through, that I'd survive to see Ki and my family again, that I could help save the people of my village from starvation . . . if it wasn't already too late for them.

I kept myself sustained by eating the inner bark of the pine trees, but it was hardly enough to keep me alive. Most of my waking hours were spent in a daze. It was hard to think about Ki or the competition when my stomach was empty. But worse than the constant hunger were the unbearably cold nights.

Even when I was curled up in my bedroll and blanket with both of my suits on and snow built up around the tent, I was freezing. Ki's body heat had warmed the tent more than I'd realized. I desperately missed his warmth. It made me regret leaving him, even though he'd been cruel. He probably hadn't even meant what he'd said. It'd been his pain talking; it had made him lash out at me.

I began to sleep during the day with the warmth of the morning sun and forced myself to walk during the night, fearful I'd freeze to death if I stopped moving. The darkness also gave me better cover. I could stay hidden from the view of competitors while searching for a familiar. If only the harsh winter winds and the relentless snow would let up.

Fifteen days had passed since I'd left Ki. I'd been alone the entire time and was slowly losing my mind. Hallucinating from hunger and loneliness, I often had conversations with myself. There'd been no signs of life since the one rabbit I'd caught. If I didn't find an animal soon I would surely starve to death. My body ached, and the dark magic within me had weakened, but I forced myself to continue on.

Wandering through the woods under the dark night's sky, it appeared to me. A white rabbit with bright blue eyes stood only a couple meters ahead of me. I stared him straight in the eyes in disbelief; it was a familiar. At first I thought it was a hallucination, but then it cocked its head as if it was analyzing me.

"Easy there, little guy. I won't hurt you." I spoke softly in hopes I could coax it with my words. His ear rotated as if he was listening, so I extended my hand to him. I attempted to inch toward him, but he took off.

Chasing after him, I forced my legs to move as fast as they could. I was weak from the lack of food and sleep, but I continued to push myself. We ran through the trees for a while, but I couldn't keep up with him. Weakness and exhaustion consumed my body, and I fell to the ground. Lying facedown in the snow, I knew I'd failed. I was at death's door. The pittance of energy I'd had left was gone. Allowing my eyes to close, I welcomed the sweet darkness, glad I would soon suffer no more.

My eyes fluttered open when a cold nose tickled my cheek. I was face-to-face with the familiar. It was my only chance, so I called upon what remained of the dark magic that lingered in my body. Chanting the binding spell Ki had made me memorize, I channeled dark energy. It flowed from me into the rabbit, and he gave no resistance.

Your heart is pure, and your love for others is strong. It is an honor to aid you. The rabbit's thoughts filled my mind. He cuddled up next to me as the binding took effect, and his true name came to me: Rafe. My joy of completing the spell was short-lived as

I realized my body was unmoving. I knew I was dying. A tear fell from my eye and froze on my cheek. I'd never see my parents again. My mind willed my body to move, but it refused. The darkness took hold of me, and I knew it was the end.

A woman's soft voice sang a lullaby that was familiar to me. Her voice was heavenly and warmed my soul. A bright light consumed me and everything around me. I was weightless, as if I'd floated out to sea. Love and happiness filled me. They were part of me; they made me whole. I'd forgotten what it was I'd been worried about.

The tiniest shadow caught my attention. It stood out against the bright light in complete contrast. I was drawn to it, reminded that there was something more important than the light. Even though I'd forgotten what that was, I knew the shadow was important. I wanted to get to it, to remember what I'd forgotten, but I couldn't move.

A deep voice was barely audible. "The prophecy will come to pass. She cannot stay here."

Confusion was followed by whispering voices, familiar but undistinguishable. It all rushed back in: my family, the farm, the Reckoning. I remembered the cold snow and the lifelessness of my own body on the verge of death.

"Kil" I screamed as his memory shook me awake. The cold air burned my lungs as I took in a breath.

"She's awake." I recognized the familiar voice; it was Midnight. My eyes darted around. I was in a tent, and blankets were folded around me tightly. They were layered on so thick that I struggled to move.

The flap to the tent opened, and Moonshine crawled in. Their eyes met mine with a smile.

"Good, you're alive. We weren't sure you'd survive the night," Moonshine said as they drew near me.

"What happened?" I asked as they started to unbundle me. Midnight's head poked through the tent's flap.

"You tell us. We thought you were dead when we found you," Midnight said in a less than interested tone.

"I thought I was dead," I replied.

"You probably would be if it wasn't for your little friend here." Moonshine pointed at the ball of fur snuggled up at my side. Rafe. I hadn't even noticed him since he blended in with all the other furs that surrounded me.

"Yeah, that obnoxious little fella kept clucking at us until we followed him," Midnight said.

"I owe you both many thanks," I replied as I was finally freed from the pile of blankets. Rafe hopped around excitedly as I tried to get up. Moonshine helped me crawl out of the tent, and Midnight offered me a hand to help me to my feet.

"You owe us nothing," Midnight said as I steadied myself, my body still weak.

"I'd be dead right now if it weren't for you two," I replied.

"And Midnight would be dead if it weren't for you," Moonshine cut in.

"Exactly," Midnight said. "A life for a life. We have repaid our debt to you."

"Now enough of all this serious talk. Let's enjoy a meal together," Moonshine said with a big smile. They motioned to a pile of fish cooking over a small fire. My jaw dropped. How had they found so many fish? Where had they all come from?

The grumble in my stomach told me not to question it, so I joined them by the fire. Its warmth was welcome, and it soothed my aching bones. I hardly waited for the fish to cool off before I tore into it.

"How long has it been since you've had food?" Midnight asked. Their orange eyes bored into me as they stared.

"Don't be rude," Moonshine replied. They gave Midnight a sideways glare.

"It's okay," I replied. "I'm sure it's quite obvious that I nearly starved to death. I haven't had much luck finding food on my own."

"That's not surprising considering how weak your magic is," Midnight replied. They turned their gaze to the fire.

"Wait, are you saying you used magic to get these fish?" I asked, confused. Magic wasn't needed to catch food, was it? I'd never actually watched Ki catch dinner—I'd just assumed he did it the same way the hunters in my village did.

"Of course we did." Moonshine smiled. "Haven't you noticed the lack of life in the woods? This whole forest is enchanted."

"I thought the winter was keeping the animals away," I replied. Midnight's burst of laughter made me jump from my seat.

"You must have spent your life living under a rock or something. Everyone knows the king uses magic to make the Reckoning more challenging. His magic keeps the animals away. If you hope to find anything you have to use your own magic to get the animals to come to you."

Midnight's words hit hard. I knew I was unaware of a lot of things due to being raised in a tiny village on the outskirts of the country, but their laughter made me feel foolish. Had Ki been using magic all those times without me knowing? Maybe I was a fool. I'd insisted I could take care of myself, but I hadn't even known I needed magic to do so.

"Don't make fun of her." Moonshine gave Midnight a slap on the back of their head. "It's not her fault she didn't have access to the same education we did." The truth in their words was painful. I was more naive than I'd thought. There was so much I still needed to learn.

"It's fine. I didn't know about the magic," I replied.

"You must be extremely lucky then. It's a miracle you've survived this long," Midnight said.

"I wasn't lucky. I was with the Darkblood Prince for most of the time, except for the past fifteen days, and as you can see, those didn't go so well for me," I replied.

"Where I sit, I see a girl who has caught herself a familiar and continues to fight for life." Moonshine smiled at me. Rafe crawled into my lap. It was as if he knew we were talking about him.

"I guess you're right," I replied. "What about you two, though? Have you found familiars?"

"No, and we don't intend to," Midnight said. Their words were more serious.

"We have no interest in serving the king," Moonshine added. "Catching a familiar would require us to continue in this life-threatening competition that we wanted no part of to begin with."

"Don't forget that being in the final ten pretty much guarantees you a position in the palace, which makes you property of the king for life," Midnight said.

"We want to return home to our family," Moonshine said. "We've just been waiting for the familiars to be found so we can be sent home."

"I'm going to be sent to the palace?" I asked as my reality set in. "But I must return home to my family. Our farm might not survive the winter without me."

"Sorry, but the final ten have never returned home in the history of the Reckoning," Midnight said. Tears filled my eyes as I thought of my home. Would I never see it again?

"Hey, but you spent a lot of time with the prince. Maybe he'd make an exception for you." Moonshine tried to cheer me up, but I knew better. Ki would never make an exception for me, not if it meant admitting he cared.

Tears dripped down my cheeks. I would never get the chance to return home. Even if I managed to gain the magic needed to save my village and my family, I wouldn't be allowed to. It was truly a cruel fate.

Don't lose hope. Rafe looked up at me from my lap. His eyes stared into mine. It was as if his thoughts were my own. Hope had gotten me through in my darkest times, and it could get me through the Reckoning as well. I would simply have to find a way to defy the odds.

"You can stay with us until the third phase begins if you

want," Midnight said. The smile on Moonshine's face was hard to miss. Their kindness gave me hope. Maybe the world could still be saved.

"Thank you," I replied, continuing to eat the fish they'd offered me. It warmed my belly after the many cold days of hunger. If I could spend a week with them I was sure I'd be back to fighting strength for the next phase of the Reckoning. Maybe if I performed well enough the king would at least allow me to visit my village before taking a permanent residence in the palace. I could even prove to Ki that I wasn't a liability.

CHAPTER 28

KI

I didn't remember much after Tyler left. As soon as the forbidden spell wore off, I lost consciousness from the intense pain. My awareness faded in and out for days—or maybe weeks—while my body tried to repair itself. I was lucky that no one stumbled upon me during those days since I'd been alone and vulnerable to any attack. My weakness would remain a secret.

Once my awareness returned to me, I found a concealed spot within the forest to build a snow-encased shelter. I knew my injuries were bad, and I needed a safe place to rest. Every inch of my body ached with pain. Its constant reminder kept me from thinking about anything else, at least for a little while.

Days passed, but my wounds hardly healed. Worse than my injuries were the thoughts that nagged at me. I'd been stupid to let Tyler leave. She could've healed me, but I'd been too proud to let her do it. Instead I was alone and gravely injured in a forest void of life.

I wasn't sure when it happened, but I'd developed a magical

link to Tyler. Once she left, I realized I could sense her essence. It was a comfort to know that she was alive, but it was also a reminder that she was gone. I began to wonder why I was even mad at her. In fact, more often than not I was fully aware of the fact that I missed her.

Tyler was just an ordinary human girl that I'd been forced to partner with, so why couldn't I get her off my mind? Her face appeared in all my dreams, and in the morning light I swore I could feel the warmth of her smile. I was obsessed, but why? Solitude had always brought me peace in the past, but now it was nearly unbearable. Weakness had taken hold of me.

I ventured from safety when I could no longer stand the loneliness. I wanted to find Tyler, and I still needed to find a familiar. It was odd that the former was more important, but I couldn't think too hard about it. I was on a mission, and I'd grown tired of the Reckoning.

A strong aura of magic drew me to it. I approached what appeared to be a fight. There was a tornado of black and yellow magic in the midst of a field, and I crouched behind a tree to take a look. As I focused on the field, the scene became clear to me.

I took in the sight of Harrison as he clung to Daniel. His eyes filled with tears, and his hands were covered in blood. Daniel was hurt. I couldn't make sense of what I saw or heard. Harrison and Daniel both confessed feelings of love for each other. When had that happened? Had they always been in love but kept it secret from me? I thought I had to have misheard, but then Daniel kissed Harrison, and an overwhelming amount of energy flowed into Harrison.

Harrison's cries made my chest tighten. It was clear that Daniel was dead, but it didn't make sense. Daniel was a warrior—how could he possibly die? The other competitors couldn't match him in strength or strategy. How had this happened? It couldn't be real.

Frozen in place, there was nothing I could do but watch in horror. The small aeni girl who had been partnered with

Harrison attacked them, but another competitor came to Harrison's rescue. I did nothing. My mind went blank as I slid to the ground, watching in silence.

Harrison clung to Daniel's body and ignored the fight. He looked as though he'd given up all will to fight as he lay on the ground. Harrison grew so still that for a moment I thought he might have also been injured, but his aura was strong. He wasn't injured, yet he appeared broken. How long had there been something between him and Daniel besides friendship? Their love must have been true in order for Harrison to give up. He didn't even bother to protect himself. It was as if he wanted to die.

I sat by the tree for a long time, watching Harrison as he lay motionless. Tears fell from my eyes as I realized my friend was gone. Daniel was dead. I'd never get to hear another one of his outrageous tales of brutality that made me feel better about my own violent tendencies. He would never be my field marshal and stand by my side as I ascended to the throne.

Even though Harrison was alive, I knew I'd lost him too. His light was gone. When I looked at him, he was no longer a beacon of innocence and positivity. His lighthearted spirit had been crushed by Daniel's death. I couldn't even begin to imagine his pain. Part of me wanted to go to him, but I had no idea what to say or how to act. What do you say to someone who's so distressed? If Tyler had been the one to die before me, I wouldn't have known what to do.

My stomach sickened just to think of it. I had to stop myself from imaging Tyler's death. It was too much to handle. My chest tightened as I sucked in a deep breath. The thought of her death terrified me to my core. It was then that I realized how important she had become. I was an idiot for not realizing it sooner. After all, on more than one occasion I'd risked my own life to save her. I was still bloody injured from the last time I'd done so.

The impossible had happened. I'd fallen in love with Tyler, a frail human girl. She didn't make me weak; she *was* my weakness. Everything finally made sense: why I was so obsessed and constantly thinking about her, why I'd refused to feed on her, why I'd pushed her away. It was love, a feeling so foreign to me that I'd rejected it. I had no idea what to do about it either.

My thoughts turned to worry as Tyler's essence disappeared. It had grown weaker with every day that passed, but now it was completely gone. I convinced myself it was just the magic, that over time whatever magical link we'd developed had just faded. It was because we'd been apart for so long. She was fine, she had to be. I couldn't allow myself to think otherwise, but I was increasingly concerned about her safety.

If Daniel could die in the Reckoning, then anyone could. The thought sobered me. I'd sustained the worst injury of my life and wasn't healing like normal, so even my own life was at risk, yet the only thing that remained on my mind was Tyler.

With Tyler's essence gone, I knew I had to find her. I had no idea where she was, so I decided to circle back to where we'd separated in hopes I could follow her trail. After walking straight through the night into the following morning, my hope was crushed. Layers of snow had covered any traces she might have left. *There's no hope. You're too weak to find her. There's nothing you can do. You're worthless, a mockery of the Darkblood line.*

For a moment I was consumed by hopelessness, but then I realized the thoughts weren't my own. I scanned the trees for what I already suspected I'd find—an imp. He hung upside down from a tree branch nearby. With his wings wrapped around his body he almost looked like a common bat, but I knew better. Imps were notorious for the mischief they caused. They were the hardest familiars to find and control. The little tricksters usually weren't worth the effort.

"Come down from there," I called out. His eyes glowed red as they peeked out from behind his wings.

"Now why would I do that?" he replied as he flipped to an upright position on the branch. He was barely a foot tall, but he stood proud. His wings extended to either side of him. In the light I could see the dark red tint of his skin.

"I have more power than you could ever dream of," I replied. Imps had very little magic of their own, and as dark creatures they were drawn to dark magic. He wouldn't be my first choice for a familiar, but I needed one, and Tyler would have a better chance of survival if the Reckoning ended faster.

"From where I'm standing, you look like you can hardly walk, so you can't be that powerful." The imp grinned. His wicked smile made my blood boil. Dark magic flowed through me, and dark crackling tendrils filled the air.

"You should mind your words when you're in the presence of royalty," I replied. The dark tendrils around me thickened as I stepped toward him.

"And what exactly do you have to offer me?" he asked.

"Do you not seek power?"

"Yes, but borrowed power only lasts so long. I'm looking for something a little more permanent," he said.

"If you bind with me you will have access to all the dark magic you could ever dream of."

"So you will gift me your magic?" the imp asked. His wording was specific. If I hadn't known any better I might have agreed and fallen into his trap, but I wouldn't be fooled so easily.

"No. I will gift you access to dark magic. You will develop your own magic in time," I replied. "Take it or leave it."

"I suppose that'll do," he replied, jumping from the branch. He came at me with incredible speed, but even in my weakened state he was no match. I snatched him out of the air as he barreled toward me.

Dark magic flowed from my hand into the imp. His entire body was consumed as I linked him to me, revealing his true name: Loki. Whether he liked it or not, he was stuck with me. My magic absorbed into his body as I released him. He wouldn't be able to venture too far from me since I'd added a proximity spell into our binding. Imps couldn't be absorbed like most familiars, and I didn't want to chance him running off.

Before I could give Loki any instructions, the metal bracelet vibrated on my wrist. "All familiars have now been found.

Everyone who remains standing shall report to the labyrinth. Please follow the glowing orb."

An orb floated out in front of me. It glowed black with dark energy and headed off in one direction. I stared at it as it floated toward the trees. It hovered in the air, waiting for me to follow it. I glanced at Loki while he flew circles around me, awaiting my instructions.

"Follow it," I said. Loki grinned and took off after the orb. I trailed behind. *Tyler will be there, she has to be. All of the competitors will be there.* I just needed to be strong for a little bit longer.

By the time we neared the labyrinth, my thoughts had run wild with panic. I was eager to see Tyler, to know that she was okay, to tell her how I felt before it was too late. She deserved to know the truth, and I needed to apologize. My words had been so cruel the last time we'd spoken.

Large tents and a crowd of servants were clustered in the open field surrounding the labyrinth. Voices filled the area. Competitors were shuffled around by commands from dark priestesses. There were only a couple of them, but their commands were easily heard.

"Competitors without familiars go to silver tents; competitors with familiars go to the black tents," a dark priestess commanded as she looked my way. I didn't care about her directions—I had to find Tyler.

It was hard to see through the swarm of servants flooding the tents. Some carried clothes, others towels, and even more carried kits that appeared to be filled with paint. They made it nearly impossible to get a look inside the tents.

I tried to peek into the silver tents, but the servants kept me out. They pushed me toward the black tents because of my familiar. I wasn't about to give up, though.

"Find Tyler," I commanded my familiar. "She's the only human female competitor." He nodded in reply and flew into the tents. I watched as he went in and out of the silver tents, and my worry increased. When he returned, I was consumed with anxiety.

"I see no human in the silver tents. Shall I check the black?" he said. Panic set in. Had she not made it to the labyrinth?

"This way, Your Highness." A servant took hold of my arm, dragging me toward the black tents. I followed her without a fight as I plotted how I would escape.

When we entered the tent, I scanned the area for competitors. It was unlikely that Tyler had caught a familiar, but I needed to be sure she wasn't here before I made an attempt to escape.

I recognized the aeni who'd been with Harrison when Daniel died. He sat in a chair while a maid painted black war stripes onto his face. I was surprised to see that he no longer wore a suit, but was instead in a black leather warrior's kilt.

In another chair sat Harrison with an identical kilt on. His tears were gone, replaced by a vengeful rage. The darkness of his aura was impossible to miss. He was so lost in his own thoughts that he didn't even notice me.

Her bright blond hair caught my eye first. It stood out against the black background of the tent. Tyler was alive. Relief washed over me as I drew closer to her. One maid combed her hair while another maid painted her face. I was so glad that I'd found her; I could finally tell her everything.

Strong arms grabbed hold of me. "This way, Your Highness," a soldier said as he pulled me away from Tyler.

"Unhand me," I said as another soldier came to help him.

"Competitors aren't allowed to interfere with the preparations," the soldier said.

"I'm not. I just need to talk to her," I replied. The soldiers pulled me to the other black tent and pushed me toward a chair.

"You'll have to wait until after. Right now you need to sit down and let these ladies do their job." Several servants walked up to me. One held a rag while the other carried a bowl of warm water.

"We're just going to clean you up," the maid with the rag

said. I didn't resist. It would have looked bad if I'd caused a scene. And if I drew that kind of attention to myself, my father would prevent me from ever seeing Tyler again, so I behaved. I had to live up to the expectations of a prince, even if I hated it.

CHAPTER 29

TYLER

Servants helped me onto a square stone platform. Its smooth surface was cool on my bare feet. I was dressed in a leather skirt and crop top that were identical to the traditional garb warriors wore in the ancient times. My long sword was fastened to my back with a leather strap that was made to match my clothes. The entire outfit was black—a tribute to the Darkblood King, no doubt. A black line had been painted across my face, right across my eyes. It probably looked ridiculous on my pale skin.

Ahead of me was an entrance to the labyrinth. At its core lay the sacred chalice of life and death. Retrieving it was the purpose of our final challenge. Nine other competitors stood around the circumference of the labyrinth on platforms identical to mine. We all had our own entrances and individual paths to take to get to the center of the maze. The king had been vague about the obstacles we would face along our routes.

I was concerned about the amount of skin my clothes left exposed, but at least the air around me was warm. It was heated by magic for the challenge and was a welcome relief from the constant cold I'd become accustomed to.

The servants departed once they were satisfied with my appearance, and the recording orbs took their place. It was the last phase of the Reckoning, and every minute was to be captured. I didn't like being put on display in an unnecessarily tight outfit. Ki probably hated the outfits just as much as I did. He didn't like being shown off either.

This is no time to be thinking about Ki. I shook myself mentally. My focus needed to be on the labyrinth, especially since I had a bad feeling about what waited for me within.

This challenge would likely be the hardest of them all, and I had to survive it on my own. No one would be there to aid me. I had my familiar, but Rafe was absorbed within me. He'd used his healing magic to restore me from near death and needed to recover, which meant he would be no help for the coming challenges. The thought clenched my stomach. I was eager for the Reckoning to be over, but one thought still plagued me. *I might not survive.*

Canon fire echoed all around me. The loud boom made me flinch. I was a few strides behind the others when I dropped from my platform, but I quickly caught up to them as I ran toward the labyrinth. A recording orb fluttered about me, watching my every move as I cleared the short distance.

Passing through the entrance without pause, I came upon a dry dirt path. Little dust clouds kicked up around me as I ran. I scanned the plain walls for traps as I made my way down the winding path. It wasn't much of a maze, with only one direction to go. My narrow path opened into a wide corridor, and I stopped in my tracks.

Before me lay a pit filled with glass shards. As I approached the pit I was horrified to find swarms of scarabs among the glass. Their skittering movements reflected off the clear glass as if the shards had been made from mirrors.

Across the center of the pit lay a narrow wooden beam, barely wide enough for a foot to stand on. The obstacle was simple enough: get to the other side without stepping into the glass shards. One little cut from the glass and the scarabs would consume me. They were bloodthirsty fiends and easily agitated. Any sudden movements would surely send them into a rage.

Inspecting the beam, I placed one foot on it to see how sturdy it was. The beam appeared to be solid since my weight wasn't enough to bow it. I inched slowly across, placing one foot in front of the other, my arms stretched out at my sides for balance. Halfway across the beam, a scarab crawled over my bare foot. I froze in place as the hairs on my legs stood on end and a shiver ran down my spine. I gently shook the fiend from my foot, and it fell to the pit floor below. I continued across the beam, but the scarabs below began to stir, upset by their fallen comrade.

My pace quickened as the scarabs' agitation increased. When I reached the other side of the pit, the scarabs had begun to crawl over its edge. They were headed straight for me. I took off in a full sprint down the narrow path before me. The scarabs followed closely at my heels. They were fast, too fast. One caught up to me and bit my foot. I cried out as a burning pain shot up my leg, but I kept running.

Another bite made me stumble as I entered a wide corridor. A fiery pit was before me. Its flames burned hot and blasted me with a wall of heat as I drew near. Stones floated in a line that spread across the pit. They were the only way to get to the other side.

With no time to think, I jumped onto the first platform as another scarab bit me. The fire kept the fiends at bay as some of them tumbled into the pit. Others skittered around madly, looking for a way to follow the blood trail.

I breathed heavily while I peeled scarabs from my legs, tossing them into the flames. The heat from the pit had me wet with sweat by the time I caught my breath. As I rested for a moment, I analyzed the floating stone path before me.

At first they all appeared to be the same, but then I noticed the tiny symbols carved into each stone. The six types of magic were represented, but only one type was on each stone. They were mixed together in no particular order. All the emblems had their own paths to the other side. The stone I stood on had a gold sun emblem etched into it, a symbol of the old Light Nation. But how could that be?

The Darkblood King had banned all light magic objects. He expressly hated all things that represented the old Light Nation. But then again, the labyrinth had been created by the original Darkblood and Lightblood families for the first Reckoning. I guessed there were things that even the king himself couldn't change.

Given the stone I stood on was sturdy, I figured the sun emblems marked the right path. I used my sword to check the stability of the nearby stones, just in case. As predicted, the stones all fell away after contact with my blade, except for the one with the sun symbol. I stepped to the stone, and it held solidly in place. Continuing onward, I stepped from stone to stone until I reached the other side of the pit. A sigh of relief escaped my lips as I leapt to the solid ground. Sweat poured down my back, and my energy drained quickly, but I had to keep moving.

Walking down the endless narrow path, I steadied my breathing. The sun beat down on me, burning my exposed skin. I quickened my pace as the temperature continued to rise. Every step was harder than the last. Sweat poured down my back, and I struggled to breathe in the hot air. I stumbled when my vision became spotty, nearly fainting. I thought it was over for me, but then darkness blanketed the path ahead.

The stone walls of the maze had a stone roof over them. I welcomed the coolness the shade provided, but the path before me was pitch-black. There was no way to tell what lay beyond. Tracing my hands along the walls on either side, I walked slowly into the darkness. I cautiously dragged my feet across the floor as I stepped, trying to find any obstacles that may be hidden.

My eyes slowly adjusted to the darkness, but I still couldn't see anything. There was no difference between having my eyes open or closed. The light of day was gone, no longer visible behind me, and the temperature dropped steadily.

I had no idea how long I continued on in that manner, or how far I'd traveled. My hair stood on end as I feared what I might stumble upon in the darkness. I jolted at the echoes of my own movements, the darkness slowly wearing down my sanity.

A sudden dip of my foot startled me. The path's floor was nonexistent in the forward direction. Another pit? I bent down slowly to touch the ground at my feet and confirmed my suspicions. The smell of water greeted me as I found the pit's edge. Reaching down lower with my hand, I was greeted by the cold touch of wetness. Water?

My body was dehydrated from the heat, but I didn't dare take a drink. There was no way to know if it was poisoned, and that was a risk I wouldn't take. I'd learned my lesson after that run-in with the sea witch. If Ki hadn't been there to save me—*no, don't think about Ki. Focus.*

I knelt at the pit's edge and stared into the water. Everything was black, except for a tiny glimmering spec in the distance. Was it the bottom of the pit? I wouldn't be sure unless I got into the water. But what awaited me in the dark depths?

The room was silent around me. I had to keep moving. I had to get through the labyrinth, so I gathered my courage and slowly lowered myself into the water. It was cold against my sunburnt skin, a welcome relief.

Before I had time to overthink it, I took a deep breath and dove down toward the glimmer. As I drew near the floor of the pit I realized the glimmer was another emblem. It was a silver crescent moon, a symbol of the Dark Nation. From the bottom I could see a trail of glowing symbols that stretched along the pit's floor. There were handles on either side of each emblem. A burning tightness filled my lungs, so I swam for the surface. I gasped for air as I broke through the water.

A loud clink echoed in the room, and the water began to push into me. It suddenly had a strong current that shoved me back against the pit's edge. There was no way I'd be able to swim against the current. I'd have to dive back down and use the handles to pull myself across. The realization made my stomach tighten. I had no idea how long the pit stretched, or how long I could hold my breath. Heck, I might not have even had the strength to pull myself against the current, but I had to. I had to make it through and prove that I wasn't weak, that I wasn't a liability.

With a deep breath, I quieted my nerves. I took another deep breath and dove to the bottom of the pit as fast as I could. The first set of handles came into sight, and I grabbed ahold of them. My muscles clenched as I pulled myself along the bottom of the pit. The water current beat hard into me, threatening to pull me from the handles, but I kept my grip.

Moving as quickly as my weakening muscles would allow, I followed the glowing emblems that lit my way. My lungs burned, desperate for air. I nearly gave up, but then a set of vertical handles appeared before me. Bubbles escaped my lips, and my vision began to blur, but I pulled myself upward. I had to get to the surface. It was just a little bit farther.

The current was even harder to overcome as I ascended. I broke through the surface of the water and hoisted myself over the pit's edge. Water escaped my lips as I coughed. Rolling onto my side, I gasped for air.

Once my breathing became steady, I reveled in the success of the moment; I'd made it. But my reprieve was short-lived. The challenge wasn't over yet. In fact, I feared it had just begun.

My hands found the walls again, and I continued my journey down the pitch-black path. I quickened my pace when light appeared at the end of the tunnel. The sun was warm on my skin when I stepped out of the darkness. I was glad to be able to see my surroundings again, even if the dirt path was all I could see.

Before me was yet another wide corridor with a deep pit. It was much deeper than any of the other pits I'd come across, and the path on the other side was at a much higher elevation than where I stood. If only I had Ki's ability to fly—not that he'd ever be able to fly again, thanks to me. *No. Stop. You can't let yourself get distracted.*

Dread crept over me as I stepped up to the pit. A bell chimed, and a strong wind shot up in a cylindrical shape before me. Its whirlwind was like a mini tornado. An identical tornado shot up farther out in the pit right as the first one died out, then another one even farther. Each new tornado rose higher than the last until the final one reached the platform on the other side.

It was silent for a moment, then the bell chimed again and the whole process repeated. I gaped at the winds in horror as I realized they were my only way to get to the path above. Would the winds be strong enough to carry my weight up? There was only one way to find out, and it would be a long fall down if I was wrong.

I considered giving up then and there. No one would blame me for wanting to live. I'd gotten into the final ten, which would provide me with rewards and bring honor to my family. But then I thought of the people in my village and how the land was slowly dying and unable to produce enough food to feed everyone. I would need considerable amounts of power to restore the lands and prevent starvation. Winning was my only option.

With my fighting spirit restored, I readied for the next bell. When it chimed, I took off in a run and leapt into the first tornado. It lifted me up and shot me into the air. My forward momentum pushed me into the next tornado as it formed. I was lifted higher and higher with each tornado. The path on the other side was in reach. I was going to make it.

The last tornado shot me up, but not as high as I needed to go. I reached out to grab for the path's edge as I nearly fell into the pit. My hands caught hold of the cliff, and I hoisted myself up. I crumbled onto solid ground, shaken. My heart raced in my chest. That was too close for comfort.

Sucking in a deep breath, I pulled myself together. The

path ahead was the only way I could go; there would be no way to turn back. I walked down the winding path, and a roof appeared overhead again. This time there were torches on the walls that lit the path, and I was grateful. I'd had enough darkness for one day.

A round room opened up before me. The walls were lined with torches and adorned with symbols for the six types of magic. It reminded me of the viewing station back home. In the middle of the room was a podium decorated with light and dark magic symbols. I investigated the podium, discovering a recessed handprint in the middle of it. I placed my hand over the print, and the room came to life.

The emblems around me glowed bright, and an image appeared on the wall in front of me. It was the same as the images created by the viewing station, except the Darkblood King was not the person I saw. Before me was a goddess with long blond hair tied back in braids. Her white dress was that of a warrior. She radiated light as she spoke.

"Congratulations for making it this far. There are two paths before you." She gestured to the two stone walls on either side of her. One was white, and the other was black. "Your answer to the following riddle will open one of the paths, so listen closely." She paused briefly before she continued. I couldn't take my eyes off of her; she was more beautiful than anyone I'd ever seen.

"It fuels your quest for power, something that is felt within. You can sense it in the world around you and see it reflected in the people you meet. It gives you strength but may also be your greatest weakness. What is it?"

Her words echoed in my mind. The answer was obvious, but there was no way it was that simple. I searched my mind for possible answers but could only think of one.

"Love," I said aloud. The room was painfully silent. Had I been wrong? What would happen if I got the riddle wrong? I was nearly in a full panic, but then the room began to vibrate and the white wall lifted, revealing a bright path beyond it.

"Venture forth, young warrior," the goddess said, "and may the light lead you to victory."

Her words weighed heavily on me. It was as though she was warning me, but of what I was unsure. I walked to the open path, leaving the goddess and her words behind. The path was brightly lit, but there were no torches in sight. It was as though the walls radiated the bright white light. My eyes could hardly stand the brightness, but I continued on. Without a backward glance, I walked into the light.

CHAPTER 30

HARRISON

I walked down the pitch-black corridor, comfortable in the darkness. The yellow glow of my familiar's magic radiated from the symbol on my hand. It was the only light that lit my path, and I could hardly see two feet in front of me. Not that it mattered, though; I preferred the darkness, the emptiness. It reflected the way I felt inside. I was numb to all emotion except for one: vengeance.

My vengeance was the only reason I continued to partake in the challenges. The Reckoning no longer mattered. I'd only entered the labyrinth to find Emm, to make sure she died by my hands.

A chuckle escaped my lips as I thought about how easy it'd been to get through the maze. The riddle had been child's play. Even an infant would know that the answer was hate. Hate was powerful and all-consuming. It fueled me on my quest for vengeance.

The sunlight blinded me as I neared the end of the corridor. My eyes adjusted as I stepped into the light, and I found myself in a large open field. Eager to find Emm, I scanned the area, but no one was around.

I was sure I was in the center of the labyrinth. Trees were scattered about the grassy plains in front of me. A hill was in the distance, and at its apex was the sacred chalice. It floated in the air, untouched. Light reflected off of it, making it glimmer. If I grabbed it, I could win the Reckoning, but then I might lose my chance for vengeance.

Emm was obsessed with winning, though. She'd even killed Daniel because of it. There was no way she wouldn't go for the chalice as soon as she spotted it. It would be the perfect bait.

Using the trees for cover, I closed the distance between myself and the chalice. As I circled the hill, I looked for competitors. No one was around. I'd reached the center first. How was it that Ki hadn't beat me? He hadn't been stationed by me at the labyrinth's entrance, but I knew he was still in the competition. The obstacles should have been easy for him, but then again, vengeance was a strong motivator.

When I caught a glimpse of light pink skin, my veins burned. Rage and dark energy radiated from me in the largest crackling aura of tendrils I'd ever created. I knew it was Emm as she ran across the field in a blur of pink. Her eyes were focused solely on the chalice, as predicted.

With perfect concentration and precision, I forced dark magic to lift from the ground at her feet. She tripped and landed face-first on the ground, but she bounced back quickly. By the time I cleared the short distance between us, she was already on her feet and prepared to fight.

"Oh, it's you. You better stay out of my way, or you'll end up like your friend," she said as she looked my way.

"Now why would I do that?" I laughed. The tendrils of energy around me increased and solidified. As the sphere of black and pink energy shielded me, the color faded from Emm's face.

"You're more powerful than you let on, but you're not the only one." Emm smirked. Her arms lifted from her sides, and the earth shifted. A cloud of dust blocked my view of her.

When the dust settled, Emm was surrounded by small balls of earth. At least, I thought they were made of the earth. She threw one at me, and it grazed my side. Blood trickled down my torso, but I ignored it. It was hardly a flesh wound. I was more concerned with what the ball was made of: metal.

"How?" I mumbled as it sank in. Emm wasn't just an ordinary earth magic user; she had an affinity for metal. But that couldn't be possible. Metal manipulators were rare, and there hadn't been a record of one being born in decades. How had she hidden herself from the Dark Nation, from the king? He would see her as a great asset.

"I could ask you the same. All those days we spent together, I never witnessed you harness the amount of power you have now," she replied, whipping several balls at me at once.

I threw my hands out, and my dark magic erupted. The sphere around me hardened, catching the metal balls. They lost their momentum and fell to the ground at my feet. I picked one up, and it fit easily in the palm of my hand.

"This is how you killed him, isn't it?" My voice cracked as the rage overtook me. Daniel was dead because of her.

Dark energy flowed into the metal ball in my hand, and I launched it back at her. Emm's hands came up to stop it. She thought her magic would be strong enough to control it, but it wasn't. The ball hit her squarely in the palm, and she shrieked as the bones in her hand shattered.

"How does it feel to be on the receiving end of your own attack?" I asked as I grabbed another ball from the ground and began to fill it with dark magic.

"You won't defeat me that easily," Emm spat. Her injured hand was held close to her chest, but her free arm lifted. The metal balls swirled in a circle in front of her until they became a blur of silver.

"Good, I don't want it to be easy. I want you to suffer as I have suffered!"

I threw the ball at her. This time she used her other balls to block it. It ricocheted away from her, but I pulled on the dark magic within it.

I didn't care that my forearms split open and blood dripped down my hands from the force of the magic. It would do as I commanded. The ball switched directions and pulled back toward Emm. She was completely unaware of it until it crashed into the back of her leg.

Her scream brought a smile to my face as she fell to the ground. In fact, I was so enthralled with my battle that I hadn't noticed when another competitor came upon us. The other competitors didn't matter to me anyway.

"Harrison! What are you doing?" Wynter's voice dissolved my smile.

"Getting my revenge. Stay back," I replied.

"You don't have to do this," Wynter pleaded as he drew closer to me.

"I said stay back!" A wave of energy pulsed from within me, and it knocked Wynter back. "This doesn't concern you."

I picked up another metal ball. The cluster of balls protecting Emm had fallen away when I hit her. She was weak.

"If you kill her, you'll lose yourself. Daniel wouldn't want that for you," Wynter said. I turned to look him in the eye. This time he hadn't stepped any closer to me, which was his only saving grace.

"You can't possibly know what Daniel would have wanted! He's dead, and she's the one who took him from me! I have nothing left to lose!"

Emm had gathered her strength while I was distracted with Wynter. Before I knew it she'd thrown another ball at me, but it bounced off the sphere shield surrounding me and headed straight for Wynter. I reacted instantly. Dark magic encased Wynter, and the ball fell to the ground in front of him. His eyes widened as he looked at me.

"No, Harrison. Don't do it," he pleaded, unable to move. My dark magic both protected him and held him in place. Warm blood dripped from my fingertips.

My hands shook with anger, and my vision turned dark. The world around me was void of color. All I could see were shades of gray. I looked back at Emm, and her eyes widened with horror. Fear could be tasted in the air around her, and I liked the taste of it. My power fed off of it.

"The chalice is yours. Just take it," Emm said through trembling lips.

"I don't want the damn chalice!" I shouted as my dark magic lifted the balls of metal from the ground. They pulled together in a line. A gray energy swirled beside Emm, and a rat appeared. It was her familiar.

"Wait, please. I'm sorry about your friend. It wasn't personal. The Reckoning made me do it. You know what it's like being alone and half-starved in the woods for days. It would make you do anything, right?" Emm said as she tried to hobble away.

Her words meant nothing to me. I wouldn't have cared if she'd begged for her life. She'd sealed her own fate the moment she killed Daniel. The rat charged at me, but I paid it no mind. With all the fury inside of me, I whipped the metal balls at Emm. She couldn't get out of the way, and the balls ripped straight through her.

"Father, forgive me," she gasped as blood spurted from her lips. Her torso hit the ground before her legs followed. I'd cut her clean in half. She was dead; I had my vengeance. With Emm dead, her bond with her familiar broke, and the rat took off.

My legs gave out, and I fell to my knees. I buried my bloodied hands in the grass beneath me. The darkness faded away, and color returned to my vision. My magic must have faded too because Wynter was freed. The earth moved around me in circles.

"Harrison!" Ki's voice echoed in my mind as hands grabbed me. "What did you do?"

"Help me stop the bleeding," Wynter said, but it wasn't to me. I turned my head and was greeted with a pair of glowing red eyes. Ki was actually here. He had a firm grip on my forearm.

"You're going to be all right," Ki said as Wynter's hands replaced his grip. Both of my arms were wrapped tightly with strips of cloth torn from Wynter's kilt.

"Can you keep him safe?" Ki said.

"I'll protect him with my life, Your Highness," Wynter replied.

"Good. I have someone else I need to find." Ki disappeared just as suddenly as he had appeared. I was numb to everything around me.

"Can you stand?" Wynter asked. Was he talking to me? He pulled on one of my arms. "Come on, get up."

Wynter pulled me to my feet, and I fell into him. He spoke in a foreign language as the world spun circles around me. It was impossible to stand on my own, but Wynter had a tight hold on me. He was stronger than he looked.

My focus returned, and the first thing I noticed were the recording orbs. There were several that fluttered around the area. I stared at one as it scanned what remained of Emm. Blood pooled around her severed body, staining the grass red. The sight of it made my stomach turn. I had to get away from it.

Wynter released me when I pulled away from him. I stumbled away from the body and the hill that held the chalice. After a few yards, I couldn't hold it in any longer. I doubled over and retched in the field. As I wiped my mouth with my arm, I noticed fresh blood dripping from my nose.

My mind flooded with emotions that I knew weren't my own. The other competitors were near; I could sense them, all of them. It was as though my head would explode. The throbbing pain was too much to bear, and I fell to the ground. I deserved the pain and wished it would end my misery.

CHAPTER 31

KI

Leaving Harrison in the hands of the aeni, I ran the perimeter of the field in an attempt to find Tyler. The other competitors had begun to emerge from the maze. I was sure one of them would grab the chalice. The Reckoning would be over soon, and I wouldn't be the winner. My father would be pissed, but I had to make sure Tyler was all right, especially after witnessing what Harrison had done to Emm.

Tyler stepped out of a passage, and I collided with her. We tumbled to the ground, and she landed on top of me. Heat rushed to my face as her hands pressed into my bare chest.

"I'm sorry," she said as she pushed herself off of me. Her face was flushed.

"I'm the one who owes you the apology," I said as I made my way to my feet. Tyler's eyes were fixated on me. She looked me up and down, and I was suddenly aware of how little my kilt covered.

"Are you hurt?" Tyler asked as she noticed the blood on my hands.

"No, it's not mine," I replied, trying to wipe my hands off on my kilt.

"The chalice?" Tyler pointed toward the hill. "You were headed away from it?" Her eyes stared into mine, and a lump caught in my throat. I took in a deep breath.

"I was looking for you," I replied.

Her eyes widened, and her cheeks turned red. The color was impossible to miss, even with the black war paint that started at her eyes and dripped down her face. Her hair was wet and covered in dirt, but she still looked beautiful.

"You were?" she asked.

Before I could reply, chaos erupted around us. The earth shook violently as it split open. I nearly lost my footing from the force of the vibrations. A boulder fell from the maze's wall, almost landing on Tyler. If she'd been a step to the left, it would have crushed her. My heart raced as I pulled her into me.

"Are you all right?" I asked. She nodded in response, but my nerves didn't calm. I scanned the area around us for potential threats.

I watched as competitors headed for the chalice. Lux and Lexa were together and ran straight for it with a pair of hyenas at their sides. The cracking earth did little to change their course. Their desire to win must have fueled them. All they could see was the prize, and they paid little mind to the destruction around them.

As they got to the bottom of the hill, it began to erupt. A volcano of golems poured from it as well as from the cracks in the earth. They ranged in size from massive to tiny. Most were human size or smaller, but the few that were ten times my size worried me. Their eyes glowed white, and they ground their teeth in agitation.

"Stay behind me," I said as I stood between Tyler and the creatures. I was her shield; nothing would touch her.

My dark magic expanded around us as the golems drew near. None of them were deterred by the magnitude of the crackling energy. They had no fear nor survival instincts. They weren't normal golems.

One of the tiny golems rushed me with incredible speed. I threw a ball of dark magic at it, and it exploded into dust. As it dissipated, I pulled my sword from my back, wanting to conserve my dark energy for maintaining the shield around Tyler. It was time to get my hands dirty.

I stepped forward as the golems rushed me. My sword had a wide reach, so I cut through a crowd of them with ease. The tiny golems were easy to kill, but larger ones emerged from nearby cracks in the earth. For every one that I destroyed, two more appeared in its place. We were greatly outnumbered, and I couldn't fight them off forever.

"I see you found the girl before I did, but it appears you're in quite the pickle," Loki said as he flew to my side.

"I don't have time for your tricks right now," I said as my sword crashed into a larger golem. It was lodged in the golem's stone abdomen. I struggled to pull it free.

The earth shook violently as the hill in the distance grew taller. Competitors and golems alike tumbled down the sides of it as it continued to become steeper. The chalice remained at its apex, continuing to get farther away by the second. We needed to seek shelter. There was no way we would be able to fight through all the golems and scale the rock formation to get to the chalice.

Glancing back, I spotted the opening in the maze that Tyler had come out of. We weren't far from it. If we could get inside and block the entrance, the golems wouldn't be able to get to us. It was our best option.

"Loki, get to Harrison and guide him to that opening over there," I commanded as I cut through another swarm of golems.

"As you wish." Loki flew off as I continued to fight.

I was surprised when a blast of dark magic came from behind me, obliterating a small golem. It was Tyler. Even though I had her tucked behind me, she still wanted to help. I shouldn't have expected anything less; she was stubborn that way—always eager to help others, even if it put her in danger.

"We need to get to that opening," I said to Tyler, and she nodded in agreement.

We inched closer to the opening. With every golem we cut down, we got another step closer to our destination. Sweat trickled down my face as I continued to fight. The weight of my sword became a burden. Its heft was great for tearing apart large opponents, but it wasn't made for long battles. My endurance was tested.

In a matter of minutes, our backs were up against the smooth stone wall of the maze. Tyler stepped into the opening but remained in the light. She continued to aid me in the fight. Her magic was strong enough to take on the tiny opponents, which left me to focus on the large ones.

Growing tired, I was more than ready to retreat when Loki and a wolf came into view. Harrison was draped over the wolf's back as they ran straight for us. The aeni trailed close behind and fought off the golems that came near them, protecting Harrison from harm.

They funneled into the opening behind me as the golems swarmed. I barely had enough space to slide into the cave before the stone bodies covered the hole. The corridor was pitch-black with the entrance covered, but I could see clearly.

The golems must have stopped at the entrance because I heard no sounds of attack. We'd made it to safety. I was relieved, but the others' hearts beat rapidly. In an attempt to reassure Tyler that everything was fine, I slid my hands down her shoulders. She jolted but then relaxed.

"Are you all right?" I asked.

"I think so. What do we do now? Those golems were everywhere," she replied.

"Looks like we'll all have to work together." Jade's voice came from the corridor, and a yellow glow lit the space; it was the wolf's energy. Harrison sat against the wall with his hands holding his head. He was in pain. The aeni was crouched beside him.

"Right, and we would trust you because?" I replied. Jade stepped into the light, and the dark eyes of a large king cobra hovered behind her shoulder.

"I live to serve the kingdom, Your Highness," she replied with a bow of her head in my direction. Her devotion made my skin crawl. The way she stared at me like I was a delicious treat disgusted me.

"Sure you do," Tyler replied. She stood rigidly in front of me. "Why should we believe you would give up a chance at winning?"

"Let's just say that I don't have to win to get what I want. If helping the prince gains me extra favor, then why not?" she replied with a wink. It made me shiver. I didn't like the sexual innuendos held within her words.

"We'll need all the help we can get if we want to survive this, so trust aside, we'll have to work together," I replied. "Let's rest while I think of a plan." As soon as I mentioned rest, Loki took up residence on the ceiling. He hung upside down with his wings wrapped around his body.

The odds were against us, but if we could all work together, we might have a shot. We were all ready for the Reckoning to be over. It had been a long couple of months, and I was tired, exhausted actually. I needed to feed; my injuries from the giant golem hadn't completely healed.

"Can we talk privately?" I whispered into Tyler's ear, but Jade glared, overhearing.

"Of course," she replied.

I led Tyler farther into the maze. Once we were far enough away from the others, I stopped. It was mostly dark, but a faint glow from the wolf's energy provided a small bit of light for Tyler. She stared up at me. I had so many things to say to her that I didn't even know where to begin. All I'd wanted for days was a chance to talk to her, and now that I had that chance I couldn't find the words.

"How's your wing feeling?" Tyler broke the silence. My words tripped over each other before I got them out.

"It'll be fine once it heals," I replied. Heat rushed to my face as my eyes stared at her bare shoulder. The bite mark remained, but the dark magic that was once within it had faded. Her pale skin teased me as it reflected the light.

"You still haven't healed? But it's been weeks." Tyler's voice was filled with worry.

"I'm sorry," I said as I knelt on the ground in front of her with my head down. "What I said before, in the woods, it wasn't true. I'm not better off without you."

"I must apologize as well," Tyler replied, joining me on the ground. "You were in pain and lashed out. I never should've left you like that. You saved my life even after I betrayed your trust, so I shouldn't have abandoned you." Her small hand touched the side of my face as she spoke. It made my skin vibrate.

"I never answered your question."

"You don't have to." Her hand was warm as it trailed down the side of my neck. I took her hands into mine.

"I was afraid," I whispered. "People don't get close to me, and I never wanted them to. So the fact that I want you here scares me. I couldn't even resist you that night when you fed yourself to me, and it terrified me that I had no control."

"You want me here?" she asked as her eyes stared into mine.

"Yes. I also want your blood," I replied. In the dark I could still see the warm smile on her face, but she didn't say anything. Had I been too forward? A lump caught in my throat as I waited for her to reply.

The space between us disappeared as Tyler pressed her body into mine. Her arms wrapped around my back, and the warmth of her bare skin touched mine. My teeth transformed as her shoulder came within biting distance. I had an intense desire for her, and it wasn't just her blood that I wanted.

As my teeth sank into her skin, a wave of relief washed over me. She didn't pull away. In fact, she squeezed me tighter, and I liked it. Her blood set every cell in my body on fire. My strength returned, and my wings unfurled as the bones within them healed completely. The dark magic within me amplified. I couldn't stop the energy from escaping.

Dark tendrils spilled into the corridor, blocking out the light. Tyler let out a soft moan that was unbearable. I wanted to ravage her right then and there; no, I *needed* to. My hands slid down the sides of her body, grabbing the underside of her thighs. I pulled her into my lap, and my bulge pressed against her.

"You should stop before you kill her," Harrison said in a monotone that brought me back to reality. My teeth released, and Tyler slumped against me as they returned to normal.

"It's not what it looks like," I said as blood dripped down my face.

"Right. So you weren't about to fuck that girl while you drained her of her life?" Harrison said as he turned to walk away. "The others are waiting for your instructions."

"Harrison, wait," I said, and he stopped in place. "Do you think you can fight?"

"Do you think you can fight?" he replied.

"Can we trust your friend?" I asked.

"You mean Wynter? He's not my friend, but yes, you can trust him. If you can trust anyone, that is." Harrison walked off down the corridor. The Reckoning had changed him so much that I hardly recognized my friend. I wondered if he thought the same was true about me.

CHAPTER 32

TYLER

Leaning against the wall of the corridor, I waited for the others to get ready. The swirls that wrapped around my hand and forearm had a faint green glow to them. Rafe's energy was weak. He'd helped me recover from the blood loss much quicker than I'd expected, but he wouldn't be much help in the coming fight. At least he would be safe while he remained within me.

"It's almost time. Do you remember the plan?" Ki asked as his eyes looked me over. The downward turn of his brows and his lack of eye contact were blatant.

"Yes, and don't worry, I've recovered," I said. His eyes finally met mine.

"Before we do this, I have something I need to tell you."

"No, don't tell me," I said, cutting him off. "You can tell me after we survive this. Anything else will just sound like goodbye, and I won't say goodbye to you." He was silent for a moment.

He sighed and pulled me into a hug as the others took their

places. "I'll keep you safe." His promise warmed my heart but did little to help my nerves.

Ki helped me onto the back of Harrison's wolf, and I was greeted with the familiar red glow of Ki's eyes. His stare burned through me, peeling back the layers of my soul and exposing my every secret. I'd never felt so vulnerable before, and I knew there was no turning back. We would win or die trying.

"No matter what happens, do not let go of him," Wynter said as his familiar crawled onto my shoulder. "If he falls he will return to me."

"I got it. I'll try to keep him safe for you," I replied. Wynter nodded and took his place in line.

"Ready?" Ki asked as Loki landed on his shoulder. The others confirmed nearly in unison. "Let's go!" he shouted, and the pile of golems covering the exit exploded. Bits of dirt and rock showered the area as light poured into the corridor. Ki ran out first with Jade and Wynter behind him. I trailed in the back with a firm grip on the wolf's mane. The only person behind me was Harrison. Ki had asked him to cover my flank.

The intense strength of Ki's magic was impossible to ignore. It radiated from him in waves that chilled my skin as he worked in unison with his familiar. Loki latched on to one of the dark tendrils that swirled around Ki. He channeled it into a stream of dark magic that slowed the golems, allowing Ki to disintegrate them with ease.

I struggled to pull my eyes away from the beauty of Ki's massive wings as he took flight. It was the first time I'd witnessed him flying in the daylight—a true wonder. The golems around him were knocked to the ground from the powerful winds his wings created.

My focus returned to my own task as my hands disappeared before my eyes. Wynter's iguana had the ability of invisibility, and he could project it onto anything he was in contact with. Even the wolf beneath me turned invisible. As long as I maintained contact with both familiars, we wouldn't be seen, but that didn't mean we couldn't be hit.

Ki, Wynter, and Jade coordinated their attacks perfectly as they cleared the path in front of me. We were headed straight toward the hill. It was a few hundred meters taller and much steeper than it was before. I could no longer see the chalice from its base, but I knew the chalice was still up there.

Lux and Lexa fought off golems with the aid of their hyena familiars as they climbed the other side of the hill. They were almost to the top. We would have to hurry to get to the chalice before them, but they weren't our only concern.

Adakk was headed straight for our group with a Bengal tiger at his side. They both looked thirsty for blood, and even though I was invisible, they had managed to cut off my path. If they spotted me, I would be done for. I was no match for the giant tlaloc and his tiger.

"I'll take care of this one. Keep going," Harrison said from behind me. I wasn't sure if he knew where I was, but the coldness in his voice kept me from questioning him. The Reckoning had changed him, and I was glad he was on our team because his aura frightened me.

"I remember you," Adakk said as Harrison stepped into his path. "You're friends with that tlaloc I beat up during the fourth challenge."

"His name was Daniel!" Harrison screamed, and energy erupted from him like a volcano. Afraid to watch the scene unfold, I kept my eyes forward. I just needed to get to the chalice.

We reached the bottom of the hill, and Ki flew ahead. I had to hold on with all my might as the wolf scaled the steep slopes. My hands slipped as my body was bounced up and down, but I didn't let go.

As we neared the top of the hill, a swarm of golems poured from its cliff. Wynter and Jade tried to keep them from me, but there were too many of them. A golem caught the wolf's foot, and I was thrown from his back.

My ears rang as I made my way to my feet. I'd landed on the flat surface of the hilltop. Lux and Lexa were only a few meters away. They looked straight at me as they cut through hordes of golems. My heart raced as I realized I could see my own hands again. The iguana and his invisibility were gone. I was completely exposed and vulnerable.

With their combined magic, Lux and Lexa launched a large golem straight at me. I had no way to stop it. The small amount of dark magic I had access to wasn't enough to change the golem's course. I closed my eyes as the golem came at me and prayed for a quick death.

A strong gust of wind knocked me from my feet, and my eyes opened in surprise. Ki and Loki stood between me and the vial duo. Dust blew about the air, but the golem was gone. It had been incinerated.

"Get the chalice. We'll take care of these two," Ki said. He didn't have to ask me twice. I got to my feet and headed toward the center of the hill.

"So we meet again. I hope you don't run off like a coward this time," Lux said as I left. Ki's anger flowed through me as I ran.

The chalice floated over the center of a bottomless pit. The opening was too wide for me to jump to the other side. If I leapt I could grab the chalice, but then I'd fall straight into the endless abyss.

Standing at the edge of the pit, I caught my breath and couldn't help but watch as Ki engaged with Lux and Lexa. His swift movements captivated me. My eyes didn't want to look away from him, so I stared. The bite mark on my shoulder tingled every time Ki used his dark magic. It drew me to him.

When sinister smiles came from Lux and Lexa, it chilled me to the bone. They were eager to fight. In fact, it appeared as though they got off on it. Were they trying to show off for Ki, or did they just have a burning desire for destruction?

Pain burst in the side of my leg as a stone struck me. I turned to the side, and another stone was heading my way. I rolled to the side, dodging it. As I got back to my feet, I spotted the source of the attack.

"I didn't come this far to lose to a human," Keerla said as

dust settled around her. "Stand aside, and I'll let you keep your life." A falcon circled over the pit; it had to be her familiar.

"I'm sorry, but I can't do that. People are counting on me," I replied.

"Suit yourself," Keerla said. The falcon came straight at me. I pulled my sword from my back, but I wasn't fast enough. Pain exploded from my arm as the falcon's claws tore into my flesh. My scream was short-lived, as a bubble of water engulfed the falcon. It writhed in the air as it tried desperately to escape the bubble.

"No!" Keerla cried as a force of wind burst the bubble. The falcon fell to the ground, and she rushed to it. I climbed to my feet and had my sword in hand by the time she finished absorbing her familiar. Her eyes looked at me with fury.

A tornado erupted around her. She had control of the winds. I took a step back. If I swung at her, my sword would get lost in the powerful winds. I would never be able to hit her through them.

"She's not the one you want. I am," Wynter said as a bubble of water floated near him.

Keerla glanced at me for a moment before turning her anger to Wynter. Her winds ripped around him and faded into a ripple on the waves he created. As they continued to fight, their magic created a hurricane. Moving out of their range, my thoughts turned to the chalice. It was up to me to get it, to end the Reckoning.

I watched as my comrades fought around me. Ki's battle with the siblings raged on in a dangerous proximity to the pit's edge. Jade and her king cobra fought off the endless hordes of golems. Wynter was caught in a storm with Keerla, and I could only imagine the bloody scene between Harrison and Adakk that I knew raged on below.

Their lives were in danger, and all I needed to do was grab the chalice. The Reckoning would be over, and the fighting would stop. Everyone would be safe. I just needed to jump the pit. So what if I didn't make it to the other side? If falling to my death meant everyone else would survive—that Ki would survive—it was worth it.

Ki slammed into the ground on the other side of the pit, his face pained. Lux had his sword drawn and was about to bring it down on Ki. Worried that Ki would be gravely injured, I took a few steps back from the pit. Summoning all my courage, I took a running start and dove for the chalice. Ki would not die because of me.

As my feet left the ground, Ki's red eyes locked with mine. He kicked Lux in the face and leapt toward me. We collided in the air over the pit, the chalice caught between our entangled bodies. In a mess of arms and legs, we fell. My stomach lurched as gravity pulled us into the pit's darkness. I thought we would fall forever, but Ki had other plans. His arm slid around me, and his wings unfurled.

My stomach clenched as our direction changed. The chalice slid free from the abrupt movement, but we caught it simultaneously. Ki held me tight as he lifted us out of the pit. The chaos around us quieted as we landed on the hill.

I had a hand on the chalice and an arm wrapped around Ki when he smiled. It was a smile I'd never seen before. He looked relieved, as if a weight had lifted from him. Happiness?

"We did it," I said, glad it was finally over, that we'd survived.

"We did," he replied with watery eyes.

He pulled me to him, and his lips found mine. The chalice dropped at our feet as I wrapped my arms around him. His lips were softer than I'd imagined, and the taste of blood still lingered on them, a taste that was oddly satisfying. My heart raced, and my skin trembled with every touch of his skin.

"I love you," he whispered between kisses.

I'd suspected his feelings but hadn't been sure he would ever admit to them. His confession moved me. My body filled with heat, and I wanted nothing more than to be with him. It didn't matter that he was the prince, a Darkblood dierdre with a thirst for blood; to me he was just Ki, a guarded, kindhearted man who shared his secrets with me even though he hid them from the world. He was a man who kept his promises, who protected me when he didn't have to. During all the time we'd spent together, he'd become dear to me. Was it love?

A powerful energy surged from within me. It was strong and pure, like nothing I'd ever experienced before. Brightness consumed us, and I had to shield my eyes. We were blasted apart by a great force, and dust clouded my view. I closed my eyes to shield them from the debris and found relief in the darkness. It was silent and peaceful compared to the chaos around me.

CHAPTER 33

KI

I coughed as I inhaled the smoke-filled air. Fires raged on around me, consuming the wooden furniture and cloth tapestries. I was in a large dining hall made of marbled stone. Its decadence reminded me of home.

The familiar clangs of metal swords echoed throughout the building, and the stone walls around me shook. Blasts of magical energy ripped through the wall to my side. Dodging the rubble that fell down around me, I realized I was caught in the middle of a war.

As I made my way through the smoke, I was greeted by the stench of death. Blood and burnt flesh could be tasted in the air. My stomach twisted as I gagged. I fought back the urge to retch as I stumbled over a pile of corpses.

The bodies of asudhs, aeni, and humans alike were scattered across my path. Whoever the enemy was, they were merciless. It was clear they weren't taking prisoners, as the bodies weren't just of men; there were women and even children lying lifeless among the wreckage. I could hardly bear to keep my eyes open as I headed toward the large door at the end of the room.

A woman's scream in the distance caused my pace to quicken. I ran through the corridor without pause. The walls crumbled around me, but I dodged the falling stones and jumped over the corpses in my path.

As I continued on, the woman's scream drew nearer. My body moved without hesitation, and I quickly realized it wasn't my own. I was a passenger, unable to control my own movements or actions. Even though I tried to force my body to change course, it wouldn't. I was forced to press on without knowledge as to why I was here or where I was headed. In fact, I didn't even know where I was.

I rounded several corners as I weaved through the building. As I burst through a large set of doors, I was greeted by the screams of life. A newborn baby cried. How could someone give birth in a war zone? I prayed the body I was in was not about to harm the child.

"My lord, she has finally come," said a young woman with a despairing smile. Her clothes were rather plain and covered in blood. She was clearly a servant or maid of some kind. Glancing around the room, I spotted another servant. The woman was much older and was preoccupied with gently wrapping something up. The baby?

"Let me hold her just once." A woman's weak voice drew my attention, and I went to her. Tears ran down my face as I embraced her with a kiss. She was immobilized in the bed, having just given birth. She was a stranger to me, but her face was familiar. I thought I'd seen her picture in a book when I was young.

"My love, our time is short. We must say goodbye," I said, but it was an older man's voice. The older lady placed the baby in the woman's arms, and she held her close to her body. She kissed the baby's forehead gently while rocking her. The crying had stopped, and everyone stared at us with tears in their eyes.

"Tyler," the woman said to the newborn in her arms. It was

an odd name for a girl, but it had to be a coincidence. There was no way the baby before me could be the same girl I'd fallen in love with.

"One day you'll discover the truth of who you are, and the world will be saved. I only hope you can forgive us for failing you." She cried as she wrapped a necklace around her baby. There was an emblem on the end of the long chain, but I didn't get a good view of it before she tucked it into the baby's blanket. She handed the baby to me, and I held her close to my chest.

"My queen, I shall see you again on the other side," I said.

"My king, I shall stand by you in this world and the next." She started to sob. I leaned in and kissed her passionately before I turned to leave.

As I raced back into the horrors of war, I finally realized where I'd seen that woman's face: in the history books. She was the Lightblood Queen, which could only mean I was witnessing the end of the king's war firsthand. But how? I'd thought I was a passenger in someone else's body and that I was simply viewing their life, but the king's war had ended nearly two decades ago. Even I didn't have the power to go back in time. I had no bloody idea what was happening to me.

My mind reeled as my body took me through the mazelike palace. I descended to a lower level, and the man I was in knew his way around even in the dim light. Without any hesitation, I felt around on a stone wall. One of the stones recessed, and a secret passage opened before me.

The path took me deeper into the ground as I quickly descended the spiral staircase. I found myself in an underground cavern when I reached the bottom. A glow from ahead lit my path. When I turned into the large altar room, I couldn't believe my eyes. The bright golden glow came from a stone in the middle of the room. It was the sunstone. I'd only ever seen pictures of it in books, and they didn't do it justice.

It was beautiful and glowed with intense power, just like the moonstone. But instead of the presence of darkness, the warmth of love radiated from the stone and drew me in. It must've been the pull of light magic. I'd never experienced anything like it before. It overwhelmed me with so much happiness that I didn't pay any attention to what my body was up to.

I'd set up a ritual circle on the ground in front of me. There were candles in the four cardinal directions, and rune stones had been placed between them. The symbols on the runes were similar to ones I'd seen before, but they weren't in Tenebrisal. It was in a language I didn't know, but it had roots in the ancient language just as Tenebrisal did. From what I could make out, it appeared to be some kind of concealment spell. That was my best guess, at least.

I held the baby at arm's length and finally got a good look at her. She had bright blue eyes and light brown hair. Her skin was fair, and her ears had a small point to them. She had the attributes of a liusaidh, so she couldn't have been my Tyler. My Tyler was human.

The baby smiled at me with an unnervingly familiar smile as I began to chant. I couldn't recognize any of the words I spoke. They were in a foreign voice and tongue. It was likely the old liusaidh language, something I'd never bothered to learn since they were all extinct.

As I continued to chant, the baby floated out of my hands and hovered in the air just above the sunstone. The stone's light shined brighter as it flowed into the baby. I worried as the magical energy consumed the child but was relieved when I heard her giggle. She was not being harmed. I assumed my concern for her came from the body I inhabited, but I also held hope for the baby's safety.

She continued to giggle as the magic changed her appearance. Her hair turned blond, and her ears rounded out. Even her skin lightened as she became human. Human? No, it couldn't be. A being's race couldn't be altered with magic. That would require more power than any one person had access to.

My chants became louder, and the magic crackled in the air. A flood of magical energy poured into the room. It came from all directions and collected around the sunstone. The energy imploded with the baby at the center of it all. What the hell?

All the light in the room was gone, except for a faint glow that surrounded the baby. I caught the baby as she floated down and hunched over her. Looking down at her bright blue eyes, I was horrified. There was no more denying it; the baby before me was Tyler, my Tyler. She was a Lightblood, the sole heir to the Light Nation. My thoughts spiraled.

"If you're seeing this, then there's still hope for the world. By now you've realized that the girl you love is in fact the only surviving member of the Lightblood family. I know it'll be hard to accept, since you yourself are a Darkblood, but she is innocent in all of this. Please keep her safe. Until the sunstone is restored, she will remain defenseless. Tell her that we're sorry and that we loved her." The man's voice strained as he spoke, and his words unnerved me.

I hadn't even begun to process the words he'd said before footsteps approached from the stairwell. A dim light filled the room as a young asudh came into view. My body was heavy, and I couldn't move.

"Your Majesty." The asudh bowed as he spoke. "I have secured transport for the princess." He held out his hands to receive the baby, and I caught a glimpse of his dark teal eyes.

"Good," I said weakly as I struggled to breathe. "No one can know who she is. Get her to the Skyys—they'll know what to do."

"Yes, Your Majesty," he said as he cradled the baby into a sling. When he turned to walk away, I finally realized what I'd just witnessed. Shock and horror froze me—not that I was able to move my body anyway. I was experiencing another person's memory, the Lightblood King's memory. Fate was cruel. Tyler Skyy, the only girl I'd ever loved, was the Lightblood Princess and my family's sworn enemy.

As darkness consumed me, I was pulled by a tingling magic. My consciousness was ripped from the memory and thrust back into my own body. Tyler's warm body was pressed against mine, and I could taste the sweetness of her lips. A bright light blinded me as magic exploded from us. I held on to her as tightly as I could, but we were thrown apart. Dazed from the impact, I struggled to focus my sight.

"Tyler?" I called out, unable to see her through the cloud of dust that lingered in the air. My thoughts were scrambled from the memory I'd just experienced. A war, a baby, a desperate king, the sunstone, the Lightbloods, Tyler—it all rushed in.

"Ki?" Tyler coughed.

The dust settled around me, and I looked up to see her. She walked toward me with the chalice in hand. My mind cleared as I remembered that the Reckoning was over. We'd gotten the chalice.

I sighed in relief. Tyler was unharmed and unchanged. She was still human. No one would have any reason to think otherwise.

"Are you okay?" she asked as she offered a hand to help me up. The metal bracelet that had once clung to her wrist was gone, and I realized mine had disappeared as well.

"I think so," I replied, accepting her hand. As I got to my feet, the other competitors approached us. They were also missing the metal bracelets that had kept us all prisoners to the Reckoning.

"What was that?" she asked. I was sure it'd been light magic, but thankfully there were no signs of magic about her. She looked perfectly normal.

"I don't know. Did you see anything strange?" I asked, curious if she'd witnessed the same memory.

"Just that bright light and burst of magic," she replied. Her warm smile lit up her face as it had so many times before, but when I looked down and her eyes met mine, I knew the truth. There was a reflection of gold in her eyes that was identical to the glow of the sunstone. Sooner or later, the world would discover who she was, and I was terrified to think of what might happen to her once they did.

"What the fuck was that?" Jade said as she approached us. Her arm glowed with the power of her absorbed familiar.

I was speechless. There was nothing I could say about the vision or the magic that had just been released. All I could do was hope the others wouldn't see the truth. Luckily, most people would find the concept of Tyler being a Lightblood pure insanity. Had I not witnessed it myself, I probably wouldn't have believed it. In fact, I didn't want to believe it at all.

My stomach clenched as reality took hold of me. I would never be able to be with Tyler. The odds had been slim before with her being a common human, but now that I knew she was a Lightblood, there was no possible future for us. At best I could hope to keep her alive and far from me and my father.

"That, my dear, was one hell of a kiss," Wynter said with a laugh. Jade clenched her teeth in disgust. Had she seen the truth? Maybe she could see right through me.

"Didn't look that great to me," Jade said. Her bitter words gave me relief. She must've just been jealous. I was thankful it wasn't more than that.

A large transport ship landed in the field below the hill. I grabbed ahold of Tyler, and we slid over the side of the hill together. Loki and the others followed behind us. The competitors who remained standing absorbed their familiars and gathered around the ship as it opened up. Loki landed on my shoulder.

I was worried by Harrison's absence, but then I spotted him in the distance. He was sprawled out on his back in the grass. Even though he was motionless, I could sense the strength of his aura.

To no one's surprise, my father stepped out of the ship first. He wore one of his more ostentatious robes with a crown to match its extravagance. A string of servants and guards followed closely behind him, and the recording orbs flew around us in a fury.

I hoped there'd been too much dust in the air for them to have recorded the exchange between me and Tyler. When we came out of that pit, I'd been so caught up in how happy I was that she was alive that I hadn't thought about the repercussions of kissing her in the public's view. If my bloody father had seen it, I would be dead for sure.

"Congratulations!" my father said with widespread arms. His smile quickly faded when his eyes landed on Tyler and the chalice in her hands. "Carrying the chalice for the prince, I see. At least someone knows their place." He glared at me.

"Actually, Your Majesty, it appears we have a tie," the dark priestess said as she stepped out from the transport ship, joining my father.

"A tie? That's preposterous! There has only ever been one champion."

"Have a look for yourself." The dark priestess pulled an orb from under her cloak. It floated in the air and replayed the last few minutes of our battle against the golem horde. She paused it at the moment Tyler and I had jumped into the pit. Our bodies were tangled together with the chalice stuck between us.

"As you can clearly see, the two competitors came into contact with the chalice at exactly the same time." The dark priestess tried to hide her smile, but it was obvious she enjoyed correcting my father.

"Fucking hell," Lux muttered. He sat at the bottom of the hill next to his sister. They both wore bitter expressions.

"So we could have won it together?" Lexa complained to her brother.

"You two sound pathetic," Adakk said. He was covered in sweat, dirt, and blood. He swayed on his feet, and I could tell that his battle with Harrison had worn him down.

"I have to agree with the tlaloc," Keerla replied.

My father stared at the evidence presented before him. His eyes twitched as he took in the situation. There was no loophole to find, no way to dispute the truth. Everyone could see that we had tied. I imagined he was pissed that a human girl had tied with his only son to win the Reckoning. Although I was sure I would pay for it later, it felt good to displease him.

"It seems you are correct, Priestess." My father collected himself, forcing a fake smile. "For the first time in history, we have two champions!" He opened his arms to the recording orbs and addressed the crowd as if he was proud to have two winners. I pitied our people, who always succumbed to his lies and false charm. He continued to rally them, but I paid no attention to what he said. I was only focused on Tyler and how I would keep her identity a secret.

CHAPTER 34

HARRISON

The grass was cool on my skin as I stared up at the sky. It was over; the Reckoning had ended. There was no reason to fight. Closing my eyes, I thought of my victory. Emm had died rightfully by my own hands. My vengeance had been served, and I'd made a bloodied mess of that pompous tlaloc Adakk. I'd been so caught up in the brutality of our fight that I probably would've killed him too if not for the bright light that dazed me.

"It's time to go," Wynter said, and my eyes fluttered open. He looked down at me with his dark gray eyes, and I sensed an air of sadness around him. "The king wants us all back at the processing center."

"Why?" I replied, closing my eyes. Anger bubbled up from within me, and my skin tingled with dark energy.

"The Reckoning is over, but we're all required to be present at the closing ceremony," Wynter replied.

"Why are you here?" My eyes opened again, and I stared up at him. He sighed, looking around as if he would find the answer on the ground beside me. Sitting up, I took a deep breath to settle my anger and dark energy. "I can feel your sadness. It clings to you when you're around me. If my presence makes you sad, then why are you here?" I said as I stood up. My face was only a few inches from his.

"Your presence does not make me sad. I'm just worried about you," he replied.

"Don't be," I said as I nudged past him and headed toward the transport ships gathered in the field.

Wynter followed me like a lost dog. I almost felt bad for him, but I couldn't think about it. If I started to think about the feelings of others, I was sure to crumble. I had to hang on to my anger; it was the only thing that kept me moving forward.

The transport ships were small, and each of them had a healer aboard. Wynter followed me onto one of the ships. We were the only ones on it besides the healer and the pilot. After we took off, the healer immediately began to fuss over me. She wanted to heal my wounds.

"Don't touch me." I slapped her hands away from my wrists when she grabbed them. Even though her touch had been gentle, I didn't like it.

"Harrison, don't be an idiot. You nearly bled out from all the magic you used earlier. Let her heal you," Wynter said. I knew he would continue to pester me if I didn't listen, so I gave in. The journey would be bad enough without him complaining the whole time.

"Fine," I replied, holding out my arms for the healer to inspect. She peeled back the bloodstained cloth and gasped.

Spirals of black energy had weaved across my skin. They curled up my right arm and spread out across the right side of my body. Unfortunately, the black markings didn't cover the crescent moon that Jess had left on my wrist. In fact, they circled around it as if to accent the damn thing.

"My word," she said. "I've never seen—"

"*Just* heal the cuts," Wynter said. The healer nodded and remained silent as she tended to my wounds. I was glad. The last thing I needed was a million questions about these marks on my body. I wasn't even sure when they'd appeared or if they were permanent. Maybe they were intended to be a reminder of all that was lost.

The anger that had been holding me together dissolved, and it all crashed in on me. Daniel was dead, and I'd become a monster. I'd ruined Jess, killed Emm, and done unspeakably degrading things to Wynter. My sins could not be absolved with prayer. Death would be the only release from my miserable existence, and I knew exactly how to get it. I would meet with the king.

My return to the processing center was similar to when I'd first arrived. Servants fussed over me. They had to get me cleaned up and dressed for the closing ceremony. This time I didn't fight them. I was eager to visit the king, so I cooperated fully. It seemed like my first visit to the center had been a lifetime ago. None of it mattered, though. I was on a mission.

Once I was dressed, the servants allowed me to leave my room. I headed straight for the king's quarters. There was a small throne room near the ballroom where the ceremonies took place. The king would be in there up until his presence was required. If I was quick I could get him to end my suffering before the ceremony.

When I came across the doors to the room, I was surprised to see that there were no guards. At first I thought the king may have been elsewhere, but the sounds of an argument came from the door. He was definitely in there.

"You will cut ties with the girl immediately, or I will take matters into my own hands!" the king shouted. "I can't believe my own son allowed himself to become so weak. It's a disgrace to our name."

"I am not weak," Ki replied. I sensed the presence of their dark auras as they argued.

"Letting yourself fall for a pitiful human girl is the greatest weakness a man can have."

"Love is not a weakness!" Ki shouted. I couldn't believe he'd become so brazen. He'd never stood up to his father in such a way before. The crash of furniture breaking told me their fight had become physical.

"You listen to me, boy. You do not love that girl. During the stress of the Reckoning, you lost your own reason and took comfort in the flesh of a woman. That is what happened, and you will not say otherwise unless you want to see her tortured. Do you understand me?"

"Yes, Father."

"Good. Now go make yourself presentable for the ceremony."

The doors to the room burst open. I barely managed to move out of the way of the swinging door. Ki emerged from the room, eyes glowing red, with a cut below his eye. His fists were clenched as he stormed down the corridor and out of sight.

"Harrison, my boy, do come in. Excuse the mess. I had to knock some sense back into that stubborn son of mine." The king's words were free of anger, but I hoped to change that. He turned a chair upright in the middle of the room and motioned for me to have a seat.

"Your Majesty, I apologize for the unannounced visit, but I needed to speak with you," I began as he took a seat on his throne. It was similar to the one in the palace back home, but it was smaller and more aged. I admired the black spikes jutting out from it.

"Nonsense—I always have time for you. What is it you need?"

"I'm afraid I must inform you of my many sins and transgressions, which occurred over the past few months. Even though you so graciously honored me and my family by promising me your daughter's hand in marriage, I'm afraid I've dishonored the union in many ways. Not only did I have premarital sex with your daughter, but I was also unfaithful to her. I know these sins are unforgivable, and I'm ready to accept the punishment."

I bowed my head respectfully, but the king's laughter caught me off guard. His laughter echoed throughout the room, and I could see tears in his eyes when I looked at him. I worried he had gone mad until he finally collected himself.

"I haven't had a good laugh like that in a long while. You almost had me there, you jokester." The king wiped the tears from his eyes as I stared in stunned silence.

"Your Majesty, I was not making a joke. I have sinned."

"Don't be so hard on yourself, lad. You're a man, and men have needs. I never actually believed my silly daughter would be able to fulfill all those needs. As far as I'm concerned, she's belonged to you since the day I promised you her hand. You're free to punish her for her slutty behavior as you see fit. And as long as you make good on your promise to marry the whore, you may fuck whomever you like. Boy or girl, it matters not to me." The king's words baffled me. He wasn't mad?

"But I—"

"Don't worry, Harrison. I have full control over what the people get to see. The recordings of you and Daniel were withheld from the public eye. His death was a great loss for us all, and his reputation will not be sullied. He will have a proper warrior's burial, and I want you to organize it. After all, you were his closest friend."

My heart sank when Daniel's name was mentioned. Tears fell from my eyes. The king would not punish me, would not give me the freedom of death. Instead he'd given me the great honor of organizing a warrior's funeral. I couldn't say no. Daniel would have wanted his life to be celebrated, and I knew him best. I would make sure his name was honored.

"Thank you, Your Majesty," I replied with a bow as I stood.

"I will see you at the ceremony." He waved me off.

The doors closed behind me as I left the room. The king had completely absolved me of all my sins. But how? I didn't deserve to go unpunished. My anger returned, and I welcomed it like an old friend. It seeped into every cell in my body. I clung to it as I headed back to my room. There was nothing left to do but wait for the ceremony to begin.

When I got to my room, I found Wynter waiting by the door. He held a tray in his hand. On it was a spread of meats, bread, and cheese, as well as a bottle of wine. I hadn't realized how hungry I was until the smell of the food reached me.

"They had a buffet for the competitors, and you weren't there, so I figured you'd be hungry," Wynter said as I opened the door. I stopped to stare him in the eyes. Remembering how much he'd enjoyed being degraded, I directed my anger at him.

"Do you enjoy being treated like shit?" I asked. He looked down, unable to keep eye contact with me. Even though he'd looked away, the flush in his cheeks was clear. It was all the answer I needed. Grabbing a fistful of his hair, I whispered into his ear.

"You better not drop one bite of this food."

Wynter's eyes avoided mine as I dragged him into the room, but he couldn't hide his grunt of pleasure. He enjoyed the forcefulness of my tight hold. I allowed him to set the tray down before throwing him to the floor. He gave little resistance as I took pleasure in abusing his body.

His lip was bleeding by the time I was done with him. I'd covered his body in scratches, and he could hardly stand. His knees already showed bruises from being forced down onto the hard floor. I didn't have any remorse for what I'd done. He practically begged for it the way he followed me around. If he wanted to act like a dog, I'd treat him like one.

I shared my food with him. Of course, I made him eat it off the floor as I threw small pieces to him, but he didn't mind. He seemed to like it, and it gave me a bit of satisfaction as well. It was like my anger found a new outlet—one I desperately needed. I just needed to have something to focus on so that I wouldn't think about anything.

We'd just finished dressing when the call came for us to assemble. It was time to line up for the ceremony. I took a look in the mirror to make sure I was presentable and was shocked by my reflection. Not only had the black marks consumed the entire right side of my body, but my left eye had turned pink. It was the same pink color that I used to see in Daniel's eyes. I hardly recognized myself.

"Why didn't you say anything about this?" I pointed to my eye as I turned, but Wynter wasn't there. In the doorway stood Jess, my fiancée and princess of the Dark Nation. She stared at me. I guessed she hardly recognized me, but she kept her composure.

"I sent your friend ahead so we could talk," Jess said, breaking the awkward silence. She wore a fluffy lavender dress that matched her eyes. A few months ago I wouldn't have been able to look away from her, but now I didn't care about how she looked, even though she had a radiant glow about her.

"You'll have to talk on the way," I replied. She offered her arm to me, and I escorted her down the halls. We'd done it so many times before, it was instinctual. I had a sense of déjà vu.

"How are you feeling?" she asked as we walked.

"I've had better days."

"I can relate to that." She sighed, and anger filled me. Did she really think that her struggles in the palace could ever compare to what I'd gone through during the Reckoning?

A surge of mixed emotions hit me, and I couldn't make sense of them. There was an air of anxiety and anticipation about Jess. I knew I was feeling her emotions, but I couldn't control it. It only added to my irritation.

"You wanted to talk to me about something?" I said as I tried to control the dark magic that swirled within me.

"Actually, I think it can wait until after the ceremony," she replied. Her anxiety overflowed, and I could taste a bit of fear. I stopped and turned to face her.

"No, you'll tell me now," I said, tired of her games. Tears welled in her eyes as a sense of shame came over me—her shame.

"I'm pregnant," she stuttered.

"Pregnant?" I replied, confused. Then the reality hit me as I processed the confession. "Is it mine?"

"Of course it is!" she replied, tears streaming down her face. "I've only ever been with you." Her emotions revealed her pain to me, and I knew she spoke the truth.

My response to her confession hurt her, but what was I supposed to think? We'd only had sex that one time, and she'd forced herself on me.

"All right, I believe you. Stop crying before you draw attention. Does anyone else know?"

"I don't think so," she replied, drying her eyes.

"Good. We can discuss this further when we get back home. For now just keep it quiet."

We continued the walk to the ballroom in silence, which gave me time to think. Apparently, I'd already produced an heir for the king. He would definitely be pleased. My spirits lifted as I realized I wouldn't be expected to lie with Jess while she was pregnant. I could probably avoid being alone with her entirely until our wedding day. The gods had shown me a bit of mercy after all.

CHAPTER 35

KI

Rage flowed through my veins as the servants cleaned me up. My father's words still burned in my mind. He wanted me to pretend Tyler meant nothing to me, to act like I'd just used her to fulfill my own lustful desires, but I hadn't. Sure, I'd fed on her multiple times, and we'd shared one kiss, but I hadn't defiled her. She was not just flesh to be used to satisfy sexual desires. I hadn't even had sexual desires until I met her. In fact, I hadn't even seen her in that way at first, but then we'd spent all that time together and I'd gotten to know her. Somehow during that time I'd unknowingly developed a desire for her.

I looked in the mirror when the servants were finished. The cut my father had left under my eye was gone; it had healed quickly. Tyler's blood had given me strength, magnified my magical abilities. The suit I wore was black with a gold vest that matched the crown I wore. It was a golden crown of leaves—the crown of a champion. I'd struggled to get it on over my newly developed horns. They'd grown longer and thicker during the Reckoning, and I was still getting used to them.

The servants had needed to cut slits in the back of my suit to allow for my wings. I couldn't hide them any longer, and they made it hard to dress. If I'd been allowed, I would've just gone topless to avoid the whole mess.

I worried others would find out about Tyler. My feelings for her had already put her on my father's radar. If he discovered who she was, there would be no way to save her from him. Why had I seen that vision? I hadn't wanted to know the truth. The truth made me feel helpless.

Every minute dragged on. I wanted to see Tyler, to know she was still safe. My mind raced and wallowed in self-torment while Loki lay comfortably in my bed. He didn't have a care in the world.

Finally, there was a knock at my door. A servant led me down the halls toward the ballroom. My heart raced as we approached the line of competitors waiting for the ceremony to begin. The servant took me to the back of the line, and my heart skipped a beat as Tyler came into view.

She wore a black dress trimmed in gold lace. A golden crown of leaves similar to mine sat atop her head. It was weaved beautifully into her braided hair. The lower half of her hair had been curled and danced about her shoulders teasingly as she moved. Her shoulders were bare, but her hair was long enough to cover the mark I'd left on her.

When Tyler spotted me, her eyes lit up. I was unable to control myself. As I reached her, I pulled her into me. Her body warmed me as it pressed into mine. I didn't want to let her go, but I knew I had to. If my father saw us together, it would only make things worse.

"People are staring," Tyler whispered as she pulled out of my embrace. I glanced around at the other competitors. They watched us closely. Wynter was all smiles, while Jade gave us a deadly glare. Lux and Lexa appeared annoyed, but Adakk and Keerla looked bored.

"It's because you look beautiful," I said, ignoring the stares. Tyler's face flushed at my words. Had I embarrassed her?

A sound from the front of the line drew my attention. The doors had been opened, and the line moved through them. Music poured from the room, getting louder as we approached the doorway. A servant waited at the entrance.

"Wait at the top of the stairs until you're announced. You'll be walking together, and the crowd will want a good view of our two champions." He was not the least bit enthusiastic. I guessed he'd coordinated too many ceremonies to take any joy in the extravagance.

I folded Tyler's arm into mine and led her into the room. My movements came naturally after the years I'd spent in the palace. It had always been my duty to escort the visiting ladies, who would talk my head off as I showed them the royal estate. I was expected to carry myself with pride regardless of the situation—even if I was being bored to death by an old woman's constant flirtations.

It was an honor to escort Tyler. We stood at the top of the stairs, waiting to be announced. My pulse quickened as the crowd's eyes turned toward us. I was overwhelmed by a sense of vulnerability as I stood next to her. Would the crowd be able to sense my feelings for her? Was there a softness in my demeanor that hadn't been there before? People stared at us with their bloody mouths half-open. I'd always hated that.

"Prince Malaki Darkblood and Tyler Elizabeth Skyy!" My father announced our names, and the crowd went wild. Their excited shouts and smiles unnerved me as I led Tyler down the stairs and toward the stage where my father waited. We walked arm in arm. Tyler smiled and waved at the people as we passed them. Was she at ease? My stomach sickened from the attention.

The crowd's cheers finally calmed when we reached the stage, taking our places beside my father. He wore a smile, but I could tell it was forced. A human champion was bad enough, but a human tying with his only son was sure to make him furious—another reason I would need to keep Tyler as far away from him as possible.

"It gives me great honor to induct my son into the hall of champions. He made new records by bringing his partner to victory with him. This lovely girl has also earned her spot in the hall of champions by overcoming the odds. Her mere survival is a shock to us all." The crowds cheered. They went wild with joy over the unusual turn of events, which would only irritate my father more.

"These nine finalists who stand before you will be inducted into the Dark Nation Army upon our return home. They have all earned the right to become our nation's protectors. I believe they all have bright futures." My father motioned toward the front of the stage where the other competitors stood with pride.

"Things have ended quite unusually this year, but since we opened the Reckoning with a dance, I find it only fitting that we end it with a dance as well. Please join our champions on the dance floor as we celebrate together." My father sent me a knowing smile, and the crowds cheered.

I took Tyler by the hand and led her onto the dance floor. The music began, and we danced. I had to keep up appearances, but I couldn't look too happy. If the people caught wind of my feelings for Tyler, my father would hurt her. He had made that clear.

"We can't look too friendly with each other," I whispered to Tyler as I twirled her around the dance floor.

"I don't understand," she replied. We both smiled as an orb came over to record us. I waited for it to fly away before I spoke again.

"My father knows about my feelings for you, and you're in danger," I said. Her smile faded. "Don't worry, I'm going to get you out of here. I remember my promise to keep you safe."

Tyler forced a smile as another orb came our way. I could tell she was worried, but she hid it well. We just needed to get through the dance. The ceremony would be over, and we could slip away. I just needed to bide time until we could make our escape. My father would come up with an excuse for her absence once she was gone. He would probably use it as a ploy to gain favor with the masses, acting as though he'd been kind enough to let a girl return home to her family.

When the song came to an end, people flooded the dance floor. The music changed, and we were lost in the crowd. It was our chance. I pushed through the crowd, holding Tyler's hand tightly. She followed me without a word. We dipped out a side door and headed toward the center's entrance.

"Where are we going?" Tyler asked.

"They keep the competitors' personal belongings in a room near the entrance. We're getting your things and leaving," I replied as I rushed down the halls. She struggled to keep up, but I didn't slow down. The sooner we were out, the safer she'd be.

"But where will we go?" she asked.

"I'm taking you home."

We got to the room, and the soldiers listened to me without question. They gave us the bag filled with Tyler's belongings, and we headed out the front entrance. Transport ships were lined up in rows. They were waiting to take the guests back to their homes. We were in luck.

I helped Tyler into one of the small ships and directed the pilot to take us to Addersfield, Tyler's hometown. My heart raced, and we both breathed heavily from our run through the center. I was finally able to relax once the ship was in the air.

"You should change out of that dress. I promise not to look," I said as I turned my back to her. I stood behind the pilot to block his view of her as well.

"It's not like you haven't seen me before," she replied. Heat rose to my face, and the pilot smiled.

"Forget you heard that," I snapped at the pilot.

"Yes, Your Highness," he replied, but his smug smile remained. I couldn't believe Tyler had said that out loud.

When Tyler finished changing, I sat down beside her. I

created a soundproof bubble out of dark magic, and it surrounded us.

"What's with this?" Tyler pointed at the bubble.

"No one else can know what I'm about to tell you," I replied. "I know this is going to be hard to understand, but you are the last living member of the Lightblood family."

"What?" Tyler laughed.

"I'm serious. When we kissed on top of the hill, I had a vision of the past. I lived through the Lightblood King's last memory. He was your father." Tyler stopped laughing.

"That doesn't make any sense. I can't be a Lightblood; I'm just an ordinary human."

"You could never be ordinary," I said, and her face turned red. "That bright light that blasted us apart, I think it was you. Your magic was awakened somehow."

"I don't know what that bright light was, but I'm sure it didn't come from me. The only magic I have is what you infected me with. Whatever you think you saw, you must be mistaken."

"I'm not mistaken. I witnessed your birth and the ritual the Lightblood King performed to change you into a human. There have to be things that have happened in your life that tell you this could be true."

Tyler frowned at me. "Just take me home."

"I'm telling you this because you need to be careful. You'll be in danger if people find out. My father will come after you if he finds out who you are," I pleaded. Tyler was silent. I could tell she didn't believe me. It was a hard pill to swallow, so I couldn't blame her, but she needed to know. Her safety depended on it.

"Please just think about it. Why else would a human be Called? Only people with the strongest affinity for magic are Called."

"It was just a mistake," she replied. "I was Called by accident."

"But you survived, and that was no accident. You even ended up as a champion. If that's possible, then isn't it possible you're a Lightblood?"

The mountainous land below had been replaced by farmlands, if you could call the barren plains farmlands. I was out of time. The transport ship began its decent. All I could do was hope that Tyler came to her senses, that she would accept who she truly was. I wanted to stay with her, but I knew that would only put her in more danger.

"Is this the right farm?" the pilot asked. My bubble dissolved.

"Yes. Here is fine," Tyler replied. The ship touched down, and the door opened. Among the barren fields sat a log cabin and a large wooden barn. It was no wonder Tyler had been starved when I met her. There was no way her family's land could produce crops.

"Please think about what I told you," I said as Tyler stood. The golden crown was still on her head, and the sunlight reflected off of it.

"I guess this is goodbye. Thank you for keeping me alive and returning me home. I am in your debt." Tyler spoke with tears in her eyes. She turned and walked away. I was speechless. Was it really goodbye? I couldn't even say it.

The love of my life walked away, and I couldn't even say goodbye.

CHAPTER 34

TYLER

My world had been turned upside down. I had to fight the tears as I kept my back to Ki. He hadn't said anything when I jumped down from the transport ship. Part of me wished that he had—that he'd stayed—but I knew he couldn't. He was the Darkblood Prince.

It was stupid for me to think we could be together. The king would never allow his son to be with a commoner. At least Ki had been able to bring me home. If I couldn't be with him, I could at least be with my family. But Ki's last words had me worried.

The Lightbloods were all dead. Their entire family had been slaughtered during the king's war. How could Ki possibly think I was a Lightblood? Sure, there'd been a strange bright light when we kissed, and maybe he really had seen a vision, but it couldn't possibly have been about me being a Lightblood. I was an ordinary human.

And yes, I had been adopted by my parents, but that didn't mean I was a Lightblood. If that were true, I'd have a great deal of power, and that kind of power was impossible to hide. I would've known if I was a Lightblood. I'd be able to sense it, wouldn't I? Ki was just confused. Maybe he'd hit his head during the blast from the bright light.

It sank in that I was finally home as the familiar dirt path crunched under my feet. The house looked just as it had when I'd left, yet it was different somehow. As the transport ship took off, I took in the fields that surrounded me. The cool air wasn't enough to calm me as I looked at the land in horror.

There was a clear division between the lands that still produced harvest and the ones that had become barren. The barren sections covered most of the fields. How long had I been gone? A few months? How had so much of the land died so quickly? We wouldn't survive without land to farm.

A tear trailed down my cheek as I took in the harsh reality: people would starve this year. My chest ached with sorrow. I needed to see my parents. Before leaving I'd worried how they'd fair without me, but with the land as it was, I knew things hadn't gone well.

I sprinted toward the farmhouse. If my parents had seen the broadcast, they would know I was alive. They'd be at home celebrating, even if my arrival was unexpected. The sounds the transport had made as it touched down and took off would have alerted them. I burst through the front door and was shocked to find the main room empty.

"Mom! Dad! I'm home!" I called out, but there was no response.

The house was empty. I double-checked every room before I ventured back outside. They must've been tending to the farm; they had to be. I called out to them as I ran around our estate. The barns and stores were empty, and the fields were quiet. There were no animals in sight. Our last few cattle must have perished while I was gone.

I took to the fields and walked the rows. Had my worst fears come true? Had my parents passed while I was gone? Had the whole village starved? I collapsed in the middle of a barren field. My tears flowed uncontrollably. The pain of my reality consumed me. All the suffering I'd endured in the Reckoning had been for nothing. I was alone. My chest clenched, and I struggled to get air into my lungs. It was as though my body would give out. There was nothing left to fight for.

As my tears fell to the ground, the earth moved. I sat up in surprise and watched as the blackened earth turned into lush green grass. The dead fields around me sprung to life. It radiated outward from where I knelt until the entire field was green. A miracle? Had I done that? No, I couldn't have. It wasn't possible. Did Rafe have that kind of power? I looked at the white paw print on my palm, but his energy was dormant.

"Tyler," said a voice from behind me, and I turned. I was greeted by dark teal eyes and a soft smile.

"Nydden!" I scrambled to my feet and cleared the distance between us. He opened his arms wide and wrapped me in a hug when I reached him. "You're alive," I sobbed into his chest, relieved to see a familiar face. He was really here, and I wasn't alone. The tension in my body relaxed.

"I'm sorry I didn't get here sooner," he replied. His arms held me tightly to him before he released me.

"Is the whole village watching the broadcast in town?" I asked, hopeful it was the explanation for my parents' absence.

"They were. Most of the villagers cleared out after the Reckoning ended. I stayed behind to escort you home, my queen." He bowed to me. His words swirled in my mind as I took a moment to process them. The village was vacated? He was taking me home? But I was already home. He'd called me his queen?

"I'm no queen," I replied.

"I'm sorry if this comes as a shock to you. When I saw the bright light that escaped you, I thought you'd become aware of who you are: the only remaining member of the Lightblood family and queen of the Light Nation." His words were spoken casually, as if it were a well-known fact.

"I don't understand," I mumbled. Why was he speaking the

same nonsense Ki had? How could they both have the same delusion? Why?

"Look around you. You've restored this land. You are a Lightblood." He gestured to the fresh grass swaying in the breeze around us. There wasn't a spot of barren land in sight. I saw it with my own eyes, but it couldn't have been because of me. Could it? Was it really true?

"How?" I asked. He extended his hand to me.

"I'll explain later. Right now we need to get you out of here," he replied. I hesitated and stared at the open hand he'd extended to me. There was so much I didn't know. I had so many questions. Nothing made sense anymore.

"Do you trust me?" he asked as I continued to stare at his hand. We'd known each other for years. He was my friend. I knew him, didn't I? He would never do anything to hurt me.

"Yes," I replied, grabbing his hand. His grip was firm as he guided me toward the forest. Our walk quickly turned into a run as we rushed through the green fields. I had no idea where we were going or what awaited me there. One thing I was sure of—my life would never be the same.

THE END

ACKNOWLEDGEMENTS

Thank you so much for reading! Publishing this book has been a dream come true, but without readers like you to share it with, it wouldn't mean a thing. If you loved *The Reckoning* the best way you can show your support is by leaving a review. It would mean the world to me.

Of course, *The Reckoning* wouldn't be what it is today without the fantastic work that was done by the staff of Enchanted Ink. Natalia Leigh has not only been an Authortube inspiration, but her amazing editorial skills and professionalism completely blew me away. And let's not forget the beautiful interior design Greg Rupel put together to really bring this book to life.

Which brings me to the artist. I enlisted my wonderfully talented friend Tiffany Davis to create the magic symbols and character art for *The Reckoning*. She really brought the magic to life through her art and I couldn't be happier.

Speaking of happiness, the next group of people I want to thank have warmed my heart by dedicating their time and energy into supporting *The Reckoning*. To my beta readers: Blue Coutell, Tiffany Davis, and Evan Young, thank you for reading the early versions of my book and helping me shape it into what it is today. You gave me hope that people would one day read and enjoy my stories. To my street team: Esme Carmichael, Kit Gulick, Elizabeth Horgan, and Gee Rubas, your help and support in the launch of my debut novel will never be forgotten. To those of you who have reviewed my book, thank you for taking the time share your thoughts and feelings about *The Reckoning.* Reviews really do make all the difference for authors.

And finally, I want to thank my family, the people who are always there to support me no matter what. Vincent Knue, Kathleen Knue, Clyde Terry, Brenda Terry, Jeffrey Knue, Kimberly Knue, Sarah Knue, and the rest of the extended Knue family, you guys know who you are and that there are far too many of you for me to list individually.

Let us not forget about my faithful lap warmers, Bunny and Charlie. They kept me company during the long hours I spent putting this whole thing together.

GLOSSARY

Addersfield: A small farming village, once part of the Light Nation, now one of the outer villages of the Dark Nation.

Aeni (uh-NEYE): Pure blooded magical races created when the gods blessed the shamans with magic.

Alterra(all-TAIR-uh): A magical world blessed by gods.

Ancient language, the: The oldest language in Alterra, and the root language that all of the languages stem from.

Apollo (uh-PALL-oh): The sun god, creator of the sunstone, and the giver of earth and fire magic.

Asudh (uh-SUD): Mix-blooded magical races created from the cross breeding of humans and aeni.

Asudhen (uh-SUD-en): The language of the asudhs, used most commonly in areas heavily populated with asudhs.

Called: To be selected to take part in the Reckoning.

Calling, the: The magical ritual performed by seers to select the participants of the Reckoning.

Common: The universal language of Alterra.

Dark Nation: The lands ruled by the Darkblood Royal family, which consists of the majority of the largest land mass in Alterra.

Dierdre (DEER-druh): A magical race with demonic origins, created by the corruption of dark magic when the moonstone made contact with a human.

Familiar: A magical creature that can bond with magic users to enhance their magical strength. Most familiars have unique abilities.

Gaia (GUY-uh): The original shaman that was blessed with earth magic.

Hecate (HEC-uh-tay): The moon goddess, creator of the moonstone, and the giver of air and water magic.

Ilmatar (ill-MA-ter): The original shaman that was blessed with air magic.

Inbetween: A patch of forest surrounded by a perfect ring of mountains, and the location where the Reckoning takes places.

Kilshore Island: An island off the west coast of the Dark Nation where the Dark Nation Army trains their soldiers.

Liusaidh (LOO-sih): A magical race with angelic origins, created by the corruption of light magic when the sunstone made contact with a human.

Nerine (nair-REEN): The original shaman that was blessed with water magic.

Reckoning, the: A deadly competition of strength and survival created by the original royal families to create warriors for their royal guards. Tradition states that the Reckoning occurs every five years and only individuals between the ages of fifteen and twenty-two can be called to take part. To be called is an honor, but glory is reserved for the champion.

Royal Guard: Elite warriors selected to protect the members of the royal family.

Sibyl (SI-bl): The goddess of spirit, creator of life, and giver of spiritual magics.

Tenebrisal (te-NEE-bree-sall): The written language of dark magic, created by the Dierdre.

Tlaloc (tlah-LAAKH): The pure blooded earth magic race known for its warrior cultures, brutality, and strength.

Tor Terran (TOR TAIR-en): A large trade city located near the northern most region of the Dark Nation.

Vulcan (VULL-can): The original shaman that was blessed with fire magic.

www.ingramcontent.com/pod-product-compliance
Lightning Source LLC
Chambersburg PA
CBHW010447310726
48979CB00018B/2838/J

* 9 7 8 1 9 5 4 5 5 4 0 0 9 *